Praise for Margaret Daley
and her novels

"Margaret Daley skillfully integrates touching
romance and a bit of mystery in
Gold in the Fire."
—*RT Book Reviews*

"Margaret Daley tells the heartwarming
tale of love winning out over doubt in
Light in the Storm."
—*RT Book Reviews*

"*Heart of the Family,* by Margaret Daley, is a
wonderful story on many levels and will have
readers shedding tears of happiness."
—*RT Book Reviews*

"*A Texas Thanksgiving* is a warm,
delightful story."
—*RT Book Reviews*

MARGARET DALEY

Gold in the Fire

&

Light in the Storm

Steeple Hill®

Published by Steeple Hill Books™

STEEPLE HILL BOOKS

Steeple
Hill®

ISBN-13: 978-0-373-65135-1

GOLD IN THE FIRE AND LIGHT IN THE STORM

GOLD IN THE FIRE
Copyright © 2004 by Margaret Daley

LIGHT IN THE STORM
Copyright © 2005 by Margaret Daley

www.SteepleHill.com

Printed in U.S.A.

CONTENTS

Books by Margaret Daley

Love Inspired

The Power of Love
Family for Keeps
Sadie's Hero
The Courage to Dream
What the Heart Knows
A Family for Tory
*Gold in the Fire
*A Mother for Cindy
*Light in the Storm
The Cinderella Plan
*When Dreams
    Come True
*Tidings of Joy

**Once Upon a Family
**Heart of the Family
**Family Ever After
A Texas Thanksgiving
Second Chance Family
†Love Lessons

*The Ladies of
    Sweetwater Lake
**Fostered by Love
†Helping Hands
    Homeschooling

Love Inspired Suspense

Hearts on the Line
Heart of the Amazon
So Dark the Night
Vanished
Buried Secrets

Don't Look Back
Forsaken Canyon
What Sarah Saw
Poisoned Secrets
Cowboy Protector

MARGARET DALEY

feels she has been blessed. She has been married more than thirty years to her husband, Mike, whom she met in college. He is a terrific support and her best friend. They have one son, Shaun.

Margaret has been writing for many years and loves to tell a story. When she was a little girl, she would play with her dolls and make up stories about their lives. Now she writes these stories down. She especially enjoys weaving stories about families and how faith in God can sustain a person when things get tough. When she isn't writing, she is fortunate to be a teacher for students with special needs. Margaret has taught for more than twenty years and loves working with her students. She has also been a Special Olympics coach and has participated in many sports with her students.

GOLD IN THE FIRE

These have come so that your faith—
of greater worth than gold, which perishes
even though refined by fire—may be proved
genuine and may result in praise, glory and honor
when Jesus Christ is revealed.

—1 *Peter* 1:7

To Laura Marie Altom, a friend who helped me
find where I belonged as a writer.
Thank you.

To Paige Wheeler, my agent,
who has been a great support.
Thank you.

To Ann Leslie Tuttle and Diane Dietz,
my two editors at Love Inspired,
who have believed in me.
Thank you.

Chapter One

Darcy O'Brien's hands shook as she brushed her hair behind her ears. She stared down at her fingers, covered with soot, the black reminding her of the charred remains of the barn only yards away. The heat from the fire chased away the early-morning chill. Smoke curled upward from the darkened boards to disappear in the fog that had rolled in to encase her in a gray cocoon. But there was nothing protective and safe about her surroundings.

Eerie. Unearthly. Darcy shivered and hugged her arms to her.

"Ma'am?"

The sound of a deep, husky voice floated to her from the swirls of smoke and fog. Her eyes stung as she searched the yard. Emerging from the shroud of gray a man appeared, dressed in a black jacket with yellow strips and black pants. He removed his fire helmet and cradled it under his arm. Dark brown hair, damp from sweat, lay at odd angles. Black smudges highlighted the hard angles of his face and emphasized the blueness of his eyes. For just a moment Darcy thought of a warrior striding purposefully toward her.

"Yes, may I help you?" she asked, pushing away her fantasy.

"That man over there said you're the one in charge." The firefighter tossed his head in the direction of Jake, one of the grooms.

The idea that she was in charge weighed heavily on her shoulders, even though it was only for a few months. She straightened, ignoring the exhaustion that cleaved to every part of her. "Yes, I am."

The firefighter stuck his hand out. "I'm Joshua Markham. I conduct the arson investigations for the department."

"Arson?"

The strong feel of his handshake reassured her. For a few seconds she forgot the past couple of hours. Then she remembered pulling the frightened horses to safety, watching the barn go up in flames, the scent of burned wood heavy in the air. But mostly she remembered trying to persuade her father to return to the main house before he collapsed. That had been the hardest task of all.

"Yes, ma'am, it's definitely a possibility. This is the third barn fire in the past few weeks."

"Please call me Darcy. 'Ma'am' reminds me of my students."

He moved away from the pile of blackened rubble.

Darcy followed. When she looked back toward the barn, all she saw was the swirls of fog. The stench of smoke clung to the air.

"When it's safe, I'll bring in my dog. I'll know more after I can take some samples and check the area out more thoroughly."

"Dog?" Her mind refused to grasp the implication of what he was saying.

"He'll be able to locate where the fire originated. We'll pinpoint what the accelerant was. If it matches the other fires, we'll know we have a serial arsonist on our hands."

"Serial arsonist? But why here?"

Joshua shrugged. "There are countless reasons why someone sets a fire. Most are for some kind of personal gain, but occasionally we find a person who just likes to set fires and watch them burn."

Darcy shuddered. Sweetwater was always such a quiet town, not like where she lived now. Even though there were nearly fifteen thousand people in Sweetwater, she still thought of it as a small, close-knit community.

"If it's arson, there'll be a thorough investigation."

"Of course."

"I'll be looking into all the reasons why someone would set a fire. That includes personal gain."

For a moment her mind went blank. Stunned, she couldn't think of a reply.

"Just thought I'd let you know."

"Why?"

"I know your father had a heart attack a few weeks

ago. Shamus Flanaghan is a respected member of our community. I don't think he had anything to do with this, but I still have to check out the possibility."

"And you want me to cushion the blow?"

The corner of his mouth quirked. "Yes, ma—Darcy. I would appreciate it."

"So in other words, you want me to help you with your investigation."

Joshua plowed his hand through his damp hair. "Well, not exactly. I just don't want to be responsible for causing your father further grief. But questions will have to be asked—and answered."

"Then you can ask me. As of last week, I'm acting as the manager of this farm until my father gets back on his feet." If she said it enough times, perhaps it would be true.

"I'll be back later with my camera and Arnold. I'll know more after I take a look around." He put his helmet on. "Good day."

Frustration churned in her stomach as she watched the firefighter walk away, the thick fog and smoke swallowing him until all she saw was a gray wall. Another shiver rippled down her spine. What in the world had she gotten herself into? A serial arsonist?

Normally this was her favorite time of day, when the sun was just peeking over the horizon, the sky lit with color, the birds chirping in the nearby trees. Even when it was foggy, there was a certain appeal to dawn, a mystery waiting to be uncovered. But now there was a real mystery. Who would want to set fires to barns filled with horses?

A pounding behind her eyes hammered at her temples. Her father raised jumpers and hunters. People from all over the country came to him. His reputation as a breeder had always been paramount to him—at times to the exclusion of even his family.

Darcy closed her eyes for a few seconds and tried to compose her shattered nerves. There was so much she had to do. She didn't know where to begin. Finally she decided she had to check on her father first, to make sure he was following his doctor's orders, before she could even take the time to assimilate this latest news.

She started up the road that led to the main house, white painted fences on either side of the asphalt. Somewhere out in those fields were some of their prize broodmares. But the fog that adhered to the ground obscured her view. She would need to make sure all the horses were accounted for—after she saw her father and reassured herself that he was all right.

She entered the house through the back door. Lizzy Johnson, the petite housekeeper, stood at the stove, shaking her head while she prepared French toast. A strand of gray hair fell forward on her forehead. With a heavy sigh, she brushed it back in place.

"What's wrong, Lizzy?"

"One thing. Shamus. He insists on eating a proper breakfast. He wanted eggs, bacon and toast. He's getting French toast. I figure that's better than a plate full of cholesterol-high eggs fried in bacon grease."

The frustration in Lizzy's voice matched her own feelings. Darcy knew how difficult her father could be. He didn't like change, and the new diet his doctor wanted him on was definitely a change.

"I'll have a word with Dad. Is he in his room resting?"

Lizzy arched a brow. "Resting? No, he's dressed and ready to go back down to the barn."

"But he promised me—" Darcy swallowed the rest of her sentence. It was hopeless. Her father didn't know how to take it easy or to follow orders. Why had she thought she would be able to help her father recover when he had never slowed down for anything in the past, not even when her mother had died? He'd put in almost a full day of work the day of the funeral.

"Child, he's in the dining room drinking his coffee. Praise the Lord, decaf. But it was a battle to get him to drink that instead of regular coffee. I'm surprised you didn't hear it down at the barn." Lizzy flipped over the pieces of bread, her gaze clouding. "How bad is it?"

"Bad. The barn is completely gone. Thankfully no one was hurt, but we lost one mare in foal. The rest of the horses we managed to save. Now I have to handle finding places to stable seventeen mares until we can rebuild the barn." Darcy thought back to what Joshua Markham had said about a serial arsonist. What if the other barns were in danger?

"And a father who won't listen to his doctor's advice."

"Yes, that, too."

"Here, I suspect you could use some of this. Just keep

it away from your father." Lizzy passed her a glass pot full of a dark brown brew. "This has lots of caffeine."

"Thanks. I can always count on you, Lizzy," Darcy murmured as she made her way into the dining room.

Pausing halfway down the long, cherry-wood table that seated twelve, she put the pot on a thick place mat. Then, instead of sitting, she gripped the back of a brocade-covered chair, leaning into it for support.

Her father glanced up from reading the newspaper. "I thought you were Lizzy with the breakfast she insists I eat. What's taking her so long? Never mind—I'm sure she's not hurrying because she doesn't think I should go down to the barn."

"You shouldn't, Dad. I can take care of everything. Did you rest at all?"

He frowned. "Rest when one of my barns is burning? What do you think?"

"When did you come back to the house?"

He looked away, busying himself with taking several sips of his coffee.

"Dad?"

"Thirty minutes ago." His sharp eyes returned to her face. "Did you really think I would go back to the house and sleep? I thought you knew me better than that."

Darcy took in the tired lines etched into his weathered face, an ashen cast to it. She noticed the slump to his shoulders and the slight trembling as he brought the cup to his lips. He was barely holding himself together, and she didn't know how to make him stop and rest be-

fore he— She wouldn't think about what could happen
to him if he didn't do what the doctor said. Their relationship might not be a strong one, but he was her father and she cared.

"Dad, there isn't anything you can do now. I can take
care of stabling the mares and seeing to the mess. That's
why I came home to help you."

"When I agreed to you coming home to help, it
wasn't for something like this. I could have lost a third
of my breeding stock last night."

Her grip on the chair tightened until pain shot up her
arms. "I'm capable of handling it."

"This is *my* life." He thumped his chest. "I need to
see to it."

Darcy pulled out the chair and sat before she collapsed. The long night was finally catching up with her,
and she felt the lack of sleep in every fiber of her being.

"If you don't take care of yourself and follow the
doctor's orders, there will be no life to see to."

"You don't mince words."

"You've always taught me to tell it like it is. You've
been home from the hospital only a few days. You aren't
supposed to deal with anything stressful, especially
something like what happened last night."

He leaned forward, clasping the edge of the table.
"Don't you understand, not knowing is more stressful
than seeing to my job."

"I came up here to check on you, then I intend to return to make sure everything is taken care of. I'll report

back to you as soon as I deal with stabling the mares. I'll keep you informed as if you're right there." The tightness in her throat threatened to cut off her words. She swallowed several times and continued. "Please let me do this for you." *Please, for once in your life, need me.*

For several moments he stared at her. Then suddenly he slumped back in the chair and dropped his head. "You win. *This* time. But I don't intend to stay in my room for long. Just as soon as I feel a little better, I'll be down at the barn."

The weak thread to his words, the fact that he'd backed down, underscored how sick her father really was. He would never admit more than he had, but she knew he was definitely feeling the effects of being up most of the night.

"Then you'll go rest and wait for me to come see you?"

He nodded.

Darcy poured herself some coffee, her hands trembling as much as her father's had. She didn't particularly like the bitter taste, but she needed a lot of caffeine to keep herself going. She decided to tell her father later about what Joshua Markham had said concerning the fire probably being the work of an arsonist. Until Joshua confirmed it, she didn't want to upset her father any more than he already was. But if there was someone going around setting fire to barns, the next few months would be more difficult than she had anticipated. Somehow she had to protect her father, even though he would fight her every inch of the way. Maybe then she would live up to what he expected.

* * *

From the paddock Darcy saw Joshua with a big black dog exploring the pile of burned rubble that had once been the broodmare barn. This afternoon was so different from earlier, when smoke had lingered in the air and the sun had been obscured. Now the sun's rays touched her face and warmed her skin. The sweet smell of freshly mowed grass peppered the air, almost wiping away the memory of the fire, the smell of charred wood—until she looked at the destruction the flames had caused.

With a sigh, she made her way toward Joshua, who ducked under the yellow tape that cordoned off the area. He strode toward his pickup with his dog on a leash and holding two metal cans.

"Did you find anything?" she asked, catching herself staring at the man, dressed in his navy-blue firefighter's uniform, his badge glittering in the sunlight. She forced herself to look down at the dog at his side before he found her staring at him.

He stored the metal cans alongside some others in the back of his truck, then secured a tarpaulin over them. "Not sure until the lab report comes back, but Arnold was very interested in several spots. I took some samples."

"He's a beauty." She rubbed the black Labrador retriever behind his ears. "How long have you had him?"

"Three years. He's garnishing quite a reputation in the state."

"Reputation?"

"He's ninety- to ninety-five-percent accurate when pinpointing the accelerant in a fire. Much better than the machine we used to have." Joshua opened the cab door and indicated to the dog to jump inside. "So when there's a questionable fire, Arnold and I get called out."

"Does that keep you busy?"

"Sometimes."

Arnold poked his head out the open window and prodded Darcy with his nose. She laughed and scratched him behind his ears some more.

"He likes you."

"I love animals."

The blue gleam in his eyes dimmed. "I'm sorry about the horse you lost in the fire."

"She was in foal. My son took it quite hard."

"Son? Was that the young man down here when I came?"

"Probably. Red hair, freckles, eight?"

"Yep. He had a few questions to ask me."

"Just a few?"

"Well, more like twenty." Joshua leaned against the cab of the truck, folding his arms across his chest.

"You got off easy. His curiosity will get him into trouble one day. I'm surprised he isn't still here."

"Said something about helping with a foal."

Darcy peered toward the second broodmare barn a paddock away. "Yes, we had one born last night. That's where I was when the fire broke out."

"It seems last night was an eventful night for you."

"And one I don't want to repeat anytime soon."

"I need to talk with your father. When would be a good time?"

"He's resting right now. I'd rather not disturb him. He didn't get any sleep last night."

"Did you?"

The probe of Joshua's gaze caused her to blush. She must look a sight—with circles under her eyes and some soot from the fire probably still on her face. She hadn't even taken the time to clean up properly. She raised her hand to wipe at her cheeks as if that would erase any evidence of the night before.

"No, not for thirty-six hours. I tried to take a nap a few hours ago, but when I closed my eyes, all I saw were flames."

"That sounds like one of my dreams. One of the hazards of being a firefighter, I guess." He pushed away from the truck. "I need to ask you some questions too. I've already interviewed the others who were here last night."

A shiver shimmered down her length when she thought back to the night before. "I'm not sure I can be of much help. All I was thinking about was getting the horses to safety." The memory of the one mare she hadn't been able to save pierced through her armor. The horse's cries would haunt her for a long time.

"I need to drop these samples off, then I'll take Arnold home. After that, I'll be back to talk to you and your father." Joshua started past her, stopped and twisted back around. "I wish we had met under better circumstances."

"So do I."

"I know this can't be easy coming home to all this."

That was definitely an understatement, she thought. But she never shared her worries with others. She'd learned a long time ago to keep her concerns to herself. She was about to make a light comment when her son appeared in the yard, yelling to get their attention. He raced toward them, skidding to a halt next to her.

Sean smiled up at Joshua. "Oh, good. You haven't left yet. Mom, did you meet Arnold? Isn't he neat? He has the best nose in the state. When something smells wrong, he'll sit."

Darcy laughed. "This chatterbox is my son, Sean O'Brien, just in case he forgot to tell you his name before."

"How's the foal?" Joshua asked, coiling the dog leash in his hand.

"She's a filly. She's all legs."

"Sorta like you, sweetie." Darcy hugged Sean to her, rubbing his head. "He's going through another one of his growth spurts."

"Aw, Mom." He squirmed from her embrace, a red tint to his cheeks that made his freckles stand out. "Do you wanna see the filly? You can pet her."

"I wish I could, but I have to finish my job first. Can I take a rain check on that offer?" Joshua tossed the leash into the truck.

"Sure. Just let me know. I know Grandpa won't mind."

"Speaking of Grandpa, did you finish mucking out those stalls you promised him you would do each day?"

Sean dropped his head, his chin on his chest.

"Just as I suspected, young man. You know he'll ask you about that when he gets up from his nap."

"I've got one done." Sean began to run toward the broodmare barn, came to a stop and glanced back at Joshua. "Don't forget about the filly."

"I won't. I'll be back out here later. Maybe you can show me then."

Beaming, Sean shouted, "Yes," and continued toward the far barn.

"Thank you."

Joshua's eyebrows rose. "For what?"

"For taking some time out of your busy schedule to see the filly." *For not rejecting my son's interest,* she added silently, thinking about all the times her husband had dismissed Sean's enthusiasm, never having any time for him.

"I'm not that busy that I can't take a little time to see an animal."

The smile that accompanied his words melted defenses that she had erected over the years. "I must warn you, if you allow him Sean will whittle his way into your life."

"I know several nice boys his age that go to my church. I would be glad to introduce him to them."

"I'm sure he'd like that. He's always in the thick of things back home."

"I understand that your father used to go to my church. From what I hear he was quite active at one time. His attendance has been spotty these past few years."

"Don't you mean nonexistent?"

Joshua kneaded the back of his neck. "Well, now that you put it that way, yes. He hasn't been in quite some time."

"More than likely thirteen or fourteen years."

"Maybe this Sunday you can get your father to attend again."

"No one can get him to do anything he doesn't want to."

"I understand." He grinned. "I need to go. I'll be back later." Joshua walked around the front of his truck and got in.

As the red pickup drove away, Darcy turned toward the burned barn. Yellow tape marked off the area, preserving the charred structure for Joshua's investigation. Scanning the pile of rubble, she couldn't imagine any evidence being left. The fire had consumed most of the barn with nothing untouched by its flames. They would have to raze the building and start over—much as she had after Clay's death.

"That must be Joshua Markham." Darcy rose from the couch when she heard the sound of an approaching vehicle.

Sean hopped up. "I'll get it."

Her father watched him race from the room. "Where does he get all that energy? I could use some."

"He's excited that Joshua's visiting."

"I expected he would have questions, especially since the Andersons' and Bakers' barns burned."

"Why didn't you tell me two other barns have burned down in the past month?"

"Didn't think it pertained to us." Beneath his usual tanned features, his skin had a sickly pallor. "Guess I was wrong. Don't see why anyone would want to go around killing horses."

Darcy heard her son's chattering as he escorted Joshua toward the den. "Shh, Dad. I don't want to frighten Sean any more than he already is. He took the mare's death hard."

"Then he shouldn't be here for the interview," her father murmured in a gruff voice, shifting in his chair as both Joshua and Sean entered the room.

"Good afternoon, Mr. Flanaghan. I hope you're feeling better."

"Shamus, please. Mr. Flanaghan makes me sound so old, and I refuse to acknowledge I'm a day over thirty." Her father waved Joshua to the couch next to Darcy. "Sean, weren't you going to help Ken with the tack?"

"Yes, but—"

"No buts, young man. Scoot."

"I want to show Joshua the new filly."

"I'll bring Joshua down to the barn before he leaves so you can show him the foal," Darcy said, aware of the man sitting only a few inches from her. The couch suddenly seemed small with Joshua's large frame next to her.

Sean stuck out his lower lip and trudged toward the door, dragging his feet. "Okay, but don't forget."

"I won't let her," Joshua said as her son disappeared into

the hallway. Joshua removed a small pad of paper from his pocket along with a pen. "I have a few questions—"

Shamus held up his hand, then placed his forefinger over his lips. "Wait a sec," he whispered. After a few seconds they heard the sound of the front door closing, and he continued. "Little boys have big ears, and Darcy doesn't want to discuss the fire in front of Sean. If you ask me, she's overprotecting him, but I'll respect her wishes."

"Dad!" A blush singed her cheeks. "I just don't think discussions about fires and horses dying is what he needs to hear."

"You have a smart boy there, Darcy. He knows exactly what happened last night."

She angled toward Joshua. "What do you want to know?" This was neither the time nor the place to get into an argument with her father concerning her methods of raising Sean. In the short time she'd been home, he'd made it plain he thought she was overprotective. There wasn't much she could say to change her father's mind.

Joshua's gaze riveted to hers, a serious expression in his eyes. "Where were you when the fire broke out?"

Chapter Two

Joshua's question brought Darcy firmly back to the business at hand—the fire. "As I said earlier, I was in the other broodmare barn helping to deliver a foal." She knew the query was necessary, but it still bothered her.

Joshua wrote something on his pad, then asked her father, "And you, sir?"

Shamus's mouth twisted into a frown as he peered away. "I was working in the office on the books."

"Dad! You were supposed to be asleep."

"Well, I wasn't. I was just checking to make sure all the orders were made."

"I did those yesterday morning, Dad—" Darcy snapped her mouth closed, suddenly remembering they had an audience.

Silence hung in the air until her father cleared his throat and said, "I didn't know anything was happening at the barn until the alarm sounded. By the time I arrived, it was engulfed in flames."

Joshua shifted toward Darcy. "What did the fire look like when you arrived?"

"Not much better. Smoke was everywhere and flames were beginning to shoot out the east side."

"And you went into the barn to get the horses out?"

"Yes. Jake was already bringing a few out. I managed to open the stall doors so the mares would at least have a chance to run to safety." The sounds of the frightened horses filled her mind all over again. Memories of the smoke-laden barn, the scent of fire everywhere, made her hug her arms to warm her chilled body.

"Did you see anything unusual or anyone who shouldn't have been there?"

Darcy shook her head, having gone over the scene many times in the past few hours, trying to come up with something that would explain the fire.

"Are you having any financial problems?"

Darcy was about to answer when her father cut in with a chuckle and said, "I wondered when you would ask me that. No, Shamrock Stables is doing fine. You may look at my books anytime. I don't need insurance money to pay my bills."

Surprised by her father's calm answer, Darcy pressed her lips together to keep from expressing her astonishment.

"Can you think of anyone, sir, who might have a grudge against you and the farm?"

"I try to do right by people, but I've made a few en-

emies in my lifetime." Her father drummed his fingers
on the arm of the leather-padded chair, a distant look in
his gray eyes. "Have Ray Anderson or John Baker
thought of anyone?"

"A few disgruntled employees, but no one who has
worked for both of them. Do any of your employees
smoke?"

"Not around my barns. I have strict rules about that.
I had to fire a groom back about six months ago
because he kept forgetting it. Caught him smoking
while he was mucking out a stall. Sent him packing that
very minute."

"Who was that, sir?"

"Angus Feehan."

Joshua jotted down the name.

"Was it started with a cigarette?" Darcy asked, thinking back to how fast the fire had developed and spread.
It had only been seven, maybe eight minutes before
she'd had to escape the barn or be trapped inside.

"I found a butt near where I think the fire started, but
I don't think it was the sole cause." Joshua rose, sliding
the notepad into his pants pocket. "That's all for the
time being."

Shamus started to stand, seemed to decide against it
and remained seated, a pinch to his mouth indicating exhaustion. "I'd like to be kept informed of your investigation. I want to know if there's a connection to the
other two fires."

"I'll let you know when I get the reports back from

the lab. But from what I've seen so far, it looks like there is a connection."

Darcy came to her feet. "Let me show you the foal."

"I can find my way to the barn if you're busy."

"That's okay. I need to check on the mares we stabled in that barn. Make sure they're settled into their new home."

Out on the front veranda Darcy paused and took a deep breath. There was still a hint of burned wood in the air, but mostly the scent of grass, flowers and earth laced the breeze. She looked toward the horizon and noticed the sun beginning its descent. A few streaks of orange and pink threaded through the blue sky like pieces of ribbon carelessly tossed about.

"It's getting close to dinnertime, Mr. Markham. Would you like to stay and eat with us?"

"Please, call me Joshua, and yes, I would like that. I don't particularly care for my own cooking."

"Neither do I." Chuckling, Darcy blushed. "I mean *my* cooking, not yours."

"You wouldn't care for mine, either."

"I think we have established we're both lousy cooks." Darcy led the way toward the broodmare barn set off to the left and farthest from the house. "I promised myself when I came this summer to have Lizzy teach me some of her dishes. Of course, now I'm wondering when I'll find the time, what with the fire and all."

"Maybe I should throw myself on Lizzy's mercy, too."

"You know Lizzy?"

"Oh, yes. She's a mainstay at Sweetwater Community Church."

"That's right. I'd forgotten that's where my mother found her and asked her to be our housekeeper."

"How long has she been working for your family?" Joshua opened a gate and stepped to the side to allow Darcy to go first into a pasture that shortened the trip to the farthest barn.

"Fourteen years. Mom died not too long after Lizzy came to work for us." One of the mares in the paddock trotted over to Darcy and nudged her. She laughed and dug into the pocket of her black jeans for a few sugar cubes, holding her palm out flat. "Bluebell won't let me leave without getting some sweets from me. She's spoiled rotten." She ran her hand over the horse's dark brown flank. "She knows she's my favorite and uses that to her advantage."

Joshua walked around the mare, making sure the horse knew where he was at all times. "She's a beauty. When is she due?"

"Not for another month. I can't wait. She always has a beautiful foal." Darcy patted Bluebell on the rump before continuing toward the far end of the field where the broodmare barn was located.

"I wish I had more time to ride."

"You're in horse country. How can you not ride?" Again Joshua opened the gate and waited for Darcy to go first. "I know. Life gets in the way."

When Darcy entered the barn, the scents of hay and

horses permeated the air. They made her feel as though she had come home. For the past ten years, since her marriage to Clay, she had spent all of her time other places—many other places—while her husband pursued his fighter-pilot career in the Navy. With his death the year before, everything had changed…and yet it hadn't. She wasn't sure what she should do with her life.

"Mom! Joshua! Come have a look. She's feeding." At the other end of the barn Sean danced in front of a stall with the biggest grin on his face. As they neared, he darted inside.

"I can see your son loves the farm," Joshua said with a laugh.

"Definitely." Darcy went into the stall with Joshua following, pushing away the guilty feeling she suddenly experienced. But it still niggled. She hadn't wanted to come home; she hadn't brought her son to see his grandfather until now.

"See. Isn't she neat?" Sean pointed to the foal nursing. "She lets me touch her. She almost fell once but she didn't."

Darcy inspected the foal who was all legs and still wobbly. The chestnut-colored coat reminded Darcy of the foal's mother. She hoped she was as good a jumper as her mother. Despite the fire, seeing the filly caused Darcy's hopes to rise. Life continued even amid problems.

"Grandpa said I could name her." Sean continued to stroke the foal.

"Have you come up with one yet?" Darcy asked, re-

membering the first time her father had let her name a
horse—a lifetime ago. So much had happened to her in
the last twenty-four years, and yet her relationship with
her father was the same—strained, at best.

"I was thinking of Big Red, but that sounds like a boy.
What do you think, Joshua?"

Joshua cocked his head and thought for a moment.
"You're probably right. The correct name will come to
you. After spending some time with her, I'm sure you'll
come up with something that fits. Naming something is
important."

Sean straightened, his shoulders thrown back, his big
grin spreading even more. "I think so. I can't just give her
any ol' name. Something real special." He peered around
Joshua. "Where's Arnold? I was hoping to see him again."

"He's at home. He worked hard today so I gave him
a treat and he's resting up. I'll bring him back some
other time."

"I never met a fire dog before."

"There aren't a lot of them around."

"How did you come up with the name Arnold?"

"My first fire captain was named Arnold. He showed
me the ropes. I wanted to honor him so I named Arnold
after him."

Sean placed his forefinger on his chin. "Hmm. That's
a thought."

"Well, young man, right now you need to get up to
the house and wash up before dinner. You know how
Lizzy is about clean hands."

"But, Mom, you and Joshua just got here."

"Joshua's coming to dinner, so you can talk to him at the table. That is, if you pass Lizzy's inspection."

"I will." He raced from the stall.

Joshua chuckled. "I don't think I've ever been used as a bribe to get someone to wash up."

"As a parent you learn to use any trick you can."

"I'm flattered."

"My son was quite taken with you and Arnold."

His smile reached deep into his blue eyes. "Maybe I can bring Arnold out here one day."

"You'll make my son's day." Darcy left the stall, and after closing its door, led the way into the barn to check each of the newly arrived mares to make sure they were settled. Joshua's quiet study of her heightened her awareness of him.

Outside, a line of oaks and maples hid the sun, dusk beginning to settle over the yard. "What made you become an arson investigator?" she asked, relishing the breeze caressing her face, cooling her cheeks.

"I decided it was the best of both worlds."

"What worlds?"

"When I was growing up, I would fluctuate between wanting to be a firefighter and a police officer. I fight fires, but I also investigate any that are suspicious in nature."

"Do you have many in Sweetwater?" Darcy thought of her hometown and the people she knew and couldn't imagine too many arsonists in the bunch.

"No, not usually, but with Arnold I cover more than just this area of Kentucky."

"But now there's a chance you have a serial arsonist in Sweetwater?"

Joshua paused at the gate to the paddock. Rolling his shoulders, he rubbed the back of his neck, apparently trying to massage a stiffness. "It's looking like that. If these fires continue, someone is going to die. I have to stop the person before that."

"You think it's one person?"

"Most likely. That's how arsonists work usually."

Darcy again stopped and greeted Bluebell before continuing across the pasture toward the main house. "Do you usually catch an arsonist?"

"Arson cases are difficult to prosecute."

She quaked at the thought that the person responsible for setting three barn fires so far would go unpunished. A mare died last night, but that could have been a person trapped in the barn. *She* could have been trapped in the barn if Jake hadn't insisted she get out before she had a chance to save the last mare. That she wasn't able to help the horse plagued her, making it doubly important that they discover who set the fire. "Then your job is quite a challenge," she murmured, hoping this case was an exception.

"Especially when we have random fires with no apparent reason. It's one thing when someone burns down a building to collect the insurance money or for some other financial reason. Usually we can catch that person. But with no connection between the fires, it's hard to know what's motivating the arsonist."

"Didn't you say some people burn buildings just to watch them burn?"

"Yes, but I don't think that's what's happening here."

Darcy mounted the steps to the veranda. "Why?"

Joshua frowned, looking back toward the place where the burned rumble of the barn lay in a large mound. "Call it a hunch. Just a feeling I can't shake. Something's driving this person—something to do with farms, barns, horses."

"That doesn't narrow down too many people in and around Sweetwater, with this being in the middle of the Bluegrass area of Kentucky."

"I know. I have my work cut out for me." Joshua held the front door open for Darcy. "But from what I understand, running a farm isn't an easy task. I'd say you have your work cut out for you, too."

"It has been a while since I worked with the horses. Until I got married, I was learning the ropes from my father while attending college." *And not doing quite the job he wanted,* Darcy thought, remembering her father's frowns and remarks when she didn't do something his way.

"Sean told me his dad died last year."

"What *hasn't* my son told you?" Darcy stopped in the middle of the entry hall and faced Joshua, thinking of her son's enthusiasm and lack of inhibition. As the saying goes, he'd never met a stranger—which thankfully had helped him make friends. They had moved a lot over the years.

"We talked this afternoon for twenty minutes nonstop."

Darcy laughed. "Nonstop on whose part, yours or his?"

"Mostly his."

"That's what I thought. He doesn't know how to keep a secret. Whenever he gets me a present, I have to open it right then and there, because he can't wait. So this past Christmas I got his picture frame he made me on December fourth, the day he finished it."

"He said something about his dad dying in a plane crash."

"Clay was a fighter pilot for the Navy. During a routine exercise he had problems with his plane and crashed. Knowing the risks he had to take in his job, I thought I was prepared. I wasn't—" A tightness in her throat prevented her from saying anything else. In fact, she wasn't even sure why she had told Joshua that. But for some reason the man was easy to talk to, and for a year she had kept a lot bottled up inside her. For most of her life she'd held her emotions close to her heart.

"I'm sorry. Death of a loved one is always difficult. I've lost both my parents over the past eight years. They were the only family I had."

A profound sadness and empathy edged each of his words and drew Darcy to him. "You didn't grow up here, did you?" Darcy felt that she would have remembered someone like him, even though she suspected a few years separated them in age.

"No. Louisville. I moved here nine years ago. I didn't want to live in a large town, but I still wanted to be close if my parents needed me."

Darcy could tell from the tone in his voice that there was more to that story. Indeed there was more to Joshua Markham than merely being a firefighter. But she was only going to be here for a few months. With her heart still scarred from her marriage to Clay, there was no way she would open herself up to any more pain, to another man.

"Mom. Joshua." Sean came running into the entry hall and slid to a stop a few feet from Darcy. "Dinner is ready. Lizzy made my favorite."

"Pizza?" Darcy breathed a sigh of relief. Suddenly the atmosphere between her and Joshua had shifted and become charged with possibilities that she wouldn't pursue.

"Naw. Spaghetti. It's my favorite now."

Darcy clasped her son's shoulder and ruffled his hair. "You have a new favorite every week. I can't keep up with them anymore."

Sean blushed and leaned closer to Joshua, cupping his mouth as though he were imparting a deep, dark secret. "Anything Lizzy makes is my favorite. She's a great cook. Wait 'til you taste her spaghetti. Mom, you should get Lizzy to show you how."

"I doubt I could match her in that department."

"Sure, Mom. You can do anything. Jake told me about the yearlings you used to break."

"A long time ago. At the ripe old age of thirty-one I'm wiser now." She placed a hand on the small of her back. "Just thinking about those days I can feel the aches and pains. Every once in a while there was one who didn't like the feel of a bit and rein or the touch of a saddle and loved to show me how much."

Sean's eyes grew round. "Did you ever break anything?"

"Only my pride from time to time."

"Maybe I can learn how?"

"Not 'til you're much older." Then in a whisper to Joshua she added, "And gone from my home."

"Mom, I heard that."

"Come on. Let's go in to eat."

When Sean raced ahead, she reached out and touched Joshua's arm to stop his forward movement. The instant her fingers grazed him she pulled her hand away.

"Will you do me a favor, Joshua?"

"What?"

"Let's not talk about the fire at dinner tonight. Dad may bring it up, but I'd rather not get him too upset."

"Sure. I don't have anything else to share about the fire until I get the lab tests back."

"Knowing my father, he'll try to pump you for information about your investigation. The doctor said he needed to reduce his stress level, which I'm not sure is possible, especially now with the fire. But I'm going to do everything I can to make his life less stressful." Will that satisfy her father…finally? she wondered.

"Good luck. I've found if the person doesn't want change, it's nearly impossible to force one on them."

"I know, especially someone as stubborn as my father. But that's why I'm here this summer."

"So in August you'll be returning home. Sean said you lived in Panama City, Florida."

"Yes, I'm a high school librarian, so luckily I could take the summer off to help Dad. This trip will be good for Sean." She wasn't so sure about herself, especially after the rocky start she and her dad had had.

"You haven't come home much?"

Darcy thought of the estranged relationship between her and her father. "No, since Clay was in the Navy we were always moving, getting settled in at a new place." She started forward, not wanting to go into the past. Going backward wouldn't change what had happened and she was tired of trying to justify why it had taken a crisis to bring her home.

After they washed their hands, Darcy stepped into the dining room as Lizzy finished putting the last serving bowl on the table. The older woman turned to leave. "Why don't you stay and join us for dinner?" Darcy asked.

Lizzy looked startled. Shaking her head she began backing toward the door. "I've got too much to do in the kitchen."

"Lizzy, you're part of the family and you have to eat." Darcy inhaled the aroma of meat sauce, seasoned with oregano, garlic and onion, flavoring the air. "It smells wonderful." She sensed Joshua's presence behind her, and a tingling awareness shivered down her spine.

Lizzy glanced toward Shamus, who was already dishing up his spaghetti. "I don't—"

"Come on, Lizzy. Joshua's joining us." Sean took the bowl from his grandfather and spooned a big helping onto his plate.

The older woman sighed. "I guess, just this once."

"I've been trying to get her to join me for dinner for years," Shamus grumbled, a frown creasing his brow. "Always said she was too busy. We must have the cleanest kitchen in the state."

"You're welcome to eat in the kitchen anytime you want." Bristling, Lizzy sat next to Sean, leaving the other side of the table for Darcy and Joshua.

Shamus motioned toward the two empty chairs. "Sit, you two. I'm hungry and this is getting cold."

"I like cold spaghetti, Grandpa."

"You like anything that doesn't move." Shamus picked up the bowl of salad but didn't put any on his plate. He passed it to Sean with a smug look thrown toward Lizzy.

The older woman pinched her lips together and focused on filling her plate with the main course. She held her petite frame rigid in the chair, her movements jerky.

At the door Darcy twisted partway around to look at Joshua. "You can always reconsider eating with us. I forget how—" She couldn't come up with an acceptable way to describe the stressful, tension-laden meals she had spent with her father over the years. He was so set in his ways that he wouldn't even eat in the kitchen when it was just him. Darcy was sure that for the past thirty-five years her father had eaten in the dining room and that was the way it would remain.

"Your father reminds me of my own."

"He does?"

"Gruff on the outside, but mush on the inside."

"Mush?" What was Joshua seeing that she had missed? Darcy wondered.

"Look at him with your son. He's listening to every word he's saying."

Darcy glanced over her shoulder at her father. His gaze was glued to Sean, who was regaling him with details of the new foal's first day. Seeing the attention her son was getting pierced defenses she'd built up over the years when trying to deal with her father.

Darcy moved into the room, continuing to feel Joshua's presence close behind her. Had her relationship with her husband colored hers with her father? Even when Clay had been home, he had rarely shown any interest in Sean. Her son was starved for male attention, and that had provoked over the years memories of her own childhood: trying to please her father and never quite succeeding.

After she slipped into the chair across from Lizzy, she filled her plate with the delicious-smelling spaghetti and meat sauce, then gave the bowls to Joshua, who took the last bit. Her father and Sean had already started eating. Lizzy cleared her throat.

Shamus looked up, confusion darkening his expression. "What?"

"I would like to say a blessing," Lizzy said in a prim and proper voice.

Eyebrows slashing downward, Shamus released his fork to clang onto his plate. "Fine."

Lizzy and Joshua bowed their heads. Watching Joshua, Sean immediately followed suit. Darcy clasped her hands together, realizing they were quivering, and stared down at her plate, feeling her father's gaze drill into her.

"Dear Heavenly Father, bless this food we are about to partake of and watch out for each one at this table. Give us the strength to seek Your guidance and the power to know when we need Your help. Amen."

Darcy lifted her head. Her father snatched up his fork, grumbling something under his breath. When her mother died, he'd stopped going to church, telling Darcy that he was just too busy. She had gone with Lizzy until she had left home, but she had always been aware of her father's disapproval.

"Grandpa, Joshua's bringing Arnold here for me to play with. I wish I had a dog."

"We'll just see what we can do about that." Darcy was about to say something when her father continued. "Every boy should have a dog."

"Dad didn't like animals. And when we lived overseas, it was hard to have one," Sean said.

"Arnold recently became a father. The puppies are

five weeks old," Joshua said as he poured ranch dressing onto his salad.

Sean's eyes grew big. "They are? Can I have one?"

"A friend of mine owns them. I can check—" Joshua swung his gaze to Darcy "—if that's okay with your mom."

The full force of his attention was directed at Darcy, causing heat to steal into her cheeks. The urge to shift nervously in her chair inundated her. "I love dogs. That sounds great." She crossed her legs, then uncrossed them. "But, Sean, you'll have to learn to take care of your puppy. It's a big responsibility."

Her son puffed out his chest. "I'm eight, Mom. I'm big enough."

"And we need to see about getting him a horse while he's here this summer." Shamus pinned Darcy with his eyes. "You had one at the age of five."

Memories assailed Darcy. She balled the napkin in her lap, her nails digging into the soft cotton material.

"My very own horse?" Sean exclaimed.

"For as long as you're here and whenever you come to visit again. It would be nice if you visited every summer."

Again Darcy felt her father's intimidating glare. She returned it with an unwavering look, though memories of never quite living up to what her father expected continued to flit through her mind, scene after disappointing scene.

"Can I, Mom?" Sean bounced up and down in his chair.

"We'll see, hon."

"Yes!" Her son pumped his fist into the air. "A dog *and* a horse."

"Your mother's right about taking care of your animals. Around my farm that is a must." Shamus broke off a piece of French bread and started to reach for the butter.

"That isn't on your diet," Lizzy said, snatching away the butter dish before his fingers touched it.

"Nothing good is on my diet," Shamus grumbled, his mouth puckered in a frown.

Before her father started in on what he couldn't eat anymore, Darcy released the tight grip on her napkin and asked, "Joshua, what made you decide to work with a dog?"

"I've been known to take in strays. My captain knew I loved animals, especially dogs, so when this opportunity came up, he encouraged me to do it. Arnold and I went through some extensive training, but it's been worth it."

"Heard you helped solve the Wright case a few months back." With narrowed eyes, Shamus stared at the butter dish sitting next to Lizzy's plate and just out of his reach.

"Wright case? What happened?" Darcy watched the silent exchange between her father and Lizzy—a battle of gazes. In the end her father turned his attention to Joshua. Darcy's mouth almost fell open.

"It was a warehouse fire in Lexington that spread to some other buildings. It was arson. We were lucky and apprehended the man responsible."

"Who?"

"An employee who had been fired and was angry at the owner."

"I came up with another name of someone you could check out," Shamus said, lifting his water glass to take a big sip. "I'd forgotten I had to let Mike Reynolds go a couple of months ago."

"He was your assistant farm manager, wasn't he?" Joshua asked, peering at Darcy.

Did he notice the stiff set to her shoulders and the tight grip she had on her glass? she wondered.

"Yeah. I didn't like his methods."

"He's working at the Colemans' farm now."

"That's what I heard."

"Dad, I think—"

Shamus swung his sharp gaze toward his daughter, a challenge in his eyes.

Darcy stiffened even more. "I don't think we need to discuss this at the dining room table." She glanced toward her son.

"Aw, Mom, I know about the fire."

"You know, Lizzy, I have to agree with Darcy. You're a terrific cook." Joshua took another bite of his spaghetti. He wished he could ease the heavy tension in the room.

The vulnerability he glimpsed in Darcy's eyes melted through his defenses. He found himself wanting to help her through the pain he knew she was experiencing. Her smile touched his heart, urging him to comfort. After Carol's betrayal he hadn't thought that possible, and was surprised by the feeling.

Lizzy blushed a nice shade of red, her eyes twinkling. "You always do know just the right thing to say, Joshua Markham."

Shamus snorted but continued eating.

Sean added, "He's right. I love your spaghetti."

Darcy slid a glance toward Joshua. Her smile reached deep into her large brown eyes, fringed in long, black lashes. The beat of his heart accelerated. He gripped his fork tighter.

"I agree with my son, Lizzy. But if I remember correctly, you make a great lasagna, too." Darcy's shoulder-length blond hair fell forward and she pushed it behind her ears.

With the conversation turning to favorite foods, Joshua sat back, watching the exchange at the table. The lively gleam in Darcy's eyes made her whole face light up. He tried to picture her breaking in a yearling, but couldn't. She was petite, not more than five foot two.

When Lizzy served sliced peaches and ice cream for dessert, Sean snapped his fingers and said, "I've got the perfect name for the new filly. Peaches."

"Not a bad name, son." Shamus frowned at Lizzy, who had handed him a bowl of peaches without the vanilla ice cream.

When Joshua's cell phone rang, everyone shifted their attention to him.

"Sorry." He retrieved his phone from his pocket and checked the message. Tension whipped down his length as he surged to his feet. "I have to leave. There's a fire at the Coleman farm."

Darcy's eyes widened and she came to her feet too, her napkin floating to the carpet. "A barn?"

A new tension descended in the room. "Yes," Joshua said as he headed toward the door.

Chapter Three

"Mom, let's stop. I want to see where Joshua works. Maybe Arnold's there." Sean bounced up and down in the front seat of the truck, pointing to the fire station at the end of the block.

"Hon, I still need to pick up some things at the store and there's a lot to do back at the farm."

"Pleease, Mom."

Pausing at the stop sign, Darcy chanced a look at her son. The eagerness in his expression shoved away all her doubts. Just because she had thought about Joshua Markham several times in the past forty-eight hours— okay, more than several times—didn't mean she couldn't pay him a visit, then go her merry way. "All right. But we can't stay long. And if he's busy, we'll need to leave."

"Sure." Sean stretched his neck to get a better look at the fire station as Darcy pulled into the driveway and parked behind the building.

"Hon, he might not be here."

"He is."

Suspicion began to form in her mind. "How do you know?"

Sean ducked his head to the side and studied the scenery out the side window as though fascinated with the brick wall several feet from the truck.

"Sean."

"Uh—" He stared down at his hands fidgeting in his lap. "I called him this morning." Her son's voice was barely audible.

"Sean, you know better than to bother a busy man."

He lifted his head, turning his appealing look on her. "But, Mom, he told me I could play with Arnold. I wanted to find out when."

"That doesn't mean you have an open invitation to visit him at work or to call him anytime you want."

"Yes, I do." His grin split his face. "He invited me this morning. Said I was welcome to come by anytime they were there."

"Only *after* you called." Darcy gripped the steering wheel and thought about backing out and escaping before anyone saw them. Her dream about the fire last night was filled with the image of the smoke and fog parting and Joshua walking toward her. Everything had dimmed except the man in the fire gear striding toward her with exhaustion evident in every line of his handsome face. Confidence had marked his stance as he'd come to a stop in front of her. His blue eyes had gleamed in the early morning light, drawing her toward him—dangerously close.

The flashback to the previous dream made beads of perspiration pop out on her upper lip. Darcy brushed them away. What am I doing? *I have no business thinking about Joshua Markham in any terms other than as a firefighter and an acquaintance.* She started to switch on the engine and leave before anyone knew they were there. She would find some excuse to give her son.

Too late. Joshua waved from the door and strode toward them.

"See. He's expecting us."

Darcy wanted to hide. She felt the heat suffuse her cheeks as the man walked to the truck, a smile of greeting on his face. The first thing she thought about was the dusty jeans and the old worn shirt she wore. Why hadn't she changed before coming into town? Why did she care? Her record with men was no good. She just had to think about her husband and father to confirm that.

Joshua stopped on her side of the truck, his face framed in her window, only a few inches from her. She rolled down the window and forced a smile to her lips. "Is this a bad time to come?" *Please let it be,* she silently added, even as she responded to his heart-melting grin, her pulse accelerating.

"It's been quiet around here."

"That's good" was all she could think to say with

the man dominating her space, his musky scent surrounding her.

"Yeah, we feel the same way."

"Where's Arnold?" Sean asked, unbuckling his seat belt.

"He's in the station. Come on in and meet the rest of the guys."

Sean hopped from the truck before Darcy could say anything. Joshua opened her door, and she slid out, glad to see her legs would support her weight. Her son ran ahead while she and Joshua walked at a leisurely pace toward the building.

"I checked with my friend about a puppy for Sean. It's fine with him. In fact, he can have the pick of the litter."

"How much are the puppies?"

"Free. He just wants to give the puppies good homes."

Darcy halted, causing Joshua to do the same. "What aren't you telling me?"

He stuffed his hands into his pockets. "I told him I didn't want the pick of the litter."

"So Sean gets it instead. I can pay for a puppy. I know teachers don't get rich teaching, but—"

"I wanted to do this for Sean."

"Why?"

"I can remember my first dog when I was growing up. Lady was so special to me. I want Sean to experience that."

"But—"

Joshua held up his hand to stop her protest. "If you

saw my house and the animals I have, you wouldn't say anything. I don't need to take on another pet."

"How many do you have?"

"Three dogs besides Arnold, two cats, a rabbit and an aquarium full of fish."

"Don't tell Sean. He'll be begging to come over."

"I've never bought one of those animals. Either people give them to me because they don't want them anymore or they are left in my yard."

He was a large, muscular man in a dangerous profession, but underneath everything he was a softie, taking in strays. There had been times when married to Clay that she'd felt like a stray, wandering from city to city looking for a permanent home. She was glad now that she and Sean had one in Panama City. This spring had been the beginning of their second year there.

Sean stood at the door to the fire station, waiting for them. He hopped from one foot to the other. "Come *on*, Mom," he finally shouted when he couldn't contain his impatience any longer.

"Do you want me to tell him about the puppy now?" Joshua said in a low voice.

"You might wait until later or he'll want you to leave your job and show him the puppy."

"I'm off on Sunday. How about after church? We can leave after the eleven o'clock service, pick up something to eat for lunch, then go to Ned's. Sean can pick out the puppy he wants."

Darcy didn't say anything for a few seconds. She'd

made plans to start going to church again with Lizzy. She'd gotten out of the habit when married to Clay. They had moved so often it had become difficult to find a place to worship where she was comfortable—at least, that was the excuse she'd given herself over the years.

"I'm sorry. I'm assuming you'll be going to church while you're home. I can meet you at Ned's place if you want."

"No. Lizzy mentioned something to me the other day."

"You can come with Lizzy, and then I can bring you and Sean home later. I should have the results back from the lab by then and I promised your father a report on what I found."

Sean danced around. "Mom! I've got to *go.*"

Joshua chuckled. "I guess we'd better get inside."

"It was that pop he drank on the way into town."

Joshua reached around Sean and pulled the door open. "The rest room is down the hall on the left."

Her son shot down the corridor and disappeared into the bathroom. They waited by the entrance until he came out into the hall. He headed straight for them with determination on his face.

"Where's Arnold?"

"Probably watching TV."

"He watches TV?"

"Yep, I'm afraid so. Nasty habit he's gotten into. The last time I saw him he was in the living area in front of the set." Joshua gestured to the right.

Sean darted ahead of them into a large room with several couches and chair. A table that sat twelve was off to one side in a spacious kitchen of gleaming stainless steel. Arnold was where Joshua had left him, perched before the big-screen television set, his head resting on his front paws.

"He really *does* watch TV," Darcy said in astonishment.

While Sean kneeled next to the black Lab, Joshua chuckled. "Like I said, a really nasty habit he developed. He likes the noise, and when a dog appears he begins to bark, which doesn't always sit well with the other guys who are trying to watch the show."

"What does he do when a cat appears?" Darcy watched her son rub the length of Arnold's back, then bury his face in his fur.

The dog rolled over, his tail wagging.

"He loves cats. His best buddy is Ringo, a white male cat that found me about two years ago and adopted us. When we're at home, they are usually inseparable."

"Hasn't Arnold heard a cat is a dog's enemy?"

"Apparently not."

An older man came into the room, Joshua introduced him to Darcy and Sean as his captain. When he left, another man, younger, entered and waved at Darcy.

"Joshua said something about you and your son coming to visit this morning." Glen hugged her. "I haven't seen you since right after high school graduation."

"We went to school together since kindergarten," Darcy said to Joshua, then turned back to Glen. "I heard you married your high school sweetheart."

"Nancy and I will have been married ten years come this July. How's your father doing? I'm sorry about the fire at the farm."

"He's the same. Thinks he can single-handedly do everything around the farm."

"That sounds like Shamus. Well, it's my turn to make lunch so I'd better get going before I have seven guys breathing down my neck." Glen made his way into the kitchen area and opened the refrigerator.

"Sean, would you like to go on a tour of the station?" Joshua asked.

Her son glanced up. "Can Arnold come too?"

"Sure, if you can get him to move from the TV set."

Sean leaped to his feet and patted his leg. "Come on, Arnold."

The black Lab lumbered to his feet and nudged Sean's hand so he would continue rubbing him behind the ear.

"I think your son has a gift with animals."

Darcy thought of all the times Sean had wanted a pet and Clay had refused to let him. She thought of how her son had taken to the farm as though he'd grown up there, doing chores, helping take care of the horses and other animals. Her throat closed. She should have brought Sean to the farm sooner. For her son's sake, she should have put her past with her father behind her. It had taken a crisis with her father to get her back home. But the minute she had stepped on Shamrock land, all her insecurities, doubts and guilt had flooded her, as though she'd never left ten years ago.

* * *

"Wait up, Darcy."

Darcy turned to see her best friend from high school hurrying toward her from the back of the church. For a few seconds she lost Jesse Bradshaw in the crowd, which was not unusual since her friend was only five feet tall. Darcy stepped to the side to allow the other parishioners to pass while she waited.

"I should berate you, Darcy O'Brien, for not coming by to see me, but I know you've had your hands full with your father's illness and the fire. I'm sorry." Jesse Bradshaw hugged Darcy. "I'm missed you." She pulled back to get a good look at Darcy. "You haven't changed a bit."

Darcy laughed. "I've missed you, Jesse, and you *have* changed." Her friend had lost twenty or so pounds, and her long brown hair was now short and feathered about her pixie-like features. The only thing the same was her green eyes—clear and sparkling with humor. Darcy turned to the side. "This is my son, Sean."

Shaking Sean's hand, Jesse said, "My son, Nate, is around here somewhere. You two will have to get together. Darcy, I'll call you this week. Let's get together for lunch. I want to know everything that's happened to you in the last ten years. E-mails just don't tell me what's really going on with you." Jesse fell into line with them to speak with the reverend.

"There's Joshua. He's waiting for us by his truck. Come on, Mom." Sean tugged on her arm.

"Joshua Markham?" Jesse asked, one brow quirked.

"Yes, he's helping Sean get a puppy." Darcy leaned toward her friend. "And that is *all*, so don't get any ideas."

Jesse held up her hand. "Who, me? Never."

Moving forward in the line, Darcy smiled at Reverend Collins and shook his hand. "I enjoyed your sermon." Out of the corner of her eye she could see her son dancing about.

"It's good to see you back home, Darcy. Don't be a stranger."

Darcy pulled Sean to her side. "And this eager young man is my son, Sean."

The reverend held out his hand. "I hope we'll get to see more of you this summer."

Sean contained his enthusiasm long enough to straighten and shake the man's hand. "Joshua introduced me to a couple of the boys in his Sunday school class. One lives down the road from Grandpa."

"That must be Brad Anderson."

"Yep." Sean glanced up at Darcy. "Can we go now? I don't want to be late."

After saying her goodbyes to Reverend Collins and Jesse, Darcy allowed her son to drag her toward Joshua. As they approached, Darcy's heart increased its beat, aware that her friend was probably watching every move she made. She didn't dare look back at Jesse and encourage her in any way.

Darcy turned her full focus on the man before her. The sight of Joshua in black slacks with a sky-blue short-sleeved shirt and a striped tie was just as compelling as the image of him in his fire gear or navy-blue fire-fighter's uniform. The bright sun beamed down on her, but that wasn't the reason she perspired more than usual. The warm greeting in Joshua's eyes did strange things to her. Her stomach flip-flopped; her pulse quickened.

"Are you ready, Sean?" Joshua asked, swinging open the passenger door of his red truck.

"Yes."

"I thought we would grab something to eat, then go to Ned's."

The wide grin on her son's face fell.

"Or, we could go to Ned's first, then eat," Joshua amended when he saw Sean's crestfallen expression.

"Yes!" Sean hopped up into the cab.

"I can't believe he's turning down a meal. That just goes to show you how important this puppy is to Sean." Darcy followed her son into the truck, relieved she wasn't pressed up against Joshua.

He shut the door and leaned forward, his head framed in the open window. "You understand, Sean, you won't be able to take the puppy home for a few more weeks."

"Can I visit my puppy?"

"I don't think Ned will mind—if it's okay with your mother."

Sean sent her a beseeching look.

"We'll work something out," she said.

Her son breathed a deep sigh of relief while Joshua rounded the front of the truck and slid behind the steering wheel.

"Actually, Ned lives about halfway to your farm on Old State Road, not too far from Sweetwater Lake."

"Maybe I could walk to his place."

"No way, young man," said Darcy. "When you get your chores done, I'll drive you. No walking along that highway."

"But, Mom—"

Joshua backed out of the parking space. "I've had a few near misses out on Old State Road. Some people think its straightaway is an invitation to race. Not a safe place to be."

Again Sean sighed, but he remained quiet.

In a short time Darcy had begun to notice the influence Joshua had over her son. For a boy hungry for male attention, Joshua was a wonderful role model. But what was going to happen when they returned to Panama City in August? She hated disappointing her son. For years he had tried to get his father interested in what he was doing, but Clay had hardly ever been around. When they'd been in the same room, it had been as though they were strangers.

As they drove toward Ned's, her son thankfully kept up a running commentary about the Sunday school class he'd joined that day, the one Joshua taught. Sean described each of the boys he'd met and gave a rundown on their likes and dislikes. She was glad he had been readily accepted by his peers, especially Brad Anderson and Nate Bradshaw, Jesse's son. Darcy relaxed and listened to Sean and Joshua.

Fifteen minutes later Joshua drove through an opened gate and down a gravel road that ended in front of a one-story, white, wooden house with an old brown barn nearby. "He's probably in the barn."

"Does he raise horses like Grandpa?" Sean exited the truck on Joshua's side.

That gave Darcy a chance to take her time and allow the two guys to go ahead of her. She heard Joshua say, "No, he takes in strays like I do. He's a firefighter at the station where I work. He doesn't have a lot of land, just a few acres. But I must say, he has more room than I do. I'm running out of places to put my animals."

Dressed in a plaid short-sleeved shirt, a man who appeared to be in his forties came out of the barn. He brushed some dust from his jeans and adjusted his navy-blue ball cap. "Right on time. I just got through feeding the animals."

Sean raced forward. "Where are the puppies?"

Ned placed a hand on the boy's shoulder and led him into the barn. Joshua waited for her by the entrance.

"I think your son is excited."

"A small understatement."

"I'm glad he enjoyed this morning. How did you like the adult class?"

"Lizzy and Jesse took me under their wing. I didn't realize there were so many new people since I last attended."

"When was that?"

"Over ten years ago."

"You never had time to come with Lizzy when you visited?"

Darcy stepped into the coolness of the barn, the familiar scents of leather, dirt and hay drifting to her. "This is the first time I've been home since I got married."

When Joshua didn't say anything for several heartbeats, Darcy felt compelled to add, "We were out of the country for half that time."

"You don't owe me an explanation."

"I know, but I didn't realize it was that long until I came home. Lizzy was quick to point that out to me."

"Not your father?"

Sean's laughter floated to her. She looked toward her son in the middle of a pen with six puppies crawling all over him. "No, my relationship with my father has been strained for years." She wasn't sure why she told Joshua that, but for some reason it felt right to confide in him, which surprised her, but he was easy to talk to and she suspected he didn't judge a person.

"You returned home when he needed you the most."

She paused a few yards from Sean so he wouldn't hear her reply. "I'm not sure my father needs me right now. He is trying to continue doing everything himself even though he is supposed to be resting and learning to take life a little easier."

"Like the fire?"

"I finally convinced him to let me take care of stabling the mares. But I don't think he rested much. He had all the book work done when I returned to the office later. But I guess sitting at a desk is better than running around the farm."

"Sometimes it's hard for a person to accept help or to even ask for it."

"That definitely describes my father."

"My father could be stubborn at times, but…" His voice faded into silence as he glanced away.

"But what?"

"I'd trade anything to have those times back. I miss our…lively discussions."

"It sounds like you had a good relationship with your father."

His intense gaze swung back to her. "It wasn't perfect, but yes, we had a good relationship."

How could she tell Joshua that she would give anything to have a good relationship with her father? How could she tell him that her father had been disappointed she wasn't a male and that she was an only child? She would never forget the time she'd overheard her parents arguing and her mother shouting at her father that she was glad they hadn't had any more children. He didn't deserve to have the son he'd always wanted, that he would have to settle for passing his farm on to a daughter. She'd run from the house and hidden in the loft of the barn, crying until there were no tears left inside. Her mother's words had explained a lot to her—her father's demands to be perfect, her father's coldness and distance. But still, it hurt to this day.

Joshua's expression softened. Darcy closed her eyes, afraid the anguish she experienced every time she remembered that day was evident in them. His finger brushed across her cheek.

"You're crying." He captured her hand and laced his fingers through hers. "Some say I'm a good listener."

Through a sheen she viewed the tenderness in his expression and wanted to go into the comfort she knew she would find in his arms. With a supreme effort she held herself back, because that wasn't her. She'd already told Joshua more than she shared with others. She attempted a smile that wavered about the corners of her mouth, then vanished.

"I think the trauma of the fire is finally catching up with me."

His gaze ensnared hers as though he were delving into her mind to read her deepest thoughts, those she kept hidden from the world.

"I know we don't know each other well," he said, "but if I—"

"Mom! Joshua! Aren't you coming?"

Darcy blinked, tugged her hand from Joshua's and started for her son. Joshua's gaze bore into her back and her steps quickened. She had been so close to telling him about her childhood—and that frightened her. She hadn't even told her husband how hard it had been growing up with warring parents and a mother who— She wouldn't think about the past. Hadn't she learned that reliving it only brought her pain?

This time when she smiled, it stayed in place. She'd become good at putting up a front for her son's sake. She entered the pen and kneeled next to Sean. "Have you decided on one yet?"

"I can't decide between this one—" he held up a male black Lab "—or this one." Scooping up the puppy into his lap, he showed her a smaller female with a lighter mark on its brow. "I think she's the runt. Which one do you like the most?"

"Son, it's your choice."

"Yeah, but what if I choose wrong?"

That innocent question brought a lump to her throat. She'd made some wrong choices that she wished she could do over, but life wasn't like that. She swallowed and replied, "Making mistakes is how we learn, but I don't think you can go wrong picking between these two adorable puppies."

The female nudged Sean's hand while the male licked him, then began gnawing on his finger. "Joshua, what do you think?"

Joshua chuckled. "I agree with your mother. It's your call."

Her son then turned his attention to Ned, who shook his head and said, "No, partner, you're on your own."

Sean's face brightened. "Mom, how about taking both? I have some money saved. I could buy the other one."

"I think, Sweetie, for your first pet we should stick to having only one." Darcy straightened, aware of Joshua standing right behind her. She always seemed to know where he was in relation to her. That shook her. "You don't have to make up your mind right this minute."

"No, why don't you play with them for a while? I have some iced tea up at the house. We'll be sitting on the porch when you're ready." Ned headed out of the barn.

Darcy backed away. She watched her son bury his face in the fur of first the female, then the male. She thought about the small yard they had in Panama City and knew one big dog was all they could handle.

"It's tough making that kind of decision," Joshua murmured as they walked from the barn.

"If the dogs were going to be smaller, we might be able to have two." She peered back once more to see Sean lying on the ground with both puppies on his chest. He was talking to them.

"It's hard setting limits."

"As a parent all I want to do is protect my son from the world and any problems that might arise."

"Impossible."

"I know." *Better than most,* she added silently, remembering being caught between two parents who had fought all the time, often using her as a referee. She had promised herself when she married that her marriage would be different. It had been, because she had given in to her husband's wishes instead of standing up for what she believed in.

She didn't believe anymore that it was possible for two people to be equal partners in a marriage. And so she would never marry again.

Chapter Four

"Mom, I don't know which puppy to take. I liked playing with both of them," Sean said, popping his last french fry into his mouth. "What do you think, Joshua?"

"Listen to your heart. You can't go wrong."

Yes, you can, Darcy thought, remembering her marriage. She'd been in love with Clay, but over the years his indifference had eroded her feelings until they had been two strangers living in the same household— much like her parents. Now she relied on her head rather than her heart when it came to important matters. Much safer.

Sean downed the rest of his soft drink. "Then I think I want the runt of the litter. She needs me."

Darcy cocked her head. "Why do you say that?"

"Because she's small like me. Probably no one will pick her. She'll need a home and someone to love her."

Her heart twisted at the pain behind her son's words.

She knew why he felt that way. Clay. Her husband over the years had made more than one comment about how small their son was. Clay had wanted Sean involved in sports and hadn't been sure if that would be possible.

"Size isn't important, Sean. It's what's inside that counts," Joshua said as he gathered up their trash and stacked it on the tray. "Until I was fifteen, I was several inches smaller than most guys in my class. Then all of a sudden I began to grow and didn't stop until I was in my early twenties. I more than made up for my lack of height as a child." Joshua slid from the booth and rose, all six feet and a few inches.

Sean craned his neck and looked at Joshua. "You think I'll be tall like you?"

"Can't say. You'll be as tall as you need to be."

Darcy slipped from the booth, followed by her son who beamed from ear to ear. Seeing Sean with Joshua only reconfirmed that her son needed a man's influence in his life. Clay hadn't been around much for Sean, and a mother just couldn't offer certain things for a boy.

"I still want the girl puppy. Maybe one day she can have a litter. I could sell all the puppies except one."

"Hold it, young man. I'm only agreeing to one dog at the moment."

"Aw, Mom, I don't mean right away. That'll be *years* from now."

"Then I'll call Ned and tell him that's your choice." Joshua held the door open for Darcy and Sean.

"Will you ask him if I can come visit her tomorrow?

I want her to get to know me so she won't be so scared when she leaves her mother."

"How do you expect to get over there?" Darcy asked while walking toward Joshua's truck in the parking lot of the fast-food restaurant.

Sean's smile grew. "You?"

Remembering how demanding her father had been about her first horse, she never wanted her son to feel he couldn't live up to his parent's expectations. "Only after you do your chores. When you're responsible for animals, their needs come before yours. If you want that horse this summer, you have to show Grandpa you can take care of it."

"It's a deal."

Joshua unlocked his truck, and Sean climbed into the front seat, followed by Darcy. Joshua backed out of the parking space and waited to pull out into traffic.

"Joshua, can I see Arnold today?"

Joshua glanced at Darcy, a question in his eyes. She shrugged, realizing she'd like to see where he lived. Did his house fit the man? She could tell a lot by a person's surroundings.

"Sure, if you promise to play catch with him. That's his favorite thing, next to TV."

"Yes!" In his excitement Sean bounced on the seat.

Ten minutes later Joshua pulled into the driveway of a one-story white cottage with a beautiful, manicured yard. Red and yellow impatiens lined the bed in front of a rock garden surrounding a century-old oak tree that shaded the house. A bird bath with several cardinals in it graced the middle of the rock garden.

Darcy followed the round stepping stones from the driveway to the porch. Off to the side sat a white wicker table and two comfortable-looking chairs with striped forest-green-and-tan cushions. A perfect place to enjoy a cup of coffee in the early morning, she thought while Joshua unlocked his house.

For a few seconds she pictured herself sitting in one of the chairs with Joshua in the other, discussing a favorite book or a movie they'd seen. He would laugh at something witty she'd said and she would—whoa. Where had that fantasy come from? She hurried inside before her thoughts took her any further.

Darcy hadn't been sure what to expect, but when she walked into Joshua's house, surprise flickered through her. One small brown dog, a mix of four or five breeds, bounded from the back of the house, yelping and jumping into the air. A large white cat stirred from the navy-blue sofa, stretched, then lumbered toward them.

"Missy, sit."

The brown mutt immediately obeyed Joshua's command. The cat weaved in and out of her legs, rubbing his body against her while purring. Another smaller cat, various shades of gray, came from the hallway at a lazy pace.

"You *do* have a lot of animals," Darcy said, bending over to pet the white cat with two different colored eyes.

"What can I say? I can't turn away a stray."

Sean kneeled on the hardwood floor next to Missy and stroked her. "Where's Arnold?"

"Out back with my other two dogs. Come on. I'll show you." Joshua started forward with Sean next to him. Joshua paused at the entrance into the kitchen and glanced back at Darcy. "Make yourself at home. I'll only be a sec."

While he was gone, Darcy scanned the living room, a large open room with a high ceiling. Beautifully carved built-in bookcases, filled with books and Indian pottery, graced one whole wall, while the others were painted a rich, deep burgundy. The room should have been dark, but the large windows with plantation shutters along the front of the house allowed sunlight to pour in. The hardwood floor in the entryway continued throughout the living room with one area rug of burgundy-and-navy between the couch and two cushioned chairs with ottomans. On the massive coffee table sat a large, black leather-bound Bible that probably had been handed down for generations.

Comfort came to mind as Darcy looked around. And a sense of warmth. A lot of care had gone into Joshua's home. The man was continually surprising her. Clay had never wanted anything to do with their houses. She'd always thought it was because they had moved so much that he had found it hard to become attached to any one place. But in reality, her husband had never viewed their houses as home.

"Grab a seat. I'll get us something to drink."

Joshua's voice startled Darcy. "I didn't hear you come in."

"Sorry. I'll whistle my approach next time."

"No, you just caught me thinking."

"About what?"

"Your house. I love it. I can tell a lot of thought went into it."

A shadow clouded Joshua's eyes. His mouth firmed into a hard line. "It did." He turned away, a rigidity to his stance. "I've got some iced tea."

He was gone before Darcy could say anything. She wondered about the sudden tension that had sparked the air. She made her way to the couch and sat. The white cat jumped up and lay in her lap. Darcy buried her fingers in his soft fur and rubbed, still pondering the change in Joshua's disposition.

"If Ringo's bothering you, just put him on the floor. He loves people and likes to make himself at home in their laps," Joshua said, coming toward her carrying two tall glasses.

She saw none of the earlier, tense expression. Maybe she had imagined it. After all, she'd given him a compliment. But some people were uncomfortable with compliments. Taking an iced tea from him, Darcy sipped, relishing the cold drink.

"I've never seen such beautiful craftsmanship before. Did these bookcases come with the house?" Darcy placed her glass on a coaster on the coffee table, wanting to recapture the ease they'd had when they'd talked earlier.

"No, I made them."

Her gaze shifted to him. "You did? How long did it take?"

"Months, working on my days off."

"Have you done other pieces of furniture?" Such craft had obviously gone into his work. There were many facets to this man.

His mouth tightened into a frown. "Yes. My bed."

Darcy almost asked to see it, but an undercurrent flowed between them as though she had journeyed into forbidden territory. Again she felt the tension take hold of Joshua and wondered about it. "You're gifted. If you ever want to stop being a firefighter, you could make a living carving furniture."

"It's just a hobby." Joshua took several large swallows of his tea, draining half the glass.

"You're a man full of interesting surprises. Most don't go to this much trouble when it's just them living alone."

His grip was so tight that his knuckles whitened on his glass. "It wasn't supposed to be just me."

"Oh?"

"I was engaged once."

"What happened?" Her teeth dug into her lower lip.

Joshua carefully put his drink on a coaster, his gaze lifting to hers. For a few seconds she glimpsed pain, until he veiled the expression and averted his look. She shouldn't have asked. She'd overstepped her bounds with the question, but she wanted to know everything about him. He interested her—more than she should allow, she realized.

She was about to rise when he finally said, "It's not really a big secret. In fact, the whole town knows. My fiancée left me at the altar last year because she was having another man's baby."

His words caught her completely by surprise and wrenched her heart. How awful. But she suspected he didn't want to hear those words. She let the silence grow while he wrestled with his demons. The clenching of his jaw and the stiffening of his body spoke of the emotions gripping him.

"I'd spent six months getting this house ready for Carol. I'd wanted everything perfect. The problem was, while I was lovingly carving the bookcases and bed, she was seeing another man. I…" His voice trailed off into the silence. He swallowed hard and reestablished eye contact with Darcy. "I should have spent the time with Carol. But I love working with my hands and this—" he swept his arm to indicate the whole house "—was my way of expressing my love for her."

"She didn't want to help?"

"She did a little, but she didn't like physical work. Computers were more her thing. She would spend hours in front of one. I need to be up and working. Sitting for too long drives me crazy."

"About the only time I sit is to read a good book. That's what I do when I have the time."

The corners of Joshua's mouth lifted in a lopsided

grin that eased the tension momentarily. "Since you're a librarian, that makes sense."

Darcy chuckled. "I guess I'd better like books or I'd be surrounded by something I don't like every day at work." She shifted on the couch, leaning back against the cushion. "Does Carol live in Sweetwater?"

"Yes. She married the man and they have—" he cleared his throat "—a seven-month-old son."

"Do you see her much?" There was a part of her that was shocked at the boldness of her questions; the other part wanted to know the answers, wanted to know Joshua.

"Not often. She used to go to the same church, but now goes to a different one across town."

"I'm sorry things didn't work out, but maybe what happened was for the best. If you aren't right for each other, it's better to discover that before the marriage rather than after." *Like I did,* Darcy thought, folding her arms over her chest.

"I keep telling myself that. The worst part about the whole situation is that it makes me doubt my judgment. How could I be so wrong about Carol? We'd known each other for years—dated for three of them."

How many times had she asked herself that very question concerning Clay? "Maybe you didn't see the true Carol. People have a way of putting up a front. The problem is, that front won't last forever. A person's true character comes out in the end."

Joshua picked up his drink and finished it in several swallows. "Speaking from experience?"

She wished she could tell him. But she wasn't used to sharing much of herself with anyone. She'd tried with Clay and he'd rejected her feelings. Between her experiences with her father and Clay, she'd learned to keep everything buried deep inside. "I was just making an observation. I'm sure everyone has dealt with people who aren't always who they seem to be."

He studied her. The silence in the room stretched to an uncomfortable level. Darcy crossed her legs, then uncrossed them.

"I suppose you're right," he finally said.

His words cut through the silence, but did nothing to relieve the tension building in Darcy. She pushed herself to her feet. "I probably should check on Sean, make sure he's staying out of trouble. It's been awfully quiet for the past twenty minutes."

"He's got three dogs to play with. When I left him, he was smiling from ear to ear while they licked him."

"That's my son. Give him an animal and he can entertain himself for hours."

"Then Sean and I have something in common."

Darcy followed Joshua through the kitchen, a sunny, cheerful room decorated in yellows and reds with dark walnut cabinets polished to a rich sheen. The tan tiled countertops and floor contrasted with the plaid wallpaper, complimenting each other.

When she stepped out onto the deck, she was taken by its beauty. A rose garden graced the east side, while a garden full of wildflowers stood along the west fence.

A pond fed by a fountain was the focal point in the rock garden along the deck. Several maple trees with two stone benches under them presented a place to seek shade in the heat of summer.

"Do you like to do yard work, too?"

Joshua glanced around, his gaze touching each garden. "Yes. I do draw the line at housework, however. I have someone come in once a week to clean for me."

"Frankly, I don't know when you would have time to do that anyway. You do like to be busy."

"There're so many things I want to do and so little time."

"Mom, watch this," Sean shouted from beneath a maple tree.

Her son held up a Frisbee and sent it sailing through the air. Arnold leaped up and caught it, then trotted back to Sean.

"Isn't he great?"

Two more dogs, one a cross between a collie and a German shepherd and the other with a lot of Chow in him, vied for Sean's attention. He tossed a ball for each of them to fetch.

"Where do you draw the line at taking in strays?" Darcy asked, turning slightly so she faced Joshua.

Sunlight danced in his blue eyes. "I haven't found that point yet. I usually manage to locate homes for my strays, but if I can't, I keep them until I find one. Every once in a while one of the strays touches me in a certain way and I end up keeping him for a pet."

"Hence the four dogs and two cats?"

He nodded, silent laughter making his eyes sparkle. "That's one of the reasons I fell in love with this house. The yard is so big."

"You know, when we return to Panama City I'm gonna have a hard time with Sean. He'll probably start wanting a larger house so he can have more pets. I won't be surprised if he doesn't start finding strays. Joshua Markham, you have made quite an impression on my son in the short time we've known you."

He straightened, satisfaction stamped on his features. "I aim to please."

That was the problem. He was pleasing to look at, pleasing to be around. She had no intention of getting serious about a man after her marriage to Clay, but she was finding that harder and harder to remember the more she was with Joshua.

"Why didn't Grandpa come with us?" Sean asked as he hopped from the car and started for the church.

"He was tired and thought he would go to bed early tonight." Darcy trailed behind her son with Lizzy at her side.

"Maybe he'll come on Sunday with us." Seeing Nate Bradshaw, Sean hurried into the building.

Lizzy stopped on the sidewalk to catch her breath. "You and I both know your father won't come on Sunday or next Wednesday night. He hasn't stepped foot in church since the day of your mother's funeral."

"I know. Maybe Sean can do what you and I couldn't—get Dad to come to church."

Lizzy shook her head. "I've been trying for the past thirteen years to no avail. He's unusually quiet about his reasons behind stopping, which in itself is a mystery. Your father is rarely quiet about anything."

As well Darcy knew. She had been on more than one occasion at the other end of her father's sharp tongue and biting opinions. She held one of the double glass doors open for Lizzy, who carried a large casserole dish for the Wednesday-night potluck dinner and church service. While Lizzy headed toward the kitchen, Darcy was letting the door close when a woman about her age with a young girl in a wheelchair approached. Smiling at the woman and child, Darcy stepped to the side to allow them into the building. The young girl, her face with an ashen complexion, grinned up at Darcy.

"Hi, I'm Darcy O'Brien."

"I'm Crystal."

Darcy glanced at the tall, slightly overweight woman with shoulder-length light brown hair and hazel eyes pushing Crystal's wheelchair.

"And I'm Crystal's mother, Tanya. Lizzy said something about Shamus Flanaghan's daughter and grandson coming home for the summer." The woman smiled, two dimples appearing in her cheeks.

"That would be me," Darcy said, responding to the upbeat, enthusiastic tone in the woman's voice and the happy expression on her face.

"Well, it's a pleasure meeting you. Lizzy has been such a dear to me and my family since the accident." Tanya started toward the rec hall, maneuvering the wheelchair around people in the foyer. "This is our first outing in a long time. Crystal's been dying to see her friends."

Inside the large room with rows of tables set for dinner, Tanya wheeled Crystal toward a group of children standing around the piano. The music director was playing and the kids were singing. When a song ended, everyone greeted Crystal, a couple of the girls hugging her. Tanya backed away and stood next to Darcy.

The woman blew out a relieved breath. "I'm glad that's over with."

"What?"

"Crystal was anxious about this first meeting."

"You said something about an accident. What happened?"

Tanya frowned, the lines on her forehead deepening into grooves. "She was taking a riding lesson when her horse got spooked and bolted. She fell and injured her spine. The doctors say she'll never walk again."

Darcy remembered her own falls from a horse and shivered. "I'm sorry." The words seemed inadequate.

"Crystal's got a great attitude. She'll be okay. That's more than I can say about her father."

The children finished singing and began moving toward the couch area with the youth minister. Tanya rushed forward to push her daughter. Darcy headed toward the kitchen to help Lizzy with the dinner setup.

"I see you met Tanya Bolton and Crystal," Lizzy said, handing Darcy a stack of plates to put on the serving table.

"Yes. When did Crystal have her riding accident?"

"Last fall. Tragic. Tom, her father, has been a hard man to live with. I try to help as much as I can, but he is so angry. Tanya had enough to cope with before the accident. Now I don't know how she does it."

Darcy came back to pick up another stack of plates. "Money problems?"

Lizzy nodded. "Crystal's accident has been very hard on the family, financially as well as emotionally. Tanya needs all the friends she can get right now." She pinned Darcy with a worried expression. "And your prayers."

"That I can give." Darcy peered through the door into the rec hall and found the woman standing by her daughter, listening to the youth minister. Her heart went out to Tanya Bolton. If something like that happened to Sean, she wasn't sure how she would handle it.

Darcy's gaze shifted away and lit upon Joshua speaking with the reverend. Her heartbeat responded with a quicker pace. He looked good to the eyes, Darcy thought, taking in Joshua dressed casually in a pair of tan slacks and navy-blue polo shirt. The blue brought out the color of his eyes.

She recalled the pain she'd seen reflected in those eyes when he'd talked about his ex-fiancée. She, too, had been through a difficult relationship, so she felt a kinship with Joshua. That was all she could allow, however. In a few months she and Sean would return to

Panama City where their home was. Sweetwater wasn't home anymore. Sometimes she wondered if it ever really had been.

Joshua caught her looking at him. A smile lit his eyes, the lines at the corners of them deepening. A dimple appeared at his mouth and held her attention for a few seconds before she averted her gaze.

She turned back toward Lizzy. "What else do you need me to do?"

"We just need to get the dishes on the table and then we're ready to eat."

"Sounds good to me. I haven't eaten since breakfast."

"Can I help you two?"

Joshua's question brought her around to face him. "Sure. As you can see, we have a lot of food." Darcy waved toward all the dishes on the counter.

Side by side she and Joshua worked to put the food out on the long serving table while Lizzy put finishing touches on some of the dishes. Seeing Joshua here this evening added a bounce to Darcy's walk, as though his presence completed the night. She shouldn't feel that way. She had every intention of leaving Sweetwater when the summer was over. She and her father couldn't stay in the same town for long. She didn't want to fall into the same old pattern she'd been in while growing up, and even while married to Clay. She was just discovering who Darcy O'Brien really was.

"I'm glad to see you here tonight." Joshua's deep,

rich voice cut into her thoughts, bringing her back to the present.

"You are?"

"Yes. I was going to call you tomorrow. Ned says that Sean can have his puppy a little earlier than usual. After your son's visit the other day, he decided that Sean would be a great owner and there wasn't any reason to wait another week."

"Have you told Sean yet?"

"No, I wanted to run it by you first."

"If I know my son, he'll want to go over to Ned's tomorrow morning before the sun rises."

Joshua laughed. "Afraid he'll have to wait a little. Ned doesn't go off duty until the afternoon."

"Sean will be beside himself. Dad has arranged for him to have a horse. He'll be riding him for the first time tomorrow morning. Are you off?"

He nodded. "Why?"

"This would be a good time for you to go riding with us. Remember you said you wanted to ride more? Well, I'm giving you the perfect excuse to. Then you can go with us to pick up the puppy, since you're the reason we're getting her."

Joshua ran a hand through his hair, thinking. "I have to confess I'm not a good rider. In fact, I'm no kind of rider."

"Then you and Sean will have something in common. Sean's only ridden a few times."

"I hope I don't regret saying yes."

"Joshua Markham, you are a man who takes risks

every day in your job. Riding a horse is much easier than fighting fires." Even as she said the last sentence, the image of Crystal in her wheelchair popped into Darcy's mind. She shivered.

"Cold?"

"No, I just thought about Crystal Bolton."

"My point exactly."

"Accidents happen all the time, Joshua. You know that. We can't worry about what might happen. If we did, we'd live in fear all the time and never get up in the morning." Another picture flashed into Darcy's thoughts: her mother locked in her bedroom with the drapes drawn all day long, sleeping and sleeping. She shook the memory from her mind, determined not to journey into the past. "You're a risk taker and you love animals. Riding is perfect for you."

Joshua held up his hand. "Okay. You've convinced me. Why the hard sell?"

"I need a referee. My father is determined to work with Sean and his horse. I'm going along to—" Suddenly she stopped, realizing what she was admitting.

Joshua moved closer, until only inches separated them. "Why are you going along, Darcy?"

"To protect my son." There, she had said it.

"From your father?"

"He taught me to ride but he isn't a very forgiving teacher. But Sean was so excited when Dad said something about it at breakfast, I didn't have the heart to say no. My father is a hard man and Sean is so impressionable." Joshua's scent, with a hint of musk, teased her senses. She should step back. She didn't. "Now that I've told you, do you still want to go?"

His eyes glinted with humor. "Only if you promise to be my teacher."

His look mesmerized her. Her mind blanked—until someone behind her coughed, reminding her that she and Joshua were not alone.

"Hi, Mike. It's good to see you. Do you need something?" Joshua glanced over Darcy's shoulder.

"That spoon in your hand for the casserole if that's not too much of an inconvenience."

Hearing the chuckle in the man's voice, Darcy spun about, feeling the heat searing her cheeks. "I'm Darcy O'Brien."

"Shamus Flanaghan's daughter?"

"Yes."

"Sorry about that," the man said belligerently before turning to spoon tuna casserole onto his plate.

Stunned, Darcy opened her mouth to say something, thought better of it and snapped her jaws closed. Anger welled up in her. It was one thing for *her* to say something about her father, but she didn't like anyone else to criticize him.

"That's Mike Reynolds, the assistant manager your father fired a few months back."

Joshua's whispered words washed over her, sending a chill down her spine. Again his nearness caused her heart to speed up, something it was doing a lot of around Joshua.

As Mike moved down the line, Darcy stepped away from the serving table to allow others to select their food. "Not a particularly friendly guy."

"I heard the Colemans let him go after the fire. He left in a huff."

"Could he be responsible for the fires?"

Joshua shrugged. "He certainly doesn't stay long at a farm. Soon it will be hard for him to be hired at all. He's garnishing quite a reputation."

"How so?"

"He's too rough with the horses."

The tightness about Joshua's mouth indicated he didn't care for Mike's techniques. "So that was the method my dad didn't like."

"Probably. Mike gets results from his horses, but at a cost."

Her father might have been tough on her when he was raising her, demanding perfection, but he was always gentle with his horses—in fact, any of the animals at the farm. She could remember once when she was a little girl wishing she had been a horse so her father would love her. Hurt, buried deep, rose and threatened to overwhelm her.

"Darcy, are you okay?"

She blinked, focusing on the here and now. Coming home had been tougher than she had thought possible. She slowly gave Joshua a nod, but inside she didn't feel all right. The fragile new life she was building for herself was beginning to unravel and she wasn't sure how to hold it together.

Chapter Five

"Dad, are you sure about this?" Darcy asked as she and her father walked toward the barn.

"I'm supposed to start exercising just so long as I don't overdo it. Yes, I'm sure."

"I can teach Sean to ride."

"I want to." Her father gave her a hard look. "I haven't been able to do much else for my only grandchild."

Guilt, just as her father had intended, swamped her. She had allowed her own feelings to get in the way of Sean knowing his grandfather. She'd been wrong, and her father was making sure she knew that.

"So Joshua Markham is coming along. What's going on there?"

Darcy stopped before they reached the barn where Joshua's red truck was parked. "Nothing, Dad, and don't imply there is."

"Mighty defensive, if you ask me."

She huffed and began walking again. "I'm not." This was going to be a long morning if her father's surly attitude was any indication.

"Mom." Sean raced toward her. "Joshua is a beginner like me."

Darcy caught sight of Joshua standing by his truck, dressed in jeans, boots and a short-sleeved plaid shirt, rubbing his thumb across the pads of his fingers. "I thought it was about time he learned to ride, since this is horse country. What do you think?"

"Yes. Are you gonna teach him while Grandpa works with me?"

Her son's eagerness took hold of her, producing a smile. "I'm gonna try. That is, if he's a quick learner." She threw the man in question a glance and noticed him ambling over to them.

"What happens if I'm not a quick learner?" Joshua asked, ruffling Sean's hair.

"It might be kinda fun to see how you handle a runaway horse."

Sean giggled and turned his face up toward Joshua's. "Mom's just kidding. She has the patience of Job."

"I may be testing that, Sean," Joshua said, laughing.

"Are we all going to stand around jawing or are we gonna ride?"

"Grandpa, I'm ready." Sean hurried after his grandfather, who was heading into the barn.

Darcy exhaled a huge breath while she watched her son and father disappear inside.

Joshua took her hand and held it between his. "Sean and Shamus will be fine."

Darcy clenched her teeth, tension in every fiber of her being. "I'm not so sure." She tugged her hand free, putting space between them.

"Don't you know grandparents' relationships with their grandchildren are different from parents' with their children?"

A lump clogged her throat. She couldn't speak for fear her emotions would pour out.

"Besides, you're gonna have your hands full dealing with me. You've got to promise me before I get up on a horse that if it bolts you'll rescue me." Again he ran his thumb over and over his fingertips.

She moistened her throat. "But aren't you the rescuer?"

"A horse, madam, isn't a burning building."

Darcy started for the entrance. "I'm so glad you clarified that for me. For a moment I was confused."

His bark of laughter followed her into the barn. She found her father and Sean at the stall of a dark brown gelding—her son's horse. Her father finished putting the saddle on, showing Sean every step. Then her father led Sea Wave over to the mounting block and tightened the cinch on the saddle before allowing Sean to get on.

"Just remember, if Sean can do this, so can you."

"You certainly know how to motivate a guy."

"I use every means I can to get the job done." Darcy flipped her hand toward a stall at the other end of the barn. "That's your horse for today. Put her saddle on." She began walking away.

Joshua grabbed her arm. "Where do you think you're going?" Panic laced his question.

"To get my mare."

"I may not know much about riding, but I do know if you don't get your saddle on securely, you will fall off the horse."

"I know. But we learn so much better from our mistakes."

He covered the area between them. "You're enjoying this way too much."

First she smiled, then she laughed. "Yes."

Somehow he shrank the space between them, his breath fanning her cheek. "I'm glad. I don't like seeing you upset. Remember we're here to have fun. Now, show me how to put on the saddle."

"First you flatter, then you demand. You have an unique way of getting what you want."

"Is it working?"

Shaking her head, she stepped around him toward the stall where his horse was. She drew in several deep breaths to still the racing of her pulse. His nearness threatened her resolve to keep an emotional distance.

Darcy brought the gray mare out into the middle of the barn to demonstrate how to secure the saddle. She was aware of Joshua's close scrutiny and her hands actually quivered. When he took the strap to tighten the girth, their fingers brushed and an electrical current zipped up her arm. She quickly moved back several paces, feeling the strong beat of her heart against her chest.

"Mom, look at me."

At the sound of her son's voice she whirled about. He was seated on Sea Wave, his posture correct, a wide grin on his face. He waved at her and she gave him a thumbs-up. While her father prepared his stallion to ride, Sean waited with the reins in his hands, watching everything his grandfather was doing.

Ten minutes later Darcy mounted her mare while Joshua surged into the saddle as though he had been doing it for years. He flashed her a grin. "I'm a quick study."

"And I get the impression not much scares you, really."

"After facing a wall of fire coming at me, you're probably right."

"What is it about men and doing risky things?"

"It's my job."

"That's what my husband used to say—and his job killed him."

"When it's my time to leave here, then it's my time. I can't let fear govern my life or I wouldn't be able to do my job."

"There's nothing wrong with a healthy dose of fear." Darcy jerked her reins to the left and set her mare into a trot.

"I agree." Joshua trailed after her, out into the sunshine. "It's what makes me pause and check out a situation before tackling it. I don't rush into a burning building without assessing it first."

"That's comforting to know." Darcy clamped her lips together before she said anything else that would give away her growing feelings for the man riding beside her.

"Watch out, Darcy O'Brien, you might actually start to care."

She shot him an exasperating look. "I care. You're a friend and I prefer that nothing happens to a friend."

"We can't live forever. What's important is what we do with our time on earth. I want no regrets when I die."

"So you don't have *any* regrets?" She pulled on the reins to halt her mare's progress, allowing her father and Sean to ride ahead.

Joshua brought his horse up next to hers. "I didn't say that. I have regrets. I'm just working on cutting them down, that's all."

"Your approach to life is a lot like my husband's was. And look what happened to him." Though their marriage hadn't been a good one, she'd lived in fear every time he'd gone up in his fighter jet. He'd loved the rush and thrill of defying the laws of nature.

"Did your husband believe in God?" Joshua shaded his eyes with his hand, his gaze intent.

"My husband believed only in himself," she said with all the bitterness that had built up in her over the years she'd been married.

"Then we aren't alike at all. I put my faith and my life in God's hands. That's not to say I don't believe in myself. I've been trained well to do what I do. There's only a certain amount of our life we can control—for the rest we just have to have faith in the Lord that He knows best."

"I wish I could feel that way."

"Why can't you?"

"Because I'm not sure I know who I am." Darcy spurred her mare forward, needing to put an end to the conversation before she confessed the struggle she was going through to discover the woman left after Clay's sudden death. Coming home had put her personal journey into a nosedive.

She caught up to her father and son on the trail to the creek as they headed into a grove of trees. There the cool breeze died, replaced by the cool shade. The scent of damp earth and pine vied with leather and horse. Several birds sang above her, while the sound of water rushing over rocks resonated through the woods.

This was her favorite place on the farm. When she was a little girl, she came here to think…or to cry. She almost hated the idea of coming here now with her father because this had been where she'd come to escape the stress of trying to be perfect for him.

Her emotions warring, she stopped near the stream and dismounted. "This place hasn't changed," she murmured, making a slow circle, taking in the tranquility that surrounded her. Physically at least…but spiritually it had changed. She wasn't the same little girl who had fought every day for her father's approval. That much she knew about herself. Somewhere along the line she'd given up. Hadn't she?

"Beautiful." Joshua came up next to her.

Sunlight shot through the openings in the tree canopy to flood the forest floor as though gold poured from the heavens to mingle with the browns and greens of earth. A merging of two worlds. Darcy wanted to dance in the streams of light, lift her face up and let them bathe her in warmth.

"Yes, it is," she said.

A yellow butterfly, soaring on an air current, passed in front of her. She watched it disappear into the thick grove on the other side of the creek and wished she could follow.

"Did you see me, Joshua?" Sean ran up to him. "Grandpa says I'm a natural."

Darcy's gaze fastened onto her father, upstream, holding the reins of both horses. Weariness showed in the deepening lines about his mouth and eyes. "Dad, why don't we sit and rest here for a while?"

He came alert. "I don't need to rest."

"You might not, but I do. I haven't been here in years and would like to enjoy it for a while."

Tension seemed to siphon from him, sagging his shoulders. "Fine. I'd forgotten this was your favorite place."

"It was, Mom?" Sean asked.

Darcy nodded, her gaze still fixed on her father as he dropped the reins and eased down onto a large boulder near the creek. Seeing him wince brought words of caution to her mouth. She dug her teeth into her lower lip to keep them inside. Her father wouldn't appreciate them.

"Are there fish in this stream?" Sean peered into the clear, cool water.

"Yes, but I don't think there are any that you would want to eat. Most are too small."

Joshua stretched his muscles. "Do you like to fish, Sean?"

"I don't know. I haven't gone fishing before."

"Well, tell you what. I'll take you one day and we'll see. Sweetwater Lake is a great place to fish."

"Can Mom come, too?"

"Sure." Joshua flashed her a grin. "That is, if you want to. You're welcome to come too, Shamus."

Her father shook his head and waved his hand. "Never did like to sit still long enough to catch anything. Too impatient for fishing."

Sean's brow furrowed. "How long do you have to sit still? I don't know if I can, either."

Joshua's wide shoulders rose in a shrug. "That depends on how the fish are biting. The place I'll take you is a good fishing hole. Probably not too long."

"Good. My teacher says I squirm too much in my desk."

"I had that same problem, but I've managed to fish." Joshua eased down onto the grass-covered ground next to Darcy and leaned back against a large oak.

Sean picked up some pebbles and tried to skip them. They plunked into the water, the sound slicing through the silence.

"It's all in which pebbles you select, son." Her father

motioned for Sean to come to him, and he began to instruct her son in how to skip rocks.

Darcy listened to her father's patient words and marveled at them. *Thank you, Lord, for that.*

"Your father's good with Sean." Joshua took a blade of grass and chewed on it.

"Yes." The word came out bitter sounding, and she immediately regretted her tone. Her own relationship with her father shouldn't color her son's.

"But he wasn't with you?"

"I can count on one hand the number of times he was patient with me when showing me something."

"Maybe he's changed. Mellowed out."

"Maybe," she said with all the cynicism she had developed over the years in regard to her father.

"Was that why you stayed away all these years?"

She clenched and unclenched her hands. "Yes. I only had so much emotional energy." *And I'd used it all up trying to keep my marriage together,* she added silently. "I know I shouldn't have stayed away. I won't again. I'm stronger now. I can deal with my father for a few weeks a year."

"That's good. Sean's connecting with his grandfather."

Darcy's gaze found her son standing next to her father, intent on what Shamus was saying. Sean picked up a pebble, examined it and tossed it back. Selecting another one, he tried it. The flat stone skipped two times across the stream.

"Way to go, Sean." Her father patted her son on the back. "You're gonna be a pro in no time."

"You think, Grandpa?"

"Sure."

Darcy turned away, her throat tight. Feeling vulnerable and guilty made each breath she took difficult. The constriction in her throat spread to encompass her chest. Sean's laughter echoed through the woods. With her eyes squeezed closed, she listened to the two men in her life and wished she felt connected.

Joshua laid his hand over hers. Her eyes snapped open and she looked into his.

"Ten years can make a difference, Darcy. Talk to your father. Let him know how you feel, especially about the past."

"How do you tell someone you love that you don't want to be around them?" Her question took even her by surprise.

"When I have a particularly difficult problem, I pray for guidance. You aren't alone. You have me. You have God—"

"Ready to head back?" Her father approached with his arm about Sean.

Darcy swallowed once, then twice before she thought she could answer. "Yes. There are still a lot of chores that need to be done."

"And a puppy to pick up," Sean said, snatching his reins.

"Here, I'll give you a leg up." Joshua pushed himself

to his feet, a groan escaping his lips. "I don't think I should have sat down. That was a big mistake. My muscles are protesting."

"If you aren't used to riding, that certainly can happen." Darcy took her reins and grabbed hold of her saddle to hoist herself up.

Joshua rolled his eyes, his first few steps toward Sean rigid. "*Now* you tell me."

"You just have to work the stiffness out, Joshua." Her father mounted his stallion and waited.

Sean vaulted into his saddle with Joshua's help. "Can we go faster on the way back to the barn?"

"Sure, once we hit the meadow—" her father paused and threw her a glance "—that is, if it's okay with your mom."

Shocked that he'd asked her opinion, Darcy nodded. While Sean and her father headed back through the woods toward the pasture, she watched Joshua pull himself into his saddle, a grimace on his face.

"Are you that sore?"

"Afraid so. I keep in shape, but obviously a whole different set of muscles is involved in riding." He stared after the disappearing pair. "Do me a favor?"

"What?"

"Let's take it slow and easy."

Darcy suppressed her laugh. "I can handle that."

But could she handle a man like Joshua? Each day she was around him she grew to like and care about him more and more. Against her nature she was finding herself confiding in him, which should be setting off alarm bells in her mind. But it felt so natural and right.... *We're just friends,* she thought—and was afraid she was lying to herself.

"Come in. Crystal has been so excited since you called." Tanya Bolton stepped to the side to allow Darcy and Sean into her house.

Sean cradled his new puppy to his chest. "At church Wednesday night Crystal told me she loved dogs. I wanted to show her my new one."

"She's back in the den. Why don't you take your puppy back there and show her?" Tanya pointed toward the hallway. "While he's doing that, would you like something to drink? I have sodas, iced tea, water?" She walked through the dining room into the kitchen.

"Water is fine." Darcy noticed the stack of dirty dishes in the sink and some pots with dried food in them left on the stove. Two houseplants on the window-sill over the sink were wilting and turning brown.

After pouring some iced water from a pitcher in the refrigerator, Tanya indicated a chair at her oak table in front of a large picture window that offered a view of the small backyard.

"Since the accident Crystal hasn't had too many of her friends over. We've been pretty tied up and haven't even had a chance to go to church until a few weeks ago."

"Sean said Crystal is in his summer Sunday school class that Joshua teaches for the upper elementary grades."

"She'll graduate to the next level next summer. She starts the sixth grade next fall—that is, if she goes to school."

Darcy lifted the glass to her lips, the cool liquid sliding down her dry throat. "Why wouldn't she?"

"Tom doesn't want her to go to school now that she's in a wheelchair." Tanya dropped her gaze to her hand that held the drink. "In fact, he isn't too happy that I'm taking her to church. He wants—" She looked at Darcy, tears in her eyes. "He thinks she's better off being home-schooled and staying here. I won't hide my daughter. I can't—" Tanya cleared her throat and took a large gulp of water. "I don't know what to do."

Darcy's heart ached for the woman sitting across from her. She reached out and covered Tanya's hand with hers. "All we can do is what we think is best. As long as I'm here, I'll help you any way I can."

Tanya choked back a sob. "Thanks. I feel so alone lately. I've lost touch with my friends. After the accident I spent every waking moment with Crystal. I'm trying to get my old life back together but—" she cleared her throat "—it's difficult sometimes, especially when I can't seem to stay on top of things that I know I should."

Darcy could relate to this woman. Making changes in one's life was never easy. "Remember, if you need help, I'm just a call away. Maybe Crystal can come visit the farm."

Horror flitted across Tanya's features. "No. Tom

would get so angry if I brought her out to your farm. I'm not even going to say anything to him about your visit."

"Well, then, we can always bring Lady over to see Crystal again if she wants."

"We'll see—" They heard a noise coming from the front of the house, and Tanya jumped, fear widening her eyes. She shot to her feet and hurried from the kitchen, saying, "I'll be back in a sec."

"I'm sorry, Mrs. Bolton. Lady got away from us."

Darcy followed the sound of her son's voice and found him in the entry hall with Tanya. Crystal had wheeled herself down the hallway. A trash can lay on its side with crumpled papers scattered over the tile floor.

"Mom, Lady likes trash cans. Isn't that funny?" Crystal patted her lap and Sean put the puppy where she indicated. "Can we go outside? Sean says he's gonna teach her to fetch."

"Crystal, you know we haven't made the deck and backyard handicap accessible yet."

Crystal pouted. "But Dad promised he would last month."

"He'll get around to it. For the time being you'll have to be satisfied with the den. But no fetching in there."

As Sean walked behind Crystal toward the den, Tanya sighed, tears springing to her eyes again. "I hate disappointing her. But she needs several ramps built in order for her to go out back. And to tell you the truth, Tom's always working. He's rarely here anymore, so I don't know when they're going to be built."

"Maybe Joshua knows someone who can build them."

Tanya's eyes grew round. "Oh, no. Tom would be furious if anyone else did it. He wants to do everything himself. He'll get to it sometime."

When they were back in the kitchen, Tanya asked, "I understand from Reverend Collins that you're just visiting for the summer, that you live in Panama City. What do you do down there?"

Darcy told Tanya about her job and the purchase of her very first house not on a Navy base, while Tanya talked about her volunteer work before her daughter's accident. The mention of the accident brought tears to Tanya's eyes and again Darcy comforted the woman, not sure how to help her. Tanya's emotions seemed so close to the surface.

Suddenly Tanya glanced at the clock over the stove and stood. "I hate to end this, but Tom will be home in an hour and I need to start dinner. Thank you so much for bringing Sean and his puppy by. Maybe he can visit another time."

Five minutes later Sean and Darcy were ushered from the house. Sean spun back to wave goodbye to Crystal, who had wheeled herself to the glass door. The forlorn look on the child's face tore at Darcy.

After the summer horse auction at the fairgrounds, Darcy decided, she would make it a point to get more involved with Crystal and Tanya. Crystal needed a friend, and Tanya needed…Darcy wasn't sure what, but the woman was close to falling apart. She intended to talk with Lizzy about Tanya Bolton. Maybe Lizzy had some suggestions to help her with the woman.

On the ride back to the farm Sean held Lady in his arms and stared out the side window. His silence was so unusual that Darcy asked, "What's wrong?"

"I'm thinking about Crystal. She doesn't leave the house much and she misses her friends. She wants a puppy like Lady."

"You know what might be nice for Crystal is a therapy dog. I'll do some research on them and say something to her mother."

"Mom, I'd like to visit again. When can I?"

"Let me see after the horse auction. My time is going to be pretty filled with that coming up. We'll be auctioning off fifteen horses."

"Can I help?"

"Sure. The more we do, the less Grandpa will have to do. It's at the end of next week."

When Darcy pulled into the farm, she headed the truck toward one of the broodmare barns. "I've got to check on the new mare. Why don't you go on up to the house and tell Lizzy we're back so she'll start dinner?"

"I'm hungry. Maybe I can get a snack." Sean hopped from the truck and let Lady down.

As he started running toward the house, Darcy shouted, "Don't spoil your dinner. No cookies or sweets."

He turned and jogged backward, Lady at his heel. "Aw, Mom."

"You heard me, young man. You can have one piece of fruit."

"He reminds me of you when you were a child."

Darcy gasped, spinning around to face Jake.

"You had quite a sweet tooth if I remember correctly."

"I still do. How's the new mare adjusting to her new home?"

"Fine. She's out in the pasture right now." Jake walked toward the barn. "I put her up next to Butterfly at the end."

"Dad thinks she'll be a good breeder."

"Your father's rarely wrong."

When it came to horses that was true, but when it came to people… She moved toward the back stall to check the mare, while Jake headed for the tack room. The scent of fresh hay gave her a feeling of having come home. She'd missed the horses and the farm—she hadn't realized how much.

"I like being a librarian," she muttered to herself, closing the door to the stall. "I like working with children."

"Should I be worried about you talking to yourself?"

Darcy peered toward the rafters, then slowly turned toward Joshua. "There are several mares within earshot."

"Oh. That makes all the difference."

She placed her hands on her waist and cocked her head. "Are you making fun of me?"

"I won't answer that. Not if I want you to do me a favor."

"What?"

"I need a date for next Thursday night."

A date? Oh, my! All her alarm bells sounded.

Chapter Six

"Yes, a date." Joshua grinned, his blue eyes glinting. "With all that has been going on I forgot about the awards dinner."

"What awards dinner?" Darcy asked.

Joshua actually turned a nice shade of red. "I'm being given an award for rescuing a woman and child from a burning house."

"What an honor!"

The blush deepened. He looked away, his thumb rubbing across his fingers. "I shouldn't have gone into the house, but I couldn't let the woman and her toddler die. I was lucky. I got them and myself out without anyone being too seriously injured. My captain was not happy about the risk I took, but the governor is giving me an award."

There was that word again—*risk*. Darcy was beginning to hate it.

"God was looking out for me that night."

"Well, I'm glad someone was." Her mouth set in a taut line, she started for the entrance.

Joshua fell into step next to her. "Why are you upset? Everything worked out okay."

"I'm not upset," she said, then realized that wasn't the truth. "One day it might not work out. Have you ever really stopped and thought about that?"

Clasping her arm in the middle of the yard, he stopped and turned her to face him. "What would you have me do? Stand by and do nothing while someone was trapped in a burning building? I had to try and get them out."

Her anger deflated. "No." Her gaze dropped to the ground. "I would have tried, too."

He placed his finger under her chin and lifted her head. His gaze locked with hers. "You did do the same thing when your barn was burning. You went in to get the horses out because you couldn't stand by and watch them burn."

She closed her eyes for a few seconds, the image of the frightened horses imprinted on her mind. When she stared into his eyes again, she felt lost in the vivid blue of his gaze. Time fell away, leaving only them.

She didn't want to care about Joshua Markham, but she did.

"Yes, I'll go. What time will you pick me up?"

"Six. We have to drive to Lexington."

"How should I dress?"

"I have to wear a suit."

"You make it sound like a sentence."

"I don't particularly like to wear a suit and tie."

"Then I guess I won't wear my jeans and boots."

His chuckle danced up her spine. "In horse country that wouldn't be too far-fetched, but since the governor and other dignitaries are going to be there, you'd better don a dress."

"The governor? This must have been a big deal."

Joshua plowed his fingers through his hair and peered over her shoulder with a wry grin on his face. "The woman I rescued was a niece of the governor's."

"So you have friends in high places."

"The only one that counts is God."

Darcy started again for the main house. She wished she had his strong faith. But doubts plagued her.

"Dinner's gonna be ready shortly. Do you want to stay?"

"Sure. Why else do you think I waited until this time to ask?"

She glanced at him, his face full of laughter. "You know, underneath it all, I think you're serious."

"For a man who hates to cook and isn't very good when he has to, you're probably right."

"So I should expect you to appear on my doorstep around seven whenever you aren't working?"

"Is that an invitation?"

The eagerness in his voice produced a laugh from Darcy. "I shouldn't encourage you."

"But I'm so adorable when I'm begging."

She shook her head and entered the house through the kitchen. Lizzy glanced up from stirring something on the stove.

"Dinner is in fifteen minutes."

"I've invited Joshua to join us again. Can I help you with anything?"

"You can get another place setting down for him. Joshua, Shamus and Sean are in the den. Will you tell them dinner is almost ready?" After Joshua left, Lizzy added, "You can also get the salad out of the refrigerator."

Darcy took a deep breath, delicious aromas enticing her. "What are we having?"

"Chicken stew. Nothing fancy, but something on your father's diet."

Darcy removed the salad from the refrigerator along with some bottles of dressing, all low fat, she noticed. "Now that Joshua's gone, what did you want to talk to me about?"

Lizzy wiped her hands on a towel tucked into the waistband of her apron. "Tanya Bolton. We've known each other too long to beat around the bush on anything. Be careful, child. Tanya is dealing with a lot of issues."

Reaching for another plate, Darcy stopped and dropped her arm to her side, spinning about to look at Lizzy. "I know she has a lot of issues. Her husband for one, her daughter's accident for another. What are you not telling me?"

Lizzy sighed heavily, leaning back against the counter and folding her arms across her chest. "Tanya is bipolar."

The room seemed to tilt for a few seconds. Darcy gripped the edge of the counter and steadied herself.

"She's been on medication for several years and was doing fine until her daughter's accident. Everything has turned upside down for Tanya. I've tried to help when I can, but her husband denies there's a problem with his wife and prefers the family not be involved with the community."

"Not a nice man if you ask me, and I haven't even met him."

"Tom has had a difficult road. A lot has happened to him in the past few years. He was doing all right until Crystal got hurt. He used to come to church regularly. He used to be involved in the community. Now he stays to himself."

"Crystal needs to be around friends. He doesn't even want her and Tanya to come to church."

"Sound like someone we know?"

"Dad." The name was wrenched from Darcy's soul, bringing back all kinds of memories of what happened after her mother died. She had so needed her father to help her to understand her loss. Her legs weakened, and Darcy slid to the floor, burying her face in her hands.

The housekeeper squatted next to her. "Now you know why I needed to warn you to be careful. Maybe you shouldn't help Tanya."

Tears stung Darcy's eyes. Memories continued to flood her. She was a teenager again, desperately trying to figure out why her mother had killed herself, need-

ing her father's comfort. Instead, she'd received anger
and coldness. He had rejected the Lord and turned away
from the church, just like Tom. Tanya and her situation
weren't the same, but there was a connection. Her
mother had suffered from manic depression too.

"But she's so alone, Lizzy."

"You're going to be gone in a few months. Do you
really want to get involved in something like that? I was
hoping I wouldn't have to tell you about Tanya because
I knew how it would affect you." Lizzy hugged her as
she had when Darcy had been trying to make sense of
her mother's death.

"I couldn't help my mother, but maybe I can help
Tanya now that I know what she's going through." Tears
coursed down her cheeks. "I've got to try."

"I figured you would say that. It isn't your battle, and
you have more than enough to handle with your father
right now."

Darcy shoved herself to her feet. "I can always count
on you to look out for me." *Is God giving me a second
chance through Tanya to understand what drove my
mother to kill herself? Would understanding Tanya's situation help me to understand my father?* Questions
bombarded her that she had no answers to.

"Child, I'm here if you need to talk."

"I know." Darcy turned back to the cabinet and retrieved a plate and glass for Joshua. "I've always been
able to count on you."

"But not your father?"

"Do I have to answer that question?" Darcy opened the drawer and selected a fork, spoon and knife.

"No. Your father can be one of the stubbornest men I've known."

"And you still work for him."

"Someone's got to watch out for him. He certainly isn't doing a very good job of it."

Seeing the slight coloring in Lizzy's cheeks made Darcy think back over the past few weeks to when the housekeeper and her father were together. Lizzy could get away with saying things to him that no one else could. He argued with her, but he also listened to what she had to say. Was there more going on between them? Lizzy had put up with him for as many years as her mother had.

"Joshua has been spending a lot of time with you and Sean. Is there something you would like to tell me?"

"Are you trying to change the subject?"

"Yes, is it working?"

Darcy laughed. "Joshua and I are friends. He's wonderful with Sean, and Sean likes to be around him."

"Just Sean." Lizzy sent her a sharp, appraising look.

"Okay, I like to be around him, too, but as you just pointed out to me, I'll be leaving in less than two months, so nothing is going to happen beyond friendship."

"If you say so." Lizzy reached for the serving bowl and a spoon. "Please set the table."

Darcy went into the dining room and arranged a place setting for Joshua, then headed for the den to see what was keeping the guys. When she entered, she heard her father and Joshua talking about the fires. Stopping at the entrance, she searched the room for her son. He wasn't there.

"All four of the fires are connected, sir. So far no one's been injured, but several horses died and a great deal of property has been destroyed."

"If I get my hands on the person responsible for doing this, he'll regret the day he was born."

"That's not looking very promising right now, unless we catch him red-handed. Arson cases can be difficult to solve, and when there's no obvious reason, it's even harder. Sometimes we find the arsonist likes to watch the fire he sets, but in this case, because of the isolation of the barns, that isn't happening. At least, where we can see him. The only crowds gathering are the people who live on the farms who are trying to rescue the horses and help put the fire out."

"What if he's hiding?"

"That's possible. Everyone's busy with the fire, so it would be hard to tell." Joshua exhaled a deep breath. "At least everyone in the area has hired additional guards to protect their barns and horses. I think that's one reason we haven't seen another fire in several weeks since the Colemans'. Maybe there won't be any more."

Her father shifted in his overstuffed chair, caught sight of her and waved her into the room. "Did you take a look at Angus Feehan? I heard he was fired from another stable a few weeks back. Pretty hotheaded man when riled."

"Riled enough to burn barns?"

Her father rubbed his chin and thought for a moment. "The more I think about him, the more it seems a strong possibility."

"We have checked him out. He doesn't have good alibis for the fires. He lives by himself and says he was home sleeping. No one to say one way or the other."

"You'd better keep an eye on him. He's got shifty eyes if you ask me."

Joshua chuckled. "The police can't arrest everyone who has shifty eyes."

"I know, but I never trusted him or Mike Reynolds. Both have reason to burn my barn."

"But the others?"

"I know Mike worked for the Andersons before coming to work for me. So he's worked for three of the four farms hit. A mighty big coincidence."

"Dad, where's Sean? Dinner is ready."

Her father labored to stand. When he saw Darcy frowning at him, he said, "I probably should get another chair to sit in. That one is getting harder and harder for an old man to get out of."

"That's the first time I've heard you refer to yourself as old."

Her father's gaze pinned her. "How would you know? You haven't been around much in the past ten years to know what I say or think."

Darcy felt as though her father had slapped her in the face. She automatically took a step back, her hand coming up to her throat.

He stalked past her, muttering, "Sean took Lady outside to…go. I'll get him."

"Sean named his dog Lady?"

Joshua's question reminded her that she wasn't alone and that she needed to regain her composure quickly or she would find herself breaking down in front of him.

"Yes." She averted her head as though she were watching her father leave, when in actuality she didn't see much through the sheen of tears.

"That was what I called my first dog."

She blinked the tears away before facing Joshua. "I know. Sean didn't think a girl dog should be called Joshua, but he liked the name Lady so he calls her that because of you."

Joshua approached her, his gaze connected to hers. "I'm sorry, Darcy."

"About what?" Her throat thickened again, and she felt the walls of the den close in on her.

Joshua gestured toward where her father had disappeared. "What I just witnessed between you and your father."

She attempted a smile that wavered about the corners of her mouth and faltered. "It's not a secret our relationship is rocky at best."

"And the added tension with the fires makes everyone on edge."

"Don't make excuses for him. The fires have nothing to do with it."

"Then what does?"

Aware of the compassion she saw in the blue depths of his eyes, she wanted to tell him everything—starting with her mother's illness and suicide. The words wouldn't come out. Instead she pressed her lips together and pivoted, heading for the dining room before she did confide in him.

What good would it do? Her mother would still be dead. Her relationship with her father would still be awful. And Joshua would own a part of her that she didn't share with others. Even Lizzy, who had been around, didn't know the depths of her agony over finding her mother and the suicide note.

Darcy ran her hand over her ice-green silk dress for probably the hundredth time since leaving the farm for Lexington. Her nerves were strung so tight she was afraid they would snap. A date! She hadn't been on one in years and wasn't sure what to do. She hoped it was like riding a bicycle because she was working herself up into a frenzy over it.

She glanced at Joshua, his large, strong hands on the steering wheel, his gaze trained forward on the highway, and wondered why she had accepted this date. It was a complication she didn't need.

But a welcome distraction, a tiny voice inside her said. The past few days at the farm had been hectic with getting ready for the horse auction. The bite of her father's words still stung from earlier today: she hadn't had all the paperwork done the way he had wished. No matter that she had never done it before and was learning—

"No frowns allowed tonight," Joshua said.

"Sorry about that. Just thinking of all the preparation that goes into selling the horses."

"That's this weekend, isn't it?"

"Yes. Dad's beside himself. He's angry that he doesn't feel one hundred percent yet, so he has to rely on me to do some of the things he's always done."

"He's a proud man. His illness has been difficult on him."

"Why is it so hard for some people to accept help?"

He flashed her grin. "Beats me. I accept all kinds of help. For instance, I need an assistant to help me with my Sunday school class for the rest of the summer. Marge had a family emergency and will be gone quite a bit." He waggled his brows. "Any takers in this truck?"

Darcy twisted around, checking the cab out. "I don't see any." She paused, then added, "Unless you're referring to me."

"How about it?"

"I won't be able to this weekend. I'll be so involved with the horse auction that I'm sure I'll meet myself coming and going."

"You can start the next Sunday, then. I'm not picky."

"Gee, I'm not sure I shouldn't be offended."

"Will it make things better if I tell you that you were the first and only person I thought to ask?"

"Now, flattery works much better."

"I aim to please." Joshua pulled into the hotel parking garage and found a place immediately on the ground level. "A good sign. This will be a nice evening."

"Of course it will, I'm your date." As they left the garage, she linked her arm through his, her spirits lifted at the prospects of spending an evening with Joshua. She wouldn't think about the farm for the next few hours. Tomorrow would be here soon enough and all the problems she'd left behind would still be there.

Darcy marveled at the beautifully decorated ballroom of the hotel. It was a study in gold and glittering crystal. Elegant. Richly ornate. "You didn't tell me half the population of Kentucky was going to be here."

"This is an annual event. The governor honors certain people who have done extraordinary things, from research scientists at the university to police officers."

"To you."

He leaned close to her ear, his breath tickling her neck. "I think you're trying to get me to blush again."

They were escorted to a table at the front of the room and seated with a police officer from Lexington and his wife, a businesswoman who financed a relief program for a small town that had suffered from a devastating tornado, and a minister and his wife who ran a program for the needy in eastern Kentucky. Darcy felt honored to be among such people.

Listening to them talk put some of Darcy's problems in perspective. Even though she was only going to be in Sweetwater for a while longer, there wasn't any reason not to become involved in the community. And she knew where she wanted to start—with Tanya and Crystal Bolton. Tanya needed help and a friend. She could do both.

By the time the awards dinner was over, Darcy had a plan. She and Joshua, plaque in hand, left the hotel after being bombarded by the press and people who wanted to congratulate Joshua for his rescue. Noticing that he blushed and continually ran his thumb over his fingers, she smiled to herself. He wasn't comfortable with all this attention, but she was glad she had come. She had seen another side of Joshua. Usually he was so self-assured, but up at the podium he was out of his element. He'd said a few words of thanks but had sat down almost immediately, having given the shortest speech of the evening.

"If I hadn't seen it with my own two eyes, I wouldn't have believed you were shy, Joshua Markham."

"I don't like crowds and I certainly don't like to give a speech in front of strangers. If you hadn't agreed to come, I'm not sure I would have shown up."

She stopped, facing him. "Not come? You're kidding! The governor was giving you a plaque honoring your heroism and you weren't going to come?"

He shrugged and reached around her to open the passenger door of his truck. "What can I say? I was a nervous wreck all day. The guys at the station were ready to demand I go home early from work."

"Going into a burning building doesn't scare you, but getting up in front of a crowd of strangers does?"

"Yep. That about sums it up."

Darcy shook her head. "I don't understand you. You get up in church and with the kids in your Sunday school class."

"That's different. I know those people and it's never about me."

"Ah, I see. So if the church gave you an award for your work you wouldn't be embarrassed?"

He nodded. "I don't do these things to call attention to myself or for any kind of reward."

"Why do you do them?"

"Because God gave me a gift and I'm using it the way He wants me to. Someone's gotta fight fires and work with the kids at church."

Darcy climbed into the cab of the truck and waited until Joshua rounded the front and slipped behind the steering wheel before saying, "I have a favor to ask."

He started the engine. "What?"

"I want to build some ramps for Crystal in her backyard so she can enjoy going outside, and I need help to do that."

"I'd love to. Have you asked Tanya and Tom?"

"Well, no, not yet, but Tanya mentioned she needed some ramps built. Do you think Tom will mind if I offer?"

"Honestly, I don't know. I haven't seen him in months, and the stories I've heard lead me to believe he might."

"That's what Tanya thought. She said something

about Tom wanting to build them himself but never getting around to it. I guess all I can do is ask. Maybe he'll surprise us all and agree."

Darcy settled in the seat and leaned her head back. Joshua switched on some soft, classical music, and the peaceful strains tempted her to close her eyes—just for a few minutes, she thought. The next thing she knew, Joshua was shaking her awake, his deep voice whispering to her.

She bolted upright, noticing he was driving down the lane that led to her house. "I didn't mean to fall asleep. You should have said something. I've been functioning for the past week on about half the sleep I require. I guess it finally caught up with me."

He breathed a deep sigh of relief. "Good. For a while there I thought it might be a statement about my scintillating conversation."

The teasing tone in his voice relaxed her. "You can drop me off at the far barn."

"Surely you aren't going to work tonight?"

"I need to check on a mare. I promised Dad I would when I came home. It was either that or *he* would have, and he was exhausted."

"And you aren't?"

"I just had an hour nap. I'm refreshed and ready to go. Besides, it should only take a minute to make sure she didn't go into labor."

"Then I'll wait for you and drive you up to the house."

"You don't have to do that."

"Yes, I do." As he stopped the truck in front of the barn, his gaze met hers.

In the yard light she saw the gleam in his eyes and the look of determination in his expression. He wouldn't take no for an answer. "Okay. I won't be long."

She slid from the cab, and as he started to open his door, she said, "Stay. You won't even know I'm gone." And she hurried toward the barn.

Inside she made her way toward the second-to-last stall as quickly as possible in three-inch high heels. After checking on the mare, who was doing fine, she closed the door and started back toward the entrance. A noise to the left of her caught her attention. She halted, suddenly wondering where the guard was. Scanning the barn, she realized she was the only other person here. The noise was probably the cat in the tack room, she thought and resumed walking.

A *crash* had her spinning around and rushing toward the tack room, heedless of the danger she might be in. Approaching the door, she lifted her arm to push it open. Suddenly it banged open and she came face to face with a short man in dirty clothes and a shaggy beard that obscured his features. But the pale blue of his eyes imprinted itself on her brain. She screamed.

He shoved past her, sending her flying back. She hit the hard-packed dirt with a *thud*. She was scrambling to her feet when she heard Joshua running toward her.

"Are you all right? What happened?"

She waved her hand toward the rear of the barn. "He went that way."

Without another word Joshua sprinted toward the back and disappeared from view. Darcy pushed herself to her feet, vaguely aware that her beautiful new silk dress was probably ruined. She kicked off her high heels, then headed after Joshua. She ran into him—literally—just outside the barn.

"Did you see the man?"

"No, he was gone. Did you know him?"

"No, he was a stranger."

"Where's your father's guard?"

"Probably making his rounds—at least, I hope so. What if something's happened to the man? What if that was the arsonist and—" She shuddered; she didn't like the direction her thoughts were taking.

Joshua drew her into his embrace. "Let's check the barn and make sure the man didn't leave anything behind. Then let's go find the guard."

"You mean that man might have rigged the barn to burn?"

Joshua gripped her hand. "Yes. On second thought, I want you to go around to my truck and wait until I check everything out."

"*No.*"

Chapter Seven

"What do you mean, no?" Anger lines carved into Joshua's face.

"I mean, no I won't go and quietly wait for you to inspect the barn for something that might cause a fire."

He thrust his face within inches of hers. "What if a fire starts while I'm in the barn?"

"Then I'll be there to help get the horses out. Every second will count if a fire starts." She tugged her hand from his and put both of hers on her waist. "And let me make it perfectly clear, I will try to save any horses I can."

"And you call *me* a risk taker. What kind of behavior is that?" He spoke in a very controlled voice while he was stalking toward the rear door of the barn.

Darcy watched him for a few seconds before she hurried after him. "What are we looking for?"

His look conveyed his displeasure at her insistence

on being in the barn. "Anything unusual." He paused at the tack room door. "He was in here?"

"Yes."

"You check the stalls while I go through this room and the storage next door."

Five minutes into the inspection the guard showed up. Darcy sent him to check the other barn with any groom still on duty. She had visions of both barns going up at the same time.

Half an hour later Darcy stood with Joshua next to his truck, staring at the barn. "I'm glad we didn't find anything. But then, who was that man and why was he in there?"

Raking his fingers through his hair—not for the first time if its disheveled look meant anything— Joshua said, "We need to get a description to the police. He could be the arsonist. Even though we didn't find anything, maybe you came before he could set the fire."

"I guess I can't postpone talking to my father any longer. I told the guard not to say anything, that I would tell Dad. But before I do, I need to check with the guard to make sure the other barn is okay. If I can tell Dad everything's all right, he might take it better." Who was she kidding? Her father wouldn't take this well at all, but getting stressed over it would only make the situation worse.

"I'll drive you."

By the time Joshua parked in front of the main house,

Darcy's shoulders sagged from exhaustion. What had started out as a delightful, fun-filled evening had evolved into a tension-filled nightmare, and she still had to face the worse part of it—her father.

Though it was after midnight, as she had suspected her father was still up in the den, reading a horse magazine. His whole life revolved around his horses and the farm. What would happen to him if the farm was destroyed by an arsonist?

"Did you two have a good time?" Shamus looked up from his magazine as Darcy and Joshua entered.

"The food was good. The people we met were interesting."

"I hear a 'but' in your voice, son."

Joshua blew out a long breath. "I could have done with a little less pomp and circumstances."

"He hates to give speeches, but he did a great job. It was short and to the point." Darcy sat across from her father while Joshua stood next to her, his hand on her shoulder giving her silent support.

"I've got the feeling you want to tell me something."

"Dad, I checked on Dragonfly and she's doing fine." Her throat parched, Darcy tried to coat it but failed. Her mouth felt stuffed with cotton. "As I was leaving, I heard something in the tack room. When I went to investigate, a man rushed out and ran me down."

Her father surged to his feet and started for the door.

"Dad, wait!"

He pivoted, anger darkening his features, his deep

gray eyes boring into her. His jaws clenched, he spoke through gritted teeth. "Where is he?"

"Gone, sir. I ran after him, but he disappeared."

"Did you know him?" Shamus asked Joshua.

"I didn't get a look at him. I was outside by my truck when I heard Darcy scream."

Her father shifted his attention to her. "Did you know him?"

She shook her head.

"What did he look like?"

"Short, dirty with a shaggy beard. His hair was dark and his eyes were a pale blue."

"Angus Feehan. That's got to be him. The last time I saw him he was growing a beard." Her father walked to the phone, put his hand on the receiver. "Did you check the barn?"

"Yes, sir. There was nothing. The guard and the groom on duty at night inspected the other one just to make sure. They even checked the new barn under construction."

Some of the tension seemed to leave Shamus as he picked up the receiver and placed a call to the police. While her father talked to the authorities, Joshua's hand on her shoulder squeezed gently, his gaze locking with hers as they walked from the room.

"I'd better go. I'm on duty tomorrow."

"Are you going to be able to come to the fairgrounds this weekend for any of the festivities?" Darcy asked when they were out in the entry hall.

"On Saturday. I'll stop by and see you. Tomorrow I'll

talk with the police about Angus and see if he has a connection to the recent fires."

"It sure would be nice to find the person before anything else happens."

"Good night, Darcy." He leaned forward and kissed her on the cheek.

As he exited, her hand came up to touch the place where his lips had been only a few seconds before. The casual gesture left her weak and shaken. It was the kind of kiss that might transpire between two friends, and yet…

It felt so good to sit for a few minutes, Darcy thought as she eased into a lawn chair under the maple tree. Shade stretched out in a large circle offering a reprieve from the heat of a late June afternoon. People milled around, looking at the horses up for sale. The crowd's murmurs vied with the sounds coming from the fairway. The aroma of popcorn and grilled meat spiced the air, chasing away the scents of horses, sweat and hay.

Her father made his way toward her, taking the empty lawn chair nearby. He moaned as he sat. "I'm sure glad this will be over soon. We've done well." He stretched his long legs out in front of him and crossed them at the ankles. "I appreciate all your work, Darcy."

For a few seconds it seemed as if her heart had stopped beating. Maybe she hadn't heard her father correctly.

He reached over and patted her arm. "You did good."

A rush of emotions swamped her, robbing her of anything like a coherent reply. She fixed her gaze on a little boy running his hand over a mare's coat, a huge grin on his face.

"Child, did you hear me?"

"Yes," she finally replied, her voice heavy and full of those emotions she was trying to get under control. Here in a crowd of people, her father was telling her she'd done a good job. A rare occurrence. "Thanks. I think the sales have gone well."

"One of the best years we've had, in spite of losing the barn a few weeks ago."

We? Not *I?* Again his statement produced a tightness in her throat that cut off the flow of words.

"I think we make a good team."

"Dad, are you all right?" *That's it. He's ill and trying to break the news gently.*

"Except for probably overdoing it today and yesterday, I'm fine. I'm nearly one hundred percent. Give me a few more weeks and there will be no stopping me." He twisted in the chair so he was looking at her. "Can't a person express their gratitude without you thinking there's something wrong?"

"Not when it's out of character."

"I realize I don't tell you how much I appreciate your efforts, but I do."

"Why now?"

"Why not?"

"That's not an answer, Dad."

"Okay, if you must know, Lizzy pointed out to me all you've been doing and that I haven't said anything to you. I realize you have given up your summer vacation to work on the farm, putting in twelve-hour days."

Ah, Lizzy. That explained everything. Disappointment surged within her. Someone had to tell him he should appreciate her efforts. Why couldn't he see that on his own?

"That's not to say I haven't seen all that you've been doing. I have. You know, girl, I'm not very good with words."

An understatement. "I'll stay this summer as long as you need me."

"Things should calm down some until fall, now that the big horse sale is over. I'll be able to work with Sean some more on riding. By the way, where is he?"

"He went with Nate to go on some of the rides. He has enough money for five of them, so he shouldn't be gone too long."

"Heard back from the police. They are charging Angus with trespassing but that's all. There isn't enough evidence for an arson charge."

"Maybe he didn't set the fires."

"Do you really believe he came back to the barn to retrieve some tack he left behind—what, three months ago?" Her father snorted. "He's lying."

"Dad, a groom found the tack he was talking about. He might not be lying."

"Oh, don't worry. I'm keeping the extra guard until this is resolved. In fact, I'm hiring another one. We have too many barns for just one. That became obvious with

Angus's little escapade." He snorted again. "Tell me, child, if he'd left tack and was so concerned about it, why didn't he just come and get it during the day?"

"From what I understand, he didn't leave the farm under the best of circumstances. Didn't you physically throw him out?"

"He was smoking in the barn! What would you have me do?" Her father rose, scanning the area. "I see some buyers over there. I'm gonna have a word with them."

He stalked off toward a group of four men near the second barn at the fairgrounds. Tact had never been her father's strong suit, Darcy thought, realizing she might have sneaked back in the dead of night for something she'd left behind, too.

"Haven't you heard frowning causes wrinkles?"

Joshua's question startled her, but she recovered quickly. "So does smiling and the sun."

He sat where her father had been only a moment before. "You know, I could stay right here and not move and probably enjoy what I like the most about the county fair."

"What?"

"People watching. People fascinate me. Like your father over there with those men. He knows them well. Even though they aren't from around here, he must see them every year at this horse auction."

"How do you know that?"

"Your father isn't a man who pats very many people on the back, but he greeted the taller man that way.

That's familiarity, and because it is unusual for your father, the relationship must be one that's developed over many years."

"Maybe they live around here."

"No. I know most of the horse people in the area. Besides, when their car pulled up, the license plate was from Tennessee."

She playfully slapped him on the arm. "You're cheating."

"I never claimed I was Sherlock Holmes."

"Dad told me the police let Angus go."

"Yep. Nothing to keep him on." Joshua settled back in the lawn chair, stretching his legs out in front of him, just as her father had.

"You want to hear something funny? I found myself sticking up for Angus with my dad. Frankly, I don't know why. Angus could very well be the arsonist."

"Darcy, isn't it obvious? You and your dad butt heads. If your father said it was sunny out, I think you would argue it was cloudy."

Darcy straightened, glaring at Joshua. "I do not. I must admit we often don't see eye to eye, but—" She couldn't finish her sentence because she realized Joshua was probably right. When she lived here and when she was married to Clay, she'd kept her opinions to herself. Lately, though, she was learning to speak her mind, which often meant she and her father didn't agree.

"I didn't used to be that way. I used to bite my tongue, literally, rather than say anything that might rock the boat."

His gaze snared hers. "So now you're standing up for yourself?"

"Yes, but it hasn't been easy and I still have a long way to go. I know I need to choose the battles I fight with my father and sometimes I don't choose wisely. I'm learning."

"That's what life is all about."

Darcy lifted her hair from her neck, letting the cool breeze caress her skin. "I suppose you've never had that kind of problem."

"Nope, but I've had more than my share of other problems."

"Hi."

Approaching them at a fast pace were Crystal and Tanya. The older woman brought the wheelchair to a halt in front of Darcy. "Crystal wanted to see the horses, so I had to wait until Tom was busy judging the pies."

Darcy stood. "I'll go get one of the yearlings we have for sale."

"I'm so glad you suggested we stop by," Tanya said in a rush, moving around as though she couldn't keep her body still.

Darcy hurried into the barn and took the nearest horse from its stall, then led her to Crystal. The young girl leaned forward and touched the yearling, her face lit with a smile.

"I've missed riding."

Tanya put a hand on her daughter's shoulder. "She doesn't blame horses for what happened to her. I have to sneak in books about horses because her father would throw them away if he found them."

Darcy blinked, trying to keep up with Tanya's rapid fire speech. "If Crystal ever wants to ride again, I would be glad to arrange something."

Crystal dropped her hand away from the animal, shaking her head. "No, that's not possible. I can't walk."

"It's possible if you want to. People with your kind of injuries do ride."

Crystal thought for a moment, then shook her head again. "Dad would never let me."

Tanya scanned the area, her gaze darting from one thing to the next, never still for any length of time. "Speaking of your father, we'd better head back to the pavilion." She whirled the wheelchair about and started toward the fairway.

Darcy took the yearling back into the barn, then returned. "You know, I've never met Tom, but—" She looked toward the area where Joshua was staring. A small man, no more than five and a half feet tall, blocked Tanya's progress.

"That's Tom."

"Oh, no. He doesn't appear to be too happy."

"Definitely an understatement. Maybe I should go over there."

Before Joshua could move, Tom took the wheelchair from Tanya and began to push his daughter toward the parking lot. Tanya followed the pair. Darcy shivered, even though the air was warm.

"Has Reverend Collins spoken with Tom?" Darcy asked. She wanted to do something to help the family that was struggling with the fallout of such a tragic accident.

"Several times, but Tom made it clear he didn't want the reverend's help."

"He hasn't gotten past the anger stage of his grief."

"Some people never do. Some people need help in dealing with their grief, but won't accept it."

Could that apply to her father? After her mother's death, all she'd seen from her father was anger. Had he moved on? She didn't know because she hadn't been around for the past ten years.

"Can you steal away for a while and get an ice cream with me?" Joshua asked, coming to stand next to her.

His presence lifted her spirits. "I've never been able to turn down ice cream. Maybe we'll see Sean on the fairway. Let me tell Dad I'm going with you for a little while."

Darcy walked toward her father, who was shaking hands with each of the four men as they were leaving. His weathered face brightened with a smile.

"They're definitely interested in two of our jumpers. I'm sure they'll be bidding on them at the evening session."

"Dad, I'm going with Joshua for an ice cream. Can I get you anything from the fairway?"

"Nope." He rubbed the back of his neck. "You've been seeing a lot of Joshua lately. Is there anything going on that I should know about?"

There was actually a twinkle in her father's dark

gray eyes that surprised Darcy. She almost forgot her father's question.

"Is there?"

Blinking, she finally replied, "Joshua and I are just friends. I'm helping him out at church with the Sunday school class."

"Is that what a few nights ago was? Funny, I would have thought you two had gone on a date. In my day that was what we called it."

Darcy lifted her shoulders in a shrug that she knew didn't convey the nonchalance she wanted to project. "That was different. He needed someone to go to the awards dinner with him."

"He couldn't go alone? I'm sure he wouldn't be the first or the last to do that."

She turned away. "I'll see you later." Her father's chuckles followed her all the way back to Joshua.

"You're blushing. What happened?"

"Nothing. Dad was just teasing me."

"Teasing you? From what I've gathered from you, that doesn't happen very often."

"If you must know, he thinks we're an item."

"And you set him straight," Joshua said, taking her by the elbow and steering her toward the fairway.

"Of course. We're just friends." And if she said it often enough, maybe she would believe it.

When had she begun to think of Joshua as more than a friend? The other evening at the awards dinner—their first official date? When he had chased

Angus? When he had given her a peck on the cheek that curled her toes?

Before she knew it, she was standing in front of the ice cream truck and Joshua was asking her what flavor she wanted. She had been so lost in thoughts of Joshua that she hadn't even realized how she'd gotten there. Boy, she had it bad!

"Hmm. I like so many. I could have a triple scoop with each layer a different flavor."

"Talk about me taking risks. Do you know what that will do to your arteries?"

"Not to mention hips. Okay, I'll settle for a double-scoop butter pecan and cookie dough ice cream." Darcy's mouth watered as she waited for the woman behind the counter to make her cone. When the lady handed it to her, Darcy took a big lick and said, "Mmm, this is delicious. Isn't life grand?"

Sean and his friend Nate ran up to them. "I'd like an ice cream cone, too."

"How about the money you were given? Where is it?" Darcy asked, knowing perfectly well it had left his hands the minute he'd gotten it.

"Gone." He gave her an innocent look, meant to appeal to her good nature.

Which wasn't too hard with Joshua next to her and a beautiful day surrounding her. She dug into the pocket of her jeans. "Okay. But you'll need to check with Ken and see if there's anything he wants you to do. Nate, do you want one, too?"

"Yes, and I can help Sean with any chore he needs to do. Mom said she'd pick me up at the barn in an hour."

"Is your mother at the pavilion showing her dolls?" Darcy remembered being the recipient of Jesse's first doll-making attempt. She still had the doll displayed in her bedroom, which had annoyed Clay.

"Yes, ma'am."

After Darcy purchased the two ice-cream cones, the boys thanked her and took off toward the barns on the edge of the fairgrounds. She caught Joshua staring at her.

"You're a good mother, Darcy O'Brien. You have a solid relationship with your son."

Heat flooded her cheeks. "A lot of the time it was just him and me. With Clay being gone so much, Sean and I became very close. I hate, though, that he doesn't have a man's influence in his life. I think that's important."

"He's taken to your father."

And you, Darcy thought. But both relationships were fleeting and hundreds of miles from their home in Panama City.

"Have you ever thought of having children? I've seen you with the kids at church and you're great with them."

His eyes conveyed a haunted look that struck a chord in Darcy. Remembering his ex-fiancée, she stepped closer, suddenly wanting to comfort him. "I'm sorry. I forgot about Carol."

"We'd talked about having children. I wanted at least three. She wasn't so sure she wanted any."

"And yet, she has a son now."

"I know I need to get past her betrayal, but we had known each other for years and I never saw it coming. It makes you doubt your judgment when something like that happens. It makes this risk taker—" he patted his chest "—cautious."

Someone jostled her, sending her into Joshua. He steadied her, so near that his breath fanned her, causing her heart to beat faster. She tilted her head to look him in the eye, and even though hundreds of people were around them, she felt no one's presence but his. He was a good, kind man who had been hurt terribly. That, they had in common. She lifted her hand to cup his jaw— strong, firm. Like the man himself.

"We're human. We make mistakes. We hopefully learn from those mistakes."

He veiled his expression. "I've learned to be very careful, not to rush into anything."

His warning, spoken in a harsh whisper, cautioned her to protect her heart. Falling in love with Joshua was a risk she wasn't willing to take. He wasn't ready for a relationship beyond friendship, and neither was she.

Darcy moved back and inhaled deeply to calm her rapidly beating heart. "I'd better get back. The afternoon auction will be starting in an hour and there are things to do."

"Can I help?"

"Surely you have something better to do than hang around a smelly barn?"

"No, I'm all yours for the afternoon."

His statement caused a hitch in her breathing. He meant nothing by that, but she began to dream of more. Her overriding thought was: How could Carol have betrayed him with another man?

Darcy headed toward the barn area, conscious of Joshua next to her. Halfway down the fairway she felt the hairs on the nape of her neck tingle. She scanned the crowd and stopped dead in her tracks when she saw Angus Feehan not three yards away, staring at her with narrowed eyes that transmitted his anger.

"What's wrong?" Joshua asked, moving to stand in front of her and blocking her view of the fired groom.

"Angus, behind you to the left."

Joshua glanced over his shoulder, stiffened and pivoted. He stalked toward the man. Angus's eyes widened, then he spun about and disappeared into the throng behind him. Joshua searched for a few minutes before returning to Darcy.

"I know this is a free country and he has every right to be here, but *why* is he here?" Darcy asked, hearing the panic in her voice.

"That was what I was going to ask him before he so conveniently vanished. Come on, let's get back to the barn." He placed his hand at the small of her back and guided her through the mass of people.

She heard raised voices coming from inside the barn where their horses were stabled for the auction. One, she knew, was her father's, and she quickened her pace. She found him arguing with Mike Reynolds, his arms waving as he spoke.

Shamus finished his tirade with "Get out before I call Security."

Mike lounged back against a stall. "Go ahead. I have every right to be here. This is public property and you can't order me off it."

Darcy stepped between the two men before they came to blows. "Dad, calm down. We aren't at Shamrock Stables." Then she turned to say to Mike, "Please go."

"Fine. But one day, old man, someone's going to knock you down a peg or two. You have no right to spread rumors about me."

"I'm only telling the truth. You shouldn't be around horses."

Darcy was glad she was standing between them, because she was sure if she hadn't been, they would have started a fistfight. She felt her father's tension and anger. She saw Mike's as he glared over her shoulder at her father. Mike huffed, then whirled about and stormed toward the entrance.

The tension remained. Darcy slowly pivoted toward her father, understanding where his anger was coming from, but realizing if he didn't control it, he would have another heart attack. "Dad, this isn't good for you."

"My heart's ticking just fine. I'm going to the arena to make sure everything is in place," he muttered, then stalked off in the opposite direction from Mike.

Joshua placed his hands on her shoulders and

kneaded. "I don't think Mike Reynolds is capable of setting the fires."

"He isn't doing very well. He's lost several jobs because of the way he handles the horses. Maybe he
blames the animals or the owners for his troubles."

"I suppose it's possible. He's certainly hotheaded
enough, but it just doesn't feel right to me."

"I hope you find the person responsible soon. I don't
know how much longer my father's going to be able to
take this."

"Since everyone heightened security at the farms, there
hasn't been a fire. And right now, with what we have, we
don't have a suspect. I'll let the police know, though,
about Angus showing up out here. It may be nothing—"

"Or it may be something. I want the person caught
but not at the expense of another fire. I guess there is no
easy answer."

"Not with arson, I'm afraid."

Even though it was hot, Darcy felt cold to the bone.
She and her father had their differences, but she was so
afraid that if the arsonist wasn't caught soon, the stress
would cause another heart attack.

*Lord, please help my father deal with his anger bet-
ter. Show me the way to help him and put a stop to this
arsonist. I know I haven't prayed much in years, but I
don't know what else to do anymore. He and Sean are
all the family I have.*

Darcy relaxed on a bale of hay that sat against the wall
of the barn. The second day of the horse auction was over

and it had gone very well. One more day and they would be finished with this big annual event. Her gaze swept the long aisle down the middle of the fairground barn, checking each stall that was occupied with a Shamrock Stables horse. One yearling stuck his head out, looking around. Several were eating. She heard the one in the last stall neighing. They had six horses left to auction off; two still had to be picked up by their new owners—they were the only animals in this barn. In the other two there were six farms represented, but Shamrock Stables was the biggest one at the county fair this year.

Everyone had worked overtime, especially her father, and she had volunteered to stay the night with the last batch of horses. Sean had wanted to join her, and she had decided at the last minute that he should go home with her father. He would have kept her up the whole night with his excitement. She couldn't afford to lose that sleep. Besides, it wasn't as if she was alone here. Every other farm had someone staying with their horses.

Darcy rose, stretched her cramped muscles and rolled her head in a full circle, trying to work the tension out. She walked to the door of the barn and looked out. She saw several grooms sitting under the large maple, talking and laughing. The noise from the fairway was diminishing as the crowd left for the evening.

Darkness had settled over the area where the barns were, but the lights from the fairway were a beacon in the night. Their brightness comforted her. Her last two years living at home, she had stayed with the horses at least one of the nights at the fair, but this year she felt edgy.

"Hi, Mrs. O'Brien. How's everything going?" One of the guards the farms had hired for the fair stopped in front of her.

"One more day and I can collapse."

"Have you even gone home since this began?"

"Yes, Friday evening."

"But you were here this morning at five, so you couldn't have been home for long."

"Just long enough to catch a few hours' sleep."

"Where are you sleeping tonight?"

"I'll be in the tack room if you need me."

"Except for a few teenagers who didn't go home when they were supposed to last night, it has been unusually quiet. Good night, Mrs. O'Brien." The guard ambled toward the next barn.

Darcy took a deep, fortifying breath and turned back into the barn. After walking its length and checking on the horses one final time, she made her way to the tack room, leaving the door open to give some light. Sitting in the corner was the cot her father had brought—a hard, uncomfortable cot with a thin blanket and a small pillow. Darcy eased down on it and listened carefully while untying her tennis shoes and removing them. The sounds of the fair were far away and faint.

Lying back, she threw the cover over herself and closed her eyes. The image of Joshua danced into her mind and brought a smile to her mouth. He had been wonderful this afternoon and evening, helping her with the horses and even bringing her something other than fattening food from the fairway to eat. The hot roast beef sandwich with cole slaw had been delicious. He was awfully good to her, she thought as she felt the effects of too little sleep. Joshua's image wavered and faded as sleep descended.

A horse's neigh pierced her dream. The scent of something burning accosted her. Darcy shot up, yanking off the blanket and surging to her feet. She rushed from the tack room into the main part of the barn; smoke billowed from the far end. The sounds of the frightened horses filled the air as quickly as the smoke did. Several were kicking their stalls. She saw one with wild eyes. She hurried to open the stall doors, trying her best not to breathe too deeply.

But still the smoke choked her as she reached the first stall. She coughed, placing her hand over her mouth and nose. Throwing the door open, she moved to the next one. She heard the horse bolting out. *One down, seven more to go.*

When she came to the fourth stall, she pulled the door open, but before she could get out of the way, the horse charged forward, the whites of his eyes all Darcy could focus on. He reared up and brought his hooves down, catching her on the shoulder. A sharp sensation like a knife cut shot through her, and she spun back against the wall. His front hooves came down again, clipping the side of her head. She sank to the dirt floor, pain radiating to every part of her. Through the smoke a man emerged, small and familiar looking, but Darcy had a hard time remembering who he was. His features wavered as she reached out to grasp him, to plead for his help. There was a searing pounding in her head as though someone were playing the bass drum inside her skull. Then darkness swallowed her up.

Chapter Eight

The insistent ringing of the phone invaded Joshua's dream about Darcy. He fumbled in the dark for the receiver, found it and brought it to his ear. "Yes."

"There's a fire at the fairgrounds. One of the barns. You need to get over there. I'm betting it's the work of the arsonist," his captain said, the sound of the sirens in the background.

"Are you on your way?" Joshua asked.

"Just about there. Get over here."

Joshua slammed the receiver down and jerked back the covers. Five minutes later, dressed in jeans and a T-shirt, he raced for his truck, fear gripping him so hard that his heart hammered against his rib cage. Darcy was in one of those barns. *Please, Lord, let her be okay.*

Thankfully there was little traffic at midnight. He sped toward the fairgrounds, thoughts of Darcy trapped in a burning barn spurring him to drive faster than was safe.

* * *

Darcy's head throbbed; every part of her was sore. A cool breeze brushed her face. When she opened her eyes, she saw that she was outside the barn, at the back, a few feet from the entrance. In the distance she heard the wail of sirens. Closer, the frantic shouts of several people and the smoke-filled air reminded her of the fire.

She started to rise and her vision blurred. Squeezing her eyes closed for a few precious seconds, she held her head, trying not to breathe too deeply. Then she attempted again to stand, this time more slowly. Her head still pulsated with pain, but she dismissed it. She had to get back inside and make sure all the horses got out.

With her gaze trained on the flames licking their way toward the back of the barn, Darcy darted inside toward the nearest stall. Nausea rose up in her and she swayed. Gripping the nearest thing, a pole, she stopped to get her bearings. She couldn't see beyond a few feet as the smoke thickened.

Please, Lord, help me rescue the horses.

The sounds of frenzied horses propelled her forward. She reached the nearest stall and swung the door open. Moving as fast as her throbbing head would allow, she got out of the way of the charging horse. It disappeared out the back door. Hugging low to the ground, she felt along the wall to the next stall and thrust it open. Plastered against the side, she watched that yearling escape to safety. She repeated the same actions at the next one.

Over the noise of the firefighters arriving and the fire

engulfing the wooden structure, she heard her name being shouted. *Joshua.* "Over here."

He appeared through the haze, dressed in jeans and a T-shirt, but with a mask and helmet on his head. In his right hand he carried an extra set. He immediately thrust the helmet and mask toward her and helped her to put it on. "Come on. You're getting out of here. The fire is out of control. It won't be long until this whole building goes," he shouted through the mask. He gripped her arm.

"No. Can't yet," she rasped, her throat burning with the effort to speak.

She only had one more stall. She wrenched herself from his grasp and started for it. Her eyes stung, her lungs seared as though the fire consumed her. But she thought she could make it and still get out. Three feet. Two.

A crashing sound behind her sped her heart to a thundering pace. She glanced over her shoulder and saw Joshua right behind her. Beyond him part of the roof near the front had fallen. A shudder ripped down her length.

"Get out. I'll get the horse." His voice vibrated with his anger. "*Now,* Darcy." He shoved her toward the rear door, not giving her a chance to think or respond.

She started back to help him—it wasn't his animal— but hands grabbed her and pulled her from the barn. Two firefighters headed into the blaze; a third, Ned, indicated she should move away from the building.

Darcy stared at the entrance, the images swimming before her eyes. She *couldn't* pass out. She had to make sure Joshua made it out. He was in there because of her. When she spied the last horse racing from the barn followed by Joshua, she sank to the ground, her legs no longer able to support her. Her whole body shook from exhaustion and spent adrenaline. Her stomach roiled; her lungs felt tight, the last good breaths squeezed from them. Ripping off the helmet and mask, she began to cough.

Across the smoky expanse, Joshua's gaze connected with hers. He walked toward her, anger marking his features and his long strides. She blinked. There were two of him, then three. The throbbing in her head intensified and each breath hurt. She cradled her face, her fingers touching a sticky substance where the horse had kicked her.

Blackness nibbled at her consciousness. She blinked again, trying to calm her reeling stomach, to push away the dark mist before her eyes.

"I can't believe you did that, Darcy," Joshua said, halting in front of her, his legs planted a foot apart, his hands on his hips.

She made the mistake of tilting her head back to peer up into his face. The blackness gobbled her up once more.

Anger gripped Joshua so tightly his muscles hurt. He stared down at Darcy, wanting to shake some sense into her. She could have died in that fire. He could take risks. She couldn't! She closed her eyes, heaved a deep breath and fell over. He stooped to catch her in his arms.

Cradling her against his chest, he felt his rage slip

from him. All his thoughts were centered on getting help for Darcy. She'd been inside too long. He brushed her hair away from her face and discovered blood oozing from a wound on the side of her head. His heart plummeted.

Dear Heavenly Father, please don't let her die.

Joshua shouted for help while laying her back on the hard ground. One of the paramedics rushed over and kneeled to check her.

Stan glanced at Joshua. "Smoke inhalation and most likely a concussion. We'll transport her to the hospital."

While Stan fetched the stretcher, Joshua stayed next to Darcy. His eyes burned from the smoke and something else he didn't want to think about. They were friends. That was all. Hadn't he told himself that enough times over the past few weeks? But…he didn't want anything to happen to her.

Joshua touched her dirt-smudged face, brushing his fingers over her skin. He laid his palm against the curve of her jaw and remembered her laughter. When she smiled, his whole world brightened to the point that it scared him.

Stan, accompanied by another paramedic, returned and they transferred Darcy to the stretcher. Joshua walked with her, holding her hand even though she had not awakened.

At the ambulance Stan asked, "Coming with us or staying?"

Torn between his duty and desire, Joshua stared at his friend, trying to decide what he should do. He had to stay. Everything inside of him demanded he do what he was good at and find the person behind the fires, and yet he didn't want to leave Darcy's side, even though there was nothing he could do for her at the hospital. He could, however, gather information and evidence to track down the arsonist before someone died. That *had* to be his priority.

He knew he had to remain at the fire; in his heart he would go with Darcy, at least in spirit, and he would pray for her fast recovery until he could be with her.

"I'm staying. Let me know what the doctor says, Stan."

"Will do." Stan peered at the barn, partially destroyed by the flames. "It looks like we'll be able to contain the fire to just this one barn. That's good news."

"Thank goodness there wasn't any wind this evening and someone quickly called in the fire."

"I'll take care of her. You go do your magic."

Joshua watched the ambulance pull away from the barn area, his heart heavy, his thoughts with Darcy. *Lord, I need Your help. Who is burning these barns? Why? Please guide me to the truth. I don't want to see anyone else get hurt. Please watch over Darcy for me and heal her. Be with her.*

The pounding in her head threatened to overwhelm Darcy and push her back into the darkness. She felt something over her mouth and wondered if she still had the mask on. No, she'd tossed it on the ground. Noises, people's voices, machines beeping and an antiseptic smell dragged her toward consciousness. She eased her eyes open.

Pale-blue walls met her inspection. A television was mounted on a shelf high in the corner. A sound to her left shifted her attention in that direction. Her father, his eyes closed, sat on the small tan sofa with Sean curled up asleep, cradled against his grandfather's side. In a chair next to the bed sat Joshua, his chin resting on his chest, his body completely relaxed in sleep.

She was in a hospital room, and from the looks of the bright sunlight streaming through the partially opened drapes it was probably late morning. Did all the horses make it? Were the firefighters able to save the other barns? Questions inundated her, demanding answers.

She removed the oxygen mask from her face and nudged Joshua's hand, which rested near hers on the bed. He stirred, lifting his head to snare her with his tired eyes. A smile tugged at the corners of his mouth, kicking her heartbeat into a faster tempo.

"I'm not sure if I should yell at you or kiss you."

"Well, if you want my opinion, I would prefer a kiss," Darcy said, her voice raw as though she hadn't used it in a long time. Her throat hurt as much as her head.

She leaned toward the bedside table to get the pitcher and pour herself some water. Joshua motioned her back and poured it for her. He supported her while she took several long sips, soothing her searing throat. His scent of musk played havoc with her senses. He was so near she could even smell his mint-flavored toothpaste. Visions of that kiss he'd mentioned danced in her mind.

When she was through drinking, he placed the glass close to her on the table. "You shouldn't have gone back in after the horses. You were lucky."

"I know, but I couldn't stand by and listen to the horses dying."

His eyes gentled. "I know." He covered her hand with his. "But you almost died last night. You gave me quite a scare."

"You weren't exactly easy on me. I thought I might never see you again when the last horse came out and you didn't."

"I wasn't far behind him."

"Those seconds seemed like an eternity."

"Then you know what I went through when I called your name and you didn't respond."

"But I did."

"Not at first. An eternity passed before I heard you."

"Mom, you're okay?" Sean asked, hopping up from the couch and rushing toward her. He threw his arms around her and hugged her. "I was so worried."

Darcy caught Joshua's "I told you so" look while she pressed her son close to her heart. Her father moved slower toward the bed, his face haggard, exhaustion evident in his expression. He bent down and kissed her on the cheek.

"Child, don't ever give us that kind of scare again. I can replace the horses. I can't replace you."

Darcy's mouth fell open. In her heart she knew her

father loved her, but he never said anything to her about his feelings. There had been times she had felt the farm was more important to him than she was. For him to say otherwise made her throat constrict. She reached for the glass and took another sip to ease the tightness.

"Did all the horses make it?"

"Yes," her father answered, stepping back to sit again on the couch.

Sean bounced onto the end of the bed. "Grandpa found the last one early this morning. Only one was injured but not seriously. I helped look for the horses."

Darcy smiled at her son. "You're becoming quite a little helper."

He puffed out his chest. "I'm not little. Grandpa said so."

"How are the other barns?"

"No damage. The firefighters were able to confine the fire to that one barn." Joshua leaned back in his chair. "Can you tell me what happened?"

Darcy touched her head where her wound was and winced. There was something at the edges of her mind that she knew was important. She closed her eyes and concentrated on the events of the past evening. What was she forgetting?

"I was asleep in the tack room when I heard something—the horses, I believe." She rubbed her forehead. *Think!* "I went out into the barn and saw the smoke. I immediately started opening the stall doors. One horse caught me with his front hooves. I went down. I—" A vague image wavered like a highway on a hot day. "I blacked out."

"In the barn?" Joshua asked, sitting forward, his elbows resting on his thighs.

"Yes, but when I woke up I was outside. Someone must have dragged me from the barn. I—" Again a featureless face materialized in her mind. She stared into space and tried to put details on that face. "I remember a man bending over me in the barn."

"Who?" Her father came to the bed again, hovering over her, his expression intense.

"I—I've seen the man before. He was small, dark hair."

"Angus. I knew it!" Her father slapped his hand against his leg. "He had no reason to be there unless he was up to no good."

She shook her head and regretted it the second she did. The pounding intensified. "Not Angus." Slowly she pieced together the image of the man leaning over her, smoke surrounding them. "I think…it was…" Slowly the haze lifted even more and features swirled into a picture of a man. "Tom Bolton."

Joshua bolted to his feet. "Are you sure?"

"I think so."

"One of the grooms saw a small man running away. He couldn't catch the man." Joshua headed for the door.

"Where are you going, son?"

"To have a little chat with Tom. It's time this stops."

The controlled anger in Joshua's voice made Darcy shudder.

* * *

Despite faint throbbing against her skull, Darcy paced from one end of her living room to the other. Joshua had said he would be here by now. She wanted to know what had happened when he talked with Tom. Other than to tell her that Tom had admitted to setting the fires, Joshua hadn't given her any details.

Her father came into the room. "Darcy, I promised the doctor you would rest. That's the only reason the doctor let you come home today. Sit. Joshua will be here when he can make it."

She pivoted toward her father, frowning. "I knew Tom Bolton was angry about his daughter's accident— but to do what he did? I don't understand."

"Grief can make a person do many things they wouldn't normally do."

Darcy wondered about the tone in her father's voice. He spoke as though he knew from experience. Was it grief over her mother's suicide he was talking about? Or grief because her mother hadn't been "normal" for much of their marriage? Darcy could still remember her mother's highs, but especially her lows, which had become more frequent as the years passed. Why hadn't her father been able to help her mother? That question she had wanted him to answer for a long time, but she'd never had the nerve to ask.

The doorbell chimed. Ignoring the pain in her head as much as possible, Darcy hurried to answer it. She threw open the door and smiled at the wonderful sight of Joshua standing on the porch. "It's about time."

"I'm only a few minutes—" he checked his watch "—okay, half an hour late. May I come in?"

She laughed and stepped to the side. "Of course. What happened when you went to see Tom? Why did he do it?"

Joshua held up his hand. "Whoa, Darcy. Let's go into the living room and sit. You should be resting. It isn't every day you get a concussion."

"You just want to drive me crazy."

Joshua waved his hand toward the living room. "My lips are sealed until you're sitting."

"Between you and Dad I'm gonna have more than my share of resting," she muttered, making her way back into the living room and sitting on the couch. She knew they were right, but waiting for Joshua had taxed her patience.

"Good evening, sir. I see you've had your hands full."

"I think she comes by it honestly. I'm not the best patient in the world, either."

"Right," Darcy interjected. "Okay, I'm sitting. Now, tell me everything."

"I found Tom at home. I think he was expecting me."

"Because I saw him."

"His hatred for horses sent him over the edge. All he could think of was to destroy every one he could. The more he was around Crystal the more angry he got about her accident, to the point he decided to set the barns on fire. I think, though, your injury last night sobered him to what he was doing."

"He didn't have to drag me from the barn. He knew

I saw him, and by helping me to escape the fire he was sealing his own fate."

"He told me the fires were about hurting what had hurt his daughter. Nothing else but that. He never wanted anyone to get hurt. That's why they were always at night when people weren't around."

"Also a good time to conceal one's movements," her father said with a snort.

Darcy sighed. "It's over. That's the main thing."

"What's sad is that I don't think Tom thought beyond his actions to what it would do to his family. When the police took Tom away, Tanya and Crystal were sobbing. I stayed to try and calm them down before giving them a ride to the police station."

"Oh, my. What will this do to them?" Darcy covered her mouth with her hand, thinking back to the times she had talked to Crystal and Tanya. They both had so many problems—and now this. "Are they still at the station?"

"No, they should be home by now. Reverend Collins came down to the police station and was going to take them home."

Darcy rose. "Will you take me to see Tanya?"

"Darcy, I don't think that's a good idea," her father said, standing too, and moving toward the entrance as though to block her exit.

"She needs a friend right now and I intend to help her and Crystal as much as possible. In fact, I think Sean should come along and bring Lady to help cheer up Crystal."

"But you're the reason Tom is in jail right now," her father said.

"I am not. *Tom* is the reason he is in jail. I want Tanya to know that I have no hard feelings toward her."

Her father's gaze pinned her. "But she may toward you."

"I still have to try to help."

Joshua came up beside her. "If I don't take you, are you going to try to drive yourself?"

She lifted her chin, determined to challenge both her father and Joshua if need be. In the past she wouldn't have, but she was discovering the power of standing up for what she believed in. And she believed that Tanya and Crystal needed her to be a friend.

"If I have to."

"Then I'll take you. Where's Sean?" Joshua asked, touching the small of her back.

The feel of his fingers honed her senses to him. She liked knowing he would be accompanying her, because she wasn't sure how Tanya would receive her. Joshua gave her the strength to do what was right.

"He's out back, trying to teach Lady some tricks."

"Lady is only seven weeks old."

"Yeah, I know. She's constantly moving. He has a hard time getting her attention."

"She'll calm down as she grows older."

"I hope so."

"I'll get Sean and Lady. Stay here until I return."

"Aye, aye, captain."

Joshua gave her an exasperated look at the entrance into the kitchen. "I mean it, Darcy. No trying to walk to the truck by yourself. Guard her, Shamus."

Her father chuckled. "Little does he know how useless that would be. Doesn't he know by now when you're determined to do something you will do it?"

"It didn't use to be like that."

"True, child, but you've changed since you got married."

"No, Dad, I changed after Clay died. What you see is the new me."

"I like it. What made you change?"

She held a deep breath for a few seconds before blowing it out through pursed lips. "I got tired of suppressing who I really was."

"Who is that?"

"I'm a work in progress at the moment. But I do know I won't keep my opinion to myself any longer."

"Tell me something I don't know."

"Grandpa, Lady sat for me."

"She did? For how long?"

"Maybe two seconds."

"I think you need to work on that trick," her father said, ruffling Sean's red hair. "In order for that to work she needs to stay seated until you tell her to move. But I do like how she's beginning to walk on a leash."

While Sean raced ahead with Lady yelping at his heels, Joshua wound his arm about Darcy's shoulders and led her to the truck.

"I can't wait to show Crystal my new trick with Lady. When she gets her own dog, I can help her train it."

"By the time she gets a dog, we may be back in Panama City."

"Oh, I forgot. Well, next summer I can help her."

On the ride to the Boltons', Darcy thought about her home in Panama City that she had been painstakingly renovating—the first one she'd spent any time on in the ten years since she'd left here. Strange, she really didn't remember much about her home and the plans she had had for it. In a short time the farm had become her home again. But the last time she'd lived here she'd lost who she was. She was determined for that not to happen again—even if it meant staying away from Shamrock Stables.

Joshua escorted her to the Boltons' front door, his arm steady about her. She liked its feel about her. Comforting. Sheltering. Like the man.

Tanya answered the doorbell immediately as though she had been expecting them. She took one look at Darcy and began to cry, throwing herself at her. Darcy hugged the woman as she sobbed against her shoulder.

"I'm so sorry to hear about Tom. I wanted to offer you my help if you'll take it." Darcy patted Tanya on the back while Sean, Lady and Joshua went into the house.

"I can't believe you're here. I thought you would hate us for what Tom nearly did to you. I'm the one who is sorry. I should have known what he was doing and made him stop. Crystal's beside herself. She has been crying all day and I can't seem to stop. What am I going to do? How will I be able to hold my head up in this town after what Tom did?"

It was Darcy's turn to clasp Tanya against her and walk into her house. "You did nothing wrong. No one's going to blame you or Crystal. I certainly don't."

Tanya's tears continued to fall unchecked down her cheeks. "All I want to do is stay in this house and never see anyone. I can't face people. I can't deal with it."

"Have you taken your medication today?" Darcy asked, remembering Tanya talking about how stressed she had been to the point of forgetting to take her medicine. From her own experience with her mother, Darcy knew that would only make the situation worse.

Tanya paused in the middle of the living room and thought for a moment. "No, I forgot."

"That's the first thing you should do. Then we'll sit in the kitchen and discuss your situation over a cup of coffee. I can make some while you're taking your medicine."

While Tanya went to get her medication, Darcy walked into the kitchen and found the counters littered with dirty dishes. She saw the coffeepot next to the sink. After washing it out, she put some coffee on to brew, then set about tidying up while she waited for Tanya to return.

Ten minutes later Tanya appeared in the doorway, her face blotchy as though she had been crying again. "I'm sorry. I took one look at myself in the mirror and broke down."

"Did you get your medicine?" Darcy asked, rinsing off the last plate to go into the dishwasher.

She held up the bottle, then opened it and poured one pill into her palm. "I know this place looks a mess, but I've been so preoccupied I haven't gotten a chance to clean up." Tanya took a glass and filled it with water, then downed her medicine.

"That's why I'm here. To help. You sit while I finish up."

"But you were just in the hospital. You shouldn't be doing anything."

Darcy motioned with her hand, dismissing Tanya's concern. "I'm fine. Besides, all I'm doing is running some water over a few dishes. Not very taxing." With the last pot in the dishwasher, she closed it, then turned slowly to face Tanya, making sure she didn't move suddenly. Her medication was helping the pain but not totally. The scent of brewing coffee saturated the air. "How do you like your coffee?"

"Black."

Darcy served Tanya her cup, then got one for herself, putting in several spoons of sugar. "The sweeter the better." When she sat across from Tanya, she continued, "Have you got a lawyer to represent Tom?"

Tanya stared at her cup.

"Tanya, do you have a lawyer?"

The woman blinked, jerking her head up. "Yes. There won't be a lengthy trial, though, since he confessed. He told me that seeing you on the ground in the barn last night shook him up, brought him to his senses. He'd never meant for a person to get hurt. He's a good man. Really."

Darcy bit her lower lip to keep from pointing out that

hurting animals wasn't okay. In her mind she felt Tom had gone a bit crazy with his daughter's accident. "Grief can do strange things to some people."

"How are Crystal and I going to live? I don't have a job. We have so many bills to pay."

"As soon as you feel up to it, I can help you with a résumé." Darcy took a sip of her coffee. "Also, Joshua and Sean want to build that ramp for Crystal so she can enjoy the backyard. What do you say?"

"I don't want to be any trouble to anyone." Tanya ran her finger around the rim of her cup, her gaze focused on its black contents.

"It looks like Sean and Lady were just what Crystal needed." Joshua entered the kitchen and took the chair next to Darcy. "I left those two laughing at Lady's attempt to roll over—or I guess more accurately, Sean's attempt to teach her a new trick."

"That's good," Tanya murmured, never lifting her gaze to Joshua.

Darcy caught his attention and shrugged. "When do you think you can start on the ramp?"

"How about Wednesday afternoon, Tanya?"

"Fine."

The listless tone in Tanya's voice worried Darcy, but she didn't know what to do. While Joshua entertained them with a description of Sean's training technique, Darcy prayed to God for guidance in helping Tanya. It had been years since she had turned to the Lord for assistance, but no matter how independent she wanted to be, she was learning her limits. Since her return home, she was quietly discovering there were some problems only the Lord could help with.

Weariness wore her down. By the time Joshua was finished with his story, Darcy didn't even have the strength to lift her cup. She had overextended herself today.

Joshua searched her features and frowned. He rose. "We'd better be going. It's been a long day for everyone."

After retrieving Sean and Lady, he escorted Darcy to his truck. His arm about her was what kept her standing.

"I'm gonna have to learn to say no to you," he whispered close to her ear.

Her neck tingled from the caress of his words. "I didn't leave you much of a choice."

"True. But you need your rest so you can help Sean and me with the ramp."

"If you could see me with a hammer, you wouldn't even suggest that."

"But I bet you'll look cute in a tool belt."

She laughed. "You stole my line."

"Come Wednesday we'll have to let Crystal and Sean decide who looks the best wearing a tool belt." He assisted her into his truck, his hand lingering on her arm longer than necessary.

He stared into her eyes for several moments, warmth and friendship offered. Then his look evolved into something beyond friendship, and her pulse rate sped. Hope flared for a heartbeat, until she thought of all the obstacles in their way. She wasn't even sure who she was. How could she ask someone to love her when she was changing? How could she love someone when she didn't know what she really wanted?

Chapter Nine

"We'll need to go get the supplies, then pick up Sean at Jesse and Nate's." Darcy climbed into Joshua's truck, looking forward to spending some time with him. The past few days, all she'd thought about was Joshua coming to her rescue in the burning barn or Joshua touching her on the hand or smiling at her with his whole face alight even down to a twinkle in his blue eyes.

"How are you feeling?"

"Much better. The headache's only a faint throb, barely noticeable."

"That's good. Don't give me a fright like that again." His expression set in a frown, Joshua threw the truck into drive and pulled away from her house.

"Where do you suggest we get the lumber for the ramp?"

"The best prices in town are at Northland Lumber."

"Isn't that a new store near the renovated downtown area?"

"Yes."

The clipped answer concerned Darcy. Was he still angry at her for taking a risk when rescuing the horses? Or was it something else? She twisted about, searching Joshua's face.

"What aren't you telling me?"

His frown deepened to a scowl. "Carol's married to the manager of Northland."

"Then we don't have to go there."

"No, I need to move on. I can't avoid going to Northland because of my ex-fiancée, especially since it's the best chance to get all the supplies in one store." He glanced at her. "I've heard that Carol wants to return to Sweetwater Community Church."

"And how do you feel about that?"

He gripped the steering wheel tighter, tension visibly moving from his face to flood his whole body. "It's one thing to see the happy family occasionally, but a completely different thing to run into them every week at church, a place I consider my sanctuary."

"Maybe she won't attend the same service as you."

"Maybe" was his tight comment.

Compelled to comfort him, Darcy laid her hand on his arm, wishing she had the right to do more. So many times he'd been there for her. "I know what it feels like to be hurt by someone you love. It knocks the breath out of you."

"It's hard to acknowledge you could have been so wrong about a person."

"Shakes your confidence in your ability to choose wisely."

"Right." His hands about the steering wheel relaxed, the rigid set to his shoulders eased.

"I've been in your shoes. I know what you're going through." *I'm still going through it,* Darcy amended silently. She wasn't entirely over her disastrous marriage to Clay. The effects of doubting her choices lingered and colored every judgment she made. She wasn't sure that would ever totally change.

"I knew there was a reason I liked you." He shifted his full attention to her while waiting at a stoplight.

Okay, she knew it was dangerous to feel warm and fuzzy, but she did. He made her feel special as no man ever had. Totally dangerous—their conversation about Carol only confirmed it. He wasn't over his ex-fiancée, might still be in love with her, even if he didn't acknowledge that to himself. Why else would he be so upset more than a year later?

Joshua parked in the lot in front of Northland Lumber. For a few seconds he just sat in the truck, staring at the entrance as though he expected Carol to come out and greet him. Darcy's throat contracted, her mouth went dry. She wanted to help him move on for a purely selfish reason. She cared about Joshua Markham.

"Were you friends with her husband?"

His jaws clenched. He sighed heavily. "Yes. We

weren't best friends or anything like that, but I knew him. We used to play on a softball team together before I got so busy I had to quit. I think that's how she met him."

"You haven't forgiven her, have you?"

His jawline hardened even more. "I'm trying. Most of the time I don't think about it. Lately I have been."

"Why now?"

Switching off the engine, he shifted so he faced her with only a foot between them. "You. You make me think of things that I'd decided might not be in my future."

The breath bottled in her lungs burned. "You know I'm as leery as you are of moving our relationship forward."

"Yes. I know why I feel that way. Why do you?"

"My marriage wasn't a partnership. I found myself suffocating. I worked hard to make sure nothing rocked the boat with Clay, and that can be very exhausting." There was so much more to the story than that, but Darcy still wasn't ready to confess all her mixed-up feelings to someone she hadn't known but a month. She and Clay had dated for a year and a half, and look what happened to that relationship. "I'm trying to discover who the real Darcy O'Brien is."

"I can tell you what I see. I see a person who is loving and caring, who is determined to do the right thing, who has taken a woman under her wing whose husband nearly killed her."

The warm, fuzzy feeling spread from the pit of her stomach to encompass her whole body. She wished she deserved his praise. "I'm helping Tanya because she is bipolar. My mother was bipolar and I want to understand the illness. As a teenager I didn't."

"So that's the only reason we're going shopping for some lumber to build a ramp? You could look the illness up on the Internet if that was all. Don't sell yourself short, Darcy."

He brushed a strand of her hair back behind her ear. The feather-soft touch curled her toes. "I couldn't help my mother. Maybe I can help Tanya. But my relationship with my mother isn't the point of this conversation."

He arched a brow. "It isn't?"

"No, we were talking about you forgiving Carol. The man I know doesn't usually hold grudges."

"I'd built in my mind my whole future around Carol. When she married Kyle, everything fell apart." He yanked his door open. "We'd better get moving if we're going to build this ramp today."

Inside the store the tension returned to Joshua's features. At any second Darcy was sure she would run into Carol coming around the next corner. When they left thirty minutes later, she hadn't even met Kyle, Carol's husband. For several miles on the drive to Nate's Joshua still held himself rigid, but slowly the tension slipped from him. Darcy breathed a sigh of relief.

After picking up Sean at Nate's, the three of them headed to the Boltons'. As she walked up to the house, Darcy wondered what kind of reception they would receive. With Tanya she never knew how she would be from one hour to the next—much like her mother had been.

Tanya threw open the door before Joshua had a chance to ring the bell. "You all are *finally* here. Crystal has been at the window for the past hour, waiting for you to come. Come in, come in."

Joshua snagged Darcy's look, his brows raised. Darcy entered while Joshua and Sean went back to the truck to begin to unload the supplies. Darcy greeted Crystal.

"I want to watch them work. Can I sit out on the deck, Mom?"

"Sure, sweetie. Be a sec, Darcy. I have some things I want to show you." Tanya rolled her daughter toward the kitchen.

After only being gone a moment, Tanya bounced back into the room, a smile on her face and an almost wild look in her eyes. "Come on back to my bedroom. I can't wait to show you what I bought."

With hesitation Darcy followed the woman in the opposite direction from the kitchen. "I'm gonna help the guys with the ramp."

"Oh, this will only take a sec." When Tanya stepped into her bedroom, she swept her arm toward the bed. "They were all on sale. I couldn't resist."

Covering the bed were mounds of clothes with the price tags still on them. On the floor nearby were ten boxes of shoes. Darcy's mouth fell open. She brought her hand up to cover her surprise.

"I thought I should go shopping for some new clothes for any job interviews I'll have. You've got to look your best if you want the job. I so appreciate you helping me with the résumé. With your help and these new clothes I'll have a job in no time, and Crystal and I won't have a worry."

Tanya talked a mile a minute. Darcy had a hard time following her conversation. She blinked and tried to focus on what the woman was saying, but all she saw was the thousands of dollars' worth of clothes on the bed—thousands of dollars that Tanya didn't have.

"What do you think?" Tanya held up a red suit, conservatively cut, and a pair of matching heels.

"Nice, but do you really need all these outfits?"

"Sure. They're perfect." Tanya took a dress from the pile and fingered the silky blue material.

"Have you taken your medication today?"

"I don't need that. I'm doing fine, Darcy. Crystal's gonna have the ramp she's wanted, the lawyer thinks that Tom can cut a deal with the district attorney because of the unusual circumstances surrounding the case. And the day is gorgeous. Great day to build a ramp. Let's go help." Tanya started for the door.

Darcy blocked her escape. "When was the last time you saw your doctor?"

"I don't need to see a doctor. I'm feeling great." Tanya pushed past Darcy and hurried down the hall.

Darcy stared at the bed and shook her head. A memory intruded: her mother standing out in front of the house while Hanson Furniture Store delivered several rooms' worth of new furniture that they had no need for and no place to put. Her mother had gone to the store for a new chair for the den and had bought thousands and thousands of dollars' worth of pieces that her father had had to return the next day—after a terrible argument between him and her mother.

When Darcy joined everyone out back, the first thing she noticed was Tanya flittering from Crystal to Joshua and Sean then back to her daughter. The woman couldn't seem to stay still. All her activity made Darcy tired just looking at her.

"Hey, I could use some help over here," Joshua called out to Darcy.

She pushed away from the door frame she'd been leaning against and made her way toward him. His gaze flickered to Tanya then back to Darcy.

"Is everything all right with Tanya?" he asked, handing her some nails to hold for him.

"No. I don't think she's taking her medicine very regularly. She's in one of her manic stages."

"You think? I believe she could climb the side of the house and not blink an eye."

Darcy peered at Crystal, who watched her mother buzz about the deck, constantly in motion but not accomplishing anything. The worried look on the child's face reminded Darcy of what she'd gone through as a child, observing her mother's bizarre behavior and not understanding.

"Sean, can you help Joshua over here?"

Her son finished stacking the lumber and hurried to her. "You bet. When do I get to hammer?"

While Joshua showed Sean what to do, Darcy strode to Crystal and pulled up a chair next to her. Tanya had disappeared inside the house. "How are you doing?"

"Okay."

If the sound of Crystal's voice was any indication, the young girl wasn't doing okay. "If something's bothering you, maybe I can help."

Her brow wrinkled, the child turned toward Darcy. "Did Mom show you her new clothes?"

"Yes."

"She got me a whole bunch of new outfits, too. I don't need any. I don't go too many places."

"Maybe your mother can take them back tomorrow."

"Maybe." Crystal studied her hands laced together in her lap.

"I'll talk with your mom and see what I can do."

"Thanks, Darcy. Is Sean going to Vacation Bible School next week?"

"You bet. That's all he's talked about lately. Are you?"

Crystal looked toward the back door. "I don't know."

"Do you want me to ask your mother if I can pick you up and take you with Sean?"

Crystal's eyes brightened. "Will you...just in case she isn't feeling too well?"

"Sure. I hear at the end they're going to have a talent show for anyone who wants to participate. Sean's talking about singing. He says you sing well. Maybe you two can do a duet."

"Me sing in front of people? I don't know about that."

"You might want to think about it. Sean's planning on asking his grandfather to come and see him perform. He might need some moral support." Especially if he couldn't get his grandpa to attend, Darcy thought. She was afraid Sean was in for a disappointment when he asked.

"I'll be there for moral support in the audience."

"Then you can sit next to me and hold my hand, because I'm going to be one nervous mother."

The child's laughter rang out, the sound a welcome change from the tension churning in the air. "You don't need me. You can do anything. Sean says so."

Embarrassment heated Darcy's cheeks. "I wish that were true. We all have our strengths and our weaknesses."

Again Crystal's gaze drifted to the back door. "Yes, I guess we do."

Darcy wanted to take the young girl into her embrace and tell her not to blame herself for her mother's illness, to seek help if she needed it. She wished she had.

"I wish I could go, Sean, but I'll be too busy that evening." Shamus spooned some oatmeal into his bowl, frowning at the cereal. "Why is the food that's good for you so bad tasting?" he mumbled, plopping the spoon back into the serving dish.

"Grandpa, you've got to come."

"No, I don't, my boy."

"But *everyone* is gonna be there. I'm singing."

"I can hear you sing here at the farm." Darcy's father poured milk onto his oatmeal, his nose wrinkling.

Darcy's stomach knotted. Sitting across from her son, she could clearly see his disappointment. He had been counting on his grandfather coming to see him. She'd tried to warn Sean that he probably wouldn't, but her son wouldn't listen to her. Her own disappointment took hold of her, forging a determination to have a word with her father after Sean left to do his chores.

Silence reigned at the dining room table. A heavy, taut silence. Darcy forced herself to eat a few bites of the oatmeal, but it settled like a lump in her stomach. She gave up trying to eat.

As soon as Sean finished his cereal, he jumped to his feet, then remembered to ask, "May I be excused?"

"Yes, honey. I'll be ready to take you to Vacation Bible School in an hour."

Without a word or look toward his grandfather, Sean raced from the room.

"Does that child know what walking is?"

"Yes, Dad." She cleared her throat, her hands twisting together in her lap. "Please reconsider going to the talent show. It's not really going to church."

"Didn't you tell me there was a service before the show?"

"Yes, but you can come late."

"Humph. I vowed I wouldn't set foot in that church after your mother died."

Darcy tossed her napkin on the table and straightened in her chair, preparing to do battle. "Why, Dad? You never told me why."

"Because it is none—" He clamped his mouth down on the last part of the sentence and glared at her. Then, with a deep breath, he continued. "God let me down. For years I was a good Christian who went to church every Sunday. All I asked of the Lord was to heal Nancy, to give my wife back to me. That didn't happen, so I stopped going."

"You can't bargain with God. He knows what's best, and sometimes we just have to accept what He plans for us rather than what we plan for ourselves."

"Is that what you really feel?"

A calm settled over Darcy, and for the first time she realized the true meaning of giving herself totally to the Lord, with no strings attached. "Yes. I know how important control is to you, but we can't control everything."

Her father splayed his hand over his heart. "I know that. These past few months have clearly shown me my limitations."

"Make your grandson happy. Come hear him sing. We don't have a big family. We need to stick together."

"Do you really feel that way?"

She nodded.

"Then why were you gone for ten years? That's not sticking together, child."

"I was wrong."

Her father shoved his chair back and stood. "No, you were angry at me and I think you still are."

Darcy came to her feet, not wanting to give her father a height advantage. Every part of her rang with her anger. "Yes, I was—I still am."

"Why?"

That one word sent the tension in the room skyrocketing. "Because you're the reason Mother killed herself."

Her father's eyes widened, then fury chased away his surprise and settled over his features. "How dare you say that! I loved your mother very much."

"Then why were you two always fighting? Why did she spend most of her days in her room, sleeping or crying, that last year? Why didn't you help her?"

He clenched his hands at his sides. "Because she wouldn't take her medication and refused to see the doctor. No matter how much I pleaded, I couldn't get her to do anything to help herself. People have to want to help themselves or nothing you do will matter." He covered the short space between them. "Why do you think I turned to the Lord? I couldn't help her. I thought maybe He could. He didn't."

A vision of her mother the last time she'd seen her flashed into her mind. "I found her, Dad, that morning, lying on her bed as though she were asleep, peaceful, except she wouldn't wake up. That's when I found the bottle of her medication by her nightstand, completely empty. I knew then that she'd taken the whole prescription at once. You never said a word to me about it. You just locked yourself in your office and worked. I *needed* you." Her whole body shook with her intense emotions, with the pain of remembering, with the image that plagued her to this day.

"Not the way I was after your mother died. I wasn't

good for anyone. I lost the woman I loved and I blamed God. But mostly I blamed myself. I should have been able to do something."

"So instead, you turned away from me *and* God."

"Don't you see, Darcy, I was never any good at words. I couldn't explain how I was feeling, let alone explain anything to you."

"How about a simple, 'I love you, Darcy.' That's all I needed. That's all I ever needed to hear from you." *And never did,* she thought, tension gripping her stomach.

"I do."

"You have a funny way of showing it. You can't even say the words now." Her true feelings, bottled up for years, spewed forward, and while a part of Darcy was taken by surprise, another part was not at all surprised. She was learning to say what she felt. He started to speak, and she cut him off, continuing. "You always demanded I do everything perfectly. I have a news flash for you, Dad, people aren't perfect. But I tried my best. And I always felt I let you down. If you must know, that's the real reason I stayed away for ten years. I couldn't stand to see the disappointment in your eyes one more time. I had all I could handle with trying to keep my marriage together with a man who was as demanding and controlling as you were. Never again."

Her father took several steps back, a sheen to his eyes. "Why didn't you say something before now?"

"Don't you dare turn everything back on me. I shouldn't have had to say anything. You're my father.

You should love me without putting conditions on that love. You should love the Lord the same way." The force of her anger prodded her toward the door of the dining room. She needed to get out of here, the air hot and suffocating, her lungs tight with each breath.

Snatching up her purse from the kitchen counter, she hurried from the house, aware of Lizzy's stunned expression as she'd flown through the kitchen. She hopped into the truck, intending to pick Sean up at the barn instead of waiting for him. Her hand trembled so badly, she had a hard time fitting the key into the ignition. When she accomplished that task, instead of starting the engine she just sat in the truck, staring out the windshield at the pasture where several mares grazed.

I'm as guilty as my father for putting conditions on my faith in the Lord, she thought. That realization struck her with the force of a hurricane, doubling her over. She rested her forehead against the steering wheel, thinking back to the times she had avoided going to church or praying because she had felt God wasn't listening to her. At the first sign of trouble she had turned away, just as her father had.

Dear Heavenly Father, please forgive me for all those years I thought I knew what was best. Help me to see Your way for me.

Sean swung the door open and climbed into the cab. "I'm all done. Let's go." He paused for a few seconds. "Mom, are you all right?"

Darcy lifted her head and focused on the most precious

thing in her life. "I'm fine. I was just thinking, that's all." She would not cry. She would not fall apart in front of her son. With seesawing emotions, she asked, "Are you all right with Grandpa not coming to hear you sing?"

He shrugged. "I guess so. Maybe he'll change his mind."

"Don't count on it, hon," she said, her hands clamping the steering wheel.

Finally Darcy started the truck and headed toward Crystal's house. After picking her up, they all made their way toward Sweetwater Community Church.

Crystal beamed. "Joshua came by and talked to Mom about a therapy dog for me. Isn't that great! I should be getting one soon."

"Then I can help you teach it some tricks," Sean said.

"Honey, I think therapy dogs are already trained," Darcy said, turning into the parking lot at the church.

"Yeah. Joshua said that if I drop a pencil, the dog can pick it up. That's so neat!"

"Way better than sitting or rolling over." Sean shifted on the seat. "I hope we're still here when you get your dog."

After parking along the sidewalk that led to the entrance, Darcy slid from the truck and came around to get Crystal out. Thankfully the child was small for her twelve years, so Darcy managed to lift her from the truck alone. But as she opened the door, Joshua walked up behind her.

"I'll get Crystal for you." He swung the wheelchair from the back and positioned it on the sidewalk.

Seeing him lifted Darcy's spirits. "Thanks. What are you doing here?"

"Myself and a few of the other firefighters at my station are the guest speakers today."

After Joshua placed Crystal in her wheelchair, Sean leaped from the truck. "I'll take her inside. Devotional starts in a few minutes. I don't want to be late."

Darcy stood next to Joshua, watching her son take care of Crystal. Her heart swelled with pride at how caring Sean was. Why couldn't her father see how important the talent show was to Sean?

"What's wrong, Darcy?"

She tilted her head to the side, looking into Joshua's beautiful blue eyes. "Nothing."

"Darcy, I'm getting pretty good at reading your moods and I've got the feeling something isn't right. Don't make me drag it out of you. I have to be ready to entertain the kids in twenty minutes."

He gave her a grin that sent her heart pounding. She said, "Dad and I had a big argument today. Sean asked him to come to the talent show on Friday evening and Dad said no. I couldn't—" Her emotions clogged her throat. She swallowed hard. "I finally told my father what I'd been carrying around for years." Tears misted her eyes, making Joshua's image blurry. "Do you know I can't remember my father ever telling me he loved me?" One tear escaped and rolled down her face.

Joshua brushed his thumb across her cheek, the touch so soft and gentle that her tears increased. Seeing them, he drew her against his rock-hard chest, his hand stroking the length of her back.

"I'm so sorry, Darcy. That can't be easy."

She cried against him, feeling the strong beat of his heart beneath her ear, soothing her, while his caress eased the disappointment she'd experienced all those years and was reliving now through Sean. For a brief moment she felt cherished by another, worthy of someone's attention.

Leaning back, she saw the wetness of her tears staining his shirt. She touched the damp place over his heart. "I didn't mean to cry like that."

"I know." He smoothed a stray strand of her hair behind her ear, then cupped her chin, compelling her to look him in the eye.

His soft expression threatened to bring on more tears. This man before her was special, someone who cared deeply for others, someone she actually might be able to love— She halted the train of her thoughts, not wanting to delve any more into her turbulent emotions, which had taken a beating that morning.

His intense gaze robbed her of thought. It held hers bound to him for a timeless moment. His other hand came up to fit along her jawline. Cradling her face, he leaned toward her.

Chapter Ten

Joshua brushed his lips across hers. Darcy's heart stopped beating for a split second, then began to hammer against her rib cage. As he settled his mouth over hers, she became lost in the sensations she hadn't ever experienced. As though Joshua realized where they were, he pulled back, his hands still cupping Darcy's face. Half veiled, his blue eyes smoldered. Reluctantly he slid his fingers away and stepped back.

Darcy sucked in a deep, calming breath, held it for a few seconds, then slowly released it between pursed lips. Joshua's kiss rocked her to her core as if he had laid claim to her. Every sensible part of her screamed that she should escape before she lost herself to him. There were so many reasons it would never work between them.

One corner of his mouth hitched in a lopsided grin. "I'd better get inside before they send out a search party. See you later."

Darcy didn't say anything, her mind swirling with all the sensations that he'd provoked in her. The one over-riding thought was that she was in over her head.

"I'm so tickled to see you and Joshua together. My only regret is that I didn't get you two together," Jesse said, approaching from behind.

Darcy glanced over her shoulder at her friend and no-ticed the calculating gleam in her eyes. "You can stop right there. There is no 'Joshua and me.' Period. End of story, Jesse Bradshaw."

"Why don't you two come over to dinner next week?"

Darcy laughed. "No way. I know about your little dinner parties. I will not be a part of one of your match-making schemes."

Jesse shrugged. "What's there to match? It looked to me like you were doing pretty well on your own." She tilted her head. "Why *isn't* there a Joshua and Darcy?"

Fluttering her hand in the air, Darcy frowned. "Be-cause—because—it wouldn't work."

"You're perfect for each other. You're much better for Joshua than Carol ever was."

"Did you get those two together?"

"They are not one of my failures, Darcy O'Brien. I'll have you know my record is quite good."

Darcy headed around her truck to the driver's side. "Well, don't get any ideas. Joshua is a friend who has taken an interest in Sean."

"Ah, a smart man. Going through your son to get past your defenses."

Darcy wrenched open the truck door. "What you see is what you get. I have no defenses." She climbed into the truck and started the engine.

Jesse opened the passenger door and poked her head into the cab. "You forget I was your best friend in high school and stood by you when your mother died. You have defenses to keep people from knowing the real you."

"Good day, Jesse."

Jesse closed the door, a knowing look on her face. As Darcy drove away, she tapped the steering wheel, nervous energy surging through her. She didn't have defenses. She didn't spill her life story to a stranger, but—who was she kidding? She knew perfectly well she was afraid to let anyone get too close, especially after her father's and Clay's rejections. She just couldn't deal with it a third time.

"Mom, do I look all right?" Sean asked, coming to a halt in front of her in the church's rec hall at the end of Vacation Bible School on Friday evening. He thrust back his shoulders and stood as tall as he could.

Darcy took in his black slacks and white short-sleeved shirt, his combed hair and clean face. "You will knock them dead."

"You think?"

"I know."

"See you after the show."

As Sean raced over to a group of boys standing near the stage, Joshua weaved his way through the crowd toward her. Darcy also saw Jesse coming from the opposite direction. She'd better warn Joshua that Jesse was up to her usual tricks. Darcy stepped forward to greet him with a smile.

"Before Jesse arrives, I must warn you that—"

Joshua chuckled. "You don't have to. I've already been subjected to twenty questions about us."

"She just doesn't understand there is no 'us.'"

"No, she's tenacious and honing in on us as we speak." He grinned. "It's good to see you, Jesse. Is Nate ready for the big talent show?"

"If Bingo will cooperate. He taught him to jump through a hoop, which usually works until something catches his eye and he runs off."

"Sean's trying to catch up with Nate on the dog tricks, but Lady isn't cooperating. We'd better get a seat. I want to sit up front."

Darcy led the way toward the front near the stage. Joshua's nearness made her spine tingle, and she was glad Jesse couldn't read minds. She would have a hard time denying that Joshua was no more than a friend if Jesse knew what she was thinking, feeling.

"Where's your dad, Darcy? I thought he would be here tonight since Sean was performing." Jesse sat on one side of Darcy while Joshua took the chair on the other side.

"He had other plans."

Joshua slid his hand over hers and held it between them. His reassuring touch chipped away at those defenses that Jesse declared she had.

The murmur of people's voices quieted. Darcy looked about, wondering why everyone had stopped talking—the show wasn't supposed to start for another ten minutes. Her gaze lit upon her father, with Lizzy next to him, striding toward her. An uncomfortable expression settled over his features. Stunned, Darcy scooted down so her father and Lizzy could sit by her.

The silence in the rec hall ended, and everyone seemed to be talking at once, greeting her father, waving at him. His uneasy expression evolved into a smile.

Her father slid into the chair next to Joshua, leaned over and said, "A guy can change his mind, too. That's not just for women."

"I'm glad you changed your mind. Sean will be thrilled to see you in the audience."

"He's the reason I'm here—him and you and Lizzy."

Her father threw the housekeeper an unreadable look that caused Darcy to wonder what had happened between them. She'd thought it strange that Lizzy said she would have to come later, that she still had something she needed to do. Lizzy had assured Sean, however, that she would be here in time to see him sing. Darcy studied the pair for a moment. She'd always thought Lizzy had a soft spot for her father, but Dad had seemed so immerse in his guilt and anger that Darcy hadn't believed her father had picked up on the signals from Lizzy.

Jesse leaned close and whispered into her ear, "It's about time those two got together."

Darcy chuckled. "They're not together—yet. And I

agree. Dad needs someone to temper him and Lizzy would be perfect for the job."

"Maybe I should invite both you and Joshua and your dad and Lizzy to dinner."

Darcy's laughter filled the silence that had descended with the opening of the curtains on the stage. She blushed and whispered, "That would send my father running for the hills. You'd better leave well enough alone. Lizzy is more than capable of pursuing it from here."

"If you say so."

Joshua squeezed her hand, drawing her attention toward him. "I heard my name mentioned and a dinner party."

"Don't worry. I discouraged Jesse from going ahead with those plans."

He blew out a relieved breath and wiped some imaginary sweat from his brow. "Boy, that's a load off my mind."

Reverend Collins came out onto the stage and announced the first act: Nate Bradshaw and his dog, Bingo. Jesse clapped and whistled. The mutt lasted through two tricks before he took off, spotting something behind the curtain. Nate ran after him, and a laughing reverend stepped onto the stage.

The next act was Crystal and Sean. Her son wheeled the young girl out onto the stage and stood next to her. They sang "Amazing Grace," Darcy's favorite, and she was proud. The blending of Sean's and Crystal's voices was sweet and moving. Darcy glanced at her father during her son's performance and saw tears in his eyes. A lump formed in her throat, threatening her own tears.

When the pair were through, Darcy jumped to her feet and clapped. Her father, Joshua, and Lizzy joined her, followed by others in the audience.

The rest of the talent show sped by in a blur. Darcy was aware of Joshua next to her, aware of his every move as if they were connected. He no longer held her hand, but her skin tingled where he had touched her. Their comfortable camaraderie was shifting, evolving into something full of mystery and…hope. Startled by the direction her thoughts were going, Darcy pushed them away.

At the end she rose.

"Dad, thank you for coming. Did you see Sean's face light up when he saw you?"

"Yes. Did you hear him sing that song? I didn't know he was so talented."

"I think back home he should join the children's choir. I don't know where he got the ability to sing like an angel. It certainly wasn't from me."

"Your mother could sing like that."

At the mention of her mother, Darcy widened her eyes. Her father had rarely talked about her mother after her death. "That's right. I remember she used to be in the choir here."

"Yes, well—" her father shuffled around, glancing at the floor "—I guess it skipped a generation."

"Shamus, I need to make sure the refreshments are

set up correctly. Will you help me?" Lizzy asked, already heading toward the kitchen off the rec hall.

"See you later."

"Will wonders never cease? Not only is my father stepping into a kitchen, but he's going to *help* in one."

"Lizzy has a way about her." Joshua scanned the room. "I see Sean wheeling Crystal to Tanya. He's following your father into the kitchen now."

"I'm jealous. Us short people miss out on so much."

"I'm glad to see your dad here. Do you think he will start attending again?"

"This morning I would have said no. Tonight I have to say I don't know. My dad used to be predictable. Not now." Darcy remembered the tears in her father's eyes when Sean sang, and wondered about them. Had the words of the song spoken to her father on a spiritual level as they had to her?

"Maybe your conversation with him opened his eyes."

"Maybe," Darcy said, deciding she would have to pursue that with her father later.

Darcy entered the office at the back of the house and found her father standing at the large window that overlooked one of the pastures. Several mares grazed with their colts and fillies not far from them. The sun paved the green grass with its golden rays and the fields were dotted with multicolored wildflowers gently swaying in the breeze.

Looking out the window with her father, Darcy

couldn't help but think that the sight before her was God's work at its best. Beautiful. Serene. She'd forgotten how much she loved the farm—or rather, had forced herself to forget.

"Dad, we're just about ready to leave for the charity auction at the church. You still going with us?"

Never taking his eyes off the scene out the window, he answered, "I told Sean I would."

Relief trembled through Darcy. Her father had been acting strangely lately and she wasn't sure anymore what to expect from him. "Are you riding with Lizzy?"

"Yep. Joshua still coming by to pick you and Sean up?"

"Yep."

Silence descended between them, not the awkward kind of the past but a tranquil one. Again Darcy was surprised by that thought. In her mind tranquility and Shamrock Stables had never gone together before.

"Joshua's a good man. Sean really likes him." Her father shifted to look at her.

"Yes, he is, and your point being?"

He chuckled. "You're getting quite good at getting to the crux of what you want to say."

"I learned from the master."

"I'm glad you think I taught you something." Sadness darkened his eyes.

"I've always thought you taught me a lot. Everything I know about horses and farming is from you."

"But that's where it stops?"

"No, Dad. You were the one who taught me about the power of God."

"Until I stopped going to church." His hand lying on the windowpane fisted. "I was wrong, Darcy. I never should have, and do you know who made me realize that?"

Throat jammed with emotions, Darcy could only shake her head.

"Your son when he sang 'Amazing Grace.' I realized I was that wretched soul in the song. I've been going through life lost and blind. When Sean finished singing, I felt a peace over me that I hadn't felt in years—since before your mother's death."

"God works in amazing ways," Darcy said in a choked voice, her own reaction to the song swamping her with intense feelings. She, too, had turned away from the Lord in many ways—until she had come home.

Her father clasped her upper arms. "Exactly. I forgot that. I forgot the Lord is in control, not me, that He does care about us and is there for us. I have let my anger at your mother get in the way of our relationship as father and daughter. I love you, Darcy. Please don't ever think otherwise."

The roughened edge to her father's voice brought tears to her eyes. "Dad" was all she could say. Every other word was whisked from her mind.

He drew her into his embrace and gave her a fierce hug. "I haven't been the father I should have been. I was too tough on you because I wanted you to be ready to run this farm when I died. There was so much to teach you and you were all I had. I…" His voice faded into the quiet.

When Darcy pulled back to stare into his face, tears streamed down her face and she didn't care. For once she wanted to show what she was feeling in her heart.

"I was wrong, Darcy."

She'd never heard him admit that, and to hear him say it twice in one day stunned her.

"I won't make that mistake with Sean. I hope you'll let him come visit every summer. I hope you'll come, too. One day—" he motioned toward the window "—all this will be yours and Sean's. If you ever care to move back here, there will always be a home for you two."

"Dad, I don't know if—"

"Shh, you don't have to say anything. I understand why you stay away. Lizzy and I have been talking about it, and I can't blame you."

"Lizzy and you?" She shouldn't be surprised by that comment because she had seen them together quite a bit since his heart attack. Once the week before, Lizzy had been sitting at the dining room table eating her breakfast and conversing with her father. The second she had entered the room, though, the housekeeper had risen and scurried into the kitchen.

"I've come to depend on Lizzy as a friend." A glint entered his eyes. "Much like you and Joshua."

"Dad," Darcy said, warning him.

He held up his palm. "I won't say another word.

We'd better get a move on or all the best items will have sold before we arrive."

"The auction isn't until the end. We eat first."

Her father started for the door. "I like that. A good plan. Fatten us up before taking our money."

"It's for a good cause. The outreach program at the church does some wonderful things."

"Yes, I know, Darcy. I'm the one who started it years ago."

"You did?" Darcy walked out of the office ahead of her father, realizing she didn't know him nearly as well as she'd thought.

"Yep. Reverend Collins and I came up with the idea over one of our Saturday morning coffees. I'm gonna hate to see him retire."

"He's retiring?" Darcy could only recall Reverend Collins as the pastor of their church. It would seem strange without him at the helm.

"He's been talking about it for the past few years. I think he will within the year."

"Mom! Grandpa!" Sean called. "Where are you? Joshua is here. We need to go." The shouts from the entry hall boomed through the house.

Darcy shook her head. "I think he wants to get going."

"With him I'm noticing it's all or nothing."

"You've about summed up my son."

"I'll go get Lizzy in the kitchen. We'll follow you all there."

"Mom!"

Darcy stepped into the foyer. "I'm right here."

"Good. Let's go." Sean raced for the door, threw it open and disappeared out onto the veranda.

Darcy faced Joshua. The small foyer grew even smaller with his presence. They were alone for the first time in a week, since the talent show. An eternity. She'd missed Joshua.

"Mom! Joshua! Let's go!"

One corner of his mouth hitched up. "Are you ready?"

She scooped up her large bag. "I am now."

On the drive to the church Sean chatted nonstop about the Fourth of July picnic, then the auction. Since the church wasn't far from Sweetwater Lake, he checked to make sure that Darcy had brought his swimming suit.

"Who's gonna be watching you all?" Darcy asked as they neared the church.

"Me for one. I volunteered to be the lifeguard from one to two."

"And have you had training?"

"Mom! Joshua can do anything."

Joshua laughed. "Listen to Sean. He's got it right. But to put your mind at rest, yes, I have had training. I was even a lifeguard for two summers as a teenager. I've also had paramedic training."

"See. I told you he could do anything."

Her son had a good case of hero worship, and the funny thing was, she did too. Joshua was the type of man she wished she'd met years ago before Clay. Then maybe she wouldn't be so cynical about love and marriage.

Joshua parked his truck near the picnic area because he had brought his grill to use for the hamburgers and hot dogs. Lizzy, in the farm's truck with her father, had their contribution to the picnic—Lizzy's German potato salad.

Sean leaped down from the cab and raced toward his friends by the playground. Darcy, next to Joshua, her side pressed against his, watched her son until he was swallowed up in the crowd of children.

"You've done such a good job with him."

Sean had left the door open and a soft breeze cooled the warming air in the cab. Her heartbeat kicked up a notch and she found beads of sweat popping out on her forehead. "My, I may have to join the kids in the lake."

"Did you bring a bathing suit?"

"Yes."

"Then you can help me lifeguard."

"But I haven't had any training."

"That's okay. You can keep me company."

The intimacy in that last sentence caused perspiration to bead on her upper lip. She wiped away the moist film only to have it quickly reappear. Before too much longer she would be drenched in sweat and it would have nothing to do with the quickly climbing heat of July.

"Aren't you afraid I might distract you from your mission?"

He cocked his head, thought for a moment and said, "Now that you mention it, you'd better stay as far away from the lake while I'm on duty as possible. You in a bathing suit would be a definite distraction."

A rivulet of sweat rolled down her face. "Boy, I'm thirsty. I see Jesse is setting up the iced tea and lemonade." Before she was tempted to stay and find out what else was a distraction for Joshua, Darcy slid across the seat and exited through the open door.

She started to make a beeline for the refreshment table, then realized there were items in the back of the truck that needed to be unloaded. The twinkle in Joshua's eyes did nothing to cool her down. She needed to seek shelter from the sun—and Joshua Markham.

After taking the lawn chairs and a blanket to the area where everyone was gathering, Darcy strode toward Jesse. Darcy snatched up a paper cup and filled it with iced tea, then dumped several packets of sugar in the cold drink.

"So you and Joshua came together," Jesse said, taking a sip of her lemonade.

Darcy rolled her eyes and started to walk away.

"Avoiding me won't work, Darcy O'Brien."

She spun about, her hand on her waist. She took a step toward her friend and lowered her voice. "Just because you were happily married doesn't mean marriage is for everyone."

Jesse glanced over Darcy's shoulder. "One Joshua Markham coming in at twelve o'clock. Be seeing you."

Before Darcy could form a retort, Jesse had escaped and Joshua had reached the refreshment table. He poured himself some tea and downed it in several swallows.

"Where's Jesse off to?"

"Probably somewhere to cause trouble. I never knew how troublesome she could be until—" Darcy clamped her lips together, realizing what she'd almost revealed to Joshua.

"Until you became the object of her matchmaking?"

"Right."

"Do you know she warned me against Carol years ago?"

"She did?" Darcy's estimation of Jesse's matchmaking skills was rising.

"Yes, said we weren't made for each other. And it turns out she was right."

"One out of how many?"

Joshua shrugged. "Who knows? She's always looking for love for everyone but herself."

"Odd, isn't it?"

"No, not really. When you've been hurt badly by love, some people would just prefer not to experience that feeling again, so they avoid it."

"But her marriage was a good one."

"Divorce or death can still produce the same kind of hurt. When you hurt because they're no longer around, it doesn't much matter how that came to be."

"Or when she leaves you at the altar?"

He checked his watch. "I'd better get moving. I'm in charge of grilling the hamburgers before my lifeguarding duty."

Darcy watched Joshua's retreating, ramrod-straight back. Why was she trying to force the issue with him?

She was no more ready for a long-term relationship than he was.

While the men grilled the food, the women laid the side dishes out on the card tables under the large oak trees in the small field between the church and Sweetwater Lake. Darcy, assisting Lizzy, scanned the gathered crowd.

"Have you seen Tanya? She said she and Crystal would be coming." Darcy uncovered the salads and baked beans.

Lizzy's brow wrinkled in a deep frown. "She was supposed to bring her brownies everyone loves, but I don't see them on the dessert table."

"I wonder if something happened."

"You know Tanya. She's forgetful and—"

Her mind racing with all kinds of scenarios, Darcy dropped the spoon and hurried toward Joshua. Reaching his side, she grabbed his arm as he flipped over a hamburger. "Can I borrow the keys to your truck?"

He took one look at her face and asked, "What's wrong?"

"Tanya and Crystal aren't here. I'm worried. I—"

Joshua handed the turner to Reverend Collins and started toward his truck. "I'll drive."

"You don't have to go. I'm probably overreacting."

"I want to go. What if something has happened? Remember my paramedic training? Tanya can be fashionably late, but not this late."

Now Darcy *was* alarmed.

Chapter Eleven

Joshua made the short drive to Tanya's house in under ten minutes. The second he stopped, Darcy was out of the truck and running up to the door. She pressed the doorbell and kept ringing.

What seemed like hours later but was actually only minutes later, Crystal answered the door, tears streaking down her face.

Darcy clasped both her arms and squatted in front of her. "Oh, baby, what's wrong?"

"Mom. She won't get out of bed to take me to the picnic like she promised."

The hammering of Darcy's heart calmed slightly. "What did she say?"

The young girl sniffed. "Not much. Just that she was tired. But she's been sleeping for the past few days almost all the time."

Darcy straightened. "I'll go talk to her and see if I can get her to come with us."

Darcy found Tanya lying on her bed, the covers tossed about as though the woman had been wrestling with them. Darcy went to the draperies and opened them to allow bright sunlight into the room. Tanya groaned and covered her head with a pillow.

Sitting on the edge of the bed next to Tanya, Darcy said, "You have a little girl in the next room crying because you aren't taking her to the picnic like you promised."

"I can't do anything right, Darcy. It's just easier to stay in here and not have to deal with things. It's not worth it anymore. It's just too much for me to deal with."

Darcy felt shaken to her core. It was worse than she had thought. Remembering her own mother and what had happened to her scared Darcy for Tanya. "I don't talk about this with many people, Tanya, but my mother was bipolar."

Tanya stirred, flinging the pillow away and looking at Darcy. "Your mother?"

"Yes. I know what Crystal's going through and it's frightening for a child. She thinks everything that is happening to you is her fault. But it's not. Something's wrong. Your medication is not working. You need to go back to the doctor, but you won't. My mother did the same thing. Finally her illness got the best of her, and I'm the one who found her when she killed herself. Is that what you want for your daughter?" She'd tried kindness. Now she was desperate and hoped tough love would prompt Tanya to get the assistance she needed to control her moods.

The woman blinked, tears rapidly filling her eyes. "No. I—I—" Her mouth moved but no words came out.

"You have a choice. You can stay here and feel sorry for yourself or you can get up, get dressed, and let me drive you to the hospital."

"Hospital?"

"I think you need to see a doctor right away, and since it's a holiday, that's the best place to go to get help immediately. Obviously things aren't working out right now. Your antidepressant isn't doing the trick. I'll help you if you'll help yourself. What do you say?" Darcy held her breath, afraid that Tanya would turn away and pull the covers over her head—like her mother had.

"What about Crystal?"

"Joshua can take her to the picnic and then to my house afterward. You don't need to worry about her. I'll take care of her. The important thing for you is to get help *now*."

Emotions battled in Tanya's expression. Finally determination glinted in her eyes. She swiped away the tears and scooted to the side of the bed. "You'll help?"

"Yes."

Slightly dazed, Tanya combed her fingers through her stringy, dirty hair. "I don't know. I look awful. I need a shower. I haven't done laundry in days. I can't go anywhere looking like this."

"Get into the shower. I'm sure we can find something for you to wear. I'll have Joshua go on and take Crystal to the picnic." Darcy assisted Tanya to her feet. She wasn't giving Tanya a choice. She wasn't going to let her end up like her mother. She hadn't been able to help her mother, but she would Tanya. Then maybe the guilt she felt would go away.

Darcy strode to the living room and motioned to Joshua, who had been telling Crystal a joke. The child's laughter died on her lips when she saw Darcy. "Your mother will be fine. I'm going to take her to see the doctor."

Worry furrowed the young girl's brow. "Why?"

"Her medicine isn't working. The doctor can help her with that. She wants you to go to the picnic and have fun. Joshua will take you and then afterward you can come to the farm and play with Sean for a while. He could use some help with Lady."

Crystal started to say something, but didn't.

Darcy kneeled in front of the child's wheelchair. "Your mother will be all right, honey. Promise." *Because I won't let anything happen to her,* she added silently, her resolve strengthening.

"I do have a book I want to show Sean."

"Go get it. Then you and Joshua can leave."

Joshua waited until the child had wheeled herself out of the living room before asking, "Is everything all right?"

"I've convinced Tanya to go to the hospital. Hopefully she will get the help she needs. Her depression is getting worse. Something's wrong."

"Are you sure you don't want me to stay or meet you at the hospital?"

"We'll be okay. Crystal needs to go to the picnic. She needs to get out as much as possible, be around friends. I don't want her upset over her mother. Just take care of her for me."

"I can do that." He moved closer, lifted his hand and brushed his finger across her cheek. "I know your mother was bipolar. Are you okay?"

His touch sent comforting waves through her. She should have realized Joshua would be perceptive enough to pick up on her own sorrow surrounding her mother. "I won't sit by and watch Tanya destroy herself if I can do anything to help her. My mother committed suicide because she wouldn't get the help she needed. I'm gonna make sure Tanya gets help." She didn't normally talk about her mother and the way she died, but with Joshua it felt right.

"Aw, Darcy. I'm sorry. I didn't know." He took her face in his hands, stepping even closer.

His scent surrounded her in a soothing cocoon. His expression, full of support, nearly undid the composure that she was determined to maintain. Tanya needed a strong friend right now.

"I know this isn't the time nor the place, but I'm here for you if you need to talk."

The constriction in her throat prevented any words from forming. She leaned closer to him until only a breath separated them. Her lips tingled in anticipation of his kiss.

"I'm ready, Joshua," Crystal said from the doorway.

Darcy jumped away from him as though she had been caught with her hand in the cookie jar. "See you two soon." Feeling a blush rise to her cheeks, she turned away and headed back toward Tanya's bedroom.

She could forget where she was when Joshua turned his charm on her. If this kept up, how was she going to be able to leave in five weeks with her heart intact?

Only two weeks until Darcy returned to Panama City. Easing down on the ground, Darcy couldn't believe how fast the summer had flown by. The dapple effect of the sunlight streaming through the trees mesmerized her. She propped herself against an oak, her legs stretched out in front, and watched the play of light on dark. Sounds—the flow of water over rocks, birds chirping, the rustle of leaves—punctuated the quiet. A crow's call pierced the air. One of the horses lifted her head and looked around, then resumed chewing on some blades of grass.

Her haven. Made even more special because Joshua was here beside her sharing it with her.

"*I'm* going to miss this," Darcy said, bringing one leg up so she could rest her arm on her knee.

"I'm going to miss it." Joshua eased down next to her. "I can't believe I don't get sore anymore when we ride."

"I'm sure Dad won't mind you coming out and going for a ride."

"It wouldn't be the same without my teacher."

She smiled. "You've been a good student."

"My teachers in high school would be surprised to hear you say that."

"You mean you weren't the model student?" She widened her eyes in mock shock.

"I know it's hard to believe, but I did visit the principal's office a few times. You know the old saying, boys will be boys."

"Don't let my son know that," Darcy said with a laugh. "I didn't get to ask you how the fishing trip went the other day. We didn't have any fish to eat that evening so I'm thinking it didn't go well."

Joshua's mouth curved downward. "Not according to my plans."

"Which were?"

"I had a big ol' catfish in mind for dinner. It just didn't oblige me."

"I don't understand why not." She shifted so she could face Joshua. "The important part was that Sean had a great time. He's now trying to talk his grandfather into going fishing. Dad won't have anything to do with it."

"I personally like to have a reason to do nothing. I'm always on the go, and to be able to sit back and wait for a fish to nibble is just fine by me."

"Why do you have to have a reason like going fishing to rest and take it easy? It's okay to do that every so often."

"This from a woman who is working twelve-hour days."

"That's so my father won't put in that kind of time."

His laughter echoed through the glade. "Darcy

O'Brien, let's face it. You love working with the horses and running the farm."

No, I don't, she wanted to retort, but she knew that was a lie. She did love working on the farm, especially now that she and her father were getting along. He was continuing to teach her about the business, but this time he was also complimenting her when he liked what she was doing.

"In two weeks I'll have to put this all behind me and go back to my regular job. School starts the third week in August and I have to get the library up and ready to go."

"Which do you prefer, books or horses?"

His simple question stole the breath from her lungs. She averted her gaze, trying to figure out how to respond, surprised she didn't have a ready answer. A month ago she would have said books without a moment's hesitation. Now she couldn't honestly say.

"Why, I like to ride a horse and read at the same time."

"Nope. I'm not letting you off that easily."

"I've almost finished my part of the Sunday school lesson for this week. I love the story of Ruth."

Joshua laid his fingers over her mouth to stop her flow of words. "And don't try to change the subject. You're always prepared for the children on Sunday morning. It must be the teacher in you."

"Technically I'm not a teacher but a librarian."

"Do you deal with children every day?"

She nodded.

"Do you teach them about how to use the different resources of the library?"

"Yes."

"Then I think you're splitting hairs."

His fingers had fallen away but were now on her upper arm, massaging slow circles into her skin. She liked that he liked to touch her. Goose bumps pricked her from head to toe. She shivered.

"Cold? It's over ninety."

No way was she going to tell him that he could make her tremble with a mere touch. The smile that tugged at the corners of his mouth told her he knew exactly the effect he had on her. She was dangerously close to giving her whole heart to him. She had to keep focused on the fact she would be leaving in two weeks and wouldn't return until Christmas.

"You never told me which it would be—horses or books?"

"Haven't you ever had two options, each with its own special benefits, that you can't choose between?"

"I doubt when all aspects are examined that they would be equal. One would stand out over the other."

"Well, then my answer is that I haven't examined all aspects and can't give you an answer."

"You didn't think you would like managing the farm, did you?"

She shook her head. "Not when I showed up two months ago. I dreaded it. Now when I get up each morning, I look forward to the day." *Partly because you are so much a part of that day,* she added silently, wishing she could deny it, because she didn't see them having a future. She didn't think she could risk her heart again. The scars from her last encounter were still healing.

"I for one like seeing your father attending church again. It's a small church and we rely on its members participating in it fully."

"And have you seen Lizzy smiling lately? I definitely think something is going on with my father and her."

"It's about time."

"Why do you say that?"

"Everyone in town except your father knows that Lizzy has been in love with him for years."

"When it comes to relationships with people my father can be a bit slow. He's great with animals, though."

"Which I'm thankful for. I found a stray cat that he said he'll take. He wants one for the new barn going up."

"Helps keep the mice population down." Darcy tossed a pebble toward the stream and heard the splash as it hit the water. "Speaking of pets, Crystal is crazy about her therapy dog. I'm so glad you were able to help her get one so fast."

"I have a few connections. A therapy dog can help her to be as independent as possible."

"She's so excited. Can't wait to show the kids at church. She's actually looking forward to school starting in the fall. She thinks Charlie will be the hit of the school."

"He probably will be. How many kids get to take a pet to school every day?"

"I'm glad I don't have to testify at Tom's trial. Since

he pleaded guilty, there won't be one. I wouldn't want to make things any worse for Crystal or Tanya."

"I think that's what made Tom not fight the charges. He'd put his family through enough already."

"They're still trying to pick up the pieces, but the church has been great to Tanya and Crystal. And Tanya even found a job yesterday."

Joshua's brows rose in surprise. "She did? Where?"

"At the bank as the receptionist. She's excited. She hasn't worked since before Crystal was born."

"When I've visited, she's been on more of an even keel."

"Yes, she's really trying to stay on her medication and promises me she will see the doctor regularly."

"She's lucky to have a friend like you."

"I just wish I could—" Her throat caught around the words she wanted to say.

"You could have helped your mother?"

She nodded, afraid to speak. Using her shoe to toy with a pebble nearby, she stared at the ground, not really seeing it. "I wish someone could have helped her. I was so young and really didn't even realize what was going on."

"But your father knew?"

Again she nodded.

"So for years you've blamed your father for what happened to your mother?"

"Yes," she said, her voice raspy. She clenched the pebble in the palm of her hand until its sharp edges cut into her skin.

"Sometimes people aren't ready to accept help, and no matter what a person does he can't change it."

"I know that now. Dad and I have talked. I know he tried to help Mom, but she just didn't or couldn't accept it. At least I know it in here—" Darcy pointed to her head "—I'm still working on knowing it in here—" She placed her hand over her heart.

"You weren't the only one affected by your mother's death. Your father was too."

"I'm discovering that. It helps to finally talk about it. For years my father wouldn't say a word about my mother, especially about how she died. There was a part of him that felt so betrayed. There was a part of me that did, too." She swung her gaze to Joshua's. "She's been gone for thirteen years, and yet almost every day that goes by, I still think about her. I never really got to say goodbye."

The rough pads of his thumbs grazed the skin under her eyes as he looked deeply into them. "A lot of people never get to say goodbye. We don't get to pick when we're going to die. People often leave behind unfinished business. That's why it's important to live your life to the fullest. Make each day count."

"I'm working on that." She laid her hands over his on her face.

Joshua bent forward and touched his mouth to hers. Her senses reeled from the sensation of his lips on hers, of his hands on her face, of his scent invading her nostrils. She was floating on clouds, soaring through the sky. Dangerous feelings bubbled to the surface—emotions of caring beyond friendship. A part of her wanted to surrender to those feelings, but years of hiding her innermost thoughts and emotions kept her from giving in to them completely.

She pulled back, his touch falling away. Something in his eyes told her that he was as surprised by the feelings generated between them as she was.

He shoved himself to his feet and extended his hand to her. "I'm on duty tonight. We'd better start back." A stiffness had entered his voice, his stance.

Darcy fitted her hand within his, and he tugged her to her feet. Releasing his grip, he walked toward his mare, untied the reins from a small tree and mounted. Darcy followed suit, her legs shaking from the emotions sweeping through her.

"Want to race back to the barn?" Joshua asked, guiding his horse from the grove of trees.

A meadow, tossed with wildflowers, stretched before Darcy. Off in the distance she saw the new barn being erected. A little to the left were three mares with their foals, grazing in the paddock.

"You do like to take risks. Are you sure?"

"I like to push my limits. I haven't ridden Patience at a full gallop yet."

"The last one to that gate over there—" Darcy gestured toward the one close to the new barn "—gets to cook a meal for the winner."

"What kind of bet is that? Neither one of us can cook."

"An interesting one." Darcy spurred her horse into a gallop.

Joshua shouted something behind her, and she glanced over her shoulder at him, laughing at his stunned expression. He prodded his horse into action. Wind whipped her hair behind her. Sunlight beat down upon her. She was one with her horse and happy, sharing something she loved with Joshua.

Her destination loomed ahead. The pounding of Joshua's horse sounded closer. Darcy was impressed. Joshua was a quick study. Slanting her head to the side, she caught sight of him out of the corner of her eye. Pushing her mare, she lengthened her lead, laughter rushing from the depths of her being at the pure joy of the contest.

She didn't slow until she made it to the gate. Reaching it first, she pulled up, twisted about in the saddle and saw Joshua only a few yards away. The expression on his face mirrored the elation she felt. Their gazes locked. Across the short expanse a connection formed and strengthened.

"I won!" Darcy said when he stopped next to her.

"You may change your mind after you eat the dinner I prepare for you."

The teasing glint in his eyes spurred her heart to beat as fast as her horse's hooves had pounded across the meadow. "Can't be any worse than what I would have fixed you."

"What a pair we make," he said with laughter, then

leaned down to open the gate and allow her to go through first.

Yes, we do make quite a pair, she thought, directing her mare toward the far barn. Next she would be thinking they were a couple. *A mistake,* her common sense warned.

When Darcy reached the barn, she swung down and began walking her mare to cool her off. Joshua fell into step next to her. A comfortable silence was only broken by the horses' hooves striking the dirt. She sighed.

"I've had a nice time, Darcy."

"So have I." She headed into the barn to brush her mare.

Inside, the cool shade offered a reprieve from the summer heat. Her father and Sean stood staring into a stall at the far end.

"What's up, you two?" Darcy asked them.

"Moonstruck is restless. She should have her foal soon," Sean said, turning toward her. "Grandpa said I can watch when the time comes."

Her father caught her eye. "Only if you give your okay, Darcy."

Pleased that her father had sought her opinion, she said, "It's about time he learns about that part of a breeding farm. Of course, Sean, most foals seem to be born at night."

Sean squared his shoulders and drew himself up to his full height. "I'll be okay. I can rest the next day."

Darcy secured the reins to a post, removed the saddle, then used a curry comb to brush the mare. With his back to her, Joshua did the same.

As he watched Shamus and Sean leaving the barn,

Joshua paused and said, "Have you ever noticed that Sean does everything your father does?"

"Yes. This morning at breakfast he asked Lizzy for a cup so he could have coffee like his grandpa. Thankfully Dad persuaded him to wait a few more years before drinking coffee. I tell you, as a parent you always have to be one step ahead of your child."

Joshua peered over his shoulder at her. "Darcy, you are lucky to have a child."

Her teeth dug into her lower lip. She remembered Joshua once talking about how he had wanted children and had been devastated when Carol had left him at the altar, destroying that dream. At thirty-three he was cynical about marriage and leery of a deep emotional relationship. They definitely *were* a pair!

Chapter Twelve

"I don't smell anything burning. That's got to be a good sign," Darcy said, entering Joshua's house for the second time since she'd met him.

Joshua splayed his hand across his chest. "I'm crushed."

Ringo sauntered over to Darcy and wound himself around her legs, purring loudly. "What are we having for dinner?"

"A surprise."

"Do you even know yet?" She inhaled a deep breath. "Come to think of it, I don't smell anything cooking."

"Okay, if you must know, Trenton's Café is delivering—" he checked his watch "—in thirty minutes."

Darcy laughed. "I love Trenton's food. A man after my own heart."

"Then you don't mind?"

Darcy couldn't resist picking up Ringo and holding him close to her, rubbing her cheek into his soft fur. "If

I had lost the bet, I would have pleaded for Lizzy to cook the dinner, and if she wouldn't have agreed, I would have done the exact same thing. So how can I mind?"

Joshua escorted her into the living room. "Good, because I have another confession to make. I tried to cook lasagna and failed miserably."

Darcy arched a brow. "Why didn't you try something easier?"

He sat on the couch, leaving her plenty of room to have a seat next to him. "Sean told me it was your favorite dish."

"You asked him? When? You've been gone these past few days." A rush of pleasure zipped through her. He had taken time away from his arson investigation in the eastern part of Kentucky to check with her son about her favorite food. Clay would never have done something like that. Her husband never even would have attempted to prepare her something to eat.

"I called him yesterday."

"That explains that silly smile he wore for half the day."

"I'm sorry about the lasagna, but thankfully Trenton's has it on their menu."

Chewing her lower lip, she glanced away from his penetrating eyes, busying herself by sitting down on the couch.

"Okay, what's up?"

Sighing, she smoothed her lime-green sundress. "Lasagna is my *son's* favorite dish, at least this week."

"You don't like it!"

"Oh, no. I like it. Really I do."

"What is your favorite food?"

"Fried shrimp. And yours?"

"A big, thick, juicy T-bone steak."

She relaxed back. "I'm glad we got that out of the way. I guess there's a lot we don't know about each other."

"We've only known each other two months."

"And I'm leaving at the end of next week." The reminder brought to mind all the reasons Darcy needed to keep herself from falling in love with Joshua. They really hadn't known each other long. She hadn't even known his favorite food, and he hadn't known hers.

Silence thickened the air. Joshua shifted on the couch, cloaking his expression and turning his attention to Ringo, who lay between them.

"In four months, I'm coming back for a week at Christmas." As she said it, the amount of time seemed inadequate. A week would pass in a flash. She would have her family obligations and Joshua would have his work.

"Sean said something about coming for the summer next year."

"I hope to. Even though Dad won't admit it, I think he would like the help." A nervous laugh escaped her. "I can't believe I'm saying that."

"You two have made amends. Now you can spend time strengthening those bonds."

But their relationship was still fragile, and with hundreds of miles between them those bonds might break. Her breath caught. Who was she referring to—her father or Joshua?

"You didn't tell me how your trip was. Was the fire caused by an arsonist?" Darcy asked, needing to change the subject. This evening was supposed to be fun and light.

"Yes. Arnold discovered where the fire started. I gathered what evidence I could. I suspect it was set for insurance purposes."

"You've got Sean debating whether to be a breeder of horses or a firefighter. He's thinking he can do both."

"Sort of like you with your books and your horses? Have you ever decided which you prefer?"

"The jury is still out on that."

The doorbell chimed. Joshua rose to answer it while Darcy stroked Ringo, curled against her side. Which did she prefer? It really didn't make any difference. She was returning to Panama City in ten days. Her trip to Sweetwater, though, had shown her how much she missed riding horses. She would have to find someplace in Panama City where she could ride. Maybe one day she could even have her own horse again.

"Dinner has arrived," Joshua announced from the doorway.

He held several boxes, and the smells drifting to Darcy promised her a delicious meal. Her stomach responded to the aroma of tomatoes, meat and bread by rumbling.

"I'm hungry. I didn't realize how much until just now."

"It isn't fried shrimp, but Trenton's makes a wonderful lasagna with bread sticks and a Caesar salad. And for dessert a chocolate fudge cake that melts in your mouth."

Pushing herself to her feet, Darcy chuckled. "You could be a walking advertisement for them."

"I eat there several times a month. I'm a regular." He waved her toward the dining room.

She passed him and entered the room, coming to a halt a few feet inside the doorway. Before her the table was laid with china, crystal and silverware, all gleaming in the soft candlelight flanking the large bouquet of lilies, carnations and roses of red and white. "I'm impressed."

"I thought since I couldn't actually cook the meal with my own two hands that I could manage to set the table. These were my parents'." He indicated the dishes and utensils. "I haven't used them before now."

Touched by his gesture, Darcy swallowed several times to clear her throat before saying, "It's beautiful."

Joshua began opening the boxes to put the contents into the serving dishes. "I remember my mother pulling all this out for Christmas, Easter and Thanksgiving. She insisted on 'going fancy,' as she called it, those three times during the year. Every other meal was with our everyday dishes."

Darcy's meals with her parents hadn't made for happy memories. If her mother showed up, there usually was an argument between her and her father before the food grew cold, especially during the last few years before her death.

"We had a series of housekeepers. Usually they didn't last—until Lizzy came along. She's a trouper. She weathered my mother's ups and downs, and now my father's sullen disposition. She's a part of the family."

Joshua pulled the chair back for her to sit. Then he pushed the chair in and unfolded the napkin to lie across her lap.

"I feel like I'm in a fancy restaurant and not dressed properly. You should have warned me."

Joshua eased into the chair next to her. "And spoil my surprise? No way." His intense gaze held her. "You look great to me."

Dressed in a simple sundress with white sandals, she felt his attention riveted to her. From the expression in his eyes, she knew she was the only woman in the world. Long ago she had given up hope of ever being cherished by a man. But now Joshua was making her wish she wasn't leaving Sweetwater next week. He teased her with all the possibilities—if only they had more time to get to know each other, if only she wasn't so afraid, if only he wasn't still dealing with his emotions concerning Carol.

Seize the moment, Darcy O'Brien. She shoved her doubts and concerns to the back recesses of her mind. She would enjoy this evening and the man she was with. She would let him make her feel special for this one night, and she would cherish the memory.

"At least you didn't greet me at the door with a tux on. That would have sent me running back home to change."

He chuckled. "I don't own a tux. If I had my way, I wouldn't even own a suit. I feel like I'm suffocating when I wear a tie."

"That's the way my dad feels. Does any man like to wear a tie?"

Joshua shrugged, then passed her the crystal bowl with the salad in it. "Beats me. Not the ones I hang with."

After dishing up the greens, Darcy took the platter with the lasagna and spooned a large portion onto her dinner plate. "I can't believe this is still hot." Selecting a warm bread stick, she gave the bowl to Joshua.

"It helps that Trenton's is only five minutes away and that I'm such a good customer."

"And Sam Trenton goes to our church."

"Not to mention his daughter is in my Sunday school class."

Darcy filled her fork with some lasagna and slid it into her mouth. Ground beef, tomatoes, noodles and several different cheeses all mixed together deliciously. "Mmm. My compliments to the chef."

"I'll tell Sam the next time I see him." Joshua bit into a bread stick. "I did make the iced tea."

"Will wonders never cease?" Darcy tasted the raspberry-flavored tea. "Mmm. My compliments to the chef."

He inclined his head. "Thank you."

For the next few minutes Darcy ate, savoring the different favors and aromas. The soft candlelight and the elegant table setting lent an intimate atmosphere to the dinner. She became transfixed by the movement of Joshua's mouth as he chewed. Fantasies played across her mind, making heat rise to her cheeks. She looked down at her nearly empty plate.

"I guess this Sunday will be our last time to teach together at church."

She looked up at him. "You're right. I hadn't realized." *Hadn't wanted to think about it.*

"I'm gonna have to find someone to replace you. Any suggestions?"

No! The thought of someone replacing her bothered her. "Maybe Jesse." Even that suggestion made her frown. Jesse was single and would be great for Joshua. Darcy should be happy if they both were happy. But she wasn't.

"She would be good. I'll have to ask her this week. With my schedule I need a partner. There are Sundays I can't come because of work."

Partner. She'd always wanted to be an equal partner with someone. She'd hoped her marriage would be that way. It hadn't been, and now she didn't know if that would ever be possible. Someone always wanted to dominate— at least from her experience with Clay and her father.

But Joshua never has, a little voice inside her retorted. That was different. They weren't married—just teaching a class together—being friends. *Is it really that different?* the voice challenged.

Joshua scooted back his chair. "Wait here. I understand presentation is everything." He hurried into the kitchen with the last container from Trenton's.

Scanning the now empty dining room, Darcy realized she would miss Joshua more than she cared to admit. Sean would miss him, too. This was the reason she hadn't wanted to pursue a friendship with him—

Who was she kidding? Their relationship was beyond friendship and that was the problem.

"Ta-da!" Joshua produced two plates with pieces of the thick chocolate cake, caramel drizzled over them in a design. A few raspberries with a sprig of mint finished off the creation. He placed her dessert in front of her, then sat. "Well, what do you think?"

His eagerness made her smile as she sliced into the cake and sampled it. "I'll have to tell Sam the next time I see him how delicious this is."

"No, the presentation. I saw a cooking show and got the idea for this from it."

"And they say you can't learn anything from television." Her smile grew. "You did good." She took another bite, enjoying the rich chocolate mixed with caramel, one of her favorite combinations.

"When you're stuck in a motel room in a strange town, there isn't much else to do except watch what's on TV."

"I find it strange that you're watching a cooking show when you don't cook."

"I don't have to cook to appreciate the food being prepared."

When she finished off the last bit of her dessert, she said, "You've got the presentation part down pat."

"That and the tea are my personal touches. Do you want any coffee?"

"No. I don't drink as much coffee in the summer as I do in the winter."

"Then let's retire to the living room." He rose, putting his linen napkin on the table next to his plate.

"How about all this?" She motioned to the dishes left.

"You're my guest. I'll clean up later."

"Our bet said nothing about you having to clean up without some help."

"It's all part of the package, especially since you insisted on driving yourself to my house." He waved her toward the living room.

Darcy took a seat on the couch. "I have to pick up Sean at Nate's later."

"I could have done that."

"I know. But you've been away, and you have to work tomorrow."

When Joshua sat, he seemed to take up most of what was left of the couch. He was only inches from her and she felt the temperature rise.

"When do you have to get Sean?"

She glanced at her watch. "Soon," she said through dry lips. She ran her tongue over them and moistened her throat.

"When are we going to talk about us?"

"Us?" she squeaked, gulping.

"You know perfectly well what I'm talking about. We have something going on between us."

"What about Carol?"

"She's history."

"Is she, Joshua?"

"She's married. What do you think?"

"I think you still haven't dealt with her betrayal. You've avoided even thinking about her."

"Why should I think about her? She isn't part of my life anymore."

His defensive tone underscored Darcy's point. "When we went to Northland for lumber you were upset because Carol's husband was the manager. You have to deal with your past before you can really move on."

"Have you dealt with yours?"

"My father and I have come to terms."

"How about your feelings concerning your husband?" Darcy stiffened.

"Just as I thought. You haven't dealt with Clay and the problems you two were having when he died."

"Why are you bringing this up now? Pushing me?"

Joshua surged to his feet and began pacing in front of the couch, rubbing his thumbs across the pads of his fingers. Then he stroked his jaw. "Because I don't want you to leave, but I realize I can't ask you to stay, either. Your job and your life is in Panama City." He came to a halt in front of her. "Yes, I *can* ask you to stay. I don't want you to leave yet. I care about you, Darcy."

Panic took hold of her. She craned her neck to look into his eyes, so full of uncertainty. She opened her mouth to reply, couldn't think of anything to say that made any sense, and snapped it closed.

"I want to see if we have a chance. Long-distance relationships are difficult at best. Won't you consider moving back to Sweetwater?"

There was a part of her that wanted to shout yes, but her defenses, put there by years of trying to be the perfect person for her father and husband, silenced her. "This is so sudden."

He kneeled and clasped her hands. "We've only begun to get to know each other. Don't leave next week."

"I need to pick up Sean. We can talk later. It's not something that I can rush into." So many emotions flew through her at the moment that she didn't know what she was feeling. She was confused, adrift. Joshua teased her with what might be, but neither one was really ready for the future. She couldn't afford that kind of risk. She had Sean to think about, not just herself.

He squeezed her hands, bringing them up to touch his chest where his heart lay beneath. "Come a little early to church on Sunday. We can talk then." He rose, releasing her.

Sunday was only a few days away. How was she supposed to make that kind of decision in such a short time? *Stay and we'll see if things work out.* Too risky.

She snatched up her purse and walked to the door. Her hand shook as she reached for the knob. Joshua gripped it at the same time she did and they touched. She pulled back, feeling burned, shocked by the electrical sensation streaking up her arm.

He had the ability to make her dream of more.

He had the ability to break her heart.

"Good night. The dinner was delicious." She escaped through the open doorway before she did something she would regret. She couldn't stay in Sweetwater, could she?

* * *

Perspiration drenched Darcy's face and neck, stinging her eyes. Quickly she lifted an arm to wipe her forehead with the sleeve of her shirt, then immediately returned her hand to help soothe the pain and panic reflected in Moonstruck's eyes, big and brown and dilated.

"You'll be all right, girl," Darcy whispered near the mare's ear. She wished she believed those words, but she felt dread. Moonstruck was one of her favorite horses at Shamrock Stables.

The mare tried to get up, but Darcy held her down while she looked back at the vet who was slowly pulling the foal from Moonstruck. Darcy brushed back damp strands of hair from her face, her gaze still trained on the vet while he attended the limp form of the foal, its glistening body barely moving.

Her worry intensified. She'd seen too much death in the past year. She felt as though a part of her was slipping away too. *This foal has to live! Please, dear Lord, breathe life into him.*

An hour later Darcy walked from the stall in the barn totally exhausted, glad that she hadn't gotten her son up for the birth as she had promised. Too many things had gone wrong from the beginning. She'd known Moonstruck would have a difficult time and she'd wanted to protect Sean from the sad reality that some foals die.

Outside she paused in the early morning and kneaded the side of her neck and shoulder, but her muscles had been coiled so tightly from the past few hours that massage did little to relieve her tension. The hot August air blasted her even though dawn had barely painted the sky with its pinks and oranges. The stifling humidity pressed in on her as she inhaled deeply, releasing the breath on a long sigh. The odors of hay, leather and horses laced the heated air, the familiar smells a reminder that her duty here would be ending when she left in a few days.

Arching her back, Darcy rolled her shoulders. She looked toward the main house but couldn't bring herself to take the first step toward it, to inform her father that they had lost a foal. Instead, she allowed her gaze to travel over the yard again, noting with satisfaction that the grooms were beginning their daily chores.

This was her home, her heritage. Could she move back to the farm and see where her relationship with Joshua would lead? He offered no promises, but he wanted to give them a chance. What did *she* want?

God give me a sign. Help me to decide what is best for everyone.

Fatigue urged her forward with leaden steps. She had to speak with her father before getting ready for church. He didn't like surprises, and she hadn't informed him that Moonstruck went into labor a little early. He'd been working so hard lately that she hadn't wanted him to miss his sleep, especially when she had discovered the foal was breech. As with Sean, she had wanted to protect her father for as long as she could.

Pushing open the back door, Darcy strode through the kitchen toward the dining room, briefly greeting

Lizzy who was starting breakfast. The scent of coffee filled the air, prodding Darcy toward the pot set near her father at the long table.

"Where have you been?" Her father brought his cup to his mouth and drank.

Darcy poured herself some coffee and sank into the chair nearby. "At the barn." She sucked in a fortifying breath and continued. "Moonstruck delivered her foal early this morning."

Her father put down his cup, a storm beginning to brew in the depths of his eyes. "Why didn't you come get me? Everything okay?"

Darcy shook her head. "We lost the foal. The vet said Moonstruck is fine, though."

Shamus shot to his feet, nearly toppling his chair. "And you didn't think I should have been there?" Anger marked his features and his words.

Slowly, because her legs trembled, Darcy stood. "No, I thought you needed your sleep more. There was nothing you could do that the vet or I didn't do. Dad, you may have forgotten, but I haven't. You had a heart attack two months ago. I came home to help relieve the stress and workload for you so you could fully recover. If you hadn't wanted me to manage the farm, then why did you agree to me coming back?"

Her father blinked as though her words had caught him by surprise. "Every birth is important."

"Yes, I know that, but you don't have to be at every one of them."

He drew himself up tall. "I always have been."

"You haven't really changed, have you?" Had she been fooling herself into believing she and her father could get along and run the farm together?

"You have. You never used to speak to me like this."

"Tell you what I'm feeling, what I think? No, I guess I didn't." Tired, disappointed, she grabbed for the cup to take it with her. "I'm going to get dressed. I have a Sunday school class to teach and a son to inform about the foal."

Darcy walked ahead of Sean, her father and Lizzy toward the church. She'd told Joshua she would come early so they could talk, but the last thing she felt like doing was having a serious discussion about her future, especially after her talk with Sean about Moonstruck and the foal. Her mind felt like mush and her body wasn't doing much better. Losing a foal on top of a night's sleep could do that to a person.

Maybe seeing Joshua's handsome face would cheer her up. She lengthened her strides toward the last classroom down the long hall.

"You will not believe the morning I've—" Darcy's words died on her lips as she entered the room.

Standing several feet apart were Joshua and Carol. She held a baby in her arms, patting him on his back, while Joshua scowled, his hands balled at his sides.

Darcy wished she could snatch her words back and silently exit the room before either one knew she had come in. No such luck. They both turned their attention toward her. The anguish she saw in Joshua's eyes made her own emotions swell inside her and threaten to choke off her next breath. In that moment she knew that she would never settle for anything less than having all of a man. She had settled all her life. She would not do that again. If Joshua wasn't over Carol, then how could they see where their relationship was heading?

"I'm sorry. I didn't mean to interrupt anything. I'll come back in fifteen minutes when the class begins." Darcy started to back out of the room.

"Don't leave. Carol's leaving. The nursery has been moved to the third room on the left."

"Thanks, Joshua. I appreciate the help." Carol glanced toward her. "You're Darcy O'Brien."

Darcy nodded, even though the woman hadn't asked a question.

"I was several years behind you in school. Are you home for good or taking a vacation?"

"Vacation. Leaving in a few days." Beneath the woman's polite tone, Darcy sensed a whole bunch of questions—the first being, what was her relationship to Joshua?

"It's nice to see you again."

When Carol disappeared through the doorway, the silence pulsated with suppressed emotions, the air churning with feelings usually banked. Anger surged in her. *How could he make me fall in love with him when he still loves Carol?* Quickly that emotion slipped away to be replaced with relief. She'd discovered his true feelings before she had committed to staying.

"It isn't what you think."

"And what do I think?"

"I am over Carol." He pronounced each word slowly to emphasize the meaning.

"Are you? Maybe you didn't catch your expression in that mirror over there—" she flipped her hand toward the far wall "—but I was lucky enough to get the full effect from where I'm standing. *You are not over her.*"

Chapter Thirteen

"Carol came in here to tell me she was rejoining this church. She didn't want me to find out by surprise." Joshua eased his hands open and crossed his arms over his chest.

"How nice of her." Darcy felt the muscles in her face lock into a smile that she knew wasn't really a smile.

"My strange look was probably because she had just asked me if I wanted to hold her son. Her question threw me off guard."

"I think her whole visit threw you off guard."

He drew in a deep breath. "I won't deny that seeing her with her child bothered me. It did. We had planned to have a family. I want children."

And you should have children, she thought. Exhaustion still clung to her as though it were a part of her. Her only desire at the moment was to sit and do nothing. But stiffness spread throughout her body.

Uncrossing his arms, he started toward her, limping.

"What's wrong?" Darcy asked, fighting the urge to back away. If he came near her, she would break down. She wanted to be a part of his life, but the encounter with Carol only emphasized the risks involved. Was she willing to take them?

"It's nothing." He waved away her concern. "There was a fire yesterday. Had some problems getting out of the house in time."

Nothing? She remembered her own close brush with a fire and knew the dangers personally. Fighting fires was a dangerous job, as her husband's had been.

Joshua clasped her upper arms, keeping a foot between them. "Listen, Darcy. Carol's in my past."

"So her and her family coming to this church each week won't bother you."

"I'm getting used to the idea. Remember, I've known she was planning to return for the past month. We won't be best friends, but I'm working on forgiving her."

"You haven't forgiven her?" His fingers burned into her skin.

"Honestly? No."

His admission underscored what she had known. It also confirmed that they couldn't have a future—at least not now. She wrenched herself free and put several feet between them.

"Seeing her son brought back all the plans and dreams I'd had. It's not always that easy to let go of that."

"Then how can you move on?"

"Stay and help me to. Take a risk, Darcy."

She shook her head, backing away some more. "I'm not one of your strays."

"I believe I know the difference between you and one of my strays."

"I can't stay. I can't do that to myself and Sean. I just can't."

Tears rose within, clogging her throat and misting her eyes. She wanted to flee, but at that very moment some of the children began to file into the room. She was trapped for the next forty-five minutes.

With his hands behind his back, Nate stopped in front of her. "Mrs. O'Brien, we sure are gonna miss you." He brought his arm around and presented her with a small bouquet of flowers, obviously picked from Jesse's garden.

Tears continued to gather in her eyes as each child gave her a token of their appreciation. Her son appeared last with a card signed by all the kids and a declaration that they were going to have a farewell party for her.

"You kept this a secret?" Darcy asked Sean as several parents brought in some lemonade and a chocolate cake.

"Yep." He puffed out his chest.

"This from the boy who makes me a present weeks before my birthday and gives it to me right away because he can't wait?"

Squaring his shoulders, he said, "This was different. I would have spoiled the surprise for everyone here if I had said something to you."

Her son was definitely growing up, and partially because of the influence of Joshua and her father. "Well, I'm impressed." She gave Sean a hug and a kiss on the cheek, which immediately caused him to screw up his face as though it wasn't something a boy of eight should get from his mother in front of a whole room full of his friends.

After a short devotional, Joshua stood before the circle of children and said to Darcy and Sean, "We wanted to show you how much we will miss both of you when you leave this week. The party is a small token of our appreciation for your filling in this summer."

"Speech. Speech," Nate called out from the back row.

Darcy moved to stand next to Joshua. "Nate Bradshaw, did your mother put you up to this?"

He nodded.

"I should have known. She knows how embarrassed I get when I have to say something in front of a crowd." *Just like Joshua,* Darcy thought with surprise.

"But you talked all summer when you taught us our lessons."

"Good point, Nate." Darcy cleared her throat, trying to keep her emotions in check. More than anything she wished she'd gotten a good night's sleep. Too many feelings were tangled up inside and so many were centered on the man next to her. All she had to do was move her arm a little and she could touch him—perhaps for the last time. Tears threatened to spill from her eyes.

"This means a lot to me." She gestured toward the table with her many gifts, mostly homemade and thus more endearing than store-bought ones. "I don't know what to say."

"How about telling us when you are coming back?" Brad Anderson asked.

"Yes, when?" Joshua asked, his gaze ensnaring hers.

"Christmas. Mom promised me we would come," Sean piped in, for which Darcy was thankful.

She didn't know if she could speak without her voice cracking. Through her misting eyes she took in all sixteen children, their faces turned toward her, their expressions, like their gifts, endearing.

"Why don't you stay?" Nate called out.

Darcy decided she needed to have a conversation with Jesse about her son asking questions he shouldn't. "My job is in Panama City," she offered, the reason suddenly sounding lame to her. A tear coursed down her cheek and she quickly brushed it away.

Why couldn't life be simpler? Why did emotions and the past have to interfere? Why couldn't Joshua love her with no strings attached? What was she afraid of? Questions bombarded her, making it difficult to keep control of her emotions. She turned away and swiped at her cheeks as the tears continued to roll down her face.

"We didn't mean to make you cry," Crystal said, wheeling herself into the room. "Sorry I'm late."

With one last brush across her cheek, Darcy spun toward Crystal, who stopped a few feet from her. She picked up a framed picture from her lap and handed it to Darcy.

She took it, her hand shaking. In the frame was a photo of her, Joshua, Sean and Crystal after they had completed the construction of the ramp. Everyone had big smiles as they showed off the product of their labor. She stared at Joshua in the picture with his tool belt around his waist and his arms about her and Sean. She and Joshua had laughed over the way the tool belt had slipped down low on her hips; if she had tried to move it would have slid completely off her. The photo would always remind her of a precious moment.

"Thank you, Crystal."

"No, thank you for the ramp and—" the child's voice faded while she dropped her head and whispered "—for my mom."

Darcy hugged Crystal. "You're welcome." When she stepped back from the girl, Darcy saw Tanya enter the room and wave to her. Who would be here for Tanya if she needed help? That question tugged at Darcy, making her decide to ask Lizzy to watch out for the woman.

The rest of the party went slowly. Darcy ate two pieces of cake and tried to laugh and smile, but inside she felt as though a part of her had died that morning. Her hopes? Her dreams? She wasn't sure, except that she felt empty. By the time the children had left to attend the service, all Darcy wanted to do was collapse into the nearest chair and lay her head down to rest. But first she needed to finish her conversation with Joshua.

After Sean had raced from the room with Nate, Darcy faced Joshua, who was throwing away the used paper plates. "We need to talk."

He jerked to his full height and swung around to stab her with his gaze. "No, we don't. I think we said all we should say. Now, if you'll excuse me, I'm reading one of the lessons today in church and I need to go over the material before it starts." He walked toward the door, his strides long and purposeful.

Darcy watched him disappear out into the hallway. He wanted her to stay but couldn't offer her any guarantees. Yes, she had friends and family in Sweetwater. But what if she came home and Joshua couldn't move on in his life? How could she see him and not have her heart break each time? It was better to put this summer behind her and go back to Panama City. She knew what she wanted now—at least she had learned that much this summer.

Then why wasn't she happier about her decision?

On Wednesday, the quiet of the sanctuary soothed Joshua as he sat in the back pew, his hands folded in his lap. Was he going to let Carol continue to rule his life? He had wanted so desperately last Sunday morning to declare to Darcy that he'd completely forgiven Carol for walking out on him and marrying another. But he couldn't lie to Darcy no matter how much he wanted her to stay in Sweetwater. Lies were not what he would base a relationship on with a woman, especially someone as special as Darcy.

Lord, I need help. How do I begin to forgive someone who hurt me so badly? What is wrong with me? I've never had this problem before.

"Joshua?" Reverend Collins stood behind him, a worried expression on his face.

"I'll close up if you need to go home."

"That's all right. I normally don't bother anyone when they are in here, but something tells me you need to talk."

Joshua felt the weight of his inability to forgive press him down. His shoulders sagged. "Yes."

The reverend came and sat beside him in the pew. "What's bothering you? Darcy leaving?"

"That's part of it. I want her to stay, but I don't have the right to ask her to."

"Why not? I've seen how you two are together. I think you need each other."

"Because I'm still harboring ill feelings toward Carol. Darcy doesn't think I've moved on and she doesn't want to risk staying, with Carol still an issue in my life."

"Oh." The reverend was silent for a few moments, then asked, "Why haven't you forgiven Carol?"

That was a good question. Joshua wasn't sure he could answer it. Since she had left him at the altar, he had tried not to think about what could have been. He had pushed his emotions into the background, refusing even to examine them. Now Darcy was forcing him to take a good hard look at his feelings concerning Carol, concerning Darcy.

"Is it your male pride speaking?"

Joshua shrugged. "That could be some of it."

"You know the verse from Proverbs—pride goeth before destruction, and an haughty spirit before a fall."

"Yes, and I'm working on it. I think I would have been all right if I hadn't been waiting for her in church in front of the whole congregation. I remembered their pitying glances for months afterwards. There had to be a better way to break the news to me."

"But that's not all?"

Plowing his fingers through his hair, Joshua frowned, staring at the back of the pew in front of him. "No. I've wanted a family for as long as I can remember. I was an only child and always said I would have a house full of children when I got married. Carol slept with another man, got pregnant by him when she was engaged to me. She had *his* child—not mine."

"What if Carol had married you, pregnant with another man's child? How would you have felt then?"

Joshua dropped his head. "Worse."

"Then Carol did the right thing by calling it off before you two got married. She only found out about the baby a few days before the wedding. She agonized over what to do."

"But she slept with Kyle."

"Yes, she made a terrible mistake and she had to face the consequences. After all, she's only human—just as we all are."

"And like Carol, I've made my share of mistakes?"

"Right. Think of all the mistakes God has forgiven you. Can you not forgive Carol this one mistake?" Reverend Collins rose. "I have some work to do in my office. Stay as long as you want."

"And be ye kind one to another, tenderhearted, forgiving one another, even as God for Christ's sake hath

forgiven you." The verse from Ephesians 4:32 popped into Joshua's mind. He knew what he must do.

Joshua marched up the steps to the front door and rang the bell. Taking a deep breath he squared his shoulders. A week ago he wouldn't even have considered doing this. Now it felt so right, he wondered why he had waited so long.

The door swung open. The woman framed in the entrance gasped.

"I know I'm probably the last person you expected to show up at your house, but may I come in?" Joshua asked, a calmness descending as if his past had been washed away.

"I just put Paul down for a nap." Carol stood to the side to allow Joshua inside. "What brings you by?"

Joshua walked into the living room where everything was in its place. Too sterile and neat for his taste, he thought as he turned to face the woman to whom he had once been engaged. "I needed to see you. I wasn't very inviting the other day at church, and I was wrong."

"I shouldn't have surprised you last Sunday."

"I knew you were thinking of returning to Sweetwater Community Church." He shook his head. "Until I did some soul searching, I was angry with you for the way you ended our engagement."

Her hands clasped in front of her, Carol averted her gaze. "I didn't handle that very well. I'm so sorry, Joshua. I had just found out I was pregnant and I knew you weren't the father. I seriously thought about going through with our wedding, but in the end I couldn't do that to you. That would have been worse than not showing up for our wedding."

"I'm the one who is sorry. I know you didn't ask me to, but I wanted to tell you I forgive you, Carol."

Her look flew back to his face. "Why are you telling me this now?"

"Because until I make amends with our situation, I can't really move on. I'm glad you're returning to the church. I know how much you enjoyed attending and I know you left because of me."

Her eyes clouded with tears; her hands twisted together. "I wasn't sure anyone would welcome me back, but last week no one said anything."

"They wouldn't, Carol. I'm learning that we're all human beings and we all make mistakes. So if God can forgive us, the least we can do is forgive each other."

She sniffed. "I appreciate you coming by."

Joshua started for the front door. Carol's words stopped him. "She's one lucky woman, Joshua. I wish you the best. You deserve it."

"Thanks." *I'll need all the luck in the world to convince Darcy to stay,* Joshua thought and headed for his truck. He wasn't finished with what he needed to do.

Darcy folded the last piece of clothing and put it into the suitcase, then closed it, the *click* of the lock sounding so final in the quiet of her childhood bedroom. She hadn't heard from Joshua since Sunday, and she would be leaving tomorrow, early in the morning. With a glance out the window, she noted the gray tones of dusk settling over the land. Less than fourteen hours…

Her heart thumped against her chest in slow, anguish-filled beats. It had only been a few days since she'd last seen Joshua and she already missed him. How was she going to make it with hundreds of miles between them?

A knock at her door disturbed her thoughts. "Come in."

Lizzy entered the room. "I found this downstairs." She handed Darcy a black sweater she'd used when her father had cranked up the air-conditioning to freezing.

"Thanks. I'd forgotten about that."

"I can always mail you anything else you leave behind."

How about Joshua? Darcy instantly thought, a smile gracing her lips for a few seconds before disappearing.

"Or, you can get it when you come back at Christmas." Lizzy sat on the bed. "Frankly, I'd hoped you would be staying, Darcy."

"You did?" Darcy asked, wondering how she was going to manage seeing Joshua at Christmas. And yet, for Sean's sake and her father's she couldn't *not* come home.

"Yeah. I thought you and Joshua were getting along quite well. Your father might not say anything to you, but he doesn't want you to leave."

"He doesn't? He told you that?"

"You know your father and words. But I've been with him for a long time and I've gotten to know him pretty well. He loves having you and Sean around."

Then why doesn't he ask me to stay? Darcy silently screamed, frustrated, even more torn up inside.

"Sean has enjoyed himself this summer."

Darcy held up her hand. "Hold it, Lizzy. No more. I know all the reasons I should stay."

"But?"

"But I can't. I just can't." Darcy turned away, busying herself rearranging her overnight bag to keep Lizzy from noticing how much her hands quivered.

"I don't see why not."

Darcy slid her eyes closed for a moment, then faced Lizzy. "Because I couldn't live in the same town as Joshua and not be with him."

"From what I've seen, you *are* with him."

Darcy sank onto the bed next to Lizzy. "He still has issues with Carol."

"Are you so sure that's the real reason you're leaving? Isn't it possible you still have issues with your husband and even your father?"

A heavy sigh whispered past Darcy's lips. "Yes, if I'm truthful with myself that's as much a reason as any."

Lizzy covered her hand on the bed. "I know your father can be a hard man, but he's trying to make things better between you. Darcy, it won't happen overnight, but if you stay away it may never get better."

"I'm coming back at Christmas," Darcy said defensively, knowing that really wasn't enough, not when she'd stayed away for ten years.

"Are you going to let your deceased husband continue to dictate how you're going to live? I've seen you change this summer and I think it's partially due to Joshua's influence. He allows a woman to be herself. He appreciates you for who you are."

"I know. But I was wrong about Clay. I thought I knew him, too."

"Some people are good at hiding behind facades. Joshua isn't one of those people. I've known him for years and he's always been very straightforward." Lizzy patted Darcy's hand. "But don't listen to me. Listen to your heart. What's it saying about Joshua?"

"I love him."

"Then why are you leaving?"

"Because I'm scared. I've been hurt before."

"So has Joshua, but he wants you to stay and see if it will work between you. Take the risk. Life is full of them. When you stop taking risks, you stop living life fully." Lizzy rose slowly, placing her hand at the small of her back. "This old body doesn't work like it used to. Think about what I said and pray for help. The Lord is wonderful to turn to when you have a dilemma."

When Lizzy closed the door behind her, Darcy stared at its dark wood, mulling over Lizzy's words. Darcy wanted to put down roots, had picked Panama City because that was the last place Clay had been stationed. But why couldn't she put down roots in her hometown? Sean needed his grandfather and, yes, Joshua if he would have her. She needed her father and most of all Joshua. Independence was great, but she would rather have interdependence—with Joshua, with her family. These past two months with Joshua had given her a glimpse of what a good relationship was like. He respected her opinions, even sought them, something Clay had never done.

Could she take the risk and stay?

"I am with you always, to the very end of the age." The verse from Matthew 28:20 was one of her favorites. She needed to remember that Jesus was with her through the bad and good times. With His strength and presence in her life, she could take the risk because she knew she would be all right in the end.

Darcy walked from her bedroom, intending to find her son, father and Lizzy to tell them she was going to stay. With each step she felt the rightness of her decision. Joshua was worth fighting for. What they had between them was good, and she was going to remind him of that. She would help him work through his issues with Carol instead of turning away from him as she had done. She had always run away from a problem in the past. Now it was her chance to stay and figure out a solution.

Downstairs she heard some laughter and headed toward the sound. In the kitchen she found her father with his arms about Lizzy, looking into the woman's eyes with an expression Darcy hadn't thought she would ever see again on her father's face. Love. Darcy's heart swelled at the sight of the two so wrapped up in each other that they hadn't heard her enter.

She coughed. They parted, looking surprised.

"I thought you were still packing," her father said, his cheeks flushed.

Lizzy began wiping down the already clean countertop with quick movements, her head turned away.

"It's okay, you two. I'm glad you've finally come to your senses, Dad. Lizzy is a wonderful woman."

His flush deepened to a scarlet red. "Yes, I know. You don't mind?"

"Of course not. No one should be alone. And with that in mind, I've come to tell you that I'm staying in Sweetwater. If you'll have me, I would like to help with the farm for the time being. You need an assistant manager. You've been working way too hard."

Her father covered the expanse between them. "Are you sure, honey? I've never felt better in my whole life than I do now, but I would love the help."

"It's that diet that Lizzy has you on, and Lizzy's influence," Darcy said with a laugh. "*Yes,* I'm sure. I want Sean to know you. And I want to see where my relationship with Joshua goes."

"Ah, a good man."

"Mom! Mom!" Sean shouted from the entrance hall. She started forward.

"Mom, Joshua's here to see you."

Darcy froze, her hand poised on the swinging door into the dining room. Her heart began to pound, her palms to sweat. She smoothed her hair back and glanced down at the shorts and oversized T-shirt she had on.

"You look great. Go get him," Lizzy said, standing again beside her father.

Darcy gave both of them a wink and pushed her way through the swinging door.

"Mom!"

"Sean, I'm right here. You don't have to shout the house down."

"Oh, I thought you were upstairs." Sean had positioned himself at the bottom step.

"And you couldn't go upstairs to get me?"

He grinned.

"I think Lizzy has some cookies for you."

Without another word, Sean raced toward the kitchen.

Darcy shifted her attention to Joshua, who stood by the front door as though positioned to leave if she wanted him to. "I'm glad you're here."

His brows rose. "I wasn't sure you'd want to see me."

"Until a while ago, I wasn't sure I wanted to see you either."

"What happened?" He took a step toward her.

Her heartbeat kicked up a notch. "I'm staying in Sweetwater. I just told Dad I want to be his assistant farm manager."

"Is that the only reason you're staying?" He came another step closer.

"No. Sean needs to stay in one place with people around him who care about him."

"True. Is that all?" Joshua moved two more steps until he was in front of her, an arm's length away.

"But mostly, I'm staying because of you."

"Why?"

"Because I love you and I want to see if there is an 'us.'"

He drew her against him. "I can tell you there definitely is an us." His lips settled over hers in a long kiss.

When he pulled back to look into her eyes, Darcy smiled, still feeling the tingling sensation his kiss had produced throughout her body. "What's changed? There's something about you that is different."

"I took your advice and dealt with my past. I went to see Carol before I came here. I told her I forgave her for leaving me at the altar." He snuggled closer. "And I meant every word I said. I want her to be happy because I'm happy. I love you, Darcy O'Brien."

"Are you sure?"

"Yes. Are you?"

"Yes. I want to stay and see where this relationship leads us." She laid her head against his chest, listening to the hammering of his heart that matched the fast tempo of hers. "We have all the time in the world to get to know each other. I'm not going anywhere, Joshua Markham."

Epilogue

Dressed in a black tuxedo, Joshua straightened to his full height, rubbing his thumbs across the tips of his fingers. Scanning the crowd in the sanctuary, he saw the expectant faces of his friends and family. Next to him stood Sean in a similar tux, a huge grin on his face.

The people in the church fell silent. The organ stopped for a few seconds, then started again. Joshua held his breath, his lungs burning. Tanya appeared in a pink satin dress pushing Crystal's wheelchair. Crystal wore the same type of dress as her mother and her dark hair was pulled on top of her head in curls with glittering stars peeking out. The young girl tossed pink rose petals down the long aisle as her mother rolled her toward the altar.

Only a moment longer, Joshua told himself, beginning to feel the constriction about his neck from his tie. Sean gave Crystal a thumbs-up when she went by him to sit next to the front pew on the left-hand side.

Then Jesse appeared at the back in a different version of the pink satin that Crystal wore. As she neared Joshua, she winked at him, then went to stand on the other side.

Suddenly the organ music changed to "The Wedding March." Everyone rose and turned to the back. Joshua forced himself to release his pent-up breath, his gaze riveted to the empty place where Darcy should be.

One second… Two… Then he saw her and pure joy swept through him. Never in his life had he seen such a beautiful sight as his soon-to-be wife walking down the aisle on her father's arm toward him, dressed in a long, cream-colored gown of lace and satin. Her smile filled his vision, his heart. He would soon have the family he'd always desired.

Darcy slipped her hand in Joshua's with all the self-assurance that she was making the best decision of her life. *What a perfect day to get married,* she thought. *Valentine's Day. A day for lovers. A day for beginnings.*

Her father kissed her on the cheek. "You take good care of her, son."

"I will, sir."

And Darcy knew Joshua would. Together they turned to face Reverend Collins as equal partners, with Darcy eager to start her new life.

* * * * *

Dear Reader,

In my first book in THE LADIES OF SWEETWATER LAKE series, *Gold in the Fire,* I explore the topic of people taking emotional risks in their lives. It is important to learn to put our trust in God and not to shy away from change. Life is full of changes that we need to embrace, but those changes can be scary.

With faith in the Lord we can be better prepared to accept the changes and risks. Darcy had to learn this with the help of Joshua. For Darcy, coming back home was full of emotional risks—first with her father, then with Joshua. But Darcy wasn't the only one in the story who had to take an emotional risk; Joshua put his life on the line many times working as a firefighter. In his personal life he didn't take any risks at all—until Darcy forced him to through her love.

In THE LADIES OF SWEETWATER LAKE, five women form a bond of friendship to help each other through tough times. Darcy's story is the first one in the series. The second book, *A Mother for Cindy,* features Jesse Bradshaw, the town matchmaker and Darcy's good friend. Then comes the third story, *Light in the Storm,* about Beth Coleman, another member of the circle of friends.

I love hearing from readers. You can contact me at P.O. Box 2074, Tulsa, OK, 74101 or visit my Web site at www.margaretdaley.com.

Best wishes,

Margaret Daley

LIGHT IN THE STORM

With us is the Lord our God
to help us and to fight our battles.
—*2 Chronicles* 32:8

To my readers—I appreciate your support.

To my local RWA chapter, Romance Writers Ink—
You are a wonderful group of writers.

Chapter One

With a huff Jane Morgan plopped into her desk. "I don't see why I have to be here."

Beth Coleman sighed, turned from watching the snow falling outside Sweetwater High School and said, "Because you'll be the topic of conversation. It's your future we'll be discussing. I thought you should have a say in it."

Flipping her long, dark brown hair behind her shoulders, Jane slouched in her desk, her arms folded over her chest, a pout firmly in place. "What future? Don't you get it? I don't want to be here."

Beth again looked at the snow coming down and wondered if this was the best time to have a parent conference. Of course, when she had contacted Jane's father yesterday, there hadn't been any snow. "Does your father have a cell phone?" Maybe she should call him and cancel until the weather was better. She could drive Jane home.

"Yes."

As with Jane's performance in class the past few weeks since the teenager had enrolled at the beginning of the second semester, Beth realized she would have to ask what the number was, because Jane wouldn't give any information unless she absolutely had to. "What is—"

"Sorry I'm late, but as you can see, the weather is getting bad." A large man with blond hair and brown eyes stood framed in the classroom doorway.

Speechless for a few seconds, Beth just stared at Jane's father. Samuel Morgan wasn't anything like her image of him when she'd talked to him briefly the day before. His voice was gruff and deep, but his looks were refined—handsome but not ruggedly so. More along the lines of a male model she'd seen in a magazine selling cologne. Whoa! Why in the world had she thought that?

Beth mentally shook her head and crossed the room. Presenting her hand, which he took in a firm grip and shook, she said, "I'm Jane's English teacher, Beth Coleman. Please come in and have a seat—unless you'd rather reschedule this meeting because of the snow. It doesn't look like it's going to let up any time soon."

He shrugged out of his heavy black wool overcoat, ran a hand through his wet, conservatively cut hair and entered the room. "No, this is too important to postpone. And besides, I'm here, so we might as well talk now. Don't you agree, Jane?"

When Samuel squeezed into the desk next to his daughter, Beth noticed how he dwarfed it, even though it was standard size for a high school class. She knew he was a minister, and yet for a brief moment he seemed more a warrior than a peacemaker.

"Sure. Why not?" Jane averted her face, staring off into space, defiance in every line of her body.

"On the phone, Miss Coleman, you said that Jane was having a problem with the work you've assigned."

Beth took a desk near the pair, scooting it around so she faced both of them. "She isn't doing any of the work. She's been here nearly two weeks and I have yet to see anything from her. We've had four graded assignments so far this semester. She has a zero right now."

"Not one grade?" Samuel asked Jane, his tension conveyed by his clenched jaw and frown.

His daughter lifted her shoulders in a shrug, but didn't say a word, her head remaining turned away.

"Is there a problem I'm not aware of?" Beth saw a flash of vulnerability appear in his dark eyes before he masked the expression. It touched a part of her that over the years had seen many single parents struggle to do the job of both mother and father.

"As I'm sure you're aware, we've just moved here." He glanced at his daughter. "Jane has never adjusted well to new towns."

"How many times have you moved?"

"This is our sixth move. I was a chaplain in the army until recently. We're both looking forward to settling down in one place."

"Adjusting to a new town can be tough. If Jane's

willing to work and stay after school to make up the assignments, I'll take them late this time."

"What do you say, Jane?" Samuel leaned forward, his hands laced together on top of the desk. His whitened knuckles indicated nothing casual in the gesture.

His daughter, silent, peered at the snow falling, as though she hadn't heard the question.

"Jane?" A firmness entered his deep, gruff voice.

She swung her gaze to her father, her pout deepening. Chewing on her bottom lip, she stared at him, several emotions vying for dominance. Anger won out over a need to please.

"Would you rather the zeros remain on your grade?" he asked with an underlying calm that amazed Beth.

Samuel Morgan was the new reverend of Sweetwater Community Church, where she attended. It was obvious that he had a great deal of patience, if his dealings with his daughter were any indication. That was comforting to know, since Reverend Collins, their previous minister, had been beloved by all in the congregation.

Jane sighed, straightening in the desk. "If you must know, I didn't understand a couple of the nts."

"Did you ask Miss Coleman for help?"

"No."

"Jane, I'll be glad to help you when you stay to complete the work. And for that matter, any other assignment you have trouble with. All you have to do is ask me for help. That's part of my job."

The teenager looked at Beth as if she thought Beth was crazy to think she was going to ask for any assistance on an assignment, especially in a class of thirty students. Beth wondered if something else was going on beneath Jane's defiance. It wasn't that unusual to see a teen rebel, but Beth sensed a troubled soul begging for help. She made a mental note to check with the young woman to see if she understood her homework assignments. Sometimes when a student moved a lot, she lost ground because curriculum wasn't always the same in each school.

"Miss Coleman, Jane will stay after school every day until she has made up her work. Since I pick her up, it shouldn't be a problem."

Beth slipped from the desk. "We can start Monday. Hopefully the weather will be clear by then."

Samuel rose. "She'll be here."

Jane shoved herself out of the desk, pushing it several inches across the hardwood floor. "Maybe we're in for a blizzard."

"We don't often have blizzards in Sweetwater," Beth said with a smile. Even as a teacher she enjoyed the occasional snow day when school was canceled.

"That's good to hear, because it sure is snowing hard now," Samuel said, looking toward the window.

"Now, that's something to pray about," Jane mumbled, starting for the door.

Samuel watched his daughter leave the classroom. "Sorry about that, Miss Coleman."

"Please call me Beth. I haven't had a chance to tell you, but I attend Sweetwater Community Church."

His brows rose. "You do? I didn't see you there last week."

"I'm sorry I missed your first Sunday, but I was taking my brother to college in Louisville. He just started this semester and he had to move into the dorm."

"Then I look forward to seeing you this Sunday." His gaze again slid to the window. "That is, if we don't have that blizzard my daughter is praying for."

Beth fitted her hand in his to shake goodbye and was conscious of something else beside its firmness—a warmth. A warmth that shot up her arm and made her very aware of the man before her. The warrior impression she'd received earlier was tempered with the calmness he'd exhibited when dealing with his daughter. He gave off mixed messages, which intrigued Beth. She suspected he was more adept at listening to other people's problems than telling anyone his.

"Tomorrow the sun will be shining. Mark my words, Reverend Morgan."

"Hope you're right, Miss—Beth. And please call me Samuel." He walked toward the door, turned back and added, "I still have a lot to do to finish moving in and bad weather definitely puts a damper on things."

Before she realized what she was really doing, Beth asked, "Can I help with anything?" The second the words were out of her mouth, she bit down on her lower lip. Her first weekend in years without any obligations, and she was volunteering to help the reverend put his house in order. When would she learn? She didn't have to be there for everyone. It was okay to take some time for herself.

He chuckled. "Thanks for the offer, but I know how many papers English teachers have to grade. My children and I will get it done...if not this weekend, then the next."

When he left, Beth walked to the window and stared at the swirling mass of white, watching for Jane and Samuel to come out the front door. When they emerged, they were quickly obscured by the blowing snow. She loved cold weather and the occasional snow they had in Sweetwater. It brought out the child she'd never been allowed to be. But this storm might be worse than she had originally thought.

Beth headed for her desk and quickly gathered those papers that the reverend had mentioned, stuffing them into her briefcase to grade over the weekend. But she promised herself as she left her classroom that she would find some time to make a snowman and give him a carrot for his nose and pieces of bark for his eyes and mouth.

After pulling her cap down over her ears and tying her wool scarf around her neck, Beth exited the school building and walked toward where she knew she had parked her white car, even though in the driving snow it wasn't visible. Halfway to the parking lot she spied her Jeep and quickened her steps. Out of the corner of her eye she saw a blue Ford Mustang with the reverend and Jane standing next to it.

Why haven't they left? Beth wondered, and changed her destination.

"Something wrong?" she asked as she approached the pair arguing while the snow blew around them.

Samuel stopped what he was going to say to his daughter and glanced toward Beth. "I was for going back inside and getting help. Jane was for hiking home." He gestured toward his car. "Won't start."

"You probably can't get anyone out here to help right now. Every tow truck will be busy just trying to haul people out of ditches. I can give you a ride home and you can see what's wrong with your car tomorrow—if this snow lets up."

"You're not going to get an argument out of me. Where are you parked?"

Beth waved her hand toward her five-year-old Jeep Cherokee. "I don't usually have too much trouble in the snow."

As they trudged toward the Jeep, Jane mumbled something under her breath. If her tight-lipped expression was any hint, Beth was glad she hadn't heard what the teenager had said. When Beth reached her car, she unlocked her doors and slid inside while Jane plopped herself in the back seat and Samuel climbed into the front.

"You're staying at the rectory, aren't you?" Beth asked, starting the engine.

"Yes. I hope it isn't too far out of your way."

"Practically on my way home."

Samuel stared out the windshield. "Can I help you scrape the windows clear of snow? I'm not sure how much good it will do, as fast as the snow is coming down."

Turning a knob on the dashboard, Beth cranked up the heat. "Let me warm up the car first, then we'll see what can be done about the windows." She peered over her shoulder. "Jane, I've got two scrapers under the front seat. Can you reach them for me?"

With her mouth slashing downward, Jane produced the two scrapers and thrust them at Beth.

"In fact, since we're inconveniencing you, Jane and I will take care of the windows while you stay warm in here," Samuel offered.

"Dad," Jane protested.

"Yes? Do you have a problem with that? You can always walk like you wanted to a few minutes ago."

Jane folded her arms across her chest, her hands clenched, and stared out the side, muttering under her breath.

Beth started to decline the offer of help, but she caught Samuel's look. He shook his head as though he knew what she was going to say and wanted her to accept their assistance. She snapped her mouth closed and gave him the scrapers.

While Samuel and Jane cleared the snow and ice built up on the windows, Beth watched, feeling guilty that she was warm while they were freezing. She didn't accept help well and this was making her very uncomfortable, especially when she saw Jane's face set in a frown, her cheeks red from the cold, her body beginning to shake because she was dressed in a short skirt with a heavy jacket that covered her only to her waist. Except for a pair of half boots, large portions of the teenager's legs were exposed to the fierce elements. At least she wore gloves, Beth thought, tapping her hand against the steering wheel to keep herself from snatching the scraper from Jane and finishing the job.

Ten minutes later father and daughter settled back into the Jeep, their sighs indicating they relished the warmth. Beth's guilt soared. She had a problem with wanting to do everything for everyone else. She had to learn to say no and to let others do for her. Darcy and Jesse were always telling her that at their Saturday get-togethers. She should listen to her friends. But it was tough to go against ingrained behavior.

Negotiating out of the parking lot, Beth drove slowly, glad that most people were off the roads and hopefully safely in their homes. "Too much longer and I'm afraid we would have been stuck at school."

Jane gave a choking sound, which caused her father to send a censuring look her way. Having raised three siblings as well as teaching high schoolers for the past fifteen years, Beth understood the inner workings of a teenage mind. Jane fitted into the category of those who hated school and would rather be anywhere but there— hence her desire to strike out and walk home in a snowstorm, even though she wasn't dressed properly for any kind of walk.

"Where were you last stationed in the army?" Beth asked, hating the silence that had descended.

With his gaze fixed on the road ahead, Samuel said, "Leavenworth."

"Where the prison is?"

"Yes."

"Stuck in the middle of nowhere," Jane offered from the back seat.

"Were you ever stationed overseas?"

"Germany and Japan, which gave us a chance to see that part of the world."

Thinking of all the places she would love to visit, Beth chanced a quick look toward Samuel. "That must have been interesting."

"If you could speak the language," Jane said.

Beth heard the pout in the teenager's voice, but didn't turn to look at her. She could imagine the crossed arms and defiant expression on the girl's face, often a permanent part of her countenance. "True. That could be a problem, but they have such wonderful programs for teaching languages. I've been using a taped series to learn Spanish."

"I always tried to learn at least some of the language when we were stationed in a country. Japanese was hard, but I found German easy, especially to read." Samuel shifted in his seat, taking his attention from the road. With a smile he asked, "Have you traveled much?"

Beth shook her head. "But that's about to change. My brother's at college, so as of a week ago I have no one left at home." Beth recalled the mixed emotions she had experienced when she had said goodbye to Daniel at school. Elation at the sense of freedom she now had mingled with sadness that he would be starting a part of his life without her.

"Are you planning on going somewhere they speak Spanish?"

"Yes, but I don't know where yet. I'm going to spread a map of Central and South America out in front of me and throw a dart. I'm going where it lands."

Samuel chuckled. "An unusual method of planning a vacation."

"It won't be a vacation. I want to live there, for a while at least."

"What about Brazil? That takes up a good portion of South America, and they speak Portuguese."

"I understand there are a lot of similarities between the two languages. If I end up in Brazil, it will just make the adventure even more exciting."

"So when are you going to throw that dart?"

"Soon. I'm thinking of having a party and inviting all my friends to be there for the big moment." Saying out loud what she had been toying with for the past few months made her firm the decision to have a party in celebration of a new phase in her life, even though she rarely threw parties.

Beth pulled up in front of the rectory, a large two-story white Victorian house that sat next to the Sweetwater Community Church. "Tomorrow call Al's Body

Shop. He should be able to help you with your car. He's a member of the church."

Jane threw open the back door and jumped out, hurrying toward the front door, her uncomfortable-looking high-heeled short boots sinking beneath the blanket of snow.

Samuel observed his daughter for a few seconds, then turned to Beth. "Thanks for the ride. You're a life-saver. Are you sure you'll be okay going home alone?"

"I'll be fine. I only live three blocks over. If it gets too bad, I can always walk and then call Al's tomorrow myself."

"At least you're more suitably dressed for a hike in the snow than my daughter. I'd better let you go." He opened the door. "I'll have a talk with Jane, and she'll be there after school on Monday."

As he climbed from the Jeep, Beth said, "See you Sunday."

Samuel plodded toward the porch while Beth inched her car away from the curb. He was thankful she had been there to help them with a ride home. Just from the short time he had been around the woman he got the impression she went out of her way to assist people when she could. He liked that about her.

Picturing Beth in his mind, he smiled. Her blue eyes had sparkled with kindness and her generous mouth had curved with a smile meant to put a person at ease. He imagined she had a hard time keeping her reddish-brown hair tamed and in control, but he liked it, because every other aspect of Miss Beth Coleman was restrained, down to her neat gray dress and matching pumps. She probably thought of her long curly hair as her bane, while he thought it softened her prim and proper facade.

Taking one last look back, Samuel noticed the white Jeep quickly disappearing in the blowing snow. The bad weather had swept through so quickly that it had caught most people off guard. The only good thing about today was that Aunt Mae had arrived before the storm.

When he entered his house, where boxes were still stacked all over the place, delicious aromas teased him, causing his stomach to rumble. At least now with Aunt Mae here, they would have a decent meal instead of his feeble attempts at cooking. There was even a chance that his house would come together before summer vacation.

Shaking off the snow that still clung to him, he stomped his feet on the mat he was sure Aunt Mae had placed in front of the door, then shrugged out of his overcoat. He took a deep breath, trying to figure out what his aunt was preparing for dinner. Onions. Garlic. Meat. Hoping it was her spaghetti, he headed toward the kitchen to see.

"Dad."

Samuel stopped in the doorway into the den and peered over the mound of boxes to find his middle child on the floor with his bottom stuck up in the air while he tried to look under the couch. "Did you lose something, Craig?"

His son straightened, one hand clutched around his

Game Boy. "Allie is hiding things again. Can't you do something about her?"

"I'll have a talk with her. How's your room coming along?" Samuel asked, realizing his son must have gotten some of his things put away or the Game Boy wouldn't be in his hand.

Craig hopped to his feet. "I'm through."

"Good, son." Samuel moved toward the kitchen, making a note to himself to check Craig's room. His son's version of clean was definitely not his.

In the kitchen Samuel found his aunt by the stove adding something to a big pot while his youngest stood on a chair next to her and stirred whatever was cooking in the big pan. "Smells wonderful. Spaghetti?"

Aunt Mae glanced over her shoulder. "Yes. That's what Allie and Craig wanted. They said something about being tired of peanut butter and jelly sandwiches."

"You know how hopeless I am in the kitchen."

She tsked. "Samuel, after over two years you'd think I would have rubbed off on you."

"Aunt Mae, don't ever go away again," Allie said in a serious voice while continuing to stir the sauce.

His aunt, a woman who obviously loved her own cooking, tousled Allie's hair. "Hopefully my sister won't hurt herself again. I didn't like being away from you all."

"Next time Aunt Kathy can come here instead of you going there." Allie laid the spoon on the counter.

Visions of Mae's older sister living with them sent

panic through Samuel. He started to say something about his eight-year-old daughter's suggestion.

Aunt Mae's blue eyes twinkled and two dimples appeared in her cheeks. "Oh, sugar, that probably wouldn't be too good of an idea. She's *very* set in her ways. Besides, she was bedridden for a week and couldn't travel."

"Well, we missed you." Allie threw her arms around Aunt Mae.

The older woman brushed back the few strands of gray hair that had come loose from her bun, fighting tears that had suddenly filled her eyes. "I missed you all."

"Is that coffee on the stove?" Samuel asked, feeling his own emotions close to the surface—which he attributed to his exhaustion. He walked to the counter where some cups were set out and retrieved one.

As Samuel poured his coffee, he corralled his emotions and shoved them to the dark recesses of his mind. Aunt Mae had been a lifesaver after his wife died. When she had arrived on his doorstep, their lives had been in total chaos. Ruth's death had hit him so hard that it had taken him months to see how much his children needed him. Thankfully Aunt Mae had been around to ease their sorrow, because he hadn't been able to— something he still felt guilty about.

"Was everything all right at school with Jane?" Aunt Mae asked, opening the refrigerator and taking out the ingredients for a salad.

"Allie!" Craig's voice echoed through the house.

His youngest daughter jumped down from the chair, scooted it back toward the table, then darted out of the kitchen.

"No doubt she hid more than Craig's Game Boy." Samuel shook his head as he heard footsteps pounding up the stairs. "Jane's having trouble in English. I'm going to check on Monday to see how she's doing in her other classes." He took a long sip of his coffee, relishing the hot drink after being out in the cold.

"She took her mother's death harder than the other two."

"She was really close to Ruth." He drank some more to ease the constriction in his throat.

"Still, something else might be going on with her, Samuel. A good prayer might help."

There was a time he had felt that way. Now he didn't know if that would help his daughter. He kissed his aunt on the cheek. "You have good intuition. I'll keep an eye on her." Shouts from above drew Samuel's attention. "I'd better go and referee those two."

"Dinner will be ready in an hour."

Samuel strode toward the stairs. He was the new minister of Sweetwater Community Church and he wasn't even sure how effective prayer was. His house was still in chaos. He longed for the time he'd felt confident in the power of the Lord—before He had taken his wife and thrown his family into turmoil. He shouldn't have taken this church assignment, but he was desperate. He wanted his old life back.

* * *

Beth took a paper cup filled with red fruit punch from the table next to the coffee urn, then backed off to allow the other parishioners to get their refreshments after the late service. Standing along the wall where all the congregation's photos hung, she watched Samuel greet each person as they came into the rec hall. Her throat parched, she drank half the juice in several swallows. Over the past few days she had thought about the man more than she should. He and Jane had even plagued her dreams last night.

Jesse Blackburn approached with a cup of coffee. "So what do you think of our new minister?"

"Interesting sermon on redemption."

"He's a widower."

"Yes, I know and, Jesse, don't you get any ideas. As they say in the movies, I'm blowing this town come summer."

Taking a sip of her coffee, Jesse stared at her over the rim of her cup. "You are?"

"Don't act innocent. You know I've been planning this ever since Daniel decided to go to college."

Jesse leaned back against the wall, a picture in non-chalance. "It seems I recall you saying something about a vacation."

"It's more than a vacation. In fact, you'll have to do the annual Fourth of July auction this year, because I won't be here."

Her good friend splayed her hand across her chest. "You're leaving *me* in charge?"

"Don't sound so surprised. You and Darcy will do a great job."

"It won't be the same without you. You've been doing it for the past ten or so years."

"And I have made very good notes for you to follow." Beth finished her punch, then crushed the paper cup into a ball. Frustration churned in her, making her feel as though she should shed her skin. "I'll help you until May. Then you're on your own."

"Boswell's a great organizer. I'll put him on it." Jesse straightened away from the wall. "Give the poor man something to do."

"How's it feel to have your own butler?"

Jesse laughed. "A bit funny, but Boswell's more like a member of the family than anything. Now, if I could just get him and Gramps to get along. Thank goodness Gramps married Susan Reed and lives at her place." She drained her coffee. "Are you sure you don't want me to have a little dinner party for the new reverend?"

"I think you *should* have a party."

Jesse's eyes widened. "You do?"

"To help introduce him to the whole congregation, not just the single women." Beth scanned the room for the man under discussion. He stood a few feet from the door, dressed in a black suit that accorded a nice contrast to his blond hair. The intent expression on his face while listening to Tanya Bolton gave Beth the impression he was a good listener, which was probably beneficial considering the needs of the people in the church. "What makes you think he's looking for a woman?"

"The romantic in me. I just hate seeing people alone."

"Jesse, I'm not alone. I have three siblings—who I grant you don't live with me anymore, but are still around. And I have my friends. Reverend Morgan has three children. And I met his aunt this morning in Sunday-school class. She lives with him. That certainly isn't alone."

"Boy, you need a man worse than I thought if you think children and an aunt are the same thing as a spouse."

"What are you two conspiring about?" Darcy Markham paused next to Beth, her hand at the small of her back.

Relieved at her friend's timely interruption, Beth smiled. "When are you going to have that baby?"

"I wish any minute, but the doctor says another month. Maybe I'll have it on my anniversary. If this child is anything like my son, he will take his sweet time. I'm not sure who is more anxious, me or Joshua."

"I sympathize with you two, but I'm glad it's you and not me." Beth's gaze caught Reverend Morgan moving away from the door and making his rounds to the various groups in the room.

"Well, I should hope so. You aren't married," Jesse said with a laugh.

Heat singed Beth's cheeks. "You know what I mean. I'm too old to have children. Besides, after raising my two brothers and sister, I'm through." After she'd turned thirty-five with no prospect of a husband, she'd given up hope of having her own children.

"Too old!" Darcy shifted her stance, rubbing her back. "You're only thirty-eight. Beth, if that's too old, then Jesse and I don't have long before we're over the hill."

"She's gonna be too busy traveling. She's leaving Sweetwater this summer and has informed me that we'll have to be in charge of the annual auction."

"Us?" Darcy pointed to her chest, then rested her hand on her stomach.

"Yes, you two. In fact, you and your husbands are invited to a party I'm having next weekend."

"A party? Isn't that Jesse's domain? You don't give parties."

Beth narrowed her eyes on Darcy, pressing her lips together. She had always been so predictable. That was about to change. "I am now. It's a celebration. I'm going to choose where I'm going this summer."

"Choose?" Jesse's brow furrowed.

"You two will just have to wait and see how. Can I count on you all coming to the celebration?"

Both Darcy and Jesse nodded their heads, big grins on their faces.

"Celebration?"

At the sound of the deep, gruff voice behind her, Beth blinked, then swallowed to coat her suddenly dry throat while the reverend stepped into view.

"I just wanted to thank you again, Beth, for rescuing

Jane and me the other day." Samuel Morgan extended his hand toward her.

She fitted hers within his and shook it, aware of the curiosity of her two friends. "It was nothing."

Still holding her hand, Samuel smiled, the warmth in his expression reaching deep into his chocolate-colored eyes. "So what are you celebrating?"

Chapter Two

My great escape, Beth thought, but decided not to voice that answer. "This is the celebration I told you about. I'm planning a long vacation and having a party to celebrate the fact."

"That's as good a reason as any to have a celebration." Samuel finally released his hold on her hand.

"You're invited if you want to come. It's next Saturday night at my house." When Beth thought she saw hesitation in his eyes, she hastened to add, "It'll be a good way for you to get to know some of the congregation in a less formal environment." Now, why had she said that? That had always been Jesse's role.

"Darcy and I will be there along with our husbands." Jesse shot a look toward Darcy that conveyed a message that Beth couldn't see. "I'll volunteer to help you with the preparations, Beth, since giving dinner parties is my specialty."

Beth knew she would have to put a stop to her friend's matchmaking scheme that she could almost see percolating in her mind. She couldn't very well exclude the reverend after he'd overheard their discussion of her celebration. Yeah, right.

"I can help, too," Darcy said, rubbing her stomach. "We can meet at your house for our Saturday-morning get-together instead of at Alice's Café."

Beth forced a smile to her lips. "Thanks," she murmured, again noticing a nonverbal exchange between Darcy and Jesse.

"Oh, I see Nick waving to me. Got to go." Jesse hugged Beth and Darcy goodbye and hurried away.

"And I need to sit down. I'm going to find Joshua and a quiet corner to rest in." Darcy kissed Beth on the cheek, then nodded toward Samuel before lumbering toward her husband, who was leaning against the piano.

That was the fastest getaway her two friends had ever made. Beth made a mental note to call them and set them straight the second she got home from church. She was not looking for a man. Didn't they know she was the plain town spinster who was a good twenty or thirty pounds overweight?

"Since that just leaves you and me, can we talk a moment in private?"

You and me. Those simple words conjured up all kinds of visions that mocked her earlier words that she wasn't looking to date. "Sure. Is something wrong?"

Samuel gestured toward an area away from the

crowd in the rec hall, an alcove with a padded bench that offered them a more quiet environment. He sat, and waited for her to do the same. She stared at the small space that allowed only two people to sit comfortably—and the reverend was a large man who took up more than his half of the bench. While she debated whether to stand or sit, a perplexed expression descended on his face. If it hadn't been for Jesse insisting on fixing her up with Samuel, she wouldn't be undecided about something as simple as sitting and talking with him, she thought.

With a sigh she sat, her leg and arm brushing against his. Awareness—a sensation she didn't deal with often—bolted through her. "What do you need to discuss?"

"Jane. She won't let me help her with her homework." He rubbed the palms of his hands together. "I'm at a loss as to what to do with her. Any suggestions?"

"Let me see how we do tomorrow when she stays after school. At the beginning of every year I give a learning-styles inventory to see how each student learns. I haven't had a chance to give it to Jane yet, but I will this week. I'll know more after that."

"Learning styles?"

"Whether she's a visual, auditory or kinesthetic learner. Then I can use that information to teach her the way she learns best."

"I appreciate any help you can give me. I suspect tomorrow when I talk with her other teachers I'm going to find she hasn't done any work for them, either."

"You said she hasn't taken her mother's death well. Have you considered counseling?"

"Tried that, and she wouldn't talk to a stranger. She just sat there, most of the time not saying a word."

"How about someone she knows?"

"Aunt Mae has tried and Jane just clammed up." He rubbed his thumb into his palm. "I've tried and haven't done much better. Jane has always been an introvert. She doesn't express her emotions much."

"Let me see what I can do," Beth said, knowing she didn't have long before she would be gone. Four months might not be long enough to establish a relationship with the teenager and get her to open up about what was bothering her. She would encourage Jane to go to the school counselor. Zoey Witherspoon was very good at her job.

Samuel rose. "I appreciate any help," he repeated. "I'm a desperate dad."

"I hear that frequently. I teach fifteen-year-olds who have raging hormones. They fluctuate between being a child and an adult, from being dependent on their parents to being independent of them."

"I was a teenager once, not that long ago, but frankly it didn't prepare me for dealing with my daughter. I think I might have a better handle on Craig when he becomes a teenager." He chuckled. "At least I hope so, since that's only a year away."

"I know what you mean. I raised two brothers and a sister. My sister was easier for me. I struggled with Daniel, my youngest brother. I'm surprised he made it through high school. He failed several subjects and had to go to school a semester longer than his classmates. I will say I saw him grow up a lot in the past six months. I think watching all his friends go off to college last summer while he had to return to high school sobered him and made him aware of some of the mistakes he'd made."

Samuel placed a hand on her arm. "Thank you."

The touch of his fingers seared her. She knew she was overreacting to the gesture, but she couldn't stop her heart from pounding against her chest. She was afraid its loud thumping could be heard across the rec hall. Even before she'd begun raising her siblings she hadn't dated much. She was plain and shy, not two aspects that drew scores of men.

"You're welcome," she finally answered, her lips, mouth and throat dry. And she had been the one to invite him to her party next Saturday night.

Jane slammed the book closed. "How are you supposed to look a word up in the dictionary when you don't have any idea how to spell it?" She slouched back in her desk, defiance in her expression.

Beth glanced up from grading a paper. "What word?"

"Perspective."

"How do you think you spell it?"

"I don't know!" The girl's frustration etched a deep frown into her features.

Beth rose and came around her desk to stand next to Jane's. "What do you think it starts with?"

"I don't—" Jane's eyes narrowed, and she looked toward the window. "With a *p*." Her gaze returned to Beth's. "But there are *thousands* of words that start with *p*."

"Let's start with the first syllable. Per."

"*P-r*—" Jane pinched her lips together, her brows slashing downward.

"Almost. It's *p-e-r*. What do you think comes next? Per*spec*tive."

Jane leaned forward, folding her arms over the dictionary. "At this rate I'll get one paragraph written by this time tomorrow. What's the use?"

"I have a dictionary of commonly misspelled words. I can lend it to you. It might help with some of the words. If it does, you can get your own copy. See if you can find it by looking up *p-e-r-s-p*." Beth knew it would be a lot faster and easier on everyone if she spelled the word completely for Jane, but she wanted to see how the teenager did. She had a feeling a lot more was going on with the young woman. Not only did she have few word attack skills, but she read with difficulty.

Jane blew out a breath and flipped the dictionary open, thumbing through the pages until she found the *p* section. With only a handful of selections to choose from, Jane pointed and said, "There." She pushed the dictionary to the side and wrote down the word, grumbling about the time it had taken to find it.

Beth made her way back to her desk. Jane had been struggling with the writing assignment for an hour. The past few days working with her after school had sent red flags waving concerning Jane's academic ability. Beth decided that when Samuel came to pick up his daughter she would have a talk with him about Jane.

Not ten minutes later Beth knew the instant Samuel appeared in the doorway. As though she had a sixth sense when it came to the man, she looked up to find him smiling at her from across the room. A dimple appeared in his left cheek, drawing Beth's attention.

The second Jane saw him she finished the sentence she had been writing and gathered up her papers. She started to slide from the desk.

"Are you through, Jane?" Samuel asked, entering.

His presence seemed to shrink the large classroom to the size of a small closet, and for the life of her, Beth couldn't understand why her pulse began to race. She suddenly worried that she looked as if she had spent the whole day in front of 150 students trying to inspire them to love literature—which she had. She felt even plainer, and wheeled her chair closer to her desk to shield her rather drab dress of gray cotton that didn't quite hide her extra pounds. Maybe she should buy a few new outfits, more updated with some splashes of color, she thought.

"Yes." Jane rose and brought the paper to Beth's desk. After plopping it down, she headed for the door. "I'm getting a drink of water and going to my locker."

The tension that churned the air left with Jane. Samuel watched his daughter disappear through the doorway before he turned toward Beth with one brow arched.

"This writing assignment was very difficult for her." Beth picked up Jane's paper and skimmed it. "And from the looks of it, she doesn't have a firm background in grammar, punctuation and spelling. Her thoughts on the subject are good ones, but she has a hard time getting them down on paper."

Samuel covered the distance between them and hovered in front of Beth's desk—way too close for her peace of mind. The dimple in his left cheek vanished as he frowned.

"What are you telling me?" He took Jane's paper and began to read.

"I think Jane needs to be tested to see if she has a learning disability."

His head shot up, his gaze riveted to hers. "A learning disability!"

"A learning disability doesn't mean that Jane isn't smart. People with normal, even high, IQs can have a learning disability that hinders them learning what they need to know. How's she doing in her other classes?"

"Not well except for geometry. She's got an A in that class. That and advanced drawing."

"Is she doing the work for the other teachers?"

"No. The same as yours. I'm trying to help her every night. She can't do anything until she gets her homework done, which basically takes her the whole evening. The Morgan household has not been a fun one this past week. I feel more like a drill sergeant than a father."

Disregarding how she imagined she looked, Beth

stood, feeling at a disadvantage sitting behind her desk. She came around beside Samuel, wanting to help, to comfort. "I think she struggles with the reading part. When I gave her the learning-styles inventory, she tested almost completely a visual learner. So much of the work in high school is from lectures. I'm not sure she's getting it. Her auditory skills seem to be weak."

"Then what do I need to do?"

"Sign permission for her to be tested. I'll refer her and our school psychologist will contact you."

"I don't know how well Jane will take this."

Beth touched his arm, the urge to comfort growing stronger the longer she was around this man. There was something about him that conveyed a troubled soul, and she had never been able to turn away from someone in need. "This can all be handled without the other students knowing."

"I don't have a choice."

As his gaze locked with hers, Beth forgot where she was for a moment. Finally when she shook off the effect he had on her senses, she said, "You always have a choice. But if she's having trouble reading it's better to know now than later."

"You don't think it's normal teenage rebellion?"

"No. I think she's using her defiant attitude as a way to cover up not knowing."

"Then refer her."

"Do you want me to talk to Jane about what I'm doing?"

"No, that's my job. I'll talk with her on the way home. I don't want her to be surprised."

"I'll be glad to help any way I can."

Again his gaze snared hers, drawing her in. "You've already done so much."

"Dad, aren't you coming?" Framed in the doorway, Jane slung her backpack over her left shoulder.

"Yes. I'll be by this time tomorrow to pick her up."

Samuel left the classroom, with his daughter walking ahead of him at a fast clip. When he stepped outside, the brisk winter air blasted him in the face. Snow still blanketed the ground, but the roads had been cleared. He found his daughter in the passenger seat of his Ford Mustang, her eyes closed, her head resting against the cushion. For a few seconds he took in her calm expression, which of late was rare, and regretted the conversation to come. But Jane needed to know what was going to happen.

Samuel started the car and drove out of the school parking lot. *Lord, I know I haven't visited with You as I should. But I need help with Jane. Please help me to find the right words to explain about the testing. Please help me to understand what is happening with my daughter.*

"What were you and Miss Coleman talking about?" Jane sat up, watching the landscape out the side window.

He took a deep, composing breath. "She wants to refer you for testing and I told her to go ahead."

Jane twisted toward him. "Testing? What kind?"

"She thinks you're struggling to read and that you might have a learning disability."

"I'm not dumb!"

"She didn't say that and I'm not, either. Your A in geometry proves that. But something's going on, Jane. Don't you want to find out what it is?"

"I'm not dumb!" Tears glistened in his daughter's eyes.

Shaken by the sight of her tears, Samuel parked his car in his driveway. Jane rarely cried. He started to reach for her to comfort her, but she glared at him. Swiping the back of her hand across her cheeks, she shoved the door open, bolted from the car and ran toward the house.

He gripped the steering wheel and let his head sag until it touched the cold plastic. He hadn't handled that well. Like everything else the past few years, he was fumbling to find the correct path. He felt as though he were lost in the desert, wandering around trying to find the promised land.

"I'm so glad you could come a little early." Beth held open the door and stepped to the side to allow Jesse into her house.

"Am I imagining things or was that panic in your voice a little while ago?" Jesse asked, following her through the living room into the dining room.

"You know I don't entertain much. I don't even know why I decided to have this party. I've got the house clean. That was easy. But do I have enough food for everyone?" Beth gestured toward the table that could seat eight if the leaf was in it, which it was.

Jesse's eyes grew round. "What color is the table-cloth? I can't tell. You've got so much food on it."

"Are you trying to tell me I overdid it?"

"How many people did you invite? The whole con-gregation plus the staff you work with?"

"I don't want anyone going hungry."

"Believe me, if they do, they have an eating disorder."

Beth scanned the table laden with three cakes, two pies, several dozen cookies and brownies, vegetable and fruit trays with two different dips each, several kinds of small sandwiches without the crust, crackers and chips with assorted spreads and a cheese ball. "I had to put the drinks in the kitchen. I ran out of room."

Jesse snatched up a carrot stick and took a bite. "So how many people are coming?"

"Besides you and Nick, Darcy and Joshua, there are the reverend, Tanya Bolton, Zoey Witherspoon, Paul Howard and Boswell."

"Boswell? He didn't say anything to me about coming."

"I saw him at the grocery yesterday when I was buying some of the food and thought he might enjoy coming. You don't mind, do you?"

"No, especially since Nate and Cindy are over at Gramps and Susan's. I'm glad Boswell's getting out. I've felt guilty about uprooting him from Chicago. He promises me that he doesn't mind living in Sweetwater, but I'm not sure I believe him." Jesse popped a potato chip into her mouth. "What do you want me to help you with?"

Beth twirled. "Do I look all right?"

"Why, Beth Coleman, I've never known you to care too much about how you look."

Regretting that she had given in to her panic and called Jesse for advice, Beth started toward the kitchen. She realized she was plain, but that didn't mean she didn't care about how she appeared to others. *Come on, Beth, don't you really mean Samuel Morgan?*

"You can wipe that smug smile off your face, Jesse. I just didn't want to be overdressed."

Jesse stopped Beth's progress with a hand on her shoulder. "I'll be serious. Turn around."

Beth faced her friend, her hands on her waist, now hoping she could pull off an "I don't care" attitude.

With a finger against her chin, Jesse studied her. "Black jeans with a cream silk blouse. Not bad. New blouse?"

The heat of a blush scored Beth's cheeks. "Yes. I haven't bought anything new in months." And except for an occasional treat to herself for Christmas and her birthday, she purchased only the basic necessities she needed for school. While her siblings had been growing up, clothing had been expensive, not to mention later helping with their college tuition.

Holding up her hands, Jesse took a step back. "Stop right there. I'm glad you're finally doing something for yourself and not just for your brothers and sister. It's about time." Her gaze skimmed the length of Beth once more. "Deep-six the tennis shoes. Heels would be better with what you have on."

"Tennis shoes go with jeans."

"But heels will look better with your blouse, which is soft and feminine. Don't you have a black pair we got last year?"

"They're awfully dressy. This is a casual party."

Jesse flipped her hand in the air, dismissing Beth's concerns. "You'll be casually elegant."

The sound of the doorbell cut through the sudden silence.

Beads of perspiration popped out on Beth's upper lip. She didn't give parties. Why had she come up with this way to kick off her new outlook on life? Bad, bad idea.

Jesse waved her toward her bedroom. "Go. I'll get the door. I don't want to see those tennis shoes."

Wiping her hand across her upper lip, Beth hurried away, wondering if she could hide for at least an hour in her bedroom. She would have been fine with just Darcy, Joshua, Jesse and Nick. She could have convinced herself that this wasn't a party she was responsible for, but the additional five people made a mockery out of that thought.

While rifling through the bottom of her closet for the box that held her black heels, she heard laughter coming from her living room and the doorbell chiming again. When she finally found the shoes, stuck way in the back, she examined them, unable to believe she had bought them. It was Jesse's fault. She'd worn them only once— to Darcy's wedding. Jesse had been with her when she had purchased them. In fact, Jesse had been the one who had insisted she buy them. On her own she never would have, and still couldn't believe she'd let Jesse talk her into them. Beth held them up, still debating whether to wear the silk-and-leather heels. They were three inches high—two more than she usually wore—with long pointed toes and no back strap. They looked uncomfortable, but actually—much to her surprise when she had tried them on at the store—they were very comfortable.

When the bell announced another arrival, Beth kicked off her tennis shoes and removed her socks, then donned the black heels. She didn't dare look at herself in her full-length mirror. She *knew* she wouldn't leave the room if she did. Hurrying as quickly as possible in her heels, she came into the foyer as Jesse opened the door to another guest—Reverend Samuel Morgan.

He peered past Jesse toward Beth and for the barest moment his eyes flashed surprise. The hammering of her heart increased, worry nibbling at her composure. What did she look like? She'd tried some new makeup she'd gotten at the grocery store yesterday and had left her curly hair down about her shoulders, probably in a wild mess by now. She wanted to whirl around, go back to her bedroom and check her appearance in her full-length mirror.

Then he smiled and her world tilted for a few seconds.

After murmuring a greeting to Jesse, Samuel came toward Beth, his long strides purposeful as if he were a man on a mission. "Thank you for including me in your celebration." He clasped her hand between his and shook it. "I haven't had a chance to do much since moving here. As you suggested, it'll be nice to meet some of my congregation in a relaxed atmosphere."

Relaxed atmosphere? There was nothing remotely relaxed about her at the moment. "I'm glad you could come." Her hand was still sandwiched between his. Suddenly she didn't feel thirty-eight but a young woman of eighteen, inexperienced but eager to learn the ways of dating. That was not to say she hadn't dated a few men over the years, but most of her time had been taken up with caring for her siblings and trying to make ends meet, first as a college student and then on the meager pay of a teacher. She definitely felt like a novice.

Finally releasing her hand, Samuel peeked into the living room, which also gave him a view of the dining-room table loaded with food. "Is everyone here?"

Beth scanned the small group of friends and nodded. "I like to cook and I just kept preparing food until I ran out of time." She actually had missed not cooking for others since Daniel had left for college.

"I'm glad I didn't have time to eat dinner before coming."

"So am I. I don't know what I'm going to do with this after you all leave."

"Freeze it," Jesse said, approaching them.

"I don't have a big enough freezer. You all are going to have to take some home with you."

"Did I hear correctly? We'll be taking doggie bags home with us?" Joshua asked, helping Darcy onto the couch.

Darcy laughed, shifting to get as comfortable as possible for a woman eight months pregnant. "I still haven't mastered the art of cooking, and poor Liz and Dad get tired of us coming to eat with them at the farm."

Joshua sat next to his wife and took her hand. "She's become quite good with one or two dishes. Sean and I don't order pizza nearly like we used to."

Darcy playfully punched Joshua on the arm. "I'm not that bad. I can prepare more than one or two."

Beth leaned close to Samuel, and immediately realized her mistake when she got a whiff of his citrusy aftershave. "Yes, she is. Just remember that when planning anything having to do with food at the church."

"I heard that, Beth Coleman. I thought you were my friend."

The laughter in Darcy's voice took the sting out of her words. "I'll give you two doggie bags, Joshua."

"Thanks. You're a good woman, Beth."

She was used to the ribbing among her and her friends, but with Samuel next to her, she couldn't help feeling as though she were on stage in front of a whole group of strangers. And that was something she avoided at all costs. She was a behind-the-scenes kind of person, never wanting to be in the limelight like Jesse and even Darcy.

"Please, everyone get a plate and eat. The drinks are in the kitchen," Beth announced, aware of Samuel's every move next to her. She felt his gaze on her and wanted to escape. She knew both Jesse and Darcy would never allow her to. This was why she didn't give parties, she remembered—too late.

"I believe you know everyone here, Samuel." Beth gestured toward her guests. "I need to see if there's enough ice for the drinks." She practically ran from the man, making a beeline for the kitchen and, she hoped, time to regroup. If she had thought this party thing through, she would have invited at least half a dozen more people, she thought. She was afraid Jesse would begin to pair everyone off and find there was no one for Samuel except either Tanya or her.

In the kitchen Boswell placed ice into his glass from the bucket that Beth had already filled. He glanced toward her when she entered.

"Do you have everything you need?" she asked, relieved he was the only one in the room.

Jesse and Nick's British manservant poured diet soda into his glass. "I swore I would never drink this stuff, but alas, the pounds are beginning to show. I can't believe I've been forced to this."

Beth suppressed a smile. "There's always water."

"You have bottled water?"

"Well, no. But the water from the tap is fine."

Horror flitted across his face. "I'll drink this."

As he left, Beth said, "And don't forget to eat. I'm sure there's something on the table that isn't fattening."

The second he was gone, Beth released a long sigh, relishing the quiet of the kitchen. Then the door swung open and Tanya entered. "I almost ran into Boswell. If it wasn't for his quick reflexes, he would have dropped his drink."

"I'd better prop the door open or there'll be an accident."

While Tanya sailed past her to the counter where the drinks were, Beth retrieved a brick she used when she wanted to leave the swinging door open between the kitchen and the dining room. As she straightened from placing it at the base of the door, she took a step back and collided with a solid wall of flesh. The scent of citrus drifted to her, and she knew Samuel was behind her.

She fixed a smile on her face and turned. "Can I get you anything to drink? I've got sodas, iced tea, decaf coffee and fruit punch. And of course, there's water." Nerves stretched taut, she listened to herself speak so fast she wondered if Samuel even understood what she said. He looked a little dazed. "Oh, and I forgot. I have hot apple cider on the stove," she added a lot more slowly.

"That sounds nice. But I can get it."

Tanya breezed by. "Beth, I'm filling in for Darcy in her Sunday-school class until after the baby comes."

"Great," Beth said to Tanya's back as she disappeared into the dining room.

"She has so much energy." Samuel followed Beth to the stove and watched her ladle a steaming cup of apple cider into a blue ceramic mug.

"That's Tanya." She poured some cider for herself.

Samuel leaned back against the counter and took a

tentative sip of his drink, surveying the kitchen. "I like your home. Very cozy."

"And small. Not now, but when my brothers and sister lived here, we met ourselves coming and going. One bathroom and four people isn't what I call an ideal situation." She was chattering again—most uncharacteristic.

"You raised all your siblings?" Samuel appeared relaxed and comfortable as though he was going to stay a while. He crossed his legs at the ankles and grasped the edge of the counter with one hand.

Dressed in black slacks and a striped gray-and-maroon shirt, he filled her kitchen with his large presence, someone who quietly commanded people's attention. She still marveled that he was a minister, when he looked more like a linebacker or a well-trained soldier. Did he work out? That question surprised her and made her gasp.

Samuel cocked his head, his brow furrowed. "Something wrong?"

She shook her head, berating herself for the folly of her thoughts. "Forgot something." *My brain,* she thought, realizing she hadn't really lied to her preacher.

"Can I help?"

"No, everything's under control." *Just as soon as I stop thinking about you.* "To answer your question, yes, I raised my brothers and sister. I was nineteen when my mother died in childbirth, and I wasn't going to let the state take them away from our home, such as it is."

"Where was your father?"

She should have realized he would ask that question. She bit the inside of her mouth, trying to transfer the mental pain she felt when her father was mentioned to a physical one instead. It didn't work. Even after nineteen years her father's abandonment bored into her heart, leaving a gaping hole she wasn't sure would ever totally heal. "He left us when my mother was six months pregnant with their fourth child. He walked out one day and we never heard from him again."

Samuel straightened from the counter. "I'm sorry. I know how inadequate those words can be at times, but it's never easy when a parent abandons a child."

"That's why I would never abandon my brothers and sister to let some stranger raise them."

"That was quite a task to take on by yourself at nineteen. You didn't have any relatives to help you?"

"We're a small family. My father had an uncle who tried to help some when he could, but he was old and set in his ways. Both of my parents were only children. My mother used to say that's why she wanted a houseful of kids. I guess my father didn't feel that way." The intense pressure in her chest made each breath difficult. She drew in several deep gulps of air, but nothing seemed to relieve the constriction. She hadn't thought about her father in a long time—most people knew it was a subject she didn't discuss.

"I can see I've distressed you." He took a step toward her, reaching to touch her arm in comfort.

She backed up against the refrigerator, feeling

trapped by the kindness in his expression. "You would think I'd be over it after nineteen years."

His arm fell to his side. "No, I don't know if a child ever totally gets over a parent walking out on her. It's hard enough on a child when one parent dies. Even though the parent doesn't choose to die, the child still experiences abandonment."

"Not just the child but the spouse, too."

The air vibrated with suppressed tension, the focus of the conversation shifting.

For a few seconds a haunted look dimmed his dark eyes, then he managed to veil his expression by lowering his lashes. "Yes."

Chapter Three

"You know, in here—" Samuel tapped the side of his head "—I know that my wife didn't choose to leave us. But in here—" he splayed his hand over his heart "—it doesn't make any difference. Pain is pain."

Beth swallowed the tightness swelling in her throat. "I think Jane's feeling the same emotions."

"I know she is. She was very close to Ruth and took her death especially hard."

But not as hard as you, Beth thought, seeing his anguish reflected in the depths of his eyes.

"Then we moved not long after that happened, and that was when I decided to resign from the army. Moving around was becoming too hard on my family, especially without their mother."

"What made you become a chaplain in the army?"

"I wanted to serve my country and God. I thought I could do it by being an army chaplain."

"But now you don't think so?" She'd heard the doubt in his voice and wondered about it.

"I discovered you can't serve two masters—at least, not me." He turned away and walked to the stove to refill his mug.

The sight of his back, his shoulders stiff with tension, told Beth that topic of conversation was finished. She could respect that. There were a lot of things she wouldn't discuss with others, and she and Samuel were practically strangers.

Even though the last thing she felt like doing at the moment was smiling, she did, needing to lighten the mood. "Tanya reminded me of something we'll need to talk about soon."

He threw her a glance over his shoulder, then slowly pivoted. "What?"

"I run the Sunday School, and since I'll be leaving in the summer, we should discuss a replacement so I can train that person this spring." She found if she voiced her plans out loud the reality of leaving Sweetwater became more real.

"Nothing like the present."

"Here? Now?"

"Well, not exactly right this minute, but how about next week some time? Why don't you come to Friday-night dinner at my house? Aunt Mae goes all out that night. For some reason she thinks we should celebrate the end of a work week. I don't think she understands I do a lot of my work on the weekend. But it's something she's done for years and I didn't have the heart to change it when she came to live with us."

"I hate to intrude on a family evening."

"Nonsense. If I entertain, it's usually then." Samuel sipped his cider, his gaze intent upon her.

The refrigerator still propped her up. Beth pushed away, surprised by the trembling in her legs—as though their conversation had affected her more than she cared to admit. "What time?"

"Six-thirty."

"Fine." She hoped she could stay awake long enough to hold an intelligent conversation. Friday nights were usually her crash night after a long week of teaching. She often would wake up around eleven, having fallen asleep in front of the television and having no idea what had been on the set earlier in the evening. "Speaking of celebrations, I think it's time I threw my dart."

"You really are going to decide where you go by throwing a dart?"

The incredulous tone of his voice made her laugh. "Yup."

Beth walked through the dining room, encouraging everyone to have a seat in the living room. Her nine guests crowded into the small area, with Jesse sitting on the arm of the lounge chair that Nick occupied and Tanya on the floor next to the sofa.

Beth went into the foyer and retrieved from the closet a tagboard and one dart. "As you can see, this is a map of Central and South America. I'm planning a trip and tonight I'm deciding where. I'd ask someone to hold the board up, but I'm afraid I might be a bit wild with the dart, so instead I'll position it on the rocking chair if Zoey doesn't mind standing for a moment—unless you want to hold it."

Her friend from school stopped rocking and leaped from the chair, horror on her face. "I'll pass. I've seen you play sports." To the group she added, "I would suggest everyone give her plenty of room. No telling where the dart will end up. I can remember the church softball game where she hit me and I wasn't anywhere near where she intended to throw the ball."

"Oh, yeah. You had a bruise on your leg for weeks after that," Darcy said, scooting closer to Joshua on the couch so Zoey could sit next to her.

Beth positioned herself in front of the tagboard, then turned around to her guests. "Hence the warning."

Several nearest her backed away. Beth squared off in front of the rocking chair, squeezed her eyes closed and tossed the dart. It clanged to the tile floor in the foyer.

"If you miss the map, does that mean you stay, Beth?" asked Paul Howard, an assistant principal at her school.

She started toward the dart. Samuel picked it up first and handed it to her. Their gazes touched for a long moment, humor deep in his eyes. She liked the way they crinkled at the corners. She liked their color—it reminded her of a piece of dark, rich chocolate that she loved to eat.

"No," she murmured, suddenly aware of the silence in the room. "It only means I try again."

Boswell and Paul moved back even farther. Half the room was clear for her next shot. Beth shook her head, closed her eyes and threw the dart without really giving it much thought, still rattled by the silent exchange a moment before with Samuel. It plunked into the tagboard. She eased one eye open and saw the dart in the middle of the map.

"Brazil." Zoey came to stand beside her and stare at the map. "Guess you'd better get some Portuguese tapes instead of the Spanish ones."

"The Amazon. How do you like heat and humidity?" Paul asked, stepping next to Zoey.

"Not to mention snakes and other unpleasant animals. Are you going to throw again?" Jesse flanked her on the other side.

With so much of South America being taken up by the Amazon, why am I surprised the dart landed there? Beth wondered. "No, I'm not going to throw again. Brazil it will be."

A mild "heat" wave had tempered the bitter cold of the past few weeks, pushing the temperature up to near fifty. But with dusk approaching quickly, the air began to chill and the sun was low behind the trees. Beth paused on her porch and looked across her brown lawn, the drabness fitting her mood perfectly. Her feet ached from standing more than usual that week at school and her mind felt muddled from the late nights she'd spent grading writing assignments until her eyes had crossed and the words had blurred.

All she wanted to do was collapse into her soft velour lounge chair, switch on her television for background noise and stare unseeing at the screen. Do nothing. For once. But this was Friday and she had told Samuel she would come to dinner. With a heavy sigh, she stuck her key into the lock and opened her front door.

A noise from the back of the house alerted her that someone was inside. She tensed, her hand clenched around the knob.

"Beth, is that you?"

Relief sagged her body against the door. Daniel was home from college. "Yes."

Her youngest brother came down the hall, drying his hair with a blue towel, wearing a pair of jeans slung low. "I just took a shower and was getting dressed to go out."

She managed to close the front door without slamming it, a remarkable feat of patience when she didn't think she had any left. "I didn't know you were coming home this weekend."

"I caught a ride with Mitch. He's taking me back on Sunday, too, so you don't need to."

"Oh." Her exhausted mind couldn't come up with anything else to say while she stared at her brother.

He hung the towel over his shoulder. "In fact, he'll be by in fifteen minutes. We're going to Pete's."

She refrained from saying "oh" again by mashing her lips together.

"We'll talk tomorrow. I'll tell you about my classes then." He turned and headed down the hall toward his bedroom.

Beth watched him disappear, irritated at herself because she was irritated at Daniel for not telling her he was coming home for the weekend. She should be happy—and she was—but he had a way of taking over the whole house. To emphasize her thought, loud music blared from his room, chasing away the silence she desired after a day spent listening to 150 students.

When she placed her stuffed briefcase and purse on the table in the foyer, she noticed the mail that Daniel must have brought into the house. On top was an envelope from the Christian Mission Institute. She tore into it with a jolt of energy. A letter welcoming her interest in their overseas program and an application caused her hands to tremble. When she filled this out, she'd be one step closer.

As she stared at the application, an image of Samuel came into her mind—of a look of vulnerability that she had seen beneath his confident surface. A man in need of a friend. Surprised by that thought, she put the letter and application on the table next to her purse. She would deal with it later when she wasn't so tired, when she wasn't picturing a man who shouldn't send her heart pounding with a smile.

Beth walked to the kitchen to find a drink with some

caffeine in it. She rummaged around in the refrigerator, positive that she'd had one cola left. Nothing. She scanned the counter and discovered the empty can by the sink along with a dirty plate and fork. Daniel.

For a brief moment she thought of making a pot of coffee and drinking it all, but decided instead to take a cool shower. Maybe that would help keep her awake while having dinner at Samuel's. Then she again visualized the handsome reverend and knew she wouldn't have any trouble staying awake, because for the past few weeks he'd haunted her dreams when she'd finally fallen asleep.

Why now? She'd never been particularly interested in a man to the point she dreamed about him.

She wasn't getting enough rest. That had to be it. Shaking her head as if that would rid her mind of the man, she started for her bedroom. Passing the laundry room, she caught sight of a *huge* mound of clothes thrown on its floor and covering most of it. Daniel. Now she knew her brother's real reason for coming home. He hadn't done any laundry since she'd dropped him off three weeks ago. Flipping on the light, she picked up a dark shirt that reeked of smoke and cologne and waded through the pile of clothes to the washer. She dropped it in, followed by another and another.

Finished with his sermon for the coming Sunday, Samuel pushed back his chair at his desk in his office and began to rise when a knock sounded at his door. "Yes?"

Tanya Bolton strode into the room. "Do you have a few minutes to talk to me?"

The troubled expression in her eyes prompted Samuel to say, "Yes, of course. What's wrong?" He gestured toward a chair.

Her eyes took on a misty look as she fought tears. She sank into the chair next to his desk. "Tom has been hurt."

"Tom?"

"My husband." Tanya folded her hands in her lap and stared at them. "He's in prison for arson. A while back he was caught burning barns in the area." She lifted her gaze to his. "He's a good man, really. He just went a little crazy after our daughter's accident. As you know, Crystal is in a wheelchair. She fell from a horse and became paralyzed. He blamed all horses after that."

"How was he hurt?" Samuel asked, realizing there was so much he didn't know about his congregation and that this put him at a disadvantage when dealing with his parishioners' problems.

"An inmate attacked him and stabbed him. He's in the infirmary. The doctor says he'll be okay, but, Reverend Morgan, I'm worried. Lately Tom has said he doesn't want me to come visit him anymore. He's never let our daughter come. I don't know what to do." Tanya twisted her hands together, the sheen of tears visible in her eyes. "I'm so afraid for Tom, my daughter, myself. What should I do?"

The question he most feared was spoken. There had been a time when Samuel had always had a ready answer, had been sure of the advice he'd given. Now he felt as though he was fumbling around in the dark, most often stumbling and falling.

"He needs me now more than ever and he won't see me." A tear slipped from Tanya's eye.

Lord, help me to say and do the right thing, Samuel prayed, aware of the silence that shouldn't have filled the office. Tanya stared at him, waiting for an answer to her problem.

"Sometimes we have to honor a person's wishes even when we don't think they are good for them. Have you prayed for guidance?"

Tanya nodded. "That's why I'm here."

Panic took hold of Samuel. Counseling was a natural part of his job, but since his wife's death he'd felt inadequate, now more than ever. How could he counsel another when he couldn't help himself?

Samuel offered his hands to Tanya. "Let's pray together."

Tanya took his hands and bowed her head.

Samuel began to pray, hoping the words would soothe a troubled soul.

Beth fingered the tortoiseshell clip that held her riotous damp hair pulled back. A few strands of her unruly mop had come loose and curled about her face. Long ago she'd given up trying to control it, and spending hours straightening it seemed like a waste of time, time she'd never had for herself. Peering down at her black jeans and heavy black-and-white sweater, she satisfied herself she was ready to ring the bell. She'd done all she could to make herself presentable in her rush to be on time for dinner, but there wasn't much she could do with her plain features. She'd started to press the buzzer when the door swept open and warmth enveloped her.

The bright lights of his foyer framed Samuel, throwing his face into the shadows, but Beth saw the smile of greeting. The welcome in his expression rivaled the warmth emanating from his house, drawing her in out of the cold.

"I hope I'm not too late. My brother unexpectedly arrived home from college with tons of laundry to be done this weekend. I wanted to get a jump start on it."

"He doesn't do his own?" After she stepped across the threshold, Samuel closed the front door behind Beth.

"His one attempt turned half his white underwear and T-shirts pink and cost a small fortune to replace." She winced at the defensive tone in her voice and tried to temper it with a grin. "It just seemed easier to do it myself. Less hassle."

Samuel started to say something, clamped his mouth closed and began to turn toward the living room. In midturn he paused and glanced over his shoulder. "Wearing pink underwear a few times will teach him pretty fast to do the laundry the correct way."

Beth bit down on her lower lip.

"I don't usually give advice unless asked." Samuel

rushed on, a frown crinkling his forehead. "But he's what, eighteen, nineteen, and mostly on his own now. He needs to learn. When you leave this summer, who will do it then?"

"You haven't said anything that Jesse, Darcy and Zoey haven't told me. I know I'm enabling. But Daniel and I had a rough few years and I decided a long time ago to pick the battles I wanted to fight with him. Laundry wasn't one of them. School was."

"Is that issue better now?"

She nodded. "He finally sees the value in a good education."

"Then move on. You're doing him a big favor teaching him how to live on his own. I wish I had known. After Ruth's death I had to learn fast if I wanted our children to have clean clothes and to eat decent meals, not to mention live in a clean environment." Without another word Samuel stepped to the side to let her go before him into his large living room.

Beth had been in this house many times when Reverend Collins lived here, so she knew the layout well. But when she entered the room, surprise took hold of her. Gone was the formal decor of the previous occupant, to be replaced with a large, comfortable sofa of navy-and-maroon plaid. There were two overstuffed maroon chairs flanking an oversize table with a tall brass lamp. The furniture was a dark cherry, richly polished and gleaming in the soft lighting. The roaring fire in the fireplace completed the impression of homey comfort and pulled her forward.

"I like what you've done. Obviously you've gotten a lot unpacked."

"Not me so much as Aunt Mae with minor help from us, especially Craig and Allie. Once she arrived the boxes disappeared totally in a week's time. She has a way of getting the kids to do stuff that would make a drill sergeant envious."

"I bet she was popular on base."

His chuckle spiced the air. "Yeah. A few sergeants came calling, especially when she was cooking certain dishes. I usually had a guest at least a couple of times a week."

"Did that bother you?"

"I'd do anything to make my aunt happy. She was a lifesaver for us after my wife died." He backed away toward the entrance. "Excuse me while I find the rest of my family and let them know you're here. Dinner shouldn't be long. I hope you're hungry. I think Aunt Mae went overboard."

"It smells wonderful," Beth said, taking a deep breath of air laced with the scents of spices, onions and meat.

"Pot roast with potatoes and carrots. I can vouch that it's delicious." Samuel left, climbing the stairs.

The crackling of the fire and the ticking of the clock on the mantel were the only noises Beth heard for a moment. Then from upstairs the children's voices drifted to her. Someone dropped something along the lines of a bowling ball from the way it sounded. Now, that's more like a house with three children in it, she thought.

She turned to the fire and stretched her hands out to

warm them. Scanning the family photographs on the mantel, Beth paused at a portrait of Samuel, his children and a beautiful woman, petite, with medium brown hair and sparkling dark eyes, dressed in a soft creation of turquoise-blue. His wife. Jane looked a lot like her, while Craig and Allie looked like their father. Ruth's beauty complemented Samuel's handsome face. They had been a stunning couple.

Beth glanced down at the bulky sweater that added a few more pounds to a body already overweight. She frowned.

The pounding of footsteps on the stairs alerted Beth to the arrival of the children—at least Craig and Allie. They entered the room as though they had been in a race, with Craig winning. They both greeted her and plopped down on the couch, Allie giving the cushion several extra bounces.

"You're Jane's teacher. I've seen you at church." Allie settled next to her brother, nudging him.

He poked his sister back. "She'll be down in a second. She's on the phone. Dad's making her get off."

Beth opened her mouth to interject something when Allie said, "She's in trouble. She called a friend long distance without telling Dad. She isn't supposed to. She didn't think Dad would find out, but he always does."

Beth clamped her lips together to keep from laughing. Samuel's children were a breath of fresh air. Jane probably didn't think so, but Beth did.

Samuel came back into the room with Jane following

him, a sullen expression on her face, which looked so much like her beautiful mother's if only the young girl would smile. "Allie," he said in warning, giving her a stern look before heading toward the kitchen.

Jane mumbled something that sounded like hello and slouched into one of the maroon chairs, her legs sprawled out in front of her, crossed at the ankles. She glared at her little brother and sister.

"It's good to see you, Jane." Beth sat in the other maroon chair.

"Oh, I forgot you got a call earlier," Craig said to Jane.

"Who?"

"Some boy, I think."

Jane straightened, leaning forward, trying to appear nonchalant but not quite coming across that way. "You think? Who was it? You know you're not supposed to answer if you can't take a message."

Craig tapped his finger against his chin and rolled his eyes toward the ceiling. "Now, let me see. Bud. No. Brad. No."

"Dad!" Jane yelled.

Craig snapped his fingers. "I know. It was Sue."

"Sue! She's not a boy."

Craig grinned. "Yeah, I know."

"Dad!"

Samuel reentered the living room with Aunt Mae behind him. "We have a guest." He peered at each of his children, ending with Jane. "Remember your manners."

Listening to the children carry on brought back

memories of when Beth had had all her siblings living at home. She had refereed many fights between them and knew exactly what Samuel had to deal with even though she had never been a parent. Those days were over with, had been for the past four years when her sister, Holly, had graduated and left her and Daniel for college.

"I need some help setting the table."

Beth started to offer, but Aunt Mae pointed to Allie and Craig. "Come on, you two. You need to earn your keep. Wash up before you get the plates."

After the children left, Aunt Mae said, "I'm glad you could join us this evening, Beth. I've heard so much about you. You do quite a bit around the church."

Beth absolutely hated compliments because she never knew what to do with them. If life were a stage production, her favorite place would be blending in with the scenery. "No more than others do."

"That's not what I hear. I know we're going to get along famously. Dinner's in ten minutes." Aunt Mae hurried back into the kitchen as a crash sounded.

Samuel skirted the chair Jane was in to sit on the couch across from his daughter. "I'm glad we have a few minutes alone. Jane, I wanted you to know I signed the papers today for you to be tested. Dr. Simpson said she would be calling you into her office over the next several weeks."

Jane's narrowed gaze flitted to Beth, then to her dad. "I can't miss class."

Samuel's eyes widened. "That's the first time you've

ever said that. Dr. Simpson assures me she won't take you from your core classes."

"I don't want to miss drawing." Jane folded her arms over her chest.

Beth was going to break one of her rules and interfere in a family discussion. "Jane, this is important for you. Dr. Simpson may be able to help you. In my class you won't have to make up any work you miss while she's testing you. That's how strongly I feel about the testing."

Jane shot to her feet, her arms stiff at her sides. "Don't you two understand? I am not dumb! I will not be tested!" With tears glistening in her eyes, she stormed from the room.

Chapter Four

Samuel stared at the doorway where Jane had disappeared, a frown marring the perfection of his features. "That didn't go well."

"No," Beth answered, uncrossing then crossing her legs again.

He swung his gaze to hers. "Any suggestions?"

The vulnerability evident in Samuel called to her, and she couldn't resist it. "Let me talk to her. Give me a few minutes." She rose and started for the stairs.

"Jane's room is the first one on the left, and thanks."

She paused at the bottom of the steps and smiled back at him. "You're welcome, but I haven't done anything yet."

Relief lit his eyes. "I'm just glad you're willing to try, because I've run out of things to do."

Beth made her way up the stairs, not quite sure what to say to Jane. *Lord, help me to approach her the right way. Help me to make her understand it's okay to ask for help, that we all have weaknesses we need to work on.*

At the closed door that Beth assumed was Jane's room, she stared at the dark wood, waiting for some kind of inspiration to strike. She had to reach the teenager or Jane would fail most of her classes.

She knew what it was like.

That was it! Beth had never talked to anyone about her struggles in school, but she was going to talk to Jane. Beth rapped several times on the door.

"Go away! I'm not hungry!" the teenager shouted from inside the room.

"Jane, it's Miss Coleman. May I have a word with you?" Beth clasped her hands together and rubbed her palms back and forth.

Silence stretched to two minutes. Then three.

Sighing, Beth started to leave.

The door swung open and Jane stood in the entrance. "I don't need to be tested."

"May I come in and talk to you?"

Jane hugged the door as if it held her up. "There's nothing you can say that will make me want to be tested."

"That may be true, but I still would like to talk to you." Beth moved toward Jane, and the teenager stepped out of the way and allowed Beth into her room.

Taking in the area before her, Beth noted the neat, organized items on the desk, dresser and bedside tables. No clothes were on the floor and even posters hung on the walls. A forest-green bedspread covered the made bed, which surprised Beth the most. It didn't look the room of any teenager she knew.

"You could give my brothers and sister lessons on keeping their rooms clean. Most of the time I never saw the floor in my youngest brother's bedroom. I think Daniel thought the floor was the trash can." Beth gestured toward the chair at the desk. "May I sit?"

"Sure." Jane shrugged and sat cross-legged on her bed, her hands grasping her knees.

After easing onto the hard-backed chair, Beth hesitated, not sure where to begin. It was part of her past she didn't dwell on. Looking at Jane, though, Beth knew that if it helped the young girl, then she had to tell her.

"Jane, when I was growing up, for years I didn't know what was wrong with me. I struggled to read, and had to memorize every word. I couldn't sound out words like the other kids. My spelling was awful. Again, because I had to memorize everything. Thankfully I was determined to read, but it didn't come easily to me, especially when confronted with new words."

Jane averted her gaze, dropping her head and rubbing her hands down her jeans.

In her lap Beth laced her fingers, their tips turning red from her tight grip. "The day my mother decided to take me to a specialist to have me tested was the best day of my life. I finally got the help I needed. Of course, at the time I didn't think it was a good thing. I was angry at my mother. I didn't want the kids to think I was different, dumb. I even told my mom I wouldn't do what the lady asked me to do." Beth paused, waiting to see if Jane would say anything.

The teenager remained quiet with her head down, her hands continuing to rub her jeans.

Drawing in a fortifying breath, Beth offered up a silent prayer for help, then said, "The other students don't have to know you're being tested. This is between you and Dr. Simpson. No one else."

Jane finally lifted her head, tears shining in her eyes. "What if they want me to be in *those* classes?"

"Special education classes?"

Jane nodded.

"I don't see a need for that. You're very smart. You just need to learn some compensating skills. Once we find out why exactly you're having problems, then we can come up with ways to level the playing field for you in your classes. Make things a little easier for you."

A tear rolled down Jane's face. She scrubbed it away. "I don't want to be different."

"We're all different. Everyone has strengths and weaknesses. Every child in the school. Some can draw like you. Others can do math as well as you. You could probably tutor some of your classmates in math. Please let us try to help you."

Another tear, then another coursed down Jane's cheeks. "I'm not dumb. I know how to read."

"I never said you didn't. But when you write, you're struggling and it takes you a lot longer to read the passages. When I'm lecturing, you aren't taking notes. Why is that, Jane?"

The teenager bit down on her bottom lip for a few seconds, then said, "Because I can't keep up with what you're saying. So what's the use?" Glaring at Beth, she uncrossed her legs and shoved herself to her feet. "Fine. Go ahead and test me."

Beth rose. "Remember, Jane, I have a master's degree in English and if I can do it, so can you. Anything is possible, but when you need help, you need to learn to accept it." Just as she had finally, with a great deal of patience from the lady who had tutored her during elementary and junior high school. She hoped Jane wasn't as stubborn as she had been.

"We'll see."

Beth headed for the door. "I bet dinner is ready by now. Are you coming down?" She took a deep breath of the air peppered with the scent of spices, bread and meat. "It sure smells wonderful."

"I guess so."

Jane followed Beth down the stairs. She felt the teenager's gaze on her the whole way to the living room where Samuel waited. His hopeful look greeted Beth and his daughter.

"Jane has agreed to the testing," Beth said, praying the girl didn't back out.

The teenager remained silent.

Relief washed over his features. "I'm glad, Jane." Samuel rose. "Aunt Mae says dinner is ready. I think

Allie and Craig are already at the table, chomping at the bit to eat."

"They're always hungry," Jane muttered as she moved toward the dining room.

Beth started toward the room, too. Samuel reached out and stopped her with a hand on her arm. She glanced back, very aware that his touch did odd things to her pulse rate.

"How did you get her to agree?" he asked, his voice pitched low.

"I told her about my learning problem in school." It wasn't something she easily shared with others because of the painful memories of her struggles, but it felt right with Samuel—and Jane. Maybe her hardship while growing up would help the teenager cope with her own problem.

"Thank you. This is one father who is grateful for any help he can get."

"Dad, I'm starved. C'mon!"

Samuel chuckled. "Craig's always impatient."

Beth entered the dining room one step ahead of Samuel. A large oblong oak table with six chairs dominated the room. Four people, seated with napkins in their laps, looked expectantly at them.

"Daddy, can I say grace tonight?"

"Sure, Allie." Samuel pulled out the chair next to his at the head of the table and waited for Beth to be seated before scooting it forward.

When he took his place he bowed his head, which was

Allie's signal to say, "God bless this food and help me to get invited to Sally Ann's party next weekend. Amen."

Beth smiled as she lifted her head.

"Who's Sally Ann?" Samuel asked, shaking out his cloth napkin and laying it in his lap.

"The most popular girl in my class. I've *got* to be invited!"

"We just moved here, honey. She may not have had a chance to get to know you yet."

"All the girls are getting invited. If I'm left out, no one will like me."

"Dad, can you pass the roast beef?" Craig asked, squirming around in his chair as though it were on fire.

Samuel looked down at the platter next to his plate and said, "Sorry." He took two slices of the meat and passed it to Beth, who was next to Craig. "Allie, they will like you. Just give them time to get to know you."

"If we didn't move around so much…" Jane let the rest of her sentence trail off into silence while she stared at her empty plate, ignoring the meat being passed around the table.

Samuel started the potatoes, then the carrots. "Hopefully that will change now that I'm out of the army, Jane."

"Good, Daddy. I'm tired of havin' to make new friends all the time." Allie scooped several potatoes onto her plate and only one small carrot.

Beth listened to the exchange at the table and remembered the days she'd had her sister and brothers at home and they had sat down to eat dinner. Some of their conversations had been lively. Now when she ate dinner the house was quiet. She often found herself with the radio on in the kitchen while she ate, because she still wasn't used to all that silence.

Jane filled her plate with the vegetables and said, "I have decided to become a vegetarian."

"Since when?" Aunt Mae asked, passing the rolls around the table.

"Since now. In biology today we saw a film on the meat packing industry. Yuck! You should have seen how—"

"I don't think we should discuss that at the table, Jane. We have a guest, remember?"

"I want to hear about it."

"Not now, Craig."

The firmness in Samuel's voice, accompanied by a frown on his face, emphasized the subject was to be dropped. Beth thought back to some of the topics her siblings had tried to discuss while eating. Thankfully she'd developed a stomach lined with iron.

For a good minute silence ruled at the table while everyone ate, their attention totally focused on their plates.

Beth took a bite of the roast beef, so tender she could cut it with her fork. "Mmm. Mae, this is delicious. Every year the women at church put out a recipe book in conjunction with the ladies' retreat. You should contribute this recipe."

"When do they do it?"

"In the fall. In fact, they'll need a person to put it together this year, since I'll be leaving and won't be able to." Beth hadn't thought about that job until she'd mentioned it to Mae. She really needed to sit down and make a list of the tasks she did at church and school and make sure someone else was lined up to do them.

Jane pinned her full attention on Beth. "You're leaving? When?"

The tone in Jane's voice chilled Beth. The expression on the teenager's face made Beth feel as though she had betrayed her. "Not until this summer. I'd never leave in the middle of the school year."

Some of the hostility evaporated as Jane looked away and picked at her potatoes with her fork. "Oh."

"I'm getting the impression you do a lot around the church." Samuel took a sip of his water.

"I like to be kept busy."

"As I've told Samuel before, working is good, but you also have to learn to play, too." Mae reached for another roll in the basket, sliced it and slathered butter on it.

"Yeah, I like to play," Craig chimed in.

"Me, too. Can I go play now, Daddy?" Allie hopped up.

Samuel lifted his hand, palm outward. "Hold it. We have company and not everyone is through with dinner yet."

Allie plopped back into the chair. "Sorry. I forgot."

"So what do you like to play with?" Beth asked, liking Samuel's youngest daughter, who was so full of energy. Beth wished she had half of it to help her get through a Friday night. Weariness nibbled at her, her shoulders aching, exhaustion stinging her eyes.

"Dolls. Daddy built me a playhouse and furniture for it. Do you want to see it?"

"I would love to, after dinner."

Allie grinned.

"How about you, Craig? What do you like to play with?"

"My Game Boy."

"My brother, Daniel, likes to do that, too."

"How old is he?"

"Nineteen. In the past few years, though, he doesn't play like he used to." Beth turned to Jane. "What do you like to do with your free time?"

She shrugged. "Listen to music. Draw."

"She drew me once. I have it up in my room. I can show you that, too." Allie gulped down the last of her milk.

"How about you, Beth?"

She looked toward Samuel and said, "Read whenever I get the chance. I've even started writing a bit. Short stories. That kind of thing."

"So you do have free time."

"Some. More now that my sister and brothers are gone." When she said the last sentence, something nagged at her. She should be celebrating that fact, but she wasn't. For years she had wanted more time for herself, and now she wasn't so sure that was really what she wanted. Maybe she was suffering from empty nest syndrome.

Samuel watched Beth stoop on the floor of Allie's bedroom and look inside the two-story Victorian dollhouse he had designed and built for his daughter over the previous year. It had been a kind of therapy for him and now that it was complete, he needed another project. He liked working with his hands. Maybe another dollhouse for the big Fourth of July auction the church always had for the outreach program.

"This is wonderful, Samuel. You're very talented."

"My daddy is the best." With her chin lifted at a proud angle, Allie stood next to Beth. "I helped Aunt Mae sew the curtains and bedspreads."

"You've thought of everything a home should have." Beth caressed the white cat curled by the fireplace with glowing logs in its grate. "Who painted the fireplace, the scenes out the windows?"

"Jane. Isn't she good?" Allie ran her finger across one large window that depicted a meadow scene with yellow, red and purple wildflowers growing abundantly in its field.

"Yes. I especially like her portrait of you over your bed." Gesturing toward the framed pen-and-ink picture of Allie that Jane had drawn, Beth pushed to her feet. "This was a family project, then?"

"Yeah, even Craig helped Daddy with sanding. He's learning to use Daddy's tools."

Beth turned to Samuel. "You have a workshop?"

"I did. I don't have one set up yet here."

"I imagine the basement could serve as a workshop. If I remember correctly, it's pretty big and only has the furnace and laundry room. They don't take up even half the space."

Samuel ran his hand through his hair, massaging the back of his neck. "I've been so busy I haven't really thought about setting up a workshop."

"You should. You're very good."

He felt his cheeks flame and was surprised at his reaction. Nothing usually threw him, but for some reason Beth's compliment had. "I've thought about making a dollhouse for the annual auction."

"That would be great! Jesse and Darcy would love it."

"Aren't you the head of the auction?"

"Yes, but I'm turning the reins over to them. Remember, I'll be gone by then."

"Oh, yeah. I forgot." The thought of having only a few months to get to know Beth bothered him. He chalked it up to the fact she was an intricate part of the church and would be sorely missed when she left.

Beth heaved a deep sigh. "I'd better be going. It's been a long week and will be a busy weekend now that Daniel is home."

"I'll walk you to your car."

"You don't have to. I know the way."

"I know. I want to." Samuel fell into step beside Beth as they made their way down the stairs to the coat closet.

He helped Beth slip into her long black wool coat with a fake fur collar. After she fitted her hands into her black leather gloves, she made her way to the kitchen to tell Aunt Mae goodbye and thank her for the delicious dinner. When they walked back to the foyer, Samuel opened his front door, a blast of cold striking him in the face.

"Really, my car is right there in your driveway."

"Wait." Samuel snagged a jacket from a hanger and quickly donned it.

Outside on the porch a cold breeze swirled about them, making Samuel instinctively draw closer to Beth in an attempt to keep her warm. She didn't move away.

"I'm not a winter person. I'm really looking forward to spring."

He chuckled. "We have less than two months till the weather gets warmer."

Beth hurried down the steps toward her car. "Nothing beats spring. The colors are breathtaking after a drab winter. God sure knew what He was doing."

At her Jeep Samuel stopped her with a hand on her arm. "Do you think it will take long to get Jane tested?"

"I'll try to push it along."

"Why didn't I see this before now?"

"Jane has probably been very good at covering up her weaknesses."

"I should have been more aware of what was going on with Jane at school."

"When a child moves from school to school, she often gets lost in the shuffle."

His chest tightened, guilt gnawing at him. "In other words, we shouldn't have moved so often."

"You didn't have a choice. That was your job."

"We always have a choice. I should have quit the army long before I did. But up until Ruth's death everything seemed fine. I can't believe I missed the signals. Ruth handled everything. I…" Samuel couldn't finish his sentence. His wife had kept the home running while he had kept the church running. It had worked, or at least until now he'd thought it had. What had he missed out on with his children? His guilt grew to knot his stomach.

"The important thing is that you're doing something about it now. Maybe I'm wrong and Jane is just rebelling."

"I don't know if I want you to be wrong or right."

Beth reached out and laid her hand over his on the car door. "Let's wait and see what the testing shows before we start throwing blame around. And even then, I strongly advise against blaming anyone or anything. It's wasted energy."

He smiled. "You're very wise, Beth Coleman. Have you thought about going into counseling?"

"I'll leave that job up to you. Teaching is what I love to do." She slid behind the steering wheel.

Samuel leaned into the car while she started it. "From what I've seen, you're very good at your job."

"And from what I've seen, you're very good at yours. The sermon last Sunday was inspiring."

He glanced away toward the streetlight that illuminated a part of his yard and the church. The building's gray stone facade mocked him. Its towering bell tower housing the brass bell that rang every Sunday jutted up toward heaven. In that moment he didn't feel worthy of setting foot in the church.

Guilt ridden, he stared at the dark shadows that surrounded the Garden of Serenity at the side of the building, where members of his congregation often found solace. In the dead of winter with snow still covering the ground he had walked its stone paths, sat on a wooden bench and looked at the pond, hoping for some kind of inspiration, and yet nothing had come to him. Instead, his sermon last Sunday had been a recycled one from when he had been in the army. He'd thought it had been an appropriate one right before Lent, concerning Jesus' mission in the days preceding His death. More than anything he had needed to reconfirm why Christ had died for them.

"Are you all right?"

Samuel blinked, tearing his gaze away from the church. "Yes, I was just thinking about the garden."

"It won't be too long before we'll have to tend to it. Spring is around the corner." Beth started her car. "But even in winter I like to visit the garden from time to time. There's a certain beauty in the starkness of nature at this time of year. And with the pine trees and holly bushes it isn't totally brown."

"Is the garden's upkeep another one of your little projects around the church?"

Beth laughed. "No, I have a brown thumb when it comes to plants. Cooking's my forte. Joshua Markham is in charge of the garden."

"Good, because I have to confess I have a *black* thumb when it comes to gardening. I've been known to kill a cactus because I underwatered it. I have to admit I can't cook, either."

"But you do beautiful things with your hands. I mean…"

Samuel heard the flustered tone in Beth's voice, but couldn't make out her features. He could imagine a blush tainting her cheeks. She blushed so easily, but the red tinge added a glow to her face, enhancing her beauty. "I know what you mean. God gives us each a talent."

"Yes, and we need to emphasize that to Jane."

"I've tried. But for some reason she doesn't think my opinion counts. She once told me I have to love her because I'm her father."

Beth sighed. "I wish that were true."

A touch of pain laced her words as though Beth knew firsthand the falseness of that conception. In a perfect world all parents would love their children and there would be no mental or physical abuse. He knew from counseling parishioners that wasn't true. Was Beth's knowledge derived from being a teacher or from personal experience? He remembered her telling him about her father leaving her mother. He shivered, thinking of the answer to that question.

Beth reached over and switched on her heater. "I'd better go before you freeze."

Samuel watched her disappear down the street, suddenly wishing that the evening wasn't over. Her caring nature added a charm to Beth Coleman that was very appealing. That observation took him by surprise.

He hadn't thought of a woman being appealing since the death of his wife, his high school sweetheart, the only person he'd ever seriously dated.

"Then if we all are in agreement, we'll put Jane on an individual education plan where she can utilize these modifications we have discussed to help her with her auditory processing problem." Dr. Simpson, the school psychologist, shuffled some papers and produced a sheet of paper, which she signed then slid across the table to Samuel. "If you'll sign here, saying that she qualifies for special education services under the category of learning disabilities, Ms. Jones will go over the IEP."

Beth noticed Jane pale and ball her hands in her lap when Nancy Simpson said "learning disabilities." The teenager's teeth dug into her lower lip. Beth's heart wrenched at the sight of the child fighting back tears.

"Jane, you should sign, too." Dr. Simpson guided the paper toward her after Samuel had penned his name.

Jane stared at the paper on the table before her. She started to say something, but her lower lip trembled. She dropped her head, her shoulders hunched over.

Sitting next to the teenager, Beth covered Jane's hand with hers. "No one needs to know you are on an IEP unless you choose to tell. This is kept strictly confidential."

"Everyone will know. They'll think I'm dumb."

The waver in the teenager's voice tightened a band about Beth's chest. She knew exactly how Jane felt. She realized Jane would have to come to terms with her disability in order to get the help she needed. That wasn't easy when she was a fifteen-year-old in a new school. Jane should have a circle of friends much as Darcy, Jesse, Zoey, Tanya and she had. Then maybe the teenage girl wouldn't feel so alone.

"It won't come from us, Jane. No one will know you'll have a copy of the teacher's notes. No one will know you have extended time for your tests. All these accommodations can be carried out without others knowing."

Jane's head jerked up, and she glared at each person sitting at the table. Tears shone in her eyes. She shoved back her chair and shot out of it. "I won't sign the paper." She rushed for the door.

Chapter Five

Samuel's gaze snagged Beth's across the empty chair between them. A dazed expression in his eyes told of his own overwhelming feelings concerning the past thirty minutes. A myriad of tests and their scores had been thrown at him, along with a list of recommendations to help Jane. He might have thought he had been prepared, but from his look Beth doubted he really had been.

Beth rose. "Let me see if I can explain again that everything will be kept private." She directed her statement to Samuel, who nodded.

She left the conference room and went in search of Jane. Beth's black pumps clicked against the tile floor, echoing in the empty hall, as she walked toward her room. Jane had probably escaped outside; she was maybe even at her father's car waiting for him at this very moment. Beth decided to grab her coat and check the parking lot. The cold chill of a late February afternoon would go right through her if she didn't.

She stepped into her classroom and halted. Jane stood at the window, her shoulders sagging forward, her chin resting on her chest, her head touching the cold pane.

"I'm not going back in there, Miss Coleman." Jane drew in a huge breath and held it for a few extra seconds. "I saw how everyone was looking at me. I don't need anyone's help. If I want to do good in school, I will."

Beth covered the space between them, stopping a few feet from Jane. "I've looked at your records from your previous schools. I know you can do well in school. Up until a few years ago your grades were good. I noticed you had some trouble in elementary school, especially with reading, but you seemed to overcome that."

Jane spun about and took a step back. "So you're wondering what happened. I don't care anymore about school. I'm—I'm…" Tears slipped from her eyes and rolled down her cheeks. As quickly as she wiped them away, more appeared.

Beth moved closer. "I know when I reached high school I started to have more trouble. The work was harder, so therefore it took longer to do my homework and assignments, to memorize what I needed to know, to read the work I needed to do. Is that what's happening?"

Jane kept her gaze turned away, but nodded.

"Some of the things we're suggesting to help you will make it easier for you. Hopefully you won't feel so overwhelmed."

Jane squared her shoulders and looked Beth in the eye. "I'm not overwhelmed. I don't care anymore."

"Why don't you?"

Her bottom lip began to tremble. Jane bit into it and looked away.

Determined to discover what was behind Jane's statement, Beth stepped even closer and laid a hand on the teenager's shoulder. "Why, Jane?"

"My grades…"

Beth moved into Jane's direct line of vision. She lifted the young girl's chin. "I care, Jane."

"My grades were important—" Jane swallowed hard "—to my mom. She helped me study when I was having trouble."

"You didn't care about having good grades?"

"No." With a sheen to her eyes Jane stared at Beth. "Yes, I wanted good grades, too."

"But that changed when your mom died?"

Jane wrenched away from Beth and crossed her arms over her chest. "Everything changed when my mom died."

Her palms sweaty, Beth curled her hands into tight fists. With a conscious effort she tried to relax against the radiator as though the conversation they were having was mundane, unimportant. "You know, Jane, you and I are a lot alike."

Jane leaned back against the other end of the radiator. "How so?"

The girl's tone of voice spoke of her doubts that a teacher and she would be alike in any way. Beth suppressed a grin and said, "I lost my mother when I was nineteen. She was my world, and when she died I didn't know what to do. There are times I still think about her and my heart breaks even after all these years."

Jane slanted a look toward her. "You do?"

"But she's always in here." Beth touched her heart. "No one can take that away from me." She ran her hand along the radiator, feeling its heat chase away the chills the memories brought. "If you want, I'll tutor you at your house. No one will need to know. It'll be between you and me. We can do it several times a week in the evening. What do you say?"

"Why would you do that?"

"Because I care what happens to you. Jane, I think you're very smart and have a lot of potential. I don't want to see you throw it away. Will you let me help you?"

"I still don't want to sign the papers."

"I know. The accommodations will be there for you to utilize if you choose to. It's not easy asking for help. I know. I've been in your shoes."

Someone cleared his throat. Beth looked toward the doorway at the same time as Jane. Samuel stood just a foot inside the room. How much had he heard? Beth wondered, and pushed herself away from the radiator. "Is the meeting over?"

"Yes. Are you ready to go home, Jane?"

"You mean I don't have to go back and sign the papers?"

"Not if you don't want to."

She straightened, her chin tilted at a proud angle. "I don't. I'm going to my locker and get my books."

When Jane left, the silence in the room grew. Beth wanted to ask if Samuel had overheard any of their conversation, but couldn't find the words. She made her way to her desk to gather up her papers. "I've offered to help Jane in the evening a couple of times a week. Is that all right with you?"

"Where?"

"Your house. She doesn't want anyone to find out."

"Do you have that kind of time?"

Beth swung her gaze to Samuel's. "I do for her. This is something I want to do, unless you object."

"No! I'm thrilled she has agreed. Maybe you can reach her. No one else has been able to since her mother died."

The touch of vulnerability always just below Samuel's surface emerged. It was obvious that his wife's death had deeply affected more than Jane. He was floundering just as much as his daughter. Could she help both father and daughter? Would she be able to before she left Sweetwater?

Lord, give me the knowledge and strength to know what to do to help both of them. They are lost and need Your love and guidance.

When Jane finished explaining the functions of each branch of government, Beth said, "I think you're ready for your government test tomorrow. What do you think?"

Jane raised one shoulder in a shrug. "I guess so."

"Did it help to have a copy of the teacher's lecture notes?"

Jane turned her head away, doodling on the piece of paper in front of her. "Yeah," she murmured in such a low voice Beth wouldn't have heard her if she hadn't been sitting right next to her at the table.

"Good. Then I'll continue to get your teachers' notes for you." Beth hoped one day that Jane would begin to ask for the notes on her own, but until then she would. Jane needed to be convinced the accommodation worked for her.

Beth knew the second Samuel appeared in the dining-room doorway. She felt the power of his gaze and met it with a smile that lightened her heart. For the past month she had been coming to his house to tutor Jane three times a week, and every time she was about to leave he would appear and they would end up talking. At first about Jane. Now their conversation covered just about every topic in the news—but nothing really personal and certainly nothing about his deceased wife. Beth wasn't sure how she could help him when he wouldn't let her in.

"Jane, there's a call for you. You can get it in my office."

Jane furrowed her brow. "I can pick up in the kitchen."

"You might want to take this call in my office."

The teenager pushed herself to her feet, dropping the pencil she had been doodling with onto the open notebook. "Who is it?"

"A boy."

"It is?" The perplexed look on Jane's face deepened as she headed toward her father's office, her steps quickening.

"Are you two through for the evening?" Samuel came into the room and stood on the other side of the table.

"Yes." Beth gathered her books and papers and stuffed them into her briefcase. "A boy calling Jane. I wonder who it is."

"I was sorely tempted to ask his name, but I suspect Jane wouldn't be too thrilled if I did. But you can bet I will be asking my daughter when she is through talking to the young man. I'm a firm believer in knowing what is going on in my children's lives. And this latest problem with Jane at school tells me I have been neglecting that responsibility. I won't do that again."

"Don't be so hard on yourself. Kids can be great at hiding things, and with you all moving so much the previous schools didn't pick up on Jane's problems, either. Sadly, that happens."

"But after only a few weeks, you saw something." Samuel skirted the table and took her briefcase from her to carry to her car.

"It's because Jane reminds me of myself at her age."

"You mentioned something about that before. You had the same kind of problems in school as my daughter?" He started for the foyer.

"Yes. I struggled for years. Actually I still do. I changed to trying to learn Portuguese on tape, but I'm not doing as well as I'd hoped. I have a hard time hearing the different sounds. I'm hoping when I live in a country it will come faster to me."

"I didn't know."

"Not many people do. I don't broadcast my diffi-culties, just as Jane doesn't. Here I am a perfectly in-telligent woman and I can't seem to learn a foreign language. It's not something I want everyone to know, so I guess we all have our secrets."

"But you shared yours with me."

"To help you to understand Jane better and why she kept so much to herself and didn't ask you for help. Haven't you had a problem you haven't asked another soul for help with?"

The frown that touched his features, his look that sliced away told Beth the answer to that question. He had his secrets, too.

Samuel busied himself by retrieving Beth's wool coat from the closet. He helped her to slip into the garment, then reached around to open the front door. "Are you sure I can't pay you for your tutoring?"

"No. We've been through this before, Samuel. I don't want your money. I'm doing this for Jane."

"Then at least let me take you out for dinner."

"I don't—"

"Please, Beth. Do this for me. I feel like I should do something for you."

She paused on the porch, looking back at Samuel framed in the doorway with the light behind him and his features in the shadows. Dinner? Like a real date? The reason she hadn't pushed him to speak about his personal life, even though she needed to know details to help him, was that she had felt it would be a mistake. The more she found out about Samuel, the more she liked him and he didn't fit into her future plans at all, especially with his ready-made family. Besides, how could she compare to his high school sweetheart, whom he had loved so much that his grief had thrown his life into turmoil, as a few of his comments had indicated?

"You don't have to do a thing. But if it's important to you, I'll go to dinner with you." The second she agreed to go out with him, a damp layer of perspiration coated her face even though it was chilly outside.

A date! What would she wear? What would they talk about? They had already exhausted every topic concerning current events. She needed help.

"Great. How about Saturday night? We could go to dinner and a movie. I'll pick you up at seven—and wear something nice."

"Okay. Where are we going?"

"It's a surprise."

"But—"

"No, Beth, I'm not going to tell you, but it will be a special place. That is the least I can do for you."

A surprise? She wasn't good with surprises, but the firm line of his jaw told her no amount of pleading would get the name of the restaurant out of him. She reached for her briefcase. "I can find my way to my car. Stay inside where it's warm."

When her hand clasped the handle, his brushed across her knuckles, sending sparks up her arm. She snatched her briefcase and spun about, hurrying down the steps. He remained in the doorway, watching her retreat. Not until she had backed out of his driveway did he close the front door.

Her hand shook on the steering wheel and a thin layer of perspiration still covered her face. It was way too hot in her car, and she didn't even have the heater on. She should have removed her coat before climbing into the Jeep.

The minute she arrived at her house, she rushed to the phone and called Jesse. "Help! I have a date."

"Okay. This isn't the end of the world, Beth. Zoey and I will help you find something to wear." Jesse opened the door to a chic dress shop along Main Street.

"I love to shop for clothes. This will be fun." Zoey followed Beth into the store, bringing up the rear.

"It may be fun for you two, but not for me. I don't like to shop." Beth scanned the racks and racks of clothing and hated the thought of trying on one dress after another. It had always made her feel so fat. "I'm not easy to fit. If it's right on the top, it isn't on the bottom."

"We all have something to contend with. I have a hard time finding clothes short enough. Not every place carries petite." Zoey went straight for the after-five dresses and began looking through them.

Jesse checked out the nice pantsuits, while Beth stood

in the middle of the store, probably looking lost if the expression on the saleswoman's face was any indication.

She hurried over to Beth. "May I be of help?"

"I'm just browsing."

Zoey turned toward the saleswoman. "She needs a special dress for a dinner date to a nice restaurant. Any suggestions?"

The older woman stepped back and allowed her gaze to trek down Beth's length. When she reestablished eye contact with Beth, she said, "I have a black number that would look great on you. We just received it and it's still in the back. Let me get it for you."

Zoey came to stand beside Beth while Jesse continued to look. "Black would look good on you."

"But I always wear black and gray. I need something different. Isn't that the object of this shopping trip? I have several nice black dresses at home." Because she'd heard once that black was slimming, she added silently.

"There are times black is appropriate. I've seen your black dresses and they aren't nice enough. Too practical. For a dinner at a nice restaurant black can be just right."

"With the right touches," Jesse added, throwing them a glance over her shoulder.

When the saleswoman walked out holding a short black dress on a hanger, its soft folds falling in a graceful pattern, Beth knew it was perfect for her—if only it fit. She took it from the older woman and headed for the dressing room. After slipping the black outfit over her head, she faced the mirror while struggling with the zipper in back. Zipping it up, she assessed herself. For once she believed that black was a slimming color.

The silk material fell in soft folds to below her knees, disguising her thighs. She immediately thought of the black shoes she had worn to her party at the end of January. They would be perfect with the dress. Its scooped neckline and thin spaghetti straps screamed for something around her neck, though. She thought of her limited jewelry and wasn't sure what she would wear to complement the outfit.

When she stepped out of the dressing room, she found both Zoey and Jesse waiting. In Zoey's hand was a red feather boa.

She handed it to Beth. "This will be perfect with it. Drape it around your neck."

Beth waved her hand toward the red boa. "I can't wear that!"

"Yes, you can. You wanted something different. This is different." Zoey draped it around Beth's neck, then moved back to evaluate the outfit. "This will knock his socks off."

Beth's eyes grew wide. "I don't want to knock our minister's socks off."

"Why not? He's single and eligible. You're single and eligible. Perfect." Jesse slowly circled her with her finger against her chin. "Yes, I believe, Zoey, that's the perfect touch."

"What was I thinking, bringing you two to help me shop for something to wear?"

"That we have good taste and won't steer you in the wrong direction." Zoey turned Beth around and gently pushed her toward the dressing room. "She'll take all of it," she said to the saleswoman.

"Next we need to visit my hair salon," Jesse called out as Beth disappeared into the room.

Beth rolled her eyes and wondered what had come over her when she had called Jesse for help. Insanity, she decided as she donned her gray wool pantsuit with its white long-sleeved shirt. Red! She never wore red!

The doorbell rang promptly at seven. Running her hand through her new shorter hair that framed her face and fell to just below her chin in soft curls, Beth took one last look at herself in the mirror and drew in a deep, cleansing breath as though that would fortify her for the rest of the evening. Why hadn't she dated more? The answer was that for so many years she had been wrapped up in raising a family and she hadn't had much time. Then most of the men she'd known had become unavailable and the available ones she'd known too well to want to date them. Now her inexperience left her a nervous wreck. Would her stomach ever stop roiling long enough for her to enjoy the dinner?

Beth quickly made her way to the foyer, checked to see if it was Samuel, then opened the front door. "Come in. I need to get my wrap. Is it cold outside?"

Samuel's face lit with a smile as his gaze took in her

attire. "Actually we have a breeze from the south and it's not too bad for March."

Backing toward the coat closet, Beth noted that Samuel was wearing a dark gray suit with a red tie. She fingered the red boa draped around her neck and hanging down her front. His gaze was riveted to her hand on it.

"I like that," he said, his voice low.

Its sound slipped down the length of her, warming every inch. Both of them had worn something red. She felt a kinship with him that surprised her, as though the color bonded them, when it really was something else—intangible, undefinable. With her gaze connected to his, Beth fumbled for her black coat with its fur collar.

Samuel stepped forward. "Here, let me get it for you." He reached around her, his arm brushing against hers, and snatched her coat off its hanger.

As he held it for her, Beth murmured, "Thank you." She was aware of him behind her, his breath fanning her neck. Her eyes slid closed and she breathed in his distinctive aftershave.

"You're beautiful tonight," he whispered close to her ear.

For the first time she actually felt beautiful. She knew she really wasn't, but his words touched her deeply, causing her pulse to race. She could not remember having a male say those words to her except her brothers when they had been young boys or when they had been trying to get something from her.

"Jesse and Zoey went shopping with me. Actually they insisted I go shopping with them and wouldn't take no for an answer."

"Who thought of this red boa?"

"Zoey. She loves red and gravitates toward anything red in a store." Beth gestured toward his tie. "Who picked out your red tie?"

A cloud descended over his expression. "My wife. Red was her favorite color."

"Oh" was all Beth could manage to say, heat suffusing her face. Her cheeks must rival her red boa, she thought.

The smile that graced Samuel's mouth seemed forced as he asked, "What is your favorite color?"

Beth grinned, not wanting the evening to start off awkwardly. "Yellow. I think some people probably think it's black or gray, because that's what I wear a lot, but I love what yellow represents—sunshine."

"Mine is green and I have no reason for liking it except that I've always felt that way since I was a little boy."

Beth moved toward the front door. "Are you going to tell me where we're going to eat dinner now?"

"Nope. It's a surprise. You'll know when we pull up to the restaurant."

"You know I don't like surprises."

"I'm still not going to tell you. I like to surprise people." Samuel pulled the door closed behind him and made sure it was locked before guiding Beth toward his Mustang, which was parked in her drive.

As Samuel backed out onto the street, Beth still felt

the impression of his fingers at the small of her back as he'd led her to his car. Her excitement grew as she thought of all the places they could be going. She rarely went out to eat except to a fast-food restaurant or Alice's Café. It had to be a very nice restaurant, since he wanted her to dress up—which excluded those places and most of the other ones in Sweetwater.

When he drove into the parking lot at the side of the best, most expensive restaurant in the county, she was at a loss for words. In all her years in Sweetwater she had never set foot inside, because she couldn't afford to eat at the place. That hadn't stopped her from dreaming about having dinner at Andre's.

"I think you've made a mistake," she said, turning slightly to face him in the car.

"A mistake?"

"Andre's is very expensive."

"I know. You won't accept money for tutoring Jane, so this is the next best thing. I want to show you how much I appreciate all the time you've spent working with my daughter."

"But—"

He pressed his fingers to her lips. "No buts, Beth. This evening is all about you."

The feel of his touch melted any reservations she had. How could she refuse?

When he escorted her into the restaurant she scanned the dimly lit room with elegantly set tables, the crystal and china gleaming in the candlelight. An arrangement of white roses adorned each table and gold utensils picked up the gold in the cream-colored china. She'd never seen anything so richly decorated except in a magazine.

After they were shown to a table set in an alcove, secluded and private, Beth opened her menu to find no prices were listed. She knew she was in trouble then. She had planned on ordering the cheapest item on the menu, but that was hard to figure out.

"Don't worry about the cost, Beth."

"But I'm on the budget committee and I know how much you make as our minister."

"Don't worry. I wouldn't have brought you here if I couldn't afford it. This won't cost me what it would have cost to hire a tutor for Jane." He laid his hand over hers on the white linen tablecloth and captured her gaze within his. "Besides, Beth, you deserve the best. You do so much for everyone else that it's about time someone did something for you."

Heat scorched her cheeks. Compliments always made her feel uneasy. She looked away and caught sight of Nick and Jesse sitting across the room from them. Her friend waved, a huge grin on her face. Suspicion began to dawn in Beth's mind.

"Did anyone suggest this restaurant to you?"

Samuel chuckled. "I got some help from one of my parishioners."

That would be the last time she confided in Jesse. Beth returned her friend's greeting with a narrowed gaze. "Jesse Blackburn?"

"Actually her husband, Nick."

"Nick!"

"I figured a man of his means would know the best place to eat in a fifty-mile radius."

"So Jesse didn't tell you I've always dreamed of having dinner at Andre's?"

One corner of his mouth hitched in a lopsided grin. "No, but thanks for letting me know my choice was a good one. It isn't every day a guy can make a lady's dream come true."

The appreciative gleam in his eyes, coupled with his heart-melting smile, sent her heartbeat racing. She dropped her gaze to the elaborate gold-and-cream china, his hand continuing to cover hers. Warmth crackled at the contact.

"What other dreams do you have, Beth Coleman? I know about traveling and seeing the world, and now this one. But surely you have others."

Her lungs expanded as she drew in a deep breath and held it for a few extra seconds. "Actually, I don't. Of course, I want my brothers and sister to do well."

His forehead creased. "Nothing else? No fame, fortune?"

"I'm a very simple person. I don't require a lot to be happy."

Samuel glanced beyond her right shoulder. "Hold that thought. I think our waiter is waiting for us to order." He slid his hand back and picked up the menu to study.

She missed his touch the second it was gone, and that

realization surprised her. She had always been sensible, never particularly getting all weak-kneed over any movie star or celebrity everyone else was raving about. Quickly she lifted her menu to peruse before she did something foolish like put her hand over his. After narrowing the choices to filet mignon and pork, she went with the roast pork with a crab stuffing, corn creamed mashed potatoes and steamed vegetables.

After the waiter took their orders, Beth leaned forward and asked, "What is one of your dreams? It's not fair for you to know two of mine and I don't know one of yours."

"Beth, haven't you heard life isn't fair?"

"Yes, and I won't accept that answer. Evading my question isn't an option."

He tapped his finger against his chin and looked toward the ceiling as though in deep thought. "Mmm. Let me see. What is a dream I've had?"

"No, what is a dream you have now?"

His eyes darkened, a somber expression descending. "To keep my family together."

She shook her head. "Your family is together."

"Not together so much as back to the way it once was before..." His words faded into silence.

"Before your wife died?"

He nodded.

"What happened?"

He opened his mouth to say something, but clamped it shut and stared off to the side of Beth. When he reestablished eye contact with her, he said, "I wasn't there for Ruth when she needed me the most. I couldn't help her. I had to watch her die from breast cancer and I could do nothing to take the pain away." He swallowed hard. "One of the last things she said to me was that she regretted most not being able to have another child with me. We'd both wanted another and had been trying for months. Then she died and I couldn't even deal with the three children I had. I was too busy grieving, questioning God for taking her from me."

The pain in his voice underscored the depth of the despair he had sunk to after his wife's death. Tears choked off her words, making it difficult to respond to him.

He pinned her with his intense gaze. "I haven't told anyone else this. I don't even know why I told you. I shouldn't have."

She reached toward him. "I'm glad you did." She suppressed her own reeling emotions to help him. "We can't go back, Samuel. You know that. We have to make a new future with what God has given us."

He clenched his jaw. "That's easy for you to say. You're looking toward your future with anticipation. You'll be leaving in a few months to fulfill one of your dreams."

"And haven't you come to Sweetwater to start a new future for you and your family?"

"Yes, but—"

"No, there aren't any buts. This is a good place to forge a new beginning. Craig and Allie seem to be a part of this town already, and I believe Jane will be soon. She's fighting it, but she is the oldest. I think a boy in one of my classes, Ryan, likes Jane. She said something about him calling her a couple of times. That's a good start."

"Yes, but—"

The waiter chose that moment to bring their salads. Samuel clamped his mouth closed in a tight, thin line while the young man placed the small plates in front of them. Beth drenched her greens with a honey mustard dressing, aware of the strained silence between her and Samuel.

When the waiter was gone, Samuel continued. "But we're not the family we once were."

"Of course not." Beth stabbed a piece of spinach with her fork and brought it to her mouth. "Your children are growing up. Their needs will be different. Even your needs will change with time."

"My needs aren't important at the moment."

"You can't neglect them, Samuel. As the head of the family, you set its tone."

His hand on his fork paused above his salad. His knuckles whitened, his jaw hard. "How did we get on such a heavy topic of conversation?"

Beth took a swallow of ice water. "I hope the weatherman is wrong about another big snow in a few days."

Tension siphoned from his expression, and he chuckled. "I didn't mean we had to resort to talking about the weather."

Beth placed her fork on her nearly empty salad plate. "What do you want to talk about? It's your call."

"This is your evening." He finished the last bite of his salad. "How's your brother doing in college?"

"I haven't heard from him in a couple of weeks, and he hasn't paid me any more surprise visits just so I could do his laundry. I took your advice and told him he would have to learn to do his own clothes and that I would be glad to give him lessons. I guess he believed me."

"Good. He'll thank you one day," Samuel said as the waiter removed the salad plates and served them their entrées.

"I hope so. He wasn't too happy when I told him."

"Aunt Mae is already teaching Craig what to do, and since Craig is learning, Allie wants to do hers."

"How about Jane?"

"Complains the whole time, but she does it." He looked down at his sirloin steak, drenched in a butter sauce. "I have to admit that I wasn't the one who insisted the children learn to do their own laundry. It was Aunt Mae. She whipped our household into shape."

"She's doing a good job at the church, too. She has volunteered to help Tanya with the Sunday-school program and she's helping Jesse and Zoey with the auction, not to mention taking over producing the recipe book."

"I thought Darcy was going to be on the committee to help with the auction."

"Darcy will help some, but with having a baby any day now, we all thought it might be better if Zoey is the other cochairwoman."

"Let's see, what other jobs do I need to find a replacement for before you leave?" Samuel held up his hand and ticked them off. "One, the budget committee, two, the ladies' retreat in the fall and…" he frowned. "I'm forgetting something."

"The bookstore."

He shook his head. "What are we going to do without you?"

She cut a piece of her pork. "Carry on."

"I'm not so sure about that, Beth. You're an important part of the church."

Suddenly she wished she was an important part of his life, and that thought shocked her. She nearly choked on the piece of meat she was chewing and had to gulp down some water. She had no business even thinking something like that. He still loved Ruth, still wore his wedding ring, had pictures of her all over his house. How could she compete with his beautiful, deceased wife? Besides, she had her own life planned—had planned for years—what she was going to do when her sister and brothers finally left their childhood home.

"Nick would be perfect for the budget committee, and by fall I think Darcy would be able to help with the ladies' retreat. Her baby will be six months old by then."

"And the bookstore?"

"Check with Felicia. She's the town librarian. She loves books and cats."

"On top of everything else, you know everyone so well. You're a fountain of information and I've come to rely on you for advice on more than how to deal with my daughter."

She'd thought her cheeks had reddened before, but nothing like they were now. She was afraid if she touched them, her fingertips would be burned.

"Your absence will leave a gaping hole in this town."

Beth held up her hand. "Stop. No more compliments. I won't know what to do if you continue."

He bent forward, again placing his hand over hers. "That's your problem. You don't know your own value to the people in Sweetwater."

Speechless, she stared into his eyes. So intent was she on Samuel, she jumped when someone stopped next to her. She slipped her hand free and brought it up to cover her heart. "Jesse, you scared me."

"Sorry about that."

Beth could tell by the impish expression on her friend's face she wasn't sorry one bit.

"I wanted to tell you before we headed out that Joshua called to tell me he was at the hospital. Darcy is in labor and should have the baby soon, according to the doctor. I told him I would let you know."

Chapter Six

"Darcy's having her baby?" Beth shot to her feet, her napkin floating to the floor. "We've got to go. I mean…" Her hand fluttered in the air.

Jesse pressed her down into her chair. "Finish eating your dinner. It will still be a while and it isn't every day you eat at Andre's. You know Darcy wouldn't be too happy with you if you cut your date short."

"We'll be along as soon as we eat." Samuel picked up Beth's napkin and gave it to her, amused by her flustered expression. "Thanks for telling us."

Beth began eating fast.

"You certainly are excited for Darcy, but you might actually want to chew your food and taste it."

Beth stopped for a few seconds, then swallowed slowly what she had in her mouth. "She's one of my best friends and she's wanted this baby so much. I think I've been through this pregnancy with her."

"Right about now she's probably wishing you were the one delivering the baby."

"I don't doubt that, but I'm glad I'm not the one having a baby."

"You don't want any children? You're so good with them."

"I'm no spring chick," she said with a gleam dancing in her eyes.

He nearly spewed out the water he was drinking. "Spring chick! You're only thirty-eight. That isn't over the hill. You're not even near the top. Please, no more talk of how old you are."

Beth forked the last of the steamed broccoli. "I have already raised three children. I've never been on my own and not had children to take care of." She slid the utensil into her mouth and took her time chewing.

To Samuel, Beth was the perfect mother, so her declaration surprised him, and yet he understood. Most nineteen-year-olds didn't have to raise three siblings all at once. Beth had, and from all he had heard from the people at church, she had done an excellent job. She deserved some time to do what she wanted.

"But that doesn't mean I won't help Darcy out with baby-sitting. I don't think she'll have trouble getting any of us to help her. Zoey, Jesse, Tanya and I will be fighting over it in no time."

After Samuel paid the bill, he pulled out Beth's chair and escorted her from the restaurant. The whole way to the hospital she tapped her fingers against the door handle as though that would speed things up.

As he neared the hospital, he slanted a look at Beth. He and Ruth had wanted more children. He still did. He tried to picture Beth with child. The image came easily to his mind. She would be a good mother. Her loving, caring way was such a natural part of her. Any child she raised would be lucky. And thirty-eight wasn't too old to have a baby!

Baby? Children? He put a halt to the direction his thoughts were going in. That wasn't in his future. He was still trying to handle the family he already had.

Samuel pulled into a parking space near the front door of the three-story hospital. He climbed from the car, intending to go around and open Beth's door. She exited more quickly than he did and hurriedly made her way to the sliding glass doors. Chuckling, especially when he thought of her comment earlier about not being a spring chick, he entered the building a few paces behind her. Beth Coleman exhibited a youthful spring to her step.

She stopped at the reception desk to ask about Darcy. Watching her talk to the woman behind the desk, Samuel noted Beth's flushed cheeks, the smile that brightened her whole face and a liveliness that gave her a fresh, wholesome look. He knew she discounted her appearance as being plain, unappealing, but she didn't see herself through his eyes. She was full of energy and enthusiasm that made her very appealing. He didn't understand why some man hadn't snapped her up.

Beth turned to him, her eyes twinkling with excitement. "Darcy's in the delivery room right now. It won't be long. Let's go to the waiting room. That's where everyone else is."

"Beth Coleman, I should have known you wouldn't be more than a few steps behind us getting here," Jesse said as Beth and Samuel entered the waiting room.

Samuel scanned the faces of his parishioners—a roomful of them, all here because of Darcy Markham. If it had been announced on the news, he wouldn't have been surprised to find half the town waiting to hear about the new baby. That was the way Sweetwater was. The town took care of its own. He was counting on that, because he needed to feel as though he belonged somewhere. He needed to reconnect with God and why he had become a minister in the first place. If not—he shuddered to think of what he would have to do if he didn't.

"You didn't think you would drop that bomb on me and I would cheerfully go on eating as though nothing was happening." Beth hugged Jesse, then Zoey and Tanya.

"You finished your meal, didn't you?" Jesse asked, stepping back against her husband, who brought his arms around her.

"Yes, but I'm not sure what I ate after you left."

Jesse captured Samuel's attention. "I'm sorry about that. I stayed away as long as I could, but I couldn't wait any longer."

Nick laughed. "You can say that again. I had to practically hog-tie her to keep her in her chair after the phone call from Joshua. She wanted to run right over that very second and announce the news to you two. Fifteen minutes was all I could persuade her to be quiet and let you eat in peace."

Jesse placed one hand on her waist. "Honestly, Beth, I've never seen you eat so slowly before."

"I wish I could have seen that," Zoey said, taking her chair again between Tanya and Darcy's father.

"Why's it taking so long?" Darcy's dad asked, his brows coming together.

Liz, his new wife, took his hand and patted it. "Babies come in their own time."

"You can say that again. With my last one I barely got to the hospital, but with my oldest I was in labor for over a day."

Having made a point of finding out about his parishioners, Samuel noticed the faraway look that appeared in Zoey's eyes as she spoke, and he realized she was thinking back to the birth of her baby daughter, a birth she'd had to go through without her husband because he was missing in action while on assignment for the DEA. He could imagine the pain she had gone through—pain that had nothing to do with delivering a baby—because he'd gone through the same kind of pain when he'd lost Ruth to breast cancer.

"Thankfully the doctor doesn't think it will be a day." Jesse plopped down across from Sean, Darcy's son. "Are you excited, kiddo?"

He nodded, but his eyelids were drooping. Liz drew him against her and rested his head against her shoulder.

At that moment Joshua came into the waiting room and everyone turned their attention toward him. "It's a little girl. She's seven pounds, eight ounces and has a great set of lungs. The doctor says she is one healthy baby."

Relief mixed with thankfulness flowed through Samuel as the room filled with everyone talking at once. He raised his hands, palms outward, and said, "I think this would be a good time to say a prayer."

"Oh, yes, let's join hands." Zoey stood and stretched out her arms on both sides of her.

With hands clasped together, Darcy's friends and family stood in a circle with their heads bowed.

Expected to lead the prayer, Samuel took a deep, cleansing breath and said, "Heavenly Father, please watch out for this newest addition to the Markham family and Sweetwater Community Church. Help us to guide her in Your ways and to bring her into Your fold. Amen."

There were a few seconds of silence then voices erupted with questions, all directed at an exhausted-looking Joshua.

"When can we see her? What is her name?" Beth asked, shifting from one foot to the other.

Joshua gave a smile so big that it seemed to encompass his whole face. "Her name is Rebecca Anne Markham, and Darcy has been asking for you, Jesse, Zoey and Tanya after she sees her father, Liz and Sean for a few minutes."

The family went with Joshua while the rest stayed in

the waiting room. Beth stood by the entrance, watching the door into Darcy's room.

"You would think she was a member of your family," Samuel said as he planted himself next to her.

"As we were growing up, I was like a big sister to her, Jesse and Zoey. So, yes, she does seem like a member of my family."

"That role came easily to you, didn't it?"

She tilted her head toward him, a question in her eyes. "As a big sister?"

"Yes."

"I guess so. That's really the only one I know except being a teacher."

"I bet your siblings think differently, especially Daniel. You were more a mother to him than a big sister."

She thought for a moment, her brow furrowed. "You're probably right. I am all he knows, since my mother died in childbirth. So my roles have been teacher, mother, sister."

"How about friend, leader, organizer—"

Beth laid her fingers against his lips. "Please, no more. I get the picture."

"Do you? You are invaluable to this town and the church. I don't think you realize that. You just go and do the things that need to be done and never really think anything about it. With your departure this summer you're trying to fill all your positions before you go. Most people don't do that. They walk away and don't look back."

Her cheeks tinged pink, Beth glanced toward Darcy's

room. "Oh, I see the family leaving." She started forward, then stopped and turned back to him. "I appreciate what you said. Really I do. But if I hadn't done those jobs, someone else would have. That's the way Sweetwater is. We take care of what is ours, and that includes you and your family."

Samuel watched her enter Darcy's hospital room with the other members of her circle of friends. Her parting words washed over him and for a long moment he didn't feel so alone in the world.

Samuel entered the front door of the church and walked toward the sanctuary. He had begun to visit with God daily again, and he cherished this time before the day really started. Normally this was his day off, but he felt compelled to visit, to check and see if everything was all right. Inside, light streamed from the stained-glass windows to illuminate his path. He headed for the front pew and came to a halt halfway down the center aisle. He wasn't alone. Tanya sat on the front pew where he often did, with her head bowed, her body shaking with sobs. He hurried forward.

"Tanya, what's wrong?" He slid in beside her.

She lifted her tear-streaked face, a piece of paper crumpled in her hands. "Tom has asked me for a divorce. I…" Sobs racked her body again as she turned away.

Samuel drew her against him. "I'm so sorry, Tanya. Have you been able to see him lately, talk to him?"

She shook her head. "He refused to let me come after

that time I went when he was injured. He was furious that I ignored his wishes then. What am I going to do?"

"Let me go visit Tom and talk with him."

Tanya latched on to Samuel's hands. "Please do. I know if he wants a divorce there is nothing I can really do to stop it. Please talk to him, make him understand I love him no matter what he did. He's Crystal's father. She needs him now more than ever."

As Samuel bowed his head to offer a prayer, he felt this was the right thing to do. He might not be able to talk Tom out of divorcing Tanya, but he had to try. Not only was Tanya hurting, but it was obvious Tom was, too.

"A picnic! What a lovely idea, Samuel," Beth said into the phone.

"Good. I'm glad you like it. Allie and Craig want to see some of the lake now that it is getting warmer. I'm counting on your preparing the food, since Aunt Mae is busy with Zoey and Jesse on the Fourth of July auction. You know how helpless I am in the kitchen."

"They're meeting without me?"

"Aunt Mae said something about you had great notes on each step of the planning and didn't want to bother you with the details, since you wouldn't be here for it."

"But still…" Beth couldn't voice aloud her dissatisfaction at not being asked to help, at least until she left Sweetwater. Yes, she had turned her duties over to others, but still she hadn't wanted to be totally out of the loop.

"Beth, you have to learn to turn it over to the ones

doing it." Samuel lowered his voice. "Enjoy some of the free time with me and my family. It's the last week in March and spring break. You need to play some."

"Well, when you put it that way... Any orders on what you all want?" Beth stared out the picture window at the pear trees laden with white flowers and the red tulips and yellow daffodils gracing the length of Felicia's house across the street.

"I'll let you surprise us. I'll bring dessert and my two youngest children and pick you up in an hour."

"How about Jane?"

"That's the best piece of news I have. She's meeting some friends at the church to help clean up the garden. Joshua organized it."

"Maybe we should help them."

"Have you forgotten my black thumb? Besides, I think Jane wants me to stay away. Ryan is one of the group. He's been calling here the past week every night."

"Then I'll see you three in an hour."

When Beth hung up she sighed heavily, still bothered that she was left out of the planning for the auction. She'd done it for the past ten years. But with the letter she had received yesterday, she knew for certain she wouldn't be here come the Fourth of July. She would be in Brazil working at a mission along the Amazon River. She still couldn't believe how fast everything was proceeding. In the next few months she had a lot to do—getting her passport, getting a physical and a whole series of shots.

But for the moment she had a picnic to plan and an

afternoon to spend with Samuel and his children. She noticed a bounce to her step as she walked into the kitchen. What was next—whistling while she worked? But she couldn't contain her excitement. For the trip or for seeing Samuel? She didn't know the answer and didn't care.

Opening the refrigerator, she inspected its contents, trying to decide what two young children would want to eat on a picnic. Remembering back to her picnics with her brothers and sister, she quickly settled on making peanut butter and jelly sandwiches with sliced fruit and chips. Nothing fancy, but then children rarely wanted that.

She set about preparing the food, then put on a new pair of jeans she had bought with Jesse the past weekend after their get-together at Alice's Café with Zoey, Tanya and Darcy, who had brought along her baby daughter. Wearing her new orange blouse and tennis shoes, Beth tied her curly hair back with an orange silk scarf, a few strands of hair escaping. She was ready to go when Samuel rang the doorbell exactly an hour after his phone call.

Beth grabbed a navy blue sweater in case she got cold from the breeze off the lake and went to answer the door. "Hi! I'm so glad you asked me to go with you all. I needed a reason not to do some yard work."

"I work hard to avoid yard work. Glad we think alike." Samuel pointed to a basket on the table in the foyer. "Is this the food?"

She nodded. "What's for dessert?"

"Nothing. The kids want to come back to the ice

cream parlor on Main and have some after our picnic. Is that okay with you?"

"Ice cream. Let's see. Next to banana cream pie, vanilla ice cream with hot caramel topping is my favorite dessert, so I guess it's okay with me."

"I hear Miller Point is a nice place to have a picnic."

"There are several places around the lake that are nice. Miller Point is fine with me."

"With spring break the kids have been eager to do some things outside. Craig and Allie brought some fishing poles to see if they can catch anything. Do you fish?"

"Nope, but I don't mind watching."

Samuel lifted the basket and allowed Beth to go first. He shut the door and made sure it was locked before descending the steps. Beth slid into the front seat and turned to greet Allie and Craig.

"Will you help me pick some wildflowers? I've seen some pretty ones from the road," Allie said as her father started the car.

"Sure. There was a time I knew the names of a lot of them. But I haven't gone wildflower picking in years." She'd been so busy doing other things she'd forgotten how much she liked doing something simple like that. She and her sister used to walk along the lake and collect wildflowers to put in a vase on the kitchen table. They had always tried to get as many different colors as possible. Her sister had called it a rainbow bouquet. "Miller Point is perfect for that. There's a meadow not far from the lake's edge."

Craig screwed up his face into a frown at the very mention of flowers. Beth added for his benefit, "You are welcome to help us, Craig. I don't want you to feel left out."

"No way. That's for girls."

"Son, when you get older, you'll realize giving flowers to a girl becomes very important to a guy," Samuel said with a smile.

"Not for me," Craig muttered, staring out the side window as his father drove toward Miller Point.

"What about Susie? Mary Ann says her older sister likes you and you like her," Allie said in a singsong voice.

"No, I don't!"

"Yes, you do. You talk to her when she calls." Allie stuck her tongue out at her brother, who returned the gesture.

Samuel slowed his car, pulled over and said, "If you two are going to fight, we can go home to do that."

Both crossed their arms, lifted their chins and turned to look out their respective car windows. Beth bit the inside of her cheek to keep a straight face. This little skirmish between brother and sister brought back bittersweet memories of raising her siblings. There had been times when they had been constantly at each other's throat and she had wondered if she would ever have any peace in the house again. Now she had more peace than she knew what to do with.

Samuel resumed driving. "Sorry about that, Beth."

"No problem. I'm used to it. You ought to hear some of the students at school."

Five minutes later Samuel pulled into a parking area near Miller Point. Allie and Craig were out of the car the second he turned off the engine. They raced toward the water, one going east along the sandy shore and the other west.

"I knew I was going to have a problem when I found out Allie's new best friend's older sister liked Craig. Allie is constantly teasing him and he isn't taking it very well."

"Sort of like he teases Jane about Ryan?"

"Yep. There are times I sneak out of the house and seek some quiet at the church."

Beth laughed. "I've been there. I know what you mean."

Samuel opened his door. "Let's spread the blanket under that maple over there." He gestured toward the largest tree in the area.

Carrying the blanket while Samuel took the basket, Beth walked beside him to the maple. Craig ran back to the car to get his fishing rod while Allie explored the shoreline, picking up some stones to examine and pocketing one.

After setting the blanket down and spreading it out so only part of it was shaded, Beth tossed back her head and let the warm rays of the sun bathe her face. Inhaling lungfuls of the rich air, she let the peacefulness of her surroundings seep into her. The chirping of the birds and the soothing serenade of the insects combined with the water lapping against the sandy beach to complete the ideal picture.

She turned toward Samuel, who had already opened the basket to peek inside. "Again I want to thank you for this wonderful suggestion. It's beautiful. Today no one should spend any time indoors."

"It's one of those perfect spring days that reconfirms God's presence." He closed the lid.

"Does the meal meet with your approval?"

"You could have brought just about anything and I wouldn't have cared less. I'm not a picky eater, as opposed to my daughters. One is a vegetarian and the other only likes peanut butter and jelly sandwiches, any kind of sweet and spaghetti." He snapped his fingers. "Oh, I almost forgot, and hamburgers and French fries."

"Not your healthiest food."

"Nope. I'm only hoping it's a brief stage she's moving through." He flipped his hand toward the basket. "But I can see you must have read Allie's mind. You have peanut butter and jelly sandwiches. How did you know?"

"Not many children their age hate PB and J sandwiches."

"True. You know children well."

"Raising three and teaching hundreds does have its advantages."

Allie raced toward the car and retrieved her fishing rod. She joined her brother, who sat on a large rock jutting out over the water. Passing her pole to Craig, Allie watched as he baited the line.

"What's he fishing with?"

"Bologna."

"Grant you, I'm not a fisherman—or is that woman? Oh, well, I'm not one of those, but I've never heard of bologna being used to lure fish to your hook."

"Allie screams if we use anything live like worms." Samuel moved back to sit on the blanket. "Surprisingly they have caught some using bologna, so Craig goes along with it."

Beth eased down next to Samuel, everything about the day feeling so right. It seemed natural to her that they were sitting and watching the two children fish as though they had for years. Samuel was easy to talk to. He made her feel important, special, very much a woman. If she hadn't had her life planned, it would have been easy to fall for him. Why had someone come along when she had stopped looking for a husband, a man to love? She had to keep focused on her trip in the summer.

Samuel rested one arm on his bent knee, never taking his gaze off his children. "How are your plans coming along? Have you heard back from the organization?"

"Yes," she said with less excitement than she would have thought. "I received my acceptance a few days ago."

"Where are you going?"

"Brazil."

"Where the dart landed?"

"Yes, that was as good a way to decide as any. The world is full of places I haven't been to." Beth crossed her legs, stretched out in front of her. "I'm going to be assigned to a mission at the upper reaches of the Amazon just before the border with Peru."

"The Amazon! That's a far cry from Sweetwater."

"Yes, but what an adventure. I've decided to keep a journal of my travels. I may write a book one day. I've always wanted to, and this will be my chance to do good for God and fill pages and pages with the new things I've learned."

"I wish I could capture your enthusiasm and give some to Jane."

"Her grades are improving. She doesn't complain to me anymore while we're working."

"That's good, since you're doing her a favor. Have I thanked you in the past week?"

Beth smiled. "Yes, every time I come over."

"Okay, I've probably carried the appreciative-dad role just a little too far, but because of you Jane is doing better and she doesn't complain like she used to about going to school."

"Soon I'm going to approach her about using the resource room when she needs help. It's staffed with two special ed teachers who assist students on IEPs with their class work, any long-term assignments and taking tests in a quiet environment where there aren't very many distractions."

"She won't do it."

"She'll need something after I'm gone if she runs into any trouble. Right now she's using me, but next year I won't be here."

Samuel flexed his hands, then curled them into fists. "I know."

The tight edge to his voice caused Beth to angle her head to look him directly in the eyes. "I want her to learn to advocate for herself and not to be ashamed of needing help with certain projects. We all need help from time to time."

"From where I'm sitting you look pretty together."

"Well, I'm not all the time."

"When?"

"The night you took me to Andre's. I was a basket case."

He quirked a brow. "You were?"

"I haven't dated much. Not very good at it when I have. If you haven't noticed, I'm shy."

"You could have fooled me. Of course, I haven't dated much either."

"So neither one of us is an expert at dating."

"I know a solution to that."

"What?"

"Go out on another date with me."

Her heart skipped a beat, then began to pound. "I…" She was at a loss for words.

"If you don't say yes soon, I'm liable to be set back years with this dating."

"By all means, we wouldn't want that."

"Then it's a yes?"

"Yes," she said with a laugh.

Chapter Seven

Beth slipped from the extra-large booth at Alice's Café to grab the coffee. She poured some for Tanya and herself. "I'm glad Alice doesn't mind us monopolizing this table for several hours." She held up the glass pot. "Any other takers?"

"No, strictly tea for me." Zoey dunked her used tea bag into her hot water and added some sugar. "I'm thinking about getting another macadamia cookie. Anyone else want one?"

Darcy placed her hand over her stomach. "Not me. It's gonna be weeks, probably months, before I can fit into my clothes again. Dieting is the pits."

Jesse raised her mug. "Here's to the day when we don't have to watch our weight."

"I'm afraid I'd be dead by that time," Beth murmured, sitting again in the booth next to Tanya.

"Me, too." Tanya cupped her chin and rested her

elbow on the table, looking despondent, deep lines carved into her expression.

"What's going on, Tanya?" Beth asked, realizing that for the past half hour her friend had said little.

A heavy sigh escaped Tanya's lips. "I didn't want to say anything, at least, not till the end, because I hate to put a damper on our gathering."

"Nonsense." Jesse waved her hand in the air. "That's what these gatherings are for. To help each other through the rough times. Has something else happened to Tom? Is he hurt again?"

Tanya shook her head, her eyes watering. "No, I…" She swallowed hard. "He wants a divorce. I received the papers a few days ago."

"You did! Why didn't you tell us immediately?" Zoey asked, stirring her green tea.

"I'm embarrassed." Tanya hung her head, staring into the black darkness of her coffee.

Beth laid her hand on her upper arm. "There's nothing for you to be embarrassed about. You can't control what Tom wants, especially with him in prison. Have you talked to him since you received the papers?"

"He doesn't want to talk with me or see me. I don't know what to do about it."

"Oh, Tanya, I'm so sorry." Tears pooled in Darcy's eyes and began to roll down her cheeks. "My hormones are running rampant." She wiped the wet tracks, only to have more tears flow. "I'm not gonna be much help. You talk to her, Beth. You're always so sensible."

Beth slipped her arm about Tanya's shoulders and pulled her friend toward her. "Give it some time. Maybe he'll come to his senses."

"I don't think so, but Reverend Morgan is going up there today to talk to Tom. He came by this morning to see how I was. I don't know what I would have done if it wasn't for our new reverend. His words have kept me focused on what's important—my daughter. I can't let this cause a setback for me. I just can't."

"Samuel does have a way about him," Beth murmured, picturing the man under discussion.

"*Samuel* does?" Jesse arched a brow. "Hmm. That sounds awfully cozy, if you ask me."

Beth shot Jesse an exasperated look. "I'm not asking you. Don't you start, Jesse Blackburn."

Tanya smiled. "You two need to stop it before Alice throws us out for causing a scene. Beth, don't you know you'll never be able to change Jesse's nature? She's a born matchmaker."

"I would refer to her as a born busybody."

"Busybody!" Jesse clasped her chest, her mouth forming a large *O*. "I can't believe you said that about me."

"If I don't shut you down immediately, you'll weave a fantasy with me marrying our minister and having his baby."

The grin on Jesse's face was pure mischief. "I don't have to. You're doing a great job of it yourself."

"Now I know why Beth is sitting at one end of the table and you at the other." Zoey shook her head, then took a swallow of her drink. "If I remember correctly, we were going to discuss Crystal's birthday coming up in a few weeks. She'll be fourteen—only two years to her sweet sixteen birthday."

"My daughter is growing up," Tanya said, pulling herself together as the conversation turned to Crystal's birthday.

Beth relaxed back, noticing that Tanya was no longer teary eyed. In fact, she was sipping her coffee and throwing herself into the party planning for her daughter. While listening to the discussion, Beth said a silent prayer that Samuel's trip to the prison would be successful.

Samuel sat at the bare table in the bare room at the prison, waiting for Tom Bolton's appearance—if he appeared, and Samuel was beginning to feel he wouldn't. He checked his watch for the third time and wondered what he should do if the man refused to see him, too. As the minutes ticked away, frustration coiled in Samuel's stomach until it ached.

Then suddenly the door swung open and a man walked in with a guard behind him. Tom limped to the table, his eyes downcast. But even though his face was averted, Samuel saw the swollen lip and cut under his eye. He blew out a breath of air, hoping God would guide him in what he should say to this man.

After Tom eased into the chair and the guard backed away to stand by the door, Tanya's husband finally lifted his gaze to Samuel's. The despair in his eyes shook Samuel to the core of his being. This was a man without hope.

Tom blinked, and the despair was replaced with anger. With his arms folded over his chest, his hands fisted and his eyes narrowed, Tom said nothing as he stared at Samuel.

Samuel coated his dry throat and scooted his chair closer to the table, placing his elbows on its wooden surface. "Your wife asked me to come and see how you were."

A nerve in the man's jaw twitched. "How does it look to you?"

"You're not doing too well."

"I guess we can't say you're blind, Reverend."

"What happened?" Samuel indicated the cuts on Tom's face.

"I walked into a brick wall. An occupational hazard in here."

"Have you reported—" Samuel glanced at the guard "—the brick wall?"

Tom shrugged, all expression shutting down completely.

"Is there anything you want me to do? Maybe I can talk to someone for you."

Again another shrug.

"I will pray for you."

"Suit yourself. It won't help, reverend. Nothing does."

The man's words held no hope, and the expression

in his eyes was weary as though he didn't care anymore about anything.

"Perhaps we can pray now."

"I stopped praying the day Crystal fell from the horse. What good is praying to a God who allows your baby to be hurt?"

Hearing Tom's anger, which mirrored his own at one time, made Samuel wince. Was that how he had sounded after Ruth died? He was ashamed of those feelings now. No good came of them except to throw his family, his life, into chaos. He wanted to help Tom see that.

"You have a beautiful daughter who is full of life. She isn't letting the fact she's in a wheelchair slow her down. She's—"

"Stop right there, Reverend, or this meeting is over. I won't listen to you talk about God and His grand plan that somehow involves my daughter being crippled. So if that's all you came to talk about, then I guess you wasted your time."

"No, that's not all," Samuel murmured, staring at Tom's closed expression. The silence lengthened into a long moment while Samuel tried to decide how to approach Tom about the divorce. He couldn't think of any way but straightforward. "Tanya doesn't want a divorce."

Tom blinked rapidly several times, then that blank look reappeared. "That's too bad, because I do."

"Will you at least see her and talk to her about it?"

Tanya's husband shook his head. "No use in wasting either one's time."

"She doesn't feel it's a waste."

"Too bad." Tom scraped the chair back and rose. "You've wasted enough of my valuable time. I have to get back to work."

The almost monotone quality to his voice sent chills down Samuel's spine. Desperation made him ask, "Don't you want to know how your family is doing?"

Tom closed his eyes for a few seconds, then opened them and looked right at Samuel, no expression whatsoever on his face. "They're better off without me. Now, if you'll excuse me."

Tom was at the door when Samuel said, "Your daughter misses you."

The man's back stiffened, but he didn't turn around or say anything to Samuel's last remark. When the guard and Tom left, Samuel scanned the bleak decor. It mirrored his feelings. He made his way out of the room and toward the guard at the end of the hall. The only result of this meeting with Tom was that he needed to prepare Tanya for the worst.

Lord, help me to be there for her in her time of need. Guide me in what I need to say to help her through this. And please be with Tom. He has lost all hope and needs it—and You—more than anyone.

Beth paused on the stone path, hesitant to go any farther into the Garden of Serenity. Samuel sat on a wooden bench near the pond with his head bent, his hands clasped together and his elbows resting on his thighs. He was a man lost in prayer.

She'd started to leave when he raised his head and peered at her. No, he was simply a man lost. His dejected expression ripped through her composure and sent her forward, her only thought to comfort. "What's wrong?"

The haunted look in his eyes shifted as though he was trying to mask it but was not quite able to. "I went to see Tom in prison."

Beth settled next to him on the bench. "I know. Tanya mentioned it earlier today at Alice's Café."

"Yeah. I forgot about your meeting with the others." He scanned the area as if he finally realized they were sitting in the middle of the church garden. "How did you find me?"

"Jane said you headed over to the church when you returned from your trip. I saw you as I was heading into the building to find you." With only a few inches separating them, she felt tension emanating from him and her concern grew. "What happened with Tom? Will he see Tanya?"

"No. He is adamant about that—and the divorce." Samuel took hold of her hand and gripped it. "I couldn't help him, Beth. I tried, but he wouldn't listen. He has turned away from the Lord."

Even though Samuel's clasp was tight, what unnerved her about his touch was its intensity, its desperation. "Sometimes there's nothing we can do to make a person listen to reason. You can't make a person believe in God's purpose."

"I have no business being a minister. I can't help my parishioners. I can't help my family. I can't help myself."

Beth sucked in a deep breath and held it until her lungs felt on fire. Such despair wrenched her heart, constricting it into a painful lump that seemed to barely beat in her chest. She covered their clasped hands with her other one and angled her body so she faced him. "Where in the world has that idea come from?"

His darkened gaze shifted to hers. "Take a good look around you."

Her throat closed around the words she wanted to say. She swallowed several times before she felt she could talk above the barest whisper. "I have. Today I sat with Tanya and listened to her sing your praises for the help you have given her through this difficult time. That doesn't sound like a person who hasn't been able to help someone. You can't help everyone. I've learned that the hard way as a teacher. You try your best and hope you can, but it doesn't always work."

"When I came to Sweetwater, I felt this was my last chance to prove myself as a minister."

She hadn't thought it possible, but his eyes became even darker, as though turmoil churned in their depths. "Last chance? You had a good record as a minister."

"Not since my wife's death. I guess you could call what has happened to me a crisis of faith. So how can a minister who is questioning God's purpose in his own life help others see God's purpose?"

"When my mother died, I was angry at God for taking her away and leaving me with three siblings to raise. I didn't know how I was going to make it. Raise them. Finish college. Have a life. We all have times in our lives when we wonder about the plans God has for us, even reject the direction He wants us to go. Just because you are a minister doesn't mean you're immune to doubts or questions concerning your faith."

"But Tom still won't see Tanya. He's still proceeding with the divorce."

"And we'll be there for Tanya. We can't control Tom's actions, but we can help Tanya deal with them."

He released a deep breath through pursed lips.

"You must keep talking to God. He's there. He's listening. Always," she added.

"I'm trying."

"That's all you can do. Try your best. As far as your family goes, your children adore you. Yes, Jane is rebelling, but that's typical of a teenager. I've seen some growth over the past few months, mainly because she knows you'll love her no matter what. That's powerful stuff when you're dealing with raging hormones."

Samuel smiled, one corner of his mouth lifting. "I guess you should know, since you've raised three teenagers and dealt with hundreds on a daily basis."

"Yes, the teacher knows best."

He chuckled. "I thought that was the father knows best."

"As my students say, *whatever.*"

Samuel straightened, removing his hand from hers. "Did you need me for something?"

For a few seconds Beth battled disappointment that they were not holding hands any longer. Then she thought of the danger in that and pushed her conflicting feelings to the back of her mind. "We were planning Crystal's birthday party in a few weeks and wanted it to be a surprise for her. Do you think we could use the rec hall for the party? Her birthday is on a Wednesday and she has youth choir practice that evening."

"That's a wonderful idea. We can have the party after the practice."

"That was what I was hoping you would say."

"What can I do to help?"

"Nothing. Tanya, Jesse, Darcy, Zoey and I have it all planned. We'll just need your presence."

"You've got that." Samuel rose and offered his hand to help her to her feet. When she stood, he moved back a step and said, "Now, about that date we discussed going on. How about going to the movies? Maybe next Saturday night?"

Date. There was that word again. "That sounds fine." *That sounds dangerous,* an inner voice taunted. "Why don't you come over for dinner at my house beforehand?"

"We can go out. I don't want you to go to any trouble."

"I know we could go out, but I like to cook and I would like to cook for you." What in the world had she just admitted to him? The ground she was standing on seemed to tremble.

His smile this time was full-fledged. "Then I can't say no. What time?"

"Let's say seven. We can go to the later movie."

"You've got yourself a date."

That was what she was afraid of, she thought, staring at his heart-melting look, the dimple in his left cheek. If she stayed any longer, she would end up a pool of liquid at his feet. She backed away.

"I'd better go. Even though I'm officially on spring break, I have tons of papers to grade. The exciting life of an English teacher." She heard herself rambling and winced inwardly.

She spun about to leave.

"Beth."

His voice called back to her. She glanced over her shoulder, steeling herself.

"Thanks for everything."

Her resolve not to fall for him was fast crumbling about her. "You're welcome. You would do the same for me." She hurried away before she decided to stay... Something she *knew* was dangerous.

"Would you like to come inside for a cup of decaf coffee?" Beth asked as Samuel escorted her to her front porch Saturday night after the movie.

He took her key from her and inserted it into her lock, then opened the door. "That sounds like a nice way to end this evening. Besides, I want to help you clean up the dishes from the dinner."

"You don't have to do that."

"I know. But I want to."

"You're a keeper. A man who wants to do dishes."

"And I do windows, too."

"How about bathrooms? That's the room I hate to clean the most." Inside her house Beth shut the front door and slipped out of her heavy sweater, draping it over a chair in the foyer.

"I can't say I'm too fond of doing the bathroom either, especially after the children use it. Thankfully Aunt Mae takes care of the housework. She has managed to get my children to help, which was something I wasn't very successful at."

"I have to admit I found it easier to do the work than plead with and prod my brothers and sister into doing their chores." She walked through the living room and dining room into the kitchen, heading for the coffeemaker. "Have a seat. This shouldn't take long."

"What about those dishes?"

"They can wait a little while longer."

"You won't get an argument out of me. What did you think of the movie?"

Beth filled the glass carafe with water and poured it into the coffee machine, then switched it on. "I liked it. It was light and funny. I wasn't in the mood for anything heavy this evening. It's nice to see two older people falling in love. So many movies are about young people, as though anyone over forty doesn't have a love life."

"I think Jane feels that way about anyone over thirty. By the way, speaking of my oldest daughter, thank you."

"What for?"

"We got her report card right after spring break and she passed all her subjects. I don't think that would have happened if you hadn't intervened."

Beth sat across from Samuel at her kitchen table. "This next nine weeks will be even better. I haven't quite convinced her to use the resource room, but I'm making headway. Hopefully by the end of the semester she will use it for the end-of-semester tests. I think it will help her to take them in a quiet environment with few distractions."

He leaned forward, clasping her hand. "What am I going to do without you next year? What's Jane going to do?"

Beth's heart thudded in her chest, its beating thundering against her eardrums. "You two will be fine." A sadness at the thought of leaving her hometown encased Beth in an icy shroud. She shivered.

"Cold?"

"No—yes. Truthfully, I am a little afraid of striking out on my own. I've never been very adventurous and I certainly haven't had a chance to travel much. I've only been to a few places, the farthest being Chicago, which isn't that far. I haven't been able to learn much of the language. What if I can't and no one understands me?"

He squeezed her hand, a gleam twinkling in his eyes. "You'll do just fine. Gesturing and body language can go a long way until you get the hang of Portuguese. I have confidence in you. You can do anything you set your mind to."

The scent of coffee brewing saturated the kitchen, adding an extra warmth to the atmosphere between them. Beth relaxed against the back of the chair, listening for the dripping to stop. "You sure know how to make a woman feel special."

"That's easy. You are special."

In that moment she felt very feminine and even pretty with Samuel's gaze trained on her, his total attention focused on her as though she was the only woman alive for him. How could a woman not feel special under those circumstances? How was she going to walk away from such a wonderful man, who made her experience things she never had?

The coffee finished perking, and Beth rose to withdraw two mugs from the cabinet above the machine. After pouring the dark brew into the cups, she asked, "Milk? Sugar?"

"Three heaping spoonfuls of sugar, please."

Surprise widened her eyes. "I can just give you the bowl of sugar and you can have it straight."

"In the army some of the coffee I had to drink was so bad that I'm not sure it was really coffee. I had to do something to make it drinkable. Now I can't have coffee without lots of sugar."

"I have my coffee blended for me. It's a shame you have to mask its rich flavor with sugar."

"Okay. Two spoonfuls. I can compromise when I have to."

Beth added the sugar to his mug, then brought it over to the table and set it in front of him. She sat cat-ercorner to him and took a tentative sip of her coffee. She loved this blend with a hint of vanilla in it.

Samuel curled his fingers around the handle and drank his doctored brew. "Mmm. This is good. We could have used you in the army."

"Maybe before I leave I can wean you off so much sugar in your coffee."

A cloud descended over his expression. "Anything is possible. How's Crystal's birthday party coming along?"

"Great. Everything's in place. Planning this has really helped Tanya take her mind off the divorce. That and your help."

"My help?"

"Don't play innocent with me. Tanya's told me about the couple of times you've stopped by her house to check up on her and talk to her. Your counseling means a lot to her. She's gone through a great deal in the past few years."

"She's lucky to have friends like you."

"I've seen Craig paying a lot of attention to Crystal during Sunday-school class lately. I think he likes her."

"He called someone last night and had a fit when Allie tried to listen. I got the feeling he was talking to a girl. Maybe it was Crystal or Susie."

"It's spring. Love is in the air."

"Is that it?" Merriment flashed in his gaze as it locked with hers. "She's an older woman. Do you think that could work?"

"Possibly," Beth answered, thinking of the few years' age difference between her and Samuel.

Silence stretched between them—visually connected but separated by a table. His look dropped to her mouth and her lips tingled. Cradling the mug between her hands, she sipped her coffee, her gaze on Samuel the whole time.

He reached across the table and took her mug, putting it down. Then he feathered his finger along her jawline before tracing the outline of her mouth. She inhaled a sharp breath. The roughened texture of his fingertip sent chills down her body.

"I don't know how you ever thought of yourself as plain. You aren't plain at all."

His words washed over her, making her care even more for this man sitting in her kitchen as though he belonged there. "With you I never have."

"Good." His hand delved into the curls of her hair and cupped the back of her head.

Tension coiled in her stomach. She was falling in love with a man who still loved his deceased wife, who wasn't over her death.

Samuel rose and drew her to her feet, his hand still in her hair. He moved so close she was sure he could feel and hear her heart pounding. His scent surrounded her as though wrapping her in a protective cocoon. He tilted her head and angled his, slanting his lips over hers.

His kiss rocked her to her core. She felt as if she were floating in the air, her heart soaring. It wouldn't take much to want to center her whole life around this man.

Panic began to eat at her composure. How could she fall in love now of all times? Samuel Morgan, and especially his family of three children, did not fit into her plans for the future—plans she'd had for years.

Chapter Eight

Beth stiffened in his arms. Samuel pulled away, dazed by the reaction that had taken hold of him when his mouth had covered hers. He felt as though he had come home. That wasn't possible. Quickly he stepped back, dropping his arms to his sides. Guilt began to gnaw at his insides. How could he forget Ruth so easily? He shouldn't have kissed Beth. They were only friends.

From the expression in her eyes, he realized her conflicting emotions raged inside as his did. She touched her mouth, rubbing her fingertips across her lips as he had done only a moment before. As he wanted to do again. He took another step back, shocked at the direction his thoughts were taking him—away from Ruth, his high school sweetheart.

He could not place his heart in jeopardy again. Beth was leaving in a few months—she had made that very clear from the beginning. He still loved his wife, even if she was gone. He couldn't betray those feelings so easily. Easily? He laughed silently at that thought. There was nothing easy about the war waging inside him. Beth made him feel like a man again. She made him feel whole, as though the fragmented parts that had split with Ruth's death were coming together.

He wouldn't apologize for the kiss, but he did say, "I shouldn't have done that. I—I'd better go."

She didn't stop him when he turned to leave. Her gaze pierced him as he headed toward the door. Outside on her porch the cool spring air flowed over him, carrying on its breeze the scent of newly blooming hyacinths from the bed in front of her house.

Why had he kissed her?

He didn't want to ruin their friendship. What if he had? He thought of their talks over the past few months and didn't know what he would do if she avoided him because of the kiss.

But too quickly summer would be here and she would be gone. Maybe it was for the best they kept their distance. As he walked toward his car he turned to the Lord, as he was doing more and more of late for guidance.

"Are you mad at Samuel?" Zoey asked while standing back and watching the children pour into the rec hall right after choir practice Wednesday evening.

Beth glanced at her friend. "Mad? What gave you that idea?"

"Usually you two are talking constantly with each other. Tonight you haven't exchanged one word and only one look that I could tell. Something's going on."

Beth stepped away from the children gathering to surprise Crystal. Tanya was going to wheel her daughter into the room on the pretext she had forgotten something at the piano. Beth leaned toward Zoey and whispered, "He kissed me the other night."

"That's great!"

"Shh." Beth glanced about, making sure no one heard Zoey's remark. Thankfully everyone's attention, even Darcy's and Jesse's was on the door into the rec hall. "No, it isn't a good thing. I'm leaving in a few months. Everything's settled except getting my passport in the mail, getting my physical and shots and packing."

"Beth, it's okay to do something spontaneous. You always have your life planned down to the last detail. Falling in love doesn't work that way."

"He kissed me. That's all. Who said anything about falling in love?" Beth could hear the panic in her voice and knew by the arched eyebrow that Zoey had, too. Again Beth looked around, hoping no one was listening. She was having a tough time explaining this to Zoey, let alone anyone else.

The children searched for hiding places while Jesse turned off the lights and told everyone to be quiet.

Zoey sidled closer to Beth and brought her hand up to

shield her lips while she whispered, "I've seen you two together. You're perfect. That's why when you didn't speak to him on Sunday after the church service as you usually do, I knew something was up. You two actually avoided each other. Then tonight the same thing happened."

"Shh. You don't want to spoil the surprise for Crystal."

"I'm not through discussing this, Beth Coleman."

"Yeah. That's what I'm afraid of."

Tanya opened the door to the rec hall and wheeled Crystal in. Someone snickered.

"Gee, Crystal, it's sure dark in here. I'd better turn on the light or I'm bound to run you into something." Tanya flipped the switch.

The children jumped up from behind chairs and the couch and yelled, "Surprise!"

Crystal's features lit with a big grin. She moved herself into the center of the room, scanning the group converging on her.

Craig playfully slugged Sean. "You almost blew the surprise."

Sean's face turned beet-red. "I couldn't help it. Cindy bet me I couldn't keep quiet."

"And you didn't. You lose." Cindy stepped around Sean and handed Crystal her present.

All the other kids began stacking gifts onto Crystal's lap until she giggled and said, "Uncle! No more. I can't see over the presents." One slid off her lap and thudded to the tile floor.

Jesse ran over to the fourteen-year-old, picked up the

dropped gift and relieved her of some of the other wrapped boxes.

Beth watched the exchange, so glad the party was a success. She noticed tears gathering in Tanya's eyes as she looked on the scene. A lump lodged in Beth's throat, and she turned away before she, too, started to cry. Her gaze found Samuel in the doorway with Allie in front of him, his hand on her shoulder. Allie held a present, but hadn't made a move toward Crystal yet. Samuel said something to Allie, then looked directly at Beth.

Across the room she felt the connection as though it were a physical link that bound them. She experienced their kiss all over again, an awareness shivering down her spine, her pulse racing, her lips tingling. All this from a mere look!

She was in deeper than she had originally thought. He affected her on so many different levels—all dangerous to her carefully made plans and dreams of the future.

"Are you going to stand there and ignore our minister all night?" Zoey whispered, giving her a gentle shove toward him.

"I have a job to do. I have to dish up the ice cream in a few minutes and you have to cut the cake to serve with the ice cream."

"Oh, yeah. Thanks for reminding me." Zoey scurried across the room toward Samuel.

Beth shook her head. Sometimes her friends could be so annoying. Usually it was Jesse who tried to fix people up, not Zoey. Well, she would be gone soon and then she wouldn't have to worry about that. But for some reason the thought of traveling and seeing some of the world didn't perk her up as it should have.

While Crystal opened her presents Beth made her way toward the kitchen to get the ice cream from the freezer. She heard the child's laughter and it filled her heart with joy. She would miss the chance to teach Crystal in a few years. For that matter, she wouldn't be instructing *any* of her friends' children. She hadn't really thought about that until now.

In the kitchen Beth paused, thinking that her mind was in turmoil too much lately. Change was good—she needed change. Her life had become so predictable and dull. She could serve the Lord and see the world. Great solution. Great plan.

With her resolve firmed, she walked to the counter. Rummaging in the drawer, she found the ice cream scoop and withdrew it.

She started to shut the drawer when she heard Samuel say, "Hold it. I need the cake slicer."

Zoey! She should have figured her friend was up to something when she hurried over to Samuel. Beth rolled her eyes toward the ceiling, then grabbed the utensil for him, berating Zoey the whole time. She was definitely getting as bad as Jesse. If she was going to be around long enough, she would love to give Zoey a taste of her own medicine. She could think of a few men she could fix Zoey up with.

With the cake slicer in hand, Beth spun about to give

it to Samuel and almost stabbed him in the chest because of his proximity. She jerked back, murmuring, "I'm sorry." The utensil clanged to the kitchen counter next to Beth. "I didn't know you were there."

He grinned. "I thought you heard me approach. I meant to reach around you and get the cake slicer."

She'd been so lost in thought about what Zoey had done that she hadn't heard a thing. Her friends were making her crazy. No, that wasn't quite right. Her see-sawing emotions concerning Samuel were making her crazy. She needed to get a handle on things. Their relationship needed to get back to the way it was last month or even last week before "the kiss."

"Thankfully no harm was done." Her breathing shallow, Beth pushed the drawer closed and placed several feet between them.

He stared at her, his gaze roaming over her features in a leisurely examination that only made her more self-conscious. The silence in the kitchen, which lengthened uncomfortably, was broken only by an occasional loud laugh from the rec hall.

Not taking her gaze from him, she shifted from one foot to the other, her mouth so parched she was afraid a gallon of water wouldn't satisfy her. "Are you slicing the cake?" She asked the first thing that popped into her mind. *Duh, Beth, of course he was, or why else would he be getting the cake slicer?*

"Yes. Zoey said something about retrieving some items from her car for the party."

Yeah, she just bet her friend had "some items" in her car. She would be curious to see what Zoey managed to scrounge up. "Then I guess we'd better get out there before the natives get restless."

Crystal finished opening her last present as Beth and Samuel emerged from the kitchen. Jesse, Darcy and Tanya all smiled toward Beth as though they knew a secret no one else did.

"It's time for cake and ice cream," Tanya announced.

"Let's sing happy birthday to Crystal first." Jesse waved the group of children toward the table where the cake was.

After everyone gathered around with Crystal in the center, the kids launched into the song, yelling and clapping at the end. The huge grin hadn't left Crystal's face the whole time.

"I think that's our cue to cut and scoop." Beth put some chocolate ice cream on the plate next to the first piece of chocolate cake with white frosting, then handed it to Crystal.

For the next ten minutes Beth scooped ice cream while Samuel stood next to her only a few inches away and sliced pieces of cake for all the children and grown-ups. The rec hall grew quiet as everyone found a place to sit and eat their treat.

"There are two pieces left. Do you want the one with a lot of frosting or the other one?" Samuel slid the cake with extra frosting, because it was a corner piece, onto one of the pink princess paper plates.

"I should say the one without much frosting, but I

won't. I love the frosting the most." Beth lifted the scoop filled with ice cream. "Want any?"

He nodded. "I can't pass up chocolate."

After she gave him what he had requested, she looked about for a chair to sit in. The only place available was the bench in the alcove or the floor. She headed for the alcove at the same time Samuel did. He glanced at her, then at the bench and shrugged.

After he eased onto the bench next to Beth, he said, "You know we need to talk about it."

"'It' meaning…?" She knew very well what he was referring to, but she wasn't going to be the one to say the word.

"The kiss. I'm not sorry I kissed you."

When she allowed herself to think about it, she wasn't either. But the kiss did complicate their relationship, which she was desperately trying to keep as simple as possible. "I'm not either, but where do we go from here?"

"I guess it's hard to go back to the way things were before I kissed you."

"Yes."

"To tell you the truth, Beth, I don't know the answer to that question. Maybe you should forget the kiss."

Forget the kiss? That could possibly be one of the hardest things she'd had to do in a long time. But because he was acting so casual about the kiss, Beth said, "Sure. We're friends, and friends kiss each other from time to time." *Yeah, right, Beth. If you keep saying that, you might convince yourself of the truth in that statement when the sun burns out.*

Samuel murmured something that sounded like a yes. He stuffed the last bite of cake into his mouth and rose. "I need to see how the adult choir practice is coming along. Bye."

He hurried away so quickly he didn't hear her say goodbye. It was just as well. If they had talked any more about kissing, she was afraid sweat would have beaded her brow and rolled down her face. How would she have explained that, when the hall was cool?

Samuel escaped from the rec hall before he did something crazy like kiss Beth in front of his parishioners. How did he think he could calmly talk about the kiss and not want to do it again? Especially since the past few days that kiss had dominated his thoughts.

She was leaving soon. He couldn't risk getting hurt—not again. He was just beginning to piece his life back together—partially due to the presence of Beth in his life as well as his family's. He had recited those same reasons not to get involved with Beth so many times over the past few days he wanted to pound something in frustration.

With a groan Samuel leaned back against the hall's wooden doors. He was in big trouble. He was afraid his heart was already involved with Beth to the point that he was going to be hurt when she left Sweetwater. Staying away from her was probably the best plan for him. He walked toward the sanctuary. He needed to feel close to God. He needed His help.

"What do you mean you haven't seen Samuel in several weeks except at church?"

Beth lifted the cup of coffee to her lips and took a drink. "Exactly that, Jesse. He's never around when I go to tutor Jane and the couple of times I've been at the church other than Sunday he hasn't been there, or at least I haven't seen him there."

Jesse shifted in the booth at Alice's Café, glancing out the picture window at the main street of Sweetwater. "It sounds like he's avoiding you."

"You think?"

Her friend frowned. "And you said it began after he kissed you and then tried to talk to you about that kiss?"

"Correct." Beth folded her arms and placed them on the table between her and Jesse.

"It's obvious. He's got cold feet."

"I know that. Jesse, I might not date a lot, but I do know what's going on here. And truthfully, Samuel's doing the right thing. Our relationship was heading toward more than friendship, and that isn't a good thing."

"Why not?"

"Because I'm committed to leaving in seven weeks and Samuel is committed to the memory of his deceased wife."

"Are you so sure about that? He kissed you!"

"One simple little kiss." She wasn't about to tell Jesse

that to her it hadn't been a simple *or* little kiss. After all, her friend was the town matchmaker. Beth caught sight of Zoey and Tanya opening the door to the café and added, "Not another word, please. I only told you about the kiss so you'd quit bugging me about Samuel."

"Fine. My lips are sealed." Jesse made a motion of turning a key by her mouth. "Even though I think we could all put our heads together and come up with a plan for you."

Beth growled her frustration as Darcy called out to Zoey and Tanya to hold the door. Darcy wheeled in a stroller with Rebecca in it, sound asleep, looking the spitting image of Joshua.

When the three ladies began settling into the oversize booth, Beth said, "I won't be able to stay too long. I'm tutoring Jane this afternoon. She has a research project due next week and we've been working extra to get it in. Let me sit on the outside." She slid across and stood while the others situated themselves.

Darcy winked. "Are you sure that's the only reason you spend so much time over at the reverend's house? I've gone by several times and have seen your car parked in the driveway."

"I don't see Samuel. He's been very busy lately. I'm seeing Jane," Beth said through clenched teeth.

Tanya took the menu lying on the table and flipped it open. "Yeah, he keeps going to the prison to try and get Tom to meet with him. Tom's refusing ever since that first meeting last month."

"Tanya, I'm so sorry. I know how much you were hoping that Tom would listen to reason." Darcy moved the blanket, revealing Rebecca in a cute pink dress with bunnies on it.

"The divorce is going through and there isn't anything to be done. Tom's turned away from God. That breaks my heart."

"Maybe when he's not so angry he'll find the Lord again." Beth checked her watch and rose. "I'd better get a move on. Sorry to cut this short, but some of you were late."

"With three kids it's hard to be on time for anything," Zoey said with a laugh. "And I brought Tanya, so that was why she was late."

Darcy gestured toward Rebecca. "She's my reason."

"That's okay. Beth and I discussed the men in our lives."

"Jesse, there are no men in my life unless you count my two brothers."

"Oh, yes, I'd forgotten. You haven't been dating anyone."

The twinkle in Jesse's eyes almost made Beth stay. She was afraid the second she left she and Samuel would be the subject of conversation at the table. "I've gone out a few times with Samuel. That's all. No big deal." She turned quickly away from her friends and headed for the door. She didn't want to dig a hole any deeper by staying and debating that with them.

Ten minutes later she arrived at Samuel's house and Jane greeted her at the door with a huge smile on her face.

"I don't have much left to do. I worked this morning. Ryan has asked me to go to the movies with him and some of his friends. Dad said yes so long as I was in a group."

Beth entered the house. "Your dad is here?" The second the question was out of her mouth she bit the inside of her cheek to keep from saying anything else.

"Yes, he's in his office writing the sermon for tomorrow."

Beth wanted to ask, "And he knew I was coming?" but refrained from making her interest too obvious. And she was definitely interested in Samuel, no matter what she had told herself or him earlier. Just the mention of his name sent her heart thudding against her chest.

Jane walked toward the dining room, where she had set up her work and the laptop she was composing on.

For the next hour Beth helped Jane hone the final draft of her research paper for history. Every sound coming from the direction of the office caused Beth to tense as though Samuel would walk into the room any second and change her whole world. By the time Jane printed out her final copy of the paper, Beth had drunk two tall glasses of water to moisten her parched throat and mouth.

Her nerves stretched taut, she read over the four pages Jane had written. "You've done a good job with this. Your history teacher will be proud of your hard work."

Jane beamed as she gathered up her papers and closed the laptop.

Footsteps from the hallway pushed Beth's composure to the edge. She slid a glance toward the door and stopped breathing for a few seconds. Samuel propped one shoulder against the jamb and smiled at her. Casual. Laid back. Appealing. Charming. All those words floated through her mind as she stared at him— blatantly, as if no one else was in the room.

Jane cleared her throat. "I'm going to go get ready for the movies."

She heard the teenager's words as though coming from afar. Every sense attuned to Samuel, Beth rose, their gazes linked. She wet her lips, then swallowed several times but nothing relieved the dryness that held her.

"I've missed you."

Samuel's words eroded her composure completely. She melted against the chair, gripping its back to keep from falling. No words came to mind.

"I've missed our talks."

That statement sparked her anger like flint against a stone. "I've been here every Monday, Tuesday and Thursday afternoon. Where have you been?" There was a part of her that was amazed she had said anything to him about his avoidance of her while she was tutoring Jane. But the other part cheered her on. She knew it was for the best that they not carry their friendship to the next level, but it was so nice to feel like a real woman for once.

"Usually at my office in the church until I see you leave."

His words caused her to blink in surprise. She didn't know what to say to the truth.

He chuckled, raising his hand, palm outward. "I admit it. I don't know what to do about us."

"Us?" she squeaked out, her voice breathless.

"Yes, us. There is an us, Beth, and you can't deny that."

"I'm not. But we won't go anywhere."

"How about we just enjoy the time we have together? I need practice dating. You need practice dating."

"We're going to practice dating?"

He nodded. "That's what I propose."

The word *propose* sent a whole different image into her mind than what he had intended. She saw herself in a long white gown, standing before a minister who wasn't Samuel because he was next to her, holding her hand. "I guess that wouldn't hurt us. I've had fun on our two dates."

"Then let's make it a third one. Jesse has invited me to a dinner at her house."

"She has?" Beth clenched the wooden slat on the back of the chair, determined to leave soon and have a word with her friend.

"Yes, she said something about inviting you and I told her I would, since I knew you would be here today."

"Do you know what one of Jesse's little dinner parties means?"

His eyes twinkled. "Yes, I've heard rumors. That's why I thought I would make it easy on her and invite you myself."

"You're too kind. I would have made her sweat some."

"I thought about doing that, but she does a lot for the church."

"You know the whole evening we'll be subjected to her matchmaking schemes."

"I think we can weather them—together."

Together. The one word stuck in her mind and kept her from thinking of anything beyond that. Again that image of her in the long white gown popped into her mind.

Worry creased his face. "Beth?"

She pulled herself away from her riotous thoughts and said, "You don't know Jesse when she sets her mind on something."

"She doesn't know me."

Some of the tension siphoned from Beth as she took in Samuel's smile, his relaxed stance. "True. We shouldn't make this easy for her."

"What do you have in mind?"

A plan began to formulate in her thoughts. She circled the table and came to stand in front of Samuel. "Let me tell you what we should do."

Chapter Nine

"You two seem awfully chummy tonight," Jesse said, handing Beth a platter with the steaks on it.

"We thought we would make it easier for you."

Jesse narrowed her gaze on Beth. "You're up to something. I can feel it."

Beth touched her chest. "Who, me?"

"Yeah, you." Jesse held the door open to allow Beth to exit the house first. "Last week you were avoiding him and now I can hardly keep you two apart."

"We've given up fighting our feelings."

Jesse's eyes grew round, and she hung back by the door, her voice low as she bent toward her to ask, "You aren't leaving this summer, then?"

"I didn't say that. Can't a gal date without it having to lead to anything permanent? I want to enjoy my last few months here. I enjoy being with Samuel." Even though she and Samuel had planned to play up their at-

traction, Beth was discovering she wasn't really play-
acting at all. She meant every word she'd said to Jesse.

Her friend's eyes widened even more. "This doesn't
sound like you." She stepped back. "Come to think of
it, you aren't dressed like the Beth I've known for years.
What have you done with her?"

Beth laughed. "I've come to my senses. You, Darcy,
Zoey and Tanya have been pushing me to wear brighter
clothes, to let my hair go, to wear some makeup." She
waved a hand down her length, indicating the teal-blue
capri pants with small beads dangling from the bottom
and the matching top with a mandarin collar and
capped sleeves.

Jesse pointed to Beth's teal sandals. "You've even
painted your toenails orange. You've never done that
before."

"Jane helped me pick out the color."

Jesse's mouth fell open.

"The guys are looking at us funny. We'd better take
the food to them." Beth left her friend by the back door
and walked toward Samuel and Nick by the grill.

Her date's eyes glittered dark fire as they roamed
over her. She nearly stumbled, and had to catch herself
before she sent the platter with their dinner flying
across the deck.

With warm humor Samuel winked at her, taking the
platter from her. "Is everything all right with Jesse?"

Nick glanced back at his wife. "I think you two foiled
her plans for the evening."

Samuel placed his arm about her shoulders. "That's too bad. What plans?"

Beth marveled at how innocent he looked. She pressed her lips together to keep her laugh inside while Nick forked the top steak and flipped it onto the grill.

"You don't know that—" Nick studied Samuel for a long moment. "You do know."

Both of them nodded as Jesse joined the group, carrying the corn on the cob wrapped in aluminum foil.

"Okay, now that you all have had some fun with me, I have to say, Beth, I do like your new look."

"Who says we're having fun with you?" Samuel drew Beth even closer and gazed into her eyes. "I like your new look *and* your old look."

Her stomach flip-flopped, her legs going weak. Samuel's grip on her tightened as she began to sink from the sensations his look sent through her. "I have to admit I like this outfit, too. Your daughter has great taste."

"Jane went with you shopping for clothes, too?" Jesse handed the corn to Nick.

"Yes."

"I'm surprised I didn't hear anything about it. That would have been hard to keep quiet in Sweetwater."

Beth grinned. "That's why we went to Lexington to shop. I didn't want the gossip hounds to work overtime."

"Believe me, when they see you, their tongues will be wagging, unless this is the extent of your new wardrobe."

"No. I bought several outfits. The next one I'm

wearing to church tomorrow and the third one to school on Monday."

"Are they all like this one?" Jesse asked Samuel.

"I don't know. I couldn't get my own daughter to tell me what Beth bought. I have to wait with the rest of you."

Jesse planted her hands on her waist. "Beth Coleman, you've always been an open book. I can't believe you are keeping secrets from us."

"And loving every minute of it."

Nick turned the steaks over. "Jesse will be up all night speculating."

The scent of grilling meat and spring flowers mingled to lace the air. Beth backed up until she felt the lounge chair and sat. "You'll just have to make the best of it, Nick. I'm sure you'll think of something to keep yourselves entertained while losing sleep."

Jesse burst out laughing.

"By the way, where are the kids?" Beth asked, observing Samuel moving around the chair to stand behind her. Her pulse quickened in anticipation of his touch.

"Cindy and Nate are at Gramps's, for the whole night."

Finally—an eternity later, in Beth's mind—Samuel settled his hands on her shoulders. Since she had come up with the scheme to give Jesse what she wanted— Beth and Samuel together as a couple—he had thrown himself wholeheartedly into the role of her boyfriend. She had thought it would be easier than fighting all the attempts by her friend to get them together. She was having second thoughts. She enjoyed his touch too much, and since they had arrived she had felt more and more comfortable with his arm around her or his hand on her.

"Jesse has gone back inside," Beth whispered, standing out in front of her friend's house, the stars shining bright in the dark sky, the night air cool but pleasant, especially with Samuel's arm around her shoulders, his warmth seeping into her to ward off any chill. "You don't have to pretend any longer."

"Pretend?"

"You know, that we're a couple. Jesse isn't looking."

"She could be spying out one of her windows as we speak."

"She isn't. I think we have convinced her we're an item, and tomorrow the whole town will know."

"I think the whole town already thinks that."

"They do?"

"Yeah. Yesterday Liz asked Aunt Mae when I was planning to propose."

Beth pulled away and squared off in front of him on the sidewalk, her hands going to her waist. "Propose! We've only been on two dates."

"Three."

"Okay. Three. Honestly, the people of Sweetwater are getting worse than Jesse ever was."

Samuel took her hands and stepped closer until little was between them, not even air. "They care about you. They want to see you happy. I think that's sweet."

"You don't have to be married to be happy. I've

been happy for the past thirty-eight years without a man. I've been—"

He lowered his head toward hers, cutting off the flow of her words. "I'm going to kiss you. I just wanted to warn you."

She nodded, a slight movement before his lips crushed down onto hers. The kiss stole her breath and any rational thought she had left. Standing on her tip-toes, plastered against him, she felt transported to a realm of the senses where she focused on his smallest detail—the dimple in his left cheek, the citrus after-shave he wore, the lines at the corners of his eyes that deepened when he smiled, the gruffness of his voice, the rough texture of his hands that he built things with. She had all those little traits memorized so that she could in-stantly recall him when he wasn't around.

When he drew back, resting his forehead on hers, she realized that he was as affected as she was by their kiss. She imagined if she laid her palm over his heart she would feel it beating as fast as hers was.

"That wasn't for the benefit of anyone but you," he whispered in the stillness.

Desperate to get control of her careening emotions, she backed away and glanced around her. "Thank goodness it's late."

"Yes, and I suppose we both need to get home. I have a sermon to deliver twice tomorrow." He took her hand and began to walk toward her street.

"After the meal Jesse prepared for us, I'm glad we're walking home."

"And it gives me a little more time with you. Private time without others around."

"Are you talking about Allie earlier this evening riding her bike alongside us as we walked over to Jesse's?"

"Not quite what someone would expect on a third date, but Allie was dying to come along and see you. I think she's jealous that Jane steals so much of your time when you're over at our house. Allie even told me the other day she needed tutoring."

"She does? I thought she got all A's."

"She had one B on her report card last time. I think she'll survive, but she said it right after you and Jane returned from Lexington."

"I'll try and plan something special with just me and her."

"You don't have to, Beth." His grasp on her hand tightened, drawing her closer to his side as they walked.

"I want to. Allie is so sweet. She reminds me of my sister when she was that age."

"And Jane reminds you of yourself?"

"There are similarities."

"Then my oldest daughter should be just fine when she grows up." Samuel paused at an intersection, looking up and down the street before crossing.

"She's almost grown up, Samuel. It won't be long before she's eighteen and heading for college."

"I know, I know. I'm not sure I'm going to like that change."

"I'm beginning to appreciate change in my life. For so many years I tried very hard to keep everything status quo. Now I'm learning to embrace change."

"Hence the new clothes and look?"

"Yes, as well as the plans to go to Brazil." She had to mention her plans. She had to ground not just him but herself in what was going to come in less than two months. She'd made a commitment to herself and the Christian Mission Institute. She didn't back down from her commitments.

Samuel turned up her oak-lined street. "What are you going to do about your house?"

"I'm keeping it. It's finally paid for. If my sister or brothers want to come back to Sweetwater, they'll have a place to stay."

"What about renting it out?"

"I don't know. I would like a place myself to come home to between assignments." She couldn't even explain to herself why she wasn't doing something with her childhood home. She envisioned herself coming back to Sweetwater from time to time to renew friendships and ground herself in the place she had come from, before heading back out into the world.

"Who's going to look after it while you're gone?"

She stopped on the sidewalk that led to her house. "You're full of questions tonight. I haven't come up with anyone yet. Any suggestions?"

"I will."

"I can't ask you—"

He brushed his fingers over her lips. "You didn't ask. I volunteered. Just as you did to tutor Jane. Let me do this for you. My house is almost back to normal, thanks to you. Jane's happier than I've seen her in a long time. I think that's your influence on her. I don't have to argue with her to get her to study. She wants to. Maybe I should ask what you have done with my daughter."

She wanted his fingers back whispering across her lips. This evening his touch had become so natural to her, as though he had been doing it for years. But she had to put a halt to the direction her thoughts were going. Dangerous territory. "I'm glad Jane is settling in. She's forming some good friends at school, and Ryan is a wonderful young man."

"I have to agree. Jane even spent the night at a friend's house last night. She's talking on the phone to her friends here in Sweetwater. She's laughing, smiling more. I'm beginning to feel the town puts something in the water. My children haven't been happier."

"We're a close community. We take care of each other."

"That's apparent all the time. When we need help at the church, there's always someone to do it. Usually more than one person. Our outreach fund is healthy."

"Speaking of the outreach fund, how's the dollhouse coming for the Fourth of July auction?"

"I should be finished very soon. If I get some time this week, I'll show you the completed house next weekend.

Then the real fun begins—making the furniture, the odds and ends for the place. It'll be a family project."

"I'd love to help. I used to love playing with my dolls when I was growing up. It'll bring back fond memories."

Samuel started up the walk to Beth's house, again reaching out and clasping her hand. "You've got yourself a deal. I know Saturdays can be busy. We could work on it on Sunday afternoons after church. I can usually corral my kids then."

The thought of doing the project with his family brought a smile to Beth's mouth. She'd missed her own family since Daniel had left for college in January. For years she had wondered what it would be like to be free of raising children. She'd made plans for that time, but hadn't really figured on how lonely it could be by herself in her now large house without three siblings. Once she was in Brazil, she would have plenty of people around her at the mission and a new life to learn.

"Then I'll pencil you and your family in for the next few Sundays." Beth stopped at the bottom of the steps that led to her porch and faced Samuel.

He took both her hands in his, bringing them up between them. "You should stay for dinner afterward. That's the least we can do for your help."

"I'd love to."

"Well, then, I guess this is good night." He began to lean toward her, hesitated, then pulled back. He squeezed her hands, then spun about and left.

Beth watched him walk away, already missing his

company. He was such a good man that maybe after she was gone Jesse could find someone for him. But when she thought about Samuel dating someone else, jealousy, something she rarely felt, sprang forth, surprising her. Maybe she wouldn't say anything to Jesse.

"Close your eyes." Samuel clasped Beth's hand to lead her into his workshop in the basement.

The scent of sawdust and paint hung in the air as she stepped through the doorway, confident that Samuel wouldn't run her into a wall or table.

"You can open your eyes now."

When she did, the first thing she saw was a modern split-level house sitting on the workbench, painted as though it was made of light brown stones with dark brown trim. "I love it!"

"I started to do a Victorian house like Allie's, but I wanted it to be as unique as Allie's, so I went with something more updated."

"It's beautiful. You could be a carpenter."

"It worked for Jesus, but I think I'll keep my day job. I'm enjoying what I'm doing again."

"Good. I'm glad to hear that. I know you were having your doubts, but as I told you before, your congregation doesn't feel you're doing a bad job at all." Beth moved closer to get a better look at the house. "You've got a deck and a hot tub. You really have gone modern."

"Do you think it will do well at the auction?"

"I can think of several people who will bid on it. Jesse will want it for Cindy and I bet Zoey will want it, too."

"I was thinking next of doing a farmhouse or a New England saltbox house. What do you think?"

"You should ask the people who will be lined up after the auction what they want, because I believe the ones who bid and don't get the split-level house will want you to do one for them. Your dollhouse is going to rival Jesse's dolls."

"It's just a hobby."

"That may be so, but it won't stop people from knocking at your door." She straightened from inspecting the different rooms. "What do you want to start with first?"

"I'll leave that decision up to you and the kids."

"Where are they?"

"Jane should be here soon. She went home with a friend after church. Allie's out back playing and Craig's picking up his room again. The first time he managed to get sidetracked and only put away one thing."

"Ah, I remember those days. With Daniel I finally had to shut the door and not go into his room—otherwise we would have been fighting all the time. I had more important battles to fight with him, like graduating from high school." Her gaze swept the neat workshop, all his tools in a certain place. "Where's Aunt Mae?"

"In the kitchen making a dessert for dinner. She was glad you agreed to stay and eat. She loves to make desserts, but only does it when we have company."

As Beth started for the stairs that led to the first floor, Samuel placed his hand at the small of her back and walked next to her as though they were back on Jesse's deck trying to make a point with her friend. For a few seconds his nearness robbed Beth of any coherent thought.

Then she realized he had asked her a question. "I'm sorry. What did you say?"

"Which room are we going to start with?"

"The den. That's the family room, the most impor-tant room in the house."

Climbing the stairs, she was aware of Samuel behind her and was glad she'd worn her new white slacks with a bright lime-green cotton shirt. No more dull shades for her. She was really getting into wearing all different colors. She figured she'd blend in with the vivid birds of the Amazon.

Samuel directed Beth to his den while he rounded up the rest of the family. She crossed to the large window overlooking the backyard and saw Allie playing in her fort at one end of the swing set. She was an adorable child. Beth could remember wishing, when she had been in her late twenties and early thirties, that she'd given birth to a baby as her friends had. But when she'd turned thirty-five she'd given up that dream and replaced it with seeing something other than Sweetwater.

What would have happened if Samuel had entered her life five years before? she wondered as Allie jumped down from the fort and ran toward the back door.

Turning away from the window, Beth drew in a deep

breath and smelled the scent of an apple pie baking. Her mouth watered in anticipation of the dessert Mae was preparing. Beth didn't make desserts for herself. In fact, she didn't cook the way she used to love to when she had her siblings at home. She needed to cook more—it had always been good therapy for her when she had been stressed. The smells that saturated a kitchen were soothing to her—bread baking, coffee perking, meat sizzling, all kinds of spices like garlic and cinnamon.

Her stomach rumbled as the children began to file into the den, chattering, laughing, filling the house with warmth. What a nice way to spend Sunday, Beth thought, making her way to the two card tables that Samuel was setting up.

Mae hurried into the room, her apron still about her waist, some flour smudged on her cheek. "Are we ready to begin?"

Allie giggled. "You've got flour on you." She pointed toward her aunt's face.

"Oh, goodness me. And I have my apron still on. Be right back." For a large woman she moved quickly from the room.

"She's always forgetting to take off her apron. I don't even notice anymore." Samuel pulled a chair out for Beth to sit in.

She did and allowed him to push it toward the table. She felt his breath on her neck and shivered.

"I'm going to sit back and let you direct this show," he whispered into her ear.

She shivered again and turned slightly to glance back at him. Big mistake. His face was only inches from hers, and she could smell the mint of his toothpaste. She could remember their last kiss the week before. She leaned away, desperately trying to calm her riotous senses. "How did I get to be so lucky?"

He shrugged, straightening away from her. "Beats me. I just know I don't know the first thing about sewing."

"But you're going to make the furniture?"

"Yep. Craig and I will, just as soon as you all decide what you want in the house."

"I can paint the walls like I did for Allie's house," Jane said. "I already helped Dad with the outside stone."

"I should have known that was your work. Very realistic." Beth examined the floor plans that Samuel unrolled. "As I told your father, I think we should start with the den."

"It'll need a television and a couch like we have." Craig plopped down next to Jane.

Before long everyone joined in discussing what the room needed, and then moved on to what they would do next. Aunt Mae came back without her apron and with her face scrubbed clean and declared that the kitchen should be the next room to tackle after the den.

The conversation swirled around Beth. She listened to the children argue about what colors to use, then lifted her hands to signal quiet. When they didn't obey, she whistled, a high shrill one that immediately quieted everyone. They all looked at her, Allie's eyes round.

A smile danced in Jane's gaze. "She did that once in class. Got our attention real fast."

"I think you punctured my eardrum." Samuel rubbed his ear.

"That was something I learned when refereeing my siblings. It's very effective." Beth took a piece of paper and a pencil. "I think I need to assign jobs to each one of you or we'll never get anything done." She checked her watch. "We have been talking around and around for the past thirty minutes and not much has been settled."

Samuel relaxed back in his chair, his gaze trained on Beth as she dealt with his children and aunt, giving them each something to start on. She was in her teacher mode and he loved seeing her at work. She would be a terrific mother. He still couldn't believe a man hadn't seen past her defenses to the woman beneath. She was loving and caring, willing to give of herself. She would be good teaching at a mission. But he couldn't help wishing she wasn't leaving soon. He was afraid she would take part of his heart with her when she did go to Brazil. He was falling in love and didn't know how to stop the plunge.

The sunlight streamed through the branches of the maple tree and crisscrossed a pattern over the stones in the path. Beth watched the light dance about as the warm spring breeze blew the branches. Everything had come to a grinding halt today, and she didn't know how to deal with it.

Going to the doctor for her physical before she traveled to Brazil was supposed to have been routine, not a big deal. Now it was. She could still remember her doctor telling her this morning after she had reviewed the results from the mammogram she'd had a few days before, "We need to do a needle biopsy. I'm scheduling you for the procedure Monday morning. If it's malignant, we'll need to operate right away."

She hadn't heard much of what the doctor had said after she'd uttered the word, *malignant.* All Beth's fears rushed through her like a raging river. Hugging her arms to her, she tried to still the tremors, but they racked her body.

She was going to leave in five weeks. If the lump was malignant, she wouldn't be able to. She— Beth couldn't think beyond that. She buried her face in her hands and desperately tried to keep the tears inside.

It might not be. She had to hold on to that hope. She had to put her faith in the Lord that He knew best.

"Beth? Are you out here?"

She lifted her head, forcing a smile to her lips, swallowing the tears lumped in her throat. She didn't want to worry Samuel with the news the doctor had given her, especially since there was a good chance nothing was really wrong. "Yes, by the pond."

Samuel appeared on the stone path, dressed in black slacks and a white knit shirt. He returned her grin with one of his own, which dimpled his left cheek and crinkled his eyes. "I was just thinking about you."

"You were?"

"Yeah. I knew you went to the doctor today. How did it go?"

The smile on her lips wavered, and it took a supreme effort on her part to keep it in place. "Fine. Fit as a fiddle." *Unless you consider the lump I have in my breast,* she added silently, not wanting to tell Samuel unless she absolutely had to. His wife had died from breast cancer. She was afraid what the news would do to him. She would protect him as long as possible.

Samuel settled on the bench next to her. "I wonder where that saying came from. I never thought of a fiddle as being fit."

She shrugged, latching on to the inane topic of conversation to keep her mind off what she didn't want to think about. "I haven't the faintest idea. A lot of sayings don't make sense." But for the life of her she couldn't come up with a single one at the moment.

"I have to admit some things in life don't make sense."

She leaned away from him and stared into his face. "Are we going to get into a big philosophical discussion?"

"We could take our government for starters. Some of the red tape is senseless. Or how about—"

She stopped his words with her fingertips, much as he had done to her in the past. "I make it a practice not to discuss politics with anyone."

The feel of his lips against her fingers sent a shock wave through her body. Not a smart move. She shifted her hand.

"Okay. Let's talk about the end of the school year.

We need to plan a party for our graduating seniors. Do you think you're up to doing that?"

"No," she replied before she realized what she was saying.

"No? Are you ill? I think that's the first time I've heard you say no."

"I'm going to be so busy the next few weeks I'm afraid I might not do the party justice. See if Zoey will." She wasn't lying to her minister, just not elaborating on what she meant by busy.

"Zoey would be good. I'll do that. I know in the past the seniors have been honored at a church service, and I still want to do that, but I would also like to do something special for them after the service. Graduating from high school is a big deal."

Beth saw Samuel's lips moving as he spoke, but for the life of her she couldn't focus on what he was saying. She kept going over what the doctor had told her and the implications of having breast cancer—what it would mean to her, to her plans for the future, to Samuel when he heard the news.

She clenched her teeth to keep from asking Samuel to pray for her. She couldn't do that to him—not to the man she loved. The revelation snatched her breath away, causing her to gasp.

"What's wrong?" Samuel asked in midsentence as he twisted around and stared at her, his sharp gaze honing in on her as though he was delving inside her mind to read her innermost thoughts.

Chapter Ten

Panic mingled with stunned bemusement. This was a secret Beth didn't want Samuel to know, especially if she did have breast cancer. She didn't want him to relive his past. Even though he didn't love her as he had his wife, he was a caring man who would feel for her if she had cancer and it would be pure agony for him. She wanted to spare him for as long as she could.

"Nothing a little rest won't take care of," she finally said. "Even though I didn't teach today, having a physical is exhausting work. All that poking and prodding. And of course, the worst is the fasting for the blood work." Beth waved her hand in the air in a flippant manner meant to dismiss the subject, and prayed that Samuel would take the hint.

"Have you eaten since the doctor's?" Samuel asked, looking at her closely, his eyes dark pinpoints.

"No, and I guess I should."

He rose in one fluid motion. "You certainly should eat. It's lunchtime. I'm taking you to Alice's Café. Do you have to get back to school?"

"No, I took the whole day off because I wasn't sure how long the physical would take."

"Good. Then let's go." He tugged on her hand to assist her to her feet.

Short of telling him what was wrong, Beth didn't see any way of getting out of having lunch with Samuel. On a normal day she would be happy to share a meal with him. But today wasn't normal. She needed to think, to make some plans, to pray.

"But I have to warn you I'm really not very hungry." Fear knotted her stomach into such a tight ball she was afraid anything she did eat would come right back up.

"Don't let Alice hear you say that."

"You're right. Maybe I should just go home. I wouldn't want to upset Alice."

Samuel stopped on the stone path and faced her. "Are you sure you're all right?"

Her panic mushroomed. She couldn't out-and-out lie to Samuel, and yet she couldn't tell him what was really wrong. She didn't want to see that look on his face when he heard she might have cancer.

He covered her forehead with his hand. "Maybe you're coming down with something."

"It's springtime. My allergies have been acting up. I'm stuffed up. I think after a good nap I'll feel much better." She skirted him on the path and started for her car in the parking lot.

He caught up with her. "Aunt Mae has a great chicken soup I can bring over later."

"Does chicken soup really work?"

"Aunt Mae swears by it."

"Sure. I'll see you later." She hurriedly climbed into her car before he asked any more questions.

Hopefully by the evening she would have her act together enough to get the chicken soup and send him on his way. Until she knew what she would have to deal with she would avoid seeing Samuel. A certain look would probably have her clinging to him for support. She couldn't do that to him, not after the ordeal he had gone through with his wife.

"I can't say anything to him." Beth stood at the window overlooking the high school parking lot, watching the rain fall in gray sheets. Dismal. The weather reflected her mood.

Zoey approached Beth and placed a hand on her shoulder. "You need to. He cares about you and he should know."

"I just can't! Right now I couldn't handle the look of fear that will appear in his eyes when he hears I was diagnosed with breast cancer, that I'm going in to have the lump removed tomorrow."

"He will hear, Beth. You can't keep this a secret. Your students will know you're gone. Jane is in your class."

"I haven't told them anything, and certainly nothing about having cancer."

"Still, Jane will tell him you weren't at school. Look at the chicken soup he brought over when you were having problems with your allergies."

Beth let her head sag forward, the tension in her neck shooting down her back and shoulders. "I know."

"He'll call your house and get your answering machine. Then he'll begin to worry, especially when you aren't at school the next day. Do you want him to go through that?"

Beth balled her hands into tight fists until her fingernails dug into her palms. "No! I want to spare him any grief. That's why I haven't said anything yet." *Even though I would love to have him hold me and tell me everything will be all right.* Her reeling emotions made her stomach constrict into a cold knot.

Rubbing her hands up and down her arms to ward off a bone-deep chill, she turned away from the rain-soaked landscape and faced her friend. "Will you tell him tomorrow for me? After I've gone into surgery?"

"Beth, you have never been a coward before. You need to tell him yourself tonight."

Tears blurred her eyes, and Zoey's face wavered in front of her. "It's too much. My cup is full."

The fear Beth had held pushed down in the dark recesses of her mind blossomed into a full-blown panic. *What if the doctor doesn't get all the cancer? What if it has spread to the lymph nodes? What if I only have a few months to live? What if...*

She squeezed her eyes shut, trying to keep the tears inside, but they leaked out, rolling down her face. "I've left everything in order in my room. A sub shouldn't have a problem. I—" Beth choked on the words lodged in her throat. She rushed past Zoey, paused at her office door and added, "Please tell him for me. I can't, Zoey. I can't do that to him."

Outside her friend's door Beth glanced up and down the hallway, relieved that it was empty. With tears flowing, she hurried to her classroom and grabbed her purse, sweater and umbrella. When she paused on the top step at the front of the school, she stared into the grayness that blanketed the parking lot and fought back the panic that had descended in Zoey's office.

She had so much to do that evening. She had to call each of her siblings and talk to them. No, she would wait to tell them later. But she did have to tell Darcy, Jesse and Tanya. She had to— The cold knot in the pit of her stomach grew. Shuddering, she slid the umbrella open and made a dash for her Jeep.

Do not think, Beth.

Do not think, Beth.

She kept chanting that sentence over and over in her mind to keep it blank of all thoughts.

Ten minutes later she arrived home to an empty, silent house. She immediately flipped on the television and turned it up loud. The noise that permeated the rooms kept the worry at bay for a few minutes while she changed her clothes and began to prepare for the next day. Then the doubts and fears came back in full force, sending her to her knees in the middle of her bedroom, a set of pajamas for the hospital clasped in her hand.

Lord, I don't know where to begin. I feel so lost and alone. Why cancer? Why now? I wanted to help people in other parts of the world. I had everything planned out. I would do Your work. Now I'm fighting for my life and so scared. Please show me what You want. Please help me.

Beth folded over, burying her face in her hands and going to the floor. What little control she'd thought she had over her life had been snatched away. The terror, the emptiness crashed down on her.

Through the sound of people talking on the television she heard the insistent ringing of her bell. She tried to ignore it, but the person at her front door wouldn't go away. The noise kept up, echoing through her mind, declaring that the outside world would not leave her alone to wallow in self-pity.

Beth rolled to her feet and trudged toward the front door, opening it without even checking who was ringing her bell, because she was so sure it was Zoey or one of her other three friends, come to talk some sense into her.

Instead, Samuel stood on her porch, his hair wet from the rain, rivulets of water running down his face. Worry darkened his eyes. Had Zoey told him already?

Please don't let it be that, Lord. I can't deal—

"Beth, what's wrong?" he shouted over the loud noise.

"Nothing." *Except that I have breast cancer. Don't look at me like that.* When he glanced toward the living room where the television was, she added, "I was in the other room and wanted to hear the show." She hoped he didn't ask which show, because she had no idea what was on at the moment or even what channel she had flipped on. That hadn't mattered at the time—she'd needed voices to fill the silence of the house.

"May I come in?" he asked, because she still blocked his entrance into her house.

No. "Sure." She stepped to the side, gripping the edge of the door so tightly that her knuckles whitened. Peering down at her casual attire, stained with paint and ripped in a few places, she said, "I wasn't expecting any guests."

He arched a brow. "'Guest' sounds so formal. I thought we were more than that."

A shaft of lightning brightened the dim foyer, followed almost immediately by a boom of thunder. "What brings you out on a night like this? If I didn't have some…housework to do, I'd be cuddled up on the couch reading a good book."

He combed his fingers through his damp hair, then rubbed the back of his neck. "I don't know. I just had an urge to see you. Is everything all right?"

How could he know something was wrong? I've been so careful not to give anything away.

Her heart seemed to come to a standstill. A tight band about her chest constricted her breathing. She masked her tension by moving past Samuel and into the living room to switch off the television that was now irritating.

"Beth?"

She spun around and pasted a smile on her face. "What could be wrong other than I have too many papers to grade and so I can't curl up on the couch and read a good book?"

"I thought you had housework to do."

"I do, then papers to grade." *It wasn't a lie,* she said silently, to soothe her conscience. She did have a few things to do around the house because she wouldn't be here for a couple of days—like watering her plants, the ones that had managed to live through the winter, and…well, that was all, but still, that chore was considered housework. She flipped her hand toward a stack of papers, most of them graded. "Those await me. So what could possibly be wrong that time won't take care of?" She managed to say the last sentence without strangling on the words, but she slid her gaze away as though immensely interested in those few papers that still needed grading.

Samuel searched her living room with his eyes, the whole time massaging his nape. "I don't know what came over me. I…" He raised his broad shoulders in a shrug.

Tell him, a little voice said inside her head.

"I guess I've been more edgy lately."

"Why?" she quickly asked, desperately wanting to center the conversation about him.

"In a few days it will be the third anniversary of Ruth's death. It's always been hard on me."

The tightness in her chest expanded. How could she add to his pain, especially at a time like this?

Chicken. You should be the one to talk to him about it, that inner voice taunted. *Not Zoey.*

But when Beth stared into his dark eyes and saw pain reflected in their depths, she knew she wouldn't say a word. Not tonight. Later she would explain her reluctance, because she knew she couldn't keep it a secret for much longer—not in Sweetwater. She loved her hometown, but this was definitely a downside to the town. Everyone knew everything eventually.

"I'm so sorry, Samuel. Losing a loved one is never easy. I wish I could help make it better for you."

He covered the distance between them. "Your presence in my life—our lives—has made it easier, Beth. Thank you."

Her fragile emotions threatened to come apart at his words. With his hair slightly tousled and wet from the rain, he looked adorable. She concentrated on the turned-up corners of his mouth and wished she could sample another kiss. She backed away before acting on her wish. That would only complicate an already complicated situation.

"I appreciate you coming over to check on me, but as you can see I'm perfectly fine." She spread her arms wide.

"You aren't gonna send a poor guy out into the driving rain without at least one cup of hot coffee?"

The hopeful gleam in his eyes unraveled her resolve to send him on his way as quickly as she could. "I guess I could take a break from…my housework for *one* cup of coffee."

He grinned. "You make the best in Sweetwater. Thanks!"

She didn't want to blush at his blatant compliment, but she felt the heat singe her cheeks and knew she had. She hurried toward the kitchen to put on some coffee.

"I thought you always had a pot on when you were here."

"I forgot when I came home." The way she was feeling she was lucky she'd made it home. "It won't take long to brew. Have a seat."

Samuel settled into a chair at the table as though he was at home in her kitchen. They had grown close over the past four months, beyond friendship, and yet all there really could be between them was friendship.

To keep busy she rifled through her cabinets until she found some chocolate cookies. "I know these are store bought, but they are very good. Want any?"

"Sure."

Beth withdrew several and placed them on a plate, then put it on the table in front of Samuel. When the coffee finished perking, she poured them each a cup and brought the sugar bowl to him.

He doctored his coffee with only one spoonful of sugar. "I can't totally give up the sweetness, but I'm working on it."

She cupped the mug between her hands and savored the warmth emanating from it. Even though it was spring outside and not chilly, she felt cold deep down inside her. "I told Jesse about the dollhouse and she is dying to see it. I told her she had to wait until the auction like everyone else."

"Good. I want to propose a prison ministry using our outreach funds. When I go to see Tom, I see so many inmates who need the Lord's guidance."

"Has anything happened with Tom?"

He shook his head, then took a long sip. "At least he's seeing me now."

"Tanya's resigned to the divorce, but she hasn't said anything to Crystal yet."

"She needs to tell her soon. Word will get out, and it's best for her to hear it from her mother."

Beth dropped her gaze to a spot halfway between them on the oak table. "She'll tell her when the time's right."

"For who?"

"Tanya. She's had to deal with a lot lately." She realized she was really talking about herself. She should be the one to talk to Samuel about her cancer, but she couldn't get the words past her lips.

"But she's not alone. God's with her and we're with her."

"Do you really feel that way?"

He looked her directly in the eye and said, "Yes. Two months ago I wouldn't have agreed, but you've made me see so much that I was refusing to see. The Lord has been with me the whole time. Just because a person prays to God doesn't mean that what he prayed about will happen. The Lord knows best, not me. I'd forgotten that."

Does He? For a few seconds her faith wavered. Then

she remembered a verse from Romans. "And we know that all things work together for good to them that love God, to them who are the called according to His purpose," she murmured.

Her hand trembled as she placed her mug on the table. *Tell him,* that inner voice pleaded.

She stared at his handsome face, the words rising within her. She opened her mouth to tell him, but as before nothing would come out. Quickly she lifted the mug again and sipped at her coffee. She could handle only so much, and telling him wasn't one of those things. Not yet.

Samuel stepped off the elevator and immediately saw Zoey pacing in front of the nurses' station. He headed for her, concerned by the worried look in her eyes. "Aunt Mae didn't tell me who was in the hospital. One of your children?"

"No." She waved him toward a waiting room across from the nurses' station, then preceded him.

When he entered the room, his gaze swept over Zoey, Darcy, Tanya and Jesse, and he knew who was in the hospital: Beth. The thought that she might be hurt slammed through him as though a truck had run over him. "What's wrong with Beth?" His question came out in a gruff whisper, but then, he was amazed his voice even worked.

"She's in surgery right now." Zoey peered toward Jesse for support, then back at Samuel. "She has breast cancer. The doctor is removing the lump."

He sank into a chair not far from him, his legs giving out. His throat closed, cutting off his air until it was difficult even to breathe. "Breast cancer," he managed to choke out, while the pressure in his chest squeezed his heart until it felt as though it were splitting into fragmented pieces.

"Yes, she found out a few days ago and the doctor wanted to operate right away." Jesse came forward. "We wanted her to tell you. She couldn't. She asked Zoey to."

Four pairs of eyes were on him, their own pain mirrored in their gazes. He couldn't look at them any longer. He dropped his head, staring unseeingly at his lap, his hands twisting together, their outline blurring.

No, not again, Lord. Why Beth? Why me?

Silence greeted his plea.

The sounds of the regional hospital cut into the quiet in his mind—beeping noises, people talking outside the waiting room, a doctor being called over the intercom system. He tried to draw air into his lungs, but a tightness gripped his chest. Light-headed, he finally looked up at the four women still staring at him, the worry on their faces now evolving into full-fledged concern.

Over three years ago he had lived through this very scene, only to lose his wife in the end because the cancer had spread so quickly. Again he took a breath, this time managing to fill his lungs partially.

Zoey sat next to him and placed her hand on his arm. "I'm so sorry. I tried to get Beth to tell you yesterday, but she said she couldn't handle it. She was still trying to deal with the fact she had cancer. Everything moved so fast once they discovered the malignant lump."

"How long has she been in surgery?" Why hadn't she been able to turn to him? He had failed her when she needed him most.

"A while. It shouldn't be much longer."

He should have been here from the beginning, but he had been out running when Zoey had called the house. He'd come as soon as he could after his aunt had told him Zoey needed him at the hospital, that she would be on the second floor in the waiting room. He should have held Beth and prayed with her last night, but instead he had sat in her kitchen drinking her coffee, talking about unimportant things, oblivious to what was really going on in her head. In his heart he'd known something was wrong, but when she hadn't said anything he hadn't pushed. He should have pushed.

For the next twenty minutes he paced the length of the room, counting his steps because he didn't want to think about what was going on with Beth. If he could numb his mind, he would be all right.

"I'm getting some coffee. Do you want any?" Darcy asked everyone.

"I could use a cup." Tanya started to lift her purse from the floor.

Samuel stopped his pacing and said, "I'll get the coffee, and it's on me."

Pivoting, he hurried from the room and went in search of the vending machine on the floor. Out in the corridor he felt as though he could breathe a little more easily without Beth's friends watching him as if they were waiting for him to explode. He had to hold himself together long enough to find out if Beth would be all right. He'd lost control once before in his life and had hurt his family in the process. He couldn't do that again, and if that meant shutting down his feelings concerning Beth, then that would be what he had to do. She had become too important to him. He would be there as her friend, but that was all. Emotionally he couldn't afford anything else.

After selecting three coffees from the vending machine, Samuel headed back to the waiting room. Approaching the group of women, he noticed a man in their midst talking to them. He rushed forward, realizing the doctor was reporting on Beth.

Smiling, Zoey looked at him. "She's going to be okay."

"I removed the lump," the doctor said. "The cancer was contained and hadn't spread to the lymph nodes."

Relief made Samuel's hand tremble as he handed the paper cups to Tanya and Darcy. "Can we see her now?"

"She's still in recovery, but I'll have the nurse tell you when she's back in her room." The doctor left the waiting room.

Jesse grabbed her purse and rummaged inside. "I'll call her sister and brothers now."

"Why aren't they here?" Samuel asked, swallowing

some of the bitter, lukewarm coffee. He winced and realized he'd forgotten the sugar that Beth was trying to wean him from.

"Beth didn't want them to come home for this. She made me promise not to call until after the operation." Jesse retrieved her cell phone and a slip of paper with some phone numbers on it. She walked to the other end of the room and began making her calls.

"I guess we're lucky she told us." Zoey went to the phone in the waiting room and began punching in some numbers as she continued, "I'm calling the school to let the secretary know what's going on."

Now that he knew Beth was going to be all right, anger started festering inside him. Beth shouldn't have kept something like this a secret—not from him. Didn't the past few months mean anything to her? He'd begun to think he meant something to her, but that was obviously not the case. Beth had told only her closest friends, and he hadn't been one of them. Her rejection hurt, fueling his anger.

"I'm going for a walk. I'll be back later," he told Beth's friends, and started for the door.

"What do we tell Beth when we see her? When will you be back?"

Samuel glanced over his shoulder and said to Zoey's questions, "I have no idea when, if ever."

He couldn't think in the hospital. He had to get away from it and try to make some sense out of his vacillating emotions.

* * *

"You told him?" Beth asked Zoey as her friend sat in the chair next to her bed.

"Yes."

Beth looked from Zoey to Jesse, then Darcy and Tanya. "Where is he?" Even though her mind was foggy from the anesthetic, concern for Samuel pushed to the forefront. She knew what the news would do to him and now she feared the worst.

"He went for a walk." Darcy glanced away from Beth as though she couldn't quite meet her eyes.

"What aren't you telling me?"

"Nothing," Jesse said too quickly.

"You don't have to protect me."

Jesse looked directly at Beth. "I'm not sure he's coming back."

Beth shouldn't have been surprised by the news and she wasn't, but disappointment that she wouldn't see Samuel flooded her. Despite not having the nerve to tell him about her cancer, she had still wanted to see him when she awakened from the operation. She loved her friends, but she needed Samuel. She needed to know he was all right. She needed him to tell her everything would be all right for her.

"I imagine this has brought back bad memories of his late wife." Beth plucked at the white cotton sheet, trying to keep her voice steady.

"He didn't look too well when I told him about

you," Zoey murmured. "I don't think I did a very good job, either."

"Nonsense, Zoey. You did fine. It's not easy breaking that kind of news to anyone. I called your siblings." Jesse moved closer to the bed.

"They aren't coming, are they?" Beth didn't want her family descending on her, not when she felt so fragile— as if she would break at any moment. She needed to be alone, to lick her wounds by herself. Or even better, she needed Samuel.

"No, they're going to respect your wishes. But Holly said you'd better call her as soon as you can. Daniel is coming home in a few weeks to check on you. I couldn't reach Ethan because he is out of the country, but I left a message on his machine."

Beth tried to smile, but the corners of her mouth quivered. "Thanks, for calling them, Jesse. I'd forgotten that Ethan was on assignment in the Middle East for his newspaper."

Weariness slid over Beth, causing her to yawn. Her eyelids drooped, then snapped open.

"I think we'd better leave you to get some rest." Zoey rose from the chair and patted Beth's arm. "We're here for you and we will be when you get home. Anything you need just ask one of us or all of us." She leaned down and gave Beth a hug.

Each one embraced Beth and said she would pray for her. Then her four best friends left her alone to her thoughts. Where was Samuel now? What had she done to him?

Please, Lord, help him and heal any pain that my illness may have caused him. I don't ever want to hurt him. I love him too much.

As the prayer slipped through her mind, she closed her eyes and pulled the sheet and blanket up to her chin. Coldness pierced her as though she had been stabbed with an icicle. She burrowed down under the covers, sleep flowing over her....

A sound penetrated her sleep-drenched mind. She shifted on the bed, trying to get up, and pain spread outward from her chest. She remembered where she was and why. Her eyes bolted open to her dimly lit hospital room, darkness beyond the window. In the shadows stood a tall, muscular man she instantly recognized as Samuel. He stared out the window into the night, his body stiff, his hands curled into fists at his sides.

Her first thought was that he had come to see her. Then she really studied his stance and saw the anger barely contained, especially when he swung around and stabbed her with his icy look, much like the coldness earlier before she'd fallen asleep.

"I just wanted to make sure you were all right with my own two eyes." He started for the door.

"Please don't leave."

Chapter Eleven

Beth's plea went straight to Samuel's heart, twisting about it and squeezing. He halted but couldn't turn toward her, not yet when he was fighting both his anger and his pain. He'd tried to walk off his anger, and had thought he had succeeded until he found himself in her hospital room. Then all his fury had returned. While she'd slept, he'd watched, alternating between wanting to leave and stay.

Still facing the door, he said, "I don't think I'd be very good company at the moment."

"I'm sorry, Samuel. I couldn't bring myself to tell you what was happening to me."

He pivoted, having come back to discover one thing. "Are you really all right?"

"I'll be fine. Time's all I need. I had reconstructive surgery at the same time, so it will take me longer to get back on my feet, but I will get back on my feet. From what the doctor said they got it all."

"Good. Now I need to go." He took a step toward the door.

"Samuel, please."

Heaving a deep sigh, he swung back toward her again. "What do you want from me, Beth? I'm dealing with this the best way I can. You didn't think enough of me to include me in what was happening to you. That clearly tells me where we stand."

"That's not why I didn't say anything to you. I care too much, Samuel. I didn't want to be the one to hurt you any further. I know what you went through with Ruth. If I could have gone through this without you ever finding out, I would have. I knew that was impossible. Not in Sweetwater." Tears ran down her face and she did nothing to stop them.

The sight of the wet tracks on her cheeks tore through his defenses, but still he stayed by the door, not daring to go to her. She'd admitted she wouldn't have said anything to him if she had thought she could get away with it. That she thought so little of him drove the hurt even further into him. His emotions were shredded and he felt half a man at the moment. He couldn't help her until he helped himself. Part of him was grounded in what had happened in the past; the other was here with Beth trying to deal with feeling left out of an important part of her life, of feeling as though he had let her down by not being by her side through the whole ordeal from the very beginning.

He gripped the handle on the door and yanked it open. "I'll see you later."

Out in the corridor he drew in a shaky breath and looked down at his hands, spread in front of him. They trembled with the force of the intense emotions coursing through him. He knew of only one way to deal with what was going on inside him.

Samuel rode the elevator to the first floor and found the chapel. Inside the small, dimly lit room he sat on the pew before the altar, folded his hands together and prayed as he had never done before. He would not go back to the man he was three years ago. That time he had nearly been destroyed. And he knew he couldn't do this by himself.

Dear Heavenly Father, I believe You brought Beth into my life for a reason. She has helped me to find my way back to You, to heal the breach in my family. Please help her. Give me the knowledge to assist her through her ordeal. Help me to overcome the pain she caused when she didn't include me in her life when she was hurting the most and needed me the most.

The serenity of the chapel seeped into his soul and soothed away the hurt as though a hand had reached inside him and stroked away the pain. She was the best thing that had happened to him in a long time. Thinking back to their discussions about Ruth, he could see why she had excluded him and faced her operation on her own. He had opened up to her as he had to no one else, but in so doing had put a barrier of fear between them when she needed him most.

Now he could either walk away from her or be there

for her as a friend—anything beyond that he wasn't
sure he was ready to give.

The nurse had come in and closed the blinds in Beth's
room. The darkness beyond her window invaded every
corner. Beth switched off all the lights except the night-
light near the bathroom and now lay in the dimness,
trying to gather her composure, pull her life together.
Even knowing Samuel's reaction to her not telling him
about the surgery and breast cancer, she didn't think she
would have done anything differently. Remembering
back to the evening before, she knew she couldn't have
come up with the right words to ease his pain with her
news. Maybe one day he would understand her motives
for keeping quiet and having Zoey tell him.

She couldn't fight her feelings any longer. She loved
him and that wasn't going to change or go away. But
how could she compete with a ghost? His deceased wife
was there between them.

She felt her tears return and determinedly squashed
them. She had cried enough the past week—because of
the cancer, because of her lost opportunity to go to
Brazil, because of Samuel and what she had known she
would do to him.

Her door swished open, and she turned her head to
see who was coming into her room. Samuel stood just
inside the entrance, a neutral expression on his face. He
moved forward. Hope flared inside her as he made his
way to her bed and sat in the chair next to her.

"It's dark in here. Were you trying to go to sleep?"

She shook her head, afraid to use her voice for fear it wouldn't work.

"Beth…" He took her hand and cupped it between his. "I'm sorry for getting angry earlier. I was purely reacting, not thinking. Can you forgive me?"

"If you'll forgive me for not having the courage to tell you myself. I wanted to. I…" She licked her dry lips and swallowed several times. "Will you hand me that glass of water on the stand?"

He reached for the peach plastic cup and gave it to her. "I won't kid you and tell you that you having breast cancer doesn't worry me because the doctor feels he got it all. In my head I know you'll be all right in time. In my heart I'll always worry about you. You're so special and very important to me."

Beth sipped her water, the cool liquid slipping down her parched throat. "That's the way I feel about you. In my head I knew I should have told you about my cancer, but in my heart I couldn't bring myself to do it. I tried. Really I did."

Leaning forward, he brushed his fingers across her moistened lips. "I know. It wasn't easy for Ruth to tell me either, and there had been no past history to contend with." When he settled back in the chair again, his hands clasped in his lap, he continued, "Now, let me make it up to you by having you come stay with us until you're back on your feet."

"I can't do—"

He held up his hand. "Shh. Yes, you can. Aunt Mae and I insist. Someone has got to take care of you for the next week or so. You didn't want your siblings to come home, so who is going to?"

Smoothing the blanket over and over, she murmured, "Me. I had planned to do it myself. I've taken care of myself for the past thirty-some years. This is no different."

"No. I won't let you do it by yourself. You need to be pampered and cared for, and I have a family who is eager to do it. I asked each one, and none of us will take no for an answer. At least consider staying with us for a few days. You've had major surgery. You shouldn't be by yourself."

Stunned by the invitation and the ardent way he asked, Beth found herself nodding, almost afraid not to from the look of determination on his face.

"Good. Then it's settled."

"You'll have to break the news to Zoey, Darcy, Jesse and Tanya. I think they had planned on taking shifts staying with me."

"They can visit you at my house."

In all her adult life she had always been the one to pamper and take care of someone. She had never been the recipient before. She might go stir crazy before the first day was over, she thought. She wasn't very good at doing nothing.

With his arm about Beth, Samuel helped her to his bed while his three children and Aunt Mae filed into his bedroom behind him. "You're going to use my room."

"I can't kick you out of your own room."

"Yes, you can and besides, you don't have a say in this." Samuel assisted her as she eased onto his bed. "I've already set up my things downstairs in my office. There's a very comfortable couch that will be fine for me."

"But—"

He shook his head. "No buts. I didn't think it would be very restful to share a room with either a fifteen- or eight-year-old. And you need your rest."

"Yes, Dr. Morgan."

Even though he grimaced, a twinkle glinted in his dark eyes. "I have a list of instructions from your doctor and I intend to carry out every last one of them."

"With our help," Allie chimed in.

Beth peered around Samuel and smiled at the young girl. "Thank you for letting me share your home."

"Dear, you're welcome anytime." Aunt Mae bustled over to the bed and began turning down the covers. "I think the best thing for you right now is to get some rest."

"That's all I've been doing the past few days. I've never had this much rest before."

"Have you ever been really sick or had an operation?" Aunt Mae fluffed up several king-size pillows and placed them against the cherry-wood headboard.

"No."

"Then you need to lie back and let us take care of you. I know what I'm doing and I'll make sure they do, too."

The older woman tossed her head in the direction of Samuel and the children. "They really are very trainable."

"Aunt Mae!" Jane exclaimed, laughter in her voice.

Samuel's aunt grinned and winked. "Now, let's take off your shoes and get you comfortable."

Beth threw a "help me" look toward Samuel. He shrugged.

When Aunt Mae started to assist Beth with her shoes, Beth shook her head and said, "I can do it. Please, I'm not an invalid yet."

"Okay. Okay." The woman backed off. "I'll go prepare dinner, then. Come on, children, I need some help in the kitchen."

The three children left the room, grumbling the whole way. Allie even glanced back and started to say something to her father.

Samuel stopped her with his hand raised. "You go with Aunt Mae. You'll get to see Beth later." Then when the children had disappeared into the hallway, he turned back to her and added, "My family can be a bit overwhelming."

Beth thought about Allie, Craig, Jane and Aunt Mae and had to agree with Samuel, but their presence warmed her. They were overwhelming in a good way, reminding her of her siblings, who had filled her house with noise and laughter.

"I'm not sure you'll get the rest you need. I forgot about how much my children like you."

Beth slipped her shoes off and scooted back against the pillows, glad that she wore a comfortable jogging suit. "Good. They can keep me from being bored. I don't do lying around very well. Never had much of a chance, raising three siblings, so I don't even know if I can do it."

"You may regret saying that in a day or two. Allie already has a whole bunch of games she wants you to play with her."

"I might be able to work some on the dollhouse."

"We're almost done and remember, no work for you. That word shouldn't even be in your vocabulary for the next week or at least a few days."

"My, I'm seeing a whole new side to you."

He dragged a padded chair to the bed and sat. "The caring, wonderful side?"

She laughed. "Hardly. More like demanding, I'm-going-to-get-my-way-no-matter-what side."

Lines of merriment appeared at the corners of his eyes, fanning outward and adding a certain whimsical appeal to his charm. "Seriously, is there anything I can get you? Do you have everything you need from your house?"

"You and Zoey did a great job of packing what I needed." She pictured Samuel helping Zoey gather her clothes and felt the heat of a blush sear her cheeks. Had he gone through her drawers and closet?

Samuel's gaze held hers for a long moment, penetratingly intense. "To put your mind at ease, Zoey wouldn't let me near your bedroom. I got the two books you wanted to read, your special blend of coffee and your address book with your stationary."

"Aunt Mae won't be offended because I brought my own coffee?"

"Not when she gets a taste of it. She'll be fighting me for a cup."

Now that she was settled, weariness washed over her. It was the middle of the afternoon. She never took naps, and yet she wanted one. She needed some coffee. "Speaking of my coffee, do you think I could get some?"

"Sure. But don't you think you should rest before dinner?"

Determined not to let her breast cancer change her life any more than it already had, she shook her head. "I don't believe in naps."

He levered himself out of the chair and hovered over her. "I'll go have Aunt Mae make some coffee and I'll share a cup with you. Then I insist you rest."

"Aye, aye, Captain."

He headed for the door. "You know I was a captain in the army."

The chuckle in his voice gave her a warm, cozy feeling as she let her eyelids close for just a moment. The scent of clean, fresh sheets teased her senses while she thought of the masculine decor in Samuel's room. Solid dark cherry-wood furniture with only a few knick-knacks adorning the surfaces fit her image of Samuel. He was solid, like the pieces of furniture, with a no-nonsense personality. And yet, on the nightstand there was a picture of his family and a Bible, both important parts of his life.

The exhaustion she'd held back claimed her, whisking her away. She fought it, but for the life of her she couldn't pry her eyes open. Sleep blanketed her.

Samuel toed open his bedroom door, since his hands were occupied with holding two mugs of the delicious-smelling coffee that was Beth's special blend. Starting across the brown carpet toward his bed, he stopped halfway when he saw Beth with her head sagging to the side on the pillows propped against the headboard, her eyes closed in sleep. She looked beautiful and at peace even though she'd had a fright this past week. The doctor felt she would make a full recovery, and Samuel prayed the man was right, because staring at Beth in his bed, sleeping, made him realize how much he cared for her, that being her friend might not be enough.

Was it love? The kind that bound two people together forever?

Frowning, he covered the distance between them and placed her mug on a coaster on his nightstand. He caught a glimpse of the framed photograph of his family. Ruth smiled at him, her hands on Allie's shoulders. Looking at his deceased wife didn't bring the usual heartache and emptiness. Samuel glanced back at Beth, knowing she was the reason he was beginning to move on with his life, relishing again the fullness of it, especially his relationship with the Lord.

But would he be placing himself in a position to be

hurt again if anything happened to Beth? What if the doctor was wrong? What if the cancer did return?

Easing onto the chair, he took a long sip of his coffee, relishing it as it slid down his throat. While he cupped the mug between his hands, he saw his wedding band on his left finger, the light gleaming in its golden depths. For the first time since he'd put it on over sixteen years ago, he was considering removing it and putting it away.

How would his children feel about him doing that?

Was he ready?

Was he in love with Beth?

Questions bombarded him as he stared at Beth in his bed. He sat drinking the rest of his coffee and watching her chest rise and fall gently as she slept. At peace. Safe.

By the time his mug was empty, Samuel knew he needed to move on. Even though his future with Beth was still very much up in the air, his first step was to take off his wedding band. Rising, he walked to his chest of drawers and pulled open the top one. With a twist he slipped the gold ring from his finger and placed it in a keepsake box.

Peering down at his bare finger, the skin where the ring had rested whiter than the rest of his hand, he waited for the feelings of guilt and sadness to inundate him. Instead, he experienced relief that he was finally moving forward in his life. Amazed, he turned toward Beth and discovered her watching him.

She screwed her face into a puzzled expression. "Are you all right?"

He nodded. "Better than I realized I would be."

Her frown deepened. "What do you mean?"

He held up his left hand. "I took off my wedding band."

Her eyes grew round. She sat up. "You did? Why?"

He strode to the chair and sat, placing his hands on his thighs, his fingers spread wide. "Because it was time. I was living in the past. That isn't good for me or my family."

"Sometimes telling ourselves what is good for us and really feeling that way are two different things."

"In my case, it isn't."

"We haven't talked about me having breast cancer. We've avoided the subject."

"And you don't want to avoid it any longer?"

"I think we need to talk about it. I know what your wife's illness did to you. I don't want to be the cause of any more pain for you."

Samuel leaned forward, sandwiching her hand between his. "I'm working on it. God and I have had some long talks lately." He hiked one corner of his mouth up. "I may not always see the big picture, but I'm trying. My main concern right now, Beth, is making sure you get back on your feet."

"If your aunt has any say, that may not be anytime soon."

"She loves to pamper, to do for others. Kinda reminds me of you."

Sadness entered Beth's expression. "I won't be able to go to Brazil in a few weeks like I had planned. The doctor said my recovery would be at least two and a half, three months." She slipped her hand free, plucking at the sheet. "I'll have to call the Christian Mission Institute to explain what happened. I hate letting anyone down."

"Most of all you?"

Her eyes gleamed with unshed tears. "I wanted to go. I have my passport. I'd bought some clothes for the jungle. I can't say my Portuguese was too great, but I am sure once I got there it would have improved. Now none of that makes any difference."

"Why do you say that? You could always leave later."

"The institute will have filled that position. They'll need someone to take my place."

"There are other positions, other groups."

Entwining the sheet about her hand, Beth shrugged. "I guess." When she brought her head up and looked him straight in the eye, she asked, "Do you think God is telling me I shouldn't leave Sweetwater?"

"That's something you have to work out with Him. I'm discovering He brought me to this town for a reason. Maybe it is to help Tanya or someone else. But the longer I am here, I know it in my heart." He patted his chest.

"How's Tanya really doing? I can tell something is wrong, but she wouldn't say what when she visited me that last time in the hospital."

"She received her divorce papers two days ago. She came to see me right after that. We prayed together."

"She should have said something to me."

"She didn't want to burden you."

She winced. "There's a lot of that going around."

"Then you understand her silence?"

"Yes." Beth straightened and reached for the phone. "But she isn't a burden. When will she realize that?" She punched in Tanya's number and waited for a good minute before hanging up. "No one's there. I'll call her later to check on her."

"I forgot. She's probably out at the farm. Crystal's riding again, with Darcy's help."

"Tanya agreed to that?"

"Crystal has been asking and asking for the past few months. Darcy has made sure that Crystal has the gentlest mare to ride."

"I have heard riding is good therapy."

"Conquering one's fears is important, too."

"Whose? Tanya's or Crystal's?"

"I think a little of both. The first time Crystal rode, Darcy told me she was white as a sheet and scared. She clenched the reins and hardly relaxed for the first twenty minutes. But by the end of the lesson she was laughing. This is the second time." He shifted in his chair. "We can learn something from Crystal."

"To meet our demons head-on?"

"Yep—she's quite a special young lady."

Beth blew out a long breath that lifted her bangs. "I'm out of commission for less than a week and look what happens. You know more about my friends and their lives than I do. Darcy didn't say a word."

"That's because the first lesson was yesterday evening."

"And they're out there again today?"

"Crystal got up this morning and insisted she go back this afternoon. Tanya couldn't say no and neither could Darcy."

She twisted her mouth into a frown. "What are they doing? Calling you every hour to give you updates?"

"Actually one of your group of friends does practically call me every hour to see how you're doing. I just ask them some questions to find out what's going on, so if you want to know I can tell you."

A smile graced her mouth. "I have some nice friends."

"Yes, you do, which says something about you."

Pink tinged her cheeks, adding some color to her pale features. She averted her face while stretching to grasp the mug. Fighting a yawn, she took a sip. "Even lukewarm this is good, and I need some caffeine if I want to stay up for dinner."

Standing, Samuel reached for her coffee and took it from her. "Take another nap. I'll bring you a tray when you're rested."

"But I don't want to be—"

"Don't, Beth. The best medicine for you is sleep. Aunt Mae's dinner can be heated up when you're ready to eat. I'll check back later."

She hid a yawn behind her hand. "I don't take naps, and certainly not two in one day."

"Then this is a good time to start the practice." He strode toward the door, opened it and glanced back to see Beth snuggle down under the covers.

He fought the urge to go back and tuck her in, as though that action would keep her safe. Her health was in the hands of the Lord now. God had brought Beth into his life for a reason. He needed to practice patience and see what the Lord had planned.

Allie clapped her hands. "I won! I won! Again!"

"You're one lucky girl," Beth said, shuffling the deck of cards.

"Can we play another game of war?"

"No, you can't, young lady. It's time for bed." Samuel entered the den and set a mug down next to Beth on the coaster on the coffee table.

She looked into it and frowned. "Milk?"

He stood next to his youngest. "You said you had a hard time falling asleep last night, so I thought this might help you. I hear warm milk is good right before bedtime."

Allie cocked her head to the side. "It's your bed-time, too?"

Tired, Beth nodded. "I didn't take as many naps today as yesterday and I think I'll have no problem sleeping tonight." She grinned. "Now I know why I don't take naps. Then I don't toss and turn during the night."

There was no way she was going to tell either Samuel or his daughter that the main reason she didn't sleep well was her dream, centered around the man standing not two feet from her. It wasn't every day she discovered she was in love. Even though he had taken off his wedding ring several days ago, that didn't mean he loved her. And even if he did, she wasn't looking for a ready-made family. She'd raised one already.

"Daddy, I want some warm milk." Allie scooted back onto the navy-and-tan couch. "I don't want to toss and turn."

He narrowed his gaze on his daughter. "You don't toss and turn. You sleep like a log."

Allie lifted her chin and crossed her arms. "But I might start tonight."

Beth chuckled. "She's got you there." She had to admit Allie was adorable, and so were Craig and Jane. Okay, she couldn't kid herself about his children. She cared about them, but enough to take on another family? Whoa! He hadn't asked her to, so why was she thinking about becoming a member of Samuel's family?

"No, this is a new stall tactic."

"You think?" Beth tried to suppress her laugh, but the exasperated look on Samuel's face made her giggle leak out.

"Eight-thirty is too early for someone my age to go to bed." Allie puffed out her chest. "Cindy isn't my age yet and she goes to bed at nine. I think I should be able to stay up at least as late as Cindy Blackburn."

Samuel squared his shoulders as if he were going to do battle. "I've got news for you, young lady—you are not Cindy Blackburn. It's still a school night and Allie Morgan goes to bed at eight-thirty." He checked his watch. "Which is right now."

"But, Daddy—"

He shook his head once. "No argument. We'll discuss your bedtime when it isn't your bedtime."

Allie pushed herself to her feet, her shoulders hunched over, a dejected look on her face. "Can we talk about it tomorrow?"

"That will depend on how fast you get ready for bed."

Allie ran from the room. The sound of her going up the stairs reminded Beth of a stampede of cattle she'd seen in a movie earlier that day while trying to do something when the children were at school and Samuel was at the church. She was afraid she drove Mae crazy with all her talk. Idleness wasn't her cup of tea.

"You've got the magic touch," Beth said, rising from the couch so Samuel didn't tower over her.

"No, you do. My kids stayed at the dining-room table long after we had eaten because of you. They enjoy your company." His look snared hers. "I enjoy your company. Are you sure you have to leave tomorrow?"

Chapter Twelve

"Yes, I've been here for four days. That's long enough." Beth knew she should move away from Samuel, but his look held her transfixed.

"What are your plans after that?"

The question that she had been avoiding since she had found out about having cancer hung between them. "I don't know," she finally answered, chilled by the uncertainty of her future. "I contacted the Christian Mission Institute and told them I couldn't take the job, but that's all I've done."

He stepped forward, taking her hand between his. "You haven't had much time to think about what you're going to do after you recover. I meant what are you going to do in the next few weeks?"

"Oh." The warmth of his hands cupping hers flowed through her, taking with it any coldness his question had produced.

"Since school is out in three weeks, you won't be going back this year, and I know firsthand—" his mouth lifted in a lopsided grin "—how you like to be kept busy."

"I could help with the auction, and I can still tutor Jane until school is out."

"She'll appreciate that and I'm sure Jesse and Zoey will appreciate any help with the auction. But what are you going to do for yourself?"

"I—I..." Beth couldn't think of anything. She wanted to say it was because Samuel was so close and robbing her of any rational thought, which was partially true. But deep down she knew the reason she couldn't think of anything was that all her life she had lived for others. The trip to Brazil had been for her, and yet now that wasn't possible.

"That's what I was afraid of, Beth. You don't know how to plan things for yourself. Tell me one thing you would like to do when you feel up to it. Is there some place you would like to go that is within a few hours of here? What do you want to do?"

An idea popped into her mind, and she smiled. "Hot air ballooning."

"Done."

"What do you mean, done?"

"I'm giving you a month to get back on your feet physically, and then you and I have a date to go hot air ballooning."

"But I don't know of anyone in Sweetwater who has one."

"That isn't your problem. Leave everything to me. For once let someone take care of you." He tugged her toward the door. "I need to say good-night to Allie. Want to come?"

"Love to."

As she followed Samuel up to the second floor and his youngest daughter's bedroom, she realized how much she looked forward to saying good-night to Allie. She missed that routine with her siblings. She missed Holly. She missed her two brothers. Tears swelled her throat. Of late she seemed more emotional, and hoped that would settle down soon.

Several books were stacked on Allie's lap as she sat in her white canopy bed, waiting for her father. "I want you to read this tonight." She held up a big thick book. "No, I think I want to hear this one." She put the first story down and selected another one. "Will you read it to me, Beth?"

Beth glanced at Samuel, who nodded. "Sure. I loved *Black Beauty*."

"I'm gonna learn to ride like Crystal."

Alarm rang through Beth's mind when she thought of the riding accident that had led to Crystal's being in a wheelchair. Beth's protective instincts came to the fore. Then she peered at Allie's eager expression and remembered what it had been like when she'd been Allie's age and wanted to ride horses. She wasn't Allie's mother, and even if she was, she would need to learn to let go. That had been a hard lesson for her while raising her siblings. Even now she still felt responsible for them, still worried about them.

"Do you know how to ride a horse?"

The little girl's question pulled Beth back to the present. "I rode when I was a teenager. I haven't since then."

"Maybe you could take lessons with me."

Clearing her throat, Beth opened the book. "We'll see."

"That always means no when Daddy says that."

Beth peered at Samuel, who stood by the door watching them, his arms folded over his chest, his shoulder cushioned against the jamb. "But it doesn't mean no when I say it. I'm just not sure of my plans once I get better. I don't want to make a promise I can't keep."

"Okay." Allie scooted over so that Beth could lean back against the headboard next to her.

Samuel couldn't take his eyes off Beth. Captivated, he observed her read to his daughter as though Allie was the most important person in Beth's life. Any lingering reservations about taking off his wedding ring were gone as he took in the picture of Beth and Allie sitting side by side, their heads bent together. His heartbeat sped up. He rubbed his sweaty palms up and down his arms.

He loved Beth Coleman. She would be a perfect mother for his children. She was good for him. She made him realize what was important in life: God, family and friends.

Then he remembered Beth's dream to travel, to serve the Lord in other parts of the world. How could he deny her that dream if he truly loved her?

* * *

A rough roar from the propane burner pierced the air, then quiet wrapped around Beth as she stared down at Sweetwater below the hot air balloon. A breeze cooled the warm June day, relieving the heat of summer. She saw her house, the church and Samuel's place, the lake with several boats on it. Jesse stood on her deck with Cindy next to her, waving at them. Beth returned the greeting as Nick came out to put his arm around his wife's shoulders and pull her close. Nate ran around the side of the house and up the stairs, joining the others.

A lump formed in Beth's throat. Jesse and Nick were so perfect for each other. Why couldn't she have found someone when she was younger? Her bout with cancer had only confirmed in her mind that she needed to do something for herself. Soon she should reapply to the Christian Mission Institute. If everything went well, in six weeks her doctor would release her, with a daily pill the only indication she'd had cancer.

The loud rushing sound cut into her thoughts as Samuel shot flames up to heat the air in the balloon. It rose above the lake, the wind stronger. The basket swayed. Beth gripped its rim to steady herself while Samuel came to stand beside her.

She slid her gaze to Samuel. "How did you arrange this?"

"With some help from Nick, who knew someone in Lexington. I told you I wanted to fulfill one of your dreams."

"You've been up in a balloon before?"

He nodded. "Quite a few times. I'm certified to fly one, so don't worry. You're safe with me."

"I'm discovering there's a lot I don't know about you."

"Isn't that what getting to know a person is all about, discovering those little things? I dated Ruth for three years and was married to her for thirteen, and she still was able to surprise me." He stepped back to hit the burner so the air in the balloon heated up.

When he returned to her side, Beth looked down at his hands clasping the railing in front of him and noticed that the area on his left finger where his wedding band used to be wasn't white anymore. In the six weeks since the surgery, she had started to dream something different. Samuel was always there to help her through any rough spots with the cancer treatment. He listened to her, especially when she felt depressed. He and his children had even helped her around the house and in her yard with chores when she had been overly tired. She wondered if, in his mind, she was taking the place of Ruth, since he had never had the chance to do those things for his wife.

After firing the burner again, Samuel stood back and studied her. "I hate to use the cliché, but a penny for your thoughts. You look so serious. This is supposed to be for fun."

She pushed away the nagging doubt and managed to smile. "I'm having fun. I just started thinking about the past six weeks. I shouldn't have."

"Why not?"

She gestured to her face. "Because of that serious expression."

"I don't want you ever to feel you can't say anything to me. I didn't like you thinking you couldn't tell me about the cancer. I hope we've gone beyond that."

She nodded, feeling closer to him in that moment than she ever had. "Then I have a question for you. For the past six weeks why have you been there every time I needed someone, sometimes when I didn't even know it? Does it have anything to do with Ruth and her fight against cancer?"

Samuel sucked in a deep breath, moving back a step and almost absently hitting the burner to keep the balloon in the air. "You don't pull any punches."

"Not anymore. You wanted to know what I was thinking."

He cocked his head to the side and looked beyond her. When he reestablished eye contact with her, he said, "I won't lie to you. Yes, it has something to do with Ruth."

Her heart skipped a beat, then began to pound, its sound thundering in her ears.

"And no, it doesn't have anything really to do with her. I don't think I can separate it so cleanly. What happened to Ruth has affected me and shaped me into the man I am today."

Vaguely Beth was aware of the silence, the fresh summer smells carried on the breeze, the warmth of the sun, but all her senses were focused on the man before her.

He covered the small space between them and drew her up against him. "I did all those things because I love you, Beth. You are a caring, compassionate woman who my children adore, who I adore."

His declaration stole her voice, her thoughts and her breath. When they all returned in a rush, tears filled her eyes and made his image blurry. "I love you, too, Samuel."

He bent forward and brushed his lips across hers before settling his mouth over hers and winding his arms around her. His kiss rocked her to her soul. Never in her life had she been kissed as though she was the most special woman in the world. Beautiful. Cherished. Loved.

She laid her head against the cushion of his shoulder, feeling the rise and fall of his chest, hearing his heartbeat beneath the thin knit of his shirt. "Where do we go from here?"

He stroked her back, his touch soft, comforting. "I don't know. I never expected to fall in love again. To tell you the truth, I didn't want to fall in love again. I never want to experience the pain and devastation that occurred after Ruth died."

She leaned back and looked into his dark eyes, shining with the love he had expressed only a moment before. But within she also saw uncertainty. "I think we take it slow and easy and see where it leads us. I'd given up on love and moved on with plans that didn't include it. Then I got cancer and things changed again."

He cupped her cheek. "I know. We never know what's really around the next corner." Rubbing his thumb across her lips, he smiled at her, but there was a sadness in the slight upturn of his mouth.

When he left her alone at the railing while he brought the hot air balloon safely to the ground, Beth closed her eyes for a few minutes, trying to assimilate what had just happened between them. Her mind felt overloaded, and she couldn't quite figure out what to do. She loved him. She loved his children. But was she prepared to take on a ready-made family...again? Would she be totally happy and content giving up on her dream? Was it fair to put Samuel in the position of going through with her what happened to his first wife? Her prognosis was good, but there was a chance the cancer could return. Massaging the sides of her temples, she realized she didn't have an answer.

Beth sat on a red plaid blanket under a large oak tree and watched the young children enjoying the church playground. Allie was swinging next to Cindy, while Sean and Nate were climbing on the jungle gym. Off to the side of the playground a group of teenagers were in the middle of a fierce volleyball game. Jane leaped into the air and smashed the ball across the net at her brother's feet, scoring a point for her team. Several of the members gave her a high five as Jane's boyfriend readied himself to serve again.

Another Fourth of July picnic and auction. But this time it was different because of Samuel and his family.

"Jane's a changed girl because of you, Beth."

She slanted a look at Zoey, who settled cross-legged on the blanket across from her. "She wanted to change or she wouldn't have, no matter what I did."

"Don't sell yourself short. You were there to help her when she needed it. You had faith in her and her ability. You're good at doing that, especially for the kids at school. They all missed you at the end of the year."

"I missed them."

Beth recalled the party her classes had thrown for her the day after school was out for the summer. Samuel had driven her to school to turn in her grades. When she'd gone to her room to input them into the computer, she had been surprised by many of her students.

"What have you decided to do come August?" Zoey smoothed the blanket in front of her, picking up a leaf and tossing it away.

"I don't know. I don't understand why I can't make a decision."

Zoey stared at Samuel talking to a group of parishioners near the tables laden with food. "I understand why you can't. Two opposing dreams are colliding. I know you've wanted to do mission work for years and were just waiting until your siblings grew up."

"Samuel told me last week that he loves me." Beth found him in the crowd, his hands gesturing as they often did when he talked. She smiled. "He's such a good man."

"You don't have to sell me on that. He's done an excellent job taking over the ministry. Somewhere in what you're saying to me I hear a 'but.'"

"I don't know if I can raise a family all over again." Beth glanced at her friend. "I don't know if he isn't confusing me with his wife, possibly subconsciously thinking he has a second chance concerning the cancer. He was devastated when he couldn't help Ruth." She motioned in Samuel's direction. "Have you taken a good look at him? He's handsome while I am…" She let her sentence trail off into the noise around them.

"What? Plain? Are you fishing for compliments, Beth Coleman?"

Beth straightened. "No."

"Well, I'm going to give them to you anyway. You *are* beautiful. I bet he's told you that, too, hasn't he?"

Beth nodded.

"Especially lately. There's a glow about you—from a look in your eyes to the way your whole face lights up, especially when Samuel is near. And you've finally gotten rid of your drab clothes." Zoey pointed toward Beth's red capri pants and red, white and blue T-shirt. "I doubt he's mixed you up with his dead wife. But as for the other doubt you have, only you can decide if taking on three more children is what you want. It's a serious, important decision and I don't envy you that. From the way his children are around you, they wouldn't mind if you did."

"We do get along, but being their mother would be different. I would be responsible for them 24/7."

"Has he asked you to marry him?"

Beth again searched out Samuel in the crowd. "Not in

so many words, but we have skirted the issue several times in the past few days. Maybe I'm jumping the gun here."

Zoey shook her head. "I don't think so. I've seen how he looks at you. He wouldn't get serious unless he meant marriage."

Samuel swung around and caught Beth staring at him. Waving, he grinned, the laugh lines at the corners of his dark eyes deep. His mere look affected her in ways she hadn't thought possible before falling in love.

"It's almost time for lunch, then the auction," Zoey said, but her voice sounded as though it came from a distance.

Beth's total attention homed in on Samuel across the churchyard near the grills where the men were cooking the hamburgers and hot dogs. She wasn't sure she deserved someone like Samuel. Even when he was struggling with his doubts concerning the Lord, he'd been a good leader of their church, taking his responsibilities seriously, caring for each member of his congregation. Without him, Beth wasn't sure Tanya would have made it through the divorce proceedings. He stood by Tanya as he had with Beth through the cancer scare and treatment.

Samuel disengaged himself from the group and headed toward her. Beth's gaze never left him as he made his way over. His stride was full of confidence, his look totally for her.

Zoey rose. "I'd better find my children and gather them for lunch or something."

Beth flicked a glance toward her friend. "Thanks for listening."

"That's what friends are for."

Samuel greeted Zoey as she walked away, then took up a spot next to Beth on the blanket, one leg bent, his arm resting on his raised knee. "What have you two been chatting about? It looked serious."

"Zoey was reading me the riot act. I've never thought of myself as pretty and she took issue with that."

"She's right. You're strong in so many ways, but when it comes to how others look at you, you don't see what we do."

"I'm working on my self-image. Taking care of a sick mother, then raising three siblings, it's never been about me, but about them."

Leaning back with his arms propping him up, Samuel scanned the people milling about. "I didn't realize how big a crowd there would be here today. You kept telling me it was a well-attended event."

"Every year the auction gets bigger and bigger. Even some people in town who aren't members of our church attend the auction."

"And the proceeds go to a worthy cause."

"Are you excited about the new prison ministry program?"

"You bet. It'll be a challenge, but then I thrive on challenges."

"How's Tom doing?"

"Not good. When he allows me to see him, he refuses

to talk about Tanya, Crystal or Sweetwater. It's as if he's cut out that part of his life."

"Maybe that's the only way he can survive prison."

A frown slashed across Samuel's features. "But he won't be in prison forever. His daughter needs her father."

"I know. It's hard when a father abandons his child."

His attention swerved to Beth. "You never talk about your own father."

"He walked out on us before Daniel was born, so what's left to say? He didn't want the responsibility of raising another child. I don't know where he is. It's as though he has vanished from our lives."

"When your mother died, did you try to find him?"

She shook her head. "I won't force myself on anyone."

"But Daniel was a baby."

"And *my* responsibility."

"You were all alone with three children."

"Ethan was only a few years younger than me, and my father's uncle helped from time to time. My great-uncle died a couple of years back and some distant relative took over his farm. That's all the family I have."

His dark gaze bored into her. "You have me and my family. I love you and when you are ready, I want to marry you."

Her breath caught in her throat. "Is that a proposal?"

His whole face shone with a smile that reached deep into his eyes. "Yes, it is. I hadn't really planned to ask at the picnic, but I won't take the words back."

"I—" She clamped her mouth shut, not sure what to say.

He touched her lips with his finger. "Don't answer right now. I know you love me, but marriage is much more than that. I want a family with you, a baby. We'll talk—"

"Daddy." Allie threw herself at her father. "It's time to eat. C'mon!" She pulled back and tugged on Samuel's hand to get him to stand.

Hovering over Beth, Samuel captured her gaze and said, "We'll talk later when it's less public. Right now we'd better eat before all the good food is gone."

The promise in his words sent a thrill through Beth. Rising, she followed the pair toward the tables lined with all types of salads, side dishes and desserts. As she piled food onto her paper plate, all she could think about was Samuel's proposal. Marriage. A family. A baby. The decision wasn't a simple yes or no. She hadn't told him yet about the offer she'd received yesterday from the Christian Mission Institute.

Samuel said goodbye to the last members of the cleanup crew as they filed out of the rec hall. When he turned back toward the table where Beth sat, adding up the purchases, he saw Zoey and Jesse join her. Aunt Mae had taken his children home, and he intended to have some quiet time with Beth just as soon as her friends left.

The whole afternoon his thoughts had been filled with his proposal to Beth. He wasn't even sure he had been too coherent when talking with others. At one point, Joshua had had to ask a question twice before he answered.

The one overriding conclusion he'd come to as the afternoon had progressed was that Beth was the right woman for him and his family. But he wasn't sure he and his family were right for her. How could he ask her to start her life over, raising a whole new family? And he had probably really frightened her when he had blurted out that he wanted a baby with her. How could he ask her to give up a dream of traveling and doing God's work? He shouldn't have been so impulsive and asked her to marry him without thinking of her needs. He didn't want her to feel obligated to marry him because she loved him and he loved her. He'd seen first-hand as a minister that wasn't always enough.

With a deep sigh he strode toward Beth, praying to God to show him the way.

"I'm so glad that the auction is over and was a success. See these." Jesse held up her hands. "I've bitten off all my fingernails. They are stubs."

"You're a natural organizer, Jesse. We pulled in more money this year than any in the past." Beth finished the tally of the proceeds and gave the sheet to her friend.

Jesse looked at it, then smiled. "This is wonderful." She passed it to Samuel. "You're the reason this was such a success this year, Beth. Zoey and I couldn't have done it without your guidance and notes. You've built the auction up until now practically the whole town turns out."

Beth laughed. "Hardly. But it was nice to see every space filled with people bidding."

"Samuel, I hope I can persuade you to build another

dollhouse. My daughter was very disappointed I didn't get it." Zoey gathered up the sale receipts and checks and placed them in a metal box.

"You're about the fifth person who has asked me that today."

Jesse winced. "Sorry, Zoey. Cindy fell in love with the dollhouse."

"That's okay. Nick made a hefty donation to our outreach program for that dollhouse and that's the most important thing. Remember last year when he bought your doll?"

Jesse got a dreamy look on her face. "Yes. Wasn't that sweet of him? And he told me right after the auction today that he was whisking me away to a secluded island in the Caribbean for a week of R and R. No kids, just the two of us."

"That's great!" Beth exclaimed. "A beach, sun and sand. That sounds wonderful after all the time you've put in with the auction."

"After our vacation I'm thinking of taking the kids with us on Nick's business trip to Europe. I may be away for most of July."

Samuel watched the wistful expression appear in Beth's eyes. Serving in the army as a chaplain, he'd done what Beth wanted to do. How could he stand in her way? Not if he truly loved her.

Zoey rose, the metal box in hand. "I don't know about you all, but I'm tired. It's been a long day and I still have to deposit the money in the bank."

"I need to leave, too. I have bags to pack and plans to make." Jesse grabbed the rest of the paperwork and glanced around. "Looks like the cleanup crew did a great job. See you."

When Zoey and Jesse left, Samuel faced Beth, taking her hand. "Do you feel up to a walk in the garden?"

She nodded, the usual sparkle in her eyes gone.

"Are you sure you're not too tired?" Samuel asked.

"No, I'm fine. I was just thinking."

Samuel headed outside with Beth next to him. "About Jesse's trip?"

"That and something I need to tell you."

"That sounds ominous."

She shrugged. "I haven't had a chance to tell you I got a letter from the Christian Mission Institute."

Samuel led Beth to the path that took them to the pond in the garden. "What did they have to say?" The beating of his heart slowed.

She took a seat on the bench, leaving him room next to her if he wanted to sit. "They have a temporary position for me at another mission near Belém in Brazil. It could work itself into a permanent position if I want, but right now a worker needs to come back to the United States for personal reasons at the beginning of August."

His chest tightened. He inhaled a deep breath, but couldn't fill his lungs.

"I'm not sure what I should do."

Again he tried to draw air into his lungs, but the band about his chest constricted his efforts. He turned away as though the goldfish in the pond were the most fascinating creatures he'd seen. Closing his eyes, he quickly asked for strength to do what was right for Beth.

When he looked back at her and saw her worry and concern, he forced a smile and said, "You have to take the position."

"But what about us? Your proposal?"

Chapter Thirteen

Samuel kept his distance, his smile gone. "You have to do this. If you don't, you'll always wonder and regret the wasted opportunity."

Her teeth dug into her bottom lip. Had something changed in the few hours since his proposal? Beth realized she wasn't very good at knowing the ins and outs of a relationship, since she'd had so few of them over the years. Why wasn't he demanding she stay and marry him?

She rose on shaky legs. "I could be gone a long time."

"I know."

She started toward the parking lot. "Then I'll call them immediately and tell them yes."

Halfway down the stone path Samuel stopped her with a hand on her arm. "Beth—"

She shook off his hand and hurried forward. Tears misted her eyes, making it difficult to see the path.

"Beth."

The plea in his voice stopped her. But she didn't turn around.

"I will be here when you are ready to get married, but I've seen people give up their dreams for another. It can build a wall between two people that is impossible to scale. When you walk down the aisle, I want it to be for all the right reasons."

Slowly she faced him. "Then I'll go."

"Why do you have to go?" Allie asked with a pout.

Beth finished zipping up her suitcase, then placed it next to her bed before answering, "They're counting on me to be there."

"But I want you here." Allie stomped her foot and pointed to the floor. "I might need someone to help me when school starts at the end of the month. I'm going into the third grade, you know."

"Your dad can help, and so can Jane."

Tears glistened in Allie's eyes. "It's not the same."

Beth sank onto the bed and motioned for Allie to come to her. She wrapped her arms around the child. "You can write me and if there's a computer at the mission, I can e-mail you, maybe even send you some pictures. I'm taking my digital camera."

"But you won't be here."

It was harder for her to leave than Beth had ever imagined, and yet she had committed herself to going to the mission and she would. Samuel was right. She needed to do this for herself. But holding Allie and having to tell her goodbye ripped at her heart.

"We'll see each other again," Beth finally whispered.

Allie pulled back. "When?"

"I'm not sure how long I'll be staying. I'm filling in for someone taking a leave, then I may stay."

"Why?"

"Because God wants me to."

"Why can't God want you to be here with us? God needs workers here, too. Others can go to the mission. Why does it have to be you?"

Beth brushed the child's hair back from her face. "I promised them I would come."

Tears streamed down her cheeks. "Do you promise to come home?"

Beth spied Samuel in the doorway, sadness in his eyes, and her heart broke into two pieces. Why had she agreed to go when she had him? Why was she so afraid to make a total commitment to his family?

Beth looked back at the little girl. "Yes, I promise to come home."

Allie threw herself at Beth and kissed her on the cheek. "Don't stay away long, please."

"Allie, I need to drive Beth to the airport. We don't want her to miss her plane."

Allie spun around. "Yes, I do, Daddy."

"Come on. The rest of the family is in the foyer waiting, Allie. Let Beth finish getting her things together."

Sighing, Allie trudged toward the door, her shoulders hunched. As she disappeared into the hallway, Beth rose.

"I'm sorry about that." Samuel came into her bedroom.

"That's okay. I knew she wasn't happy with me."

"I tried to explain to her last night, but I guess I wasn't successful." He pulled up the handle on the suitcase so he could roll it toward the door.

"I'm sorry."

He halted and turned back to her. "About what?"

"About causing Allie any pain, about us."

Letting go of the suitcase, he strode the few feet to her and clasped her upper arms. "You have nothing to be sorry for. You have to do this. That doesn't mean we are happy about it, but we will live through it. If you decide working at the mission is what you need to do, then I will learn to accept that decision." He pulled her to him. "I love you. I want what's best for you."

His words comforted and yet pained her at the same time. She laid her head against his heart, needing to hear its steady, strong beat, so much like the man.

"Right now my family needs Sweetwater and what it can offer them. You need the mission near Belém. We'll be here when you want to come home." He leaned back and framed her face, his intense gaze on her.

When he lowered his head and covered her mouth with his, she melted against him and poured all her love into the kiss. The memory of it would have to last her a long time. Savoring the taste of him on her lips, she finally pulled away.

"I only have a few things to gather for the plane ride. I'll be out in a minute."

Watching him leave with her big suitcase, Beth managed to keep herself together until he was gone. Then the tears came, rolling down her face unchecked.

God, why isn't life as easy as Allie thinks it is?

The rain fell in gray sheets outside the window at the mission. Beth stared at the line of trees marking the edge of the clearing where the jungle began. Eight weeks had slipped by. She loved working in the school with the small children, and if she cared to, the director wanted her to stay on permanently.

But every day for the past eight weeks she had missed Samuel and his children. She felt good about the work she was doing for the Lord, but there was an emptiness inside her she couldn't fill with her prayers.

God needs workers here, too.

Beth remembered Allie's plea to her that last day in Sweetwater. She hadn't been able to get the child's words out of her mind. She didn't have to go thousands of miles from home to do God's work. There was a need in Sweetwater, as there was any place.

Was she ready for a family? Because Samuel came with one. In fact, he wanted more children. After working with the young children at the mission she knew she wanted to be a mother in every sense of the word, from giving birth to raising the child, as she had her siblings.

She had a lot of love inside her—love she wanted to give to Samuel and his children. She needed to go home, and hoped that Samuel still wanted her as his wife, since he hadn't mentioned it in his e-mails.

Beth rose from the desk and walked to the open window, listening to the steady downpour. Through the gray she caught sight of some orchids growing in a tree. Such beauty here. Raw. Untamed. She was glad she had experienced this, but without Samuel it didn't mean much. He defined her life, made her complete, and it had taken coming to Brazil for her to realize that fully.

The sound of children's feet alerted her to the beginning of class. She turned from the window and greeted her pupils as they entered the classroom.

"I thought I would find you here, Dad." Jane slipped into the pew next to Samuel at the front of the church.

He glanced at his watch. "School's out already?"

Jane grinned. "Has been for an hour."

"How was it today? Any problems?"

"Don't worry, Dad. I'll get help if I need it from whoever I need to. Beth taught me that, to ask for help."

"Beth taught us all something."

"What did she teach you?"

He sighed. "To trust in the Lord. To turn to Him when things are hard to deal with."

"Is that why you come in here every day before coming home?"

He chuckled. "I work here."

"It's more than that, Dad."

"True. Yes, I like to talk with God before going home. This place—" he scanned the sanctuary "—is comforting."

"It reminds you of Beth?"

He nodded. "She was so much a part of this church."

"Everyone misses her. Do you think she misses us?"

"In her e-mails she says she does."

"Then why doesn't she come home?"

"She will if it's meant to be."

"How can you sit there and calmly say that?"

He turned to face his daughter. "Because I have faith that the Lord will do what is best for all of us."

"Beth is best for us."

He took his oldest daughter's hand between his. "I hope He sees it that way. I hope she does. That's all I can do, hon. Hope and pray."

Jane rose. "I will, too. Maybe it will be enough."

As his daughter started for the door, it opened. Jane gasped and hurried forward. Not able to see who it was, Samuel pushed to his feet and turned toward the back. Jane threw her arms around the person still partially hidden, but Samuel knew who it was.

He rushed down the aisle as Jane pulled Beth into full view. He stopped, taking in the sight of the woman he loved. From her expression he knew she had come home for good.

"I'm leaving," Jane said, but her words sounded so far away.

All Samuel could see was Beth's beautiful smiling

face that glowed with a promise of love. She took a step toward him. He moved forward. Then somehow they were in each other's arms.

He kissed her on the forehead, the cheek, then the mouth. "Why didn't you let me know you were coming? I could have picked you up at the airport."

"I wanted to surprise you, and it looks like I did. I took a chance you were still at the church. When I couldn't find you in your office, I thought you might be in here."

"You did?"

"Call it a hunch. It was good to see Jane. Is she really doing all right in school? She wrote me she was."

"The first nine weeks will be over soon and she has good grades so far, but she works hard for them."

"How are Allie and Craig?"

"There isn't a day Allie doesn't ask about you. And Craig is on a football team. It's his whole life right now."

"I can't wait to see them."

He cupped her face, his fingers delving into her curls. "Will you marry me?"

"Why do you think I came back?"

"I'll take that as a yes."

"Yes, that's a yes. For years I thought I wanted the single life, not having to be responsible for anyone but me. I was wrong. I missed not having a family. It took going thousands of miles away to finally realize that, but I want children and a husband. I want my own family. I want you and the kids."

"No more traveling?"

She smiled. "I didn't say that. I've decided to organize mission trips for our youth every summer. It's something we have talked about doing but haven't done yet. Now is the time. Our outreach program is expanding, especially with the success of events like the auction."

"You are never going to change. Already home less than an hour and you have a new job."

"Speaking of a job, I'm going to substitute for the remainder of the school year. One of the teachers in the English department is going on maternity leave in a few weeks and I'm going to take over her classes until the end of the semester."

"It doesn't bother you not to have your own classes?"

"No, because I think I'll be busy making plans for my wedding."

"Not to mention the mission trip for next summer."

She snuggled closer. "You know I can't stay idle."

"Have you ever thought of having your own child?"

"Ever since I met you, many times," she said with a laugh. "But I can't wait too long. I'm pushing forty."

Samuel wound his arm about her shoulders and headed for the door. "Then we need to get married soon."

Out in the foyer of the church the front door burst open and in raced Allie and Craig. Both practically tackled Beth in their enthusiasm to greet her.

"Hold it, you two. Let her breathe," Samuel said, watching his family show their love as though Beth had always been their mother.

"Jane told us you were back." Allie enclosed her arms about Beth's waist and pressed her head to her chest.

"I made a promise to a young lady that I had to keep."

Allie bent back to look up into Beth's face. "I knew something was up when you didn't answer my latest e-mail right away."

"Why don't you two go let Aunt Mae know there will be one more for dinner?"

Allie and Craig hurried toward the house.

"When I see you and your family, I can't imagine why I thought I needed to go to Brazil in the first place."

"What's ten weeks, three days—" he checked his watch "—eight hours and twenty-four minutes in the grand scheme of things?"

"An eternity when you are away from the one you love."

Epilogue

"Look, that's Jane!" Allie pointed toward the stage in the high school auditorium.

Beth's chest swelled as she watched Jane walk to the superintendent of Sweetwater schools and shake his hand, then take her high school diploma from the principal. The past few years hadn't been easy for Jane, but she had done it and with a good grade point average. She would be heading to the University of Kentucky in the fall.

Tears clogged Beth's throat as she thought of Jane telling her that she wanted to be a teacher and help students as Beth had.

Samuel laid his hand on her arm, pulling her attention toward her husband.

"Jane owes you a lot."

"Samuel, I owe her a lot. She has given me so much."

"Mama, eat."

Her sixteen-month-old son wiggled out of Aunt

Mae's arms and climbed over his father to get to Beth's lap. She rummaged in her large purse and found a plastic bag of cereal for Garrett. He plunged his chubby fingers inside and stuffed some of the round O's into his mouth.

Samuel leaned close to her ear and whispered, "Will you be okay when Jane leaves home?"

"No, but I'll deal with it. Besides, I'm going to be extra busy next year."

"Have you decided to go back to teaching?"

She shook her head. "No, we're having another baby."

Samuel pulled back, his dark eyes round. "We are?"

"Yes, around the middle of January."

He slipped his arm around her. "Beth Morgan, I love you."

* * * * *

Dear Reader,

I hope you enjoyed Beth and Samuel's story in
Light in the Storm. I am a high school teacher who
has worked with students with learning disabilities.
It is important to convey to them that they have
strengths as well as weaknesses. Sometimes we
dwell on our weaknesses and our self-esteem suffers
for it. Yes, we need to be aware of what we need to
work on, but no one is perfect. Jane needed to learn
that in this story, as did Beth and Samuel.

Another aspect of my story was Beth's battle with
breast cancer. With it being one of the common
forms of cancer for women, I wanted to stress the
importance of early detection. One way is monthly
self-examination. There is a Buddy Check program
that advocates a woman forming a partnership with
a friend or family member; each reminds the other
to self-check monthly.

I love hearing from my readers. You can contact
me at P.O. Box 2074, Tulsa, OK 74101, or visit my
Web site at www.margaretdaley.com.

Best wishes,

Margaret Daley